A CO… GHOST STORIES

EDIT… SON DOWSE

Murder, Mystery & Mayhem

YoungWriters

A YOUNG WRITERS ANTHOLOGY

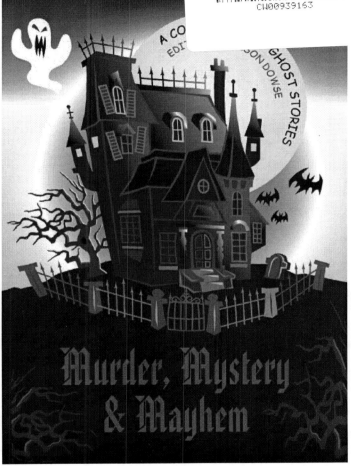

First published in Great Britain in 2005 by
Young Writers, Remus House,
Coltsfoot Drive, Peterborough, PE2 9JX
Telephone (01733) 890066
www.youngwriters.co.uk

SB ISBN 1 84602 204 5

Disclaimer

Young Writers has maintained every effort to publish stories that will not cause offence. Any stories, events or activities relating to individuals should be read as fictional pieces and not construed as real-life character portrayal.

Foreword

Young Writers was established in 1991 and has been passionately devoted to the promotion of reading and writing in children and young adults ever since. The quest continues today. *Young Writers* remains as committed to engendering the fostering of burgeoning poetic and literary talent as ever.

This year, *Young Writers* are happy to present a dynamic and entertaining new selection of the best creative writing from a talented and diverse cross section of some of the most accomplished secondary school writers around. Entrants were presented with four inspirational and challenging themes.

'Myths And Legends' gave pupils the opportunity to adapt long-established tales from mythology (whether Greek, Roman, Arthurian or more conventional eg The Loch Ness Monster) to their own style.

'A Day In The Life Of . . .' offered pupils the chance to depict twenty-four hours in the lives of literally anyone they could imagine. A hugely imaginative wealth of entries were received encompassing days in the lives of everyone from the top media celebrities to historical figures like Henry VIII or a typical soldier from the First World War.

Finally 'Short Stories', in contrast, offered no limit other than the author's own imagination while 'Hold The Front Page' provided the ideal opportunity to challenge the entrants' journalistic skills asking them to provide a newspaper or magazine article on any subject of their choice.

Murder, Mystery & Mayhem: A Collection Of Ghost Stories is ultimately a collection we feel sure you will love, featuring as it does the work of the best young authors writing today. We hope you enjoy the work included and will continue to return to *Murder, Mystery & Mayhem: A Collection Of Ghost Stories* time and time again in the years to come.

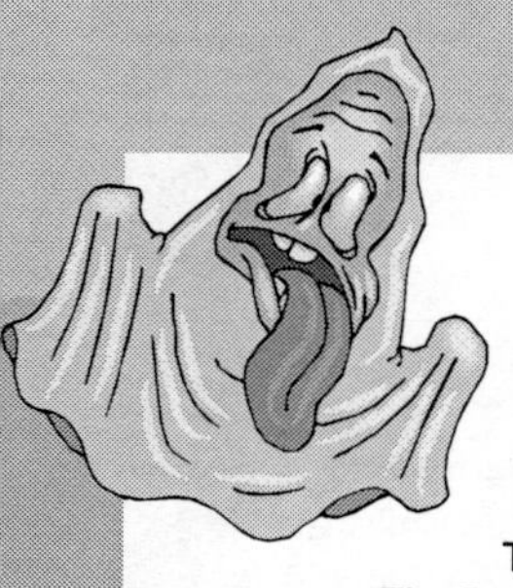

Contents

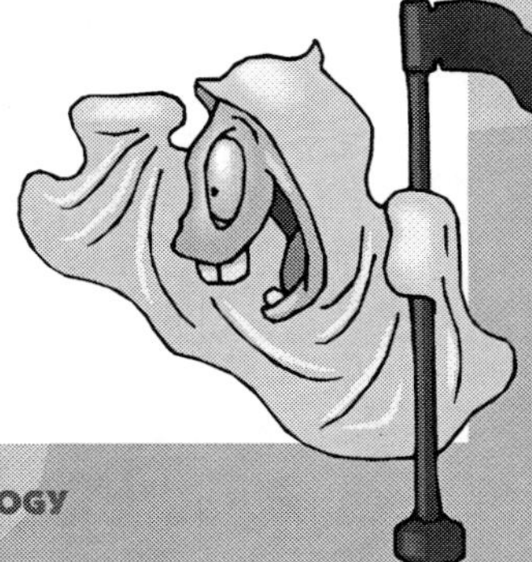

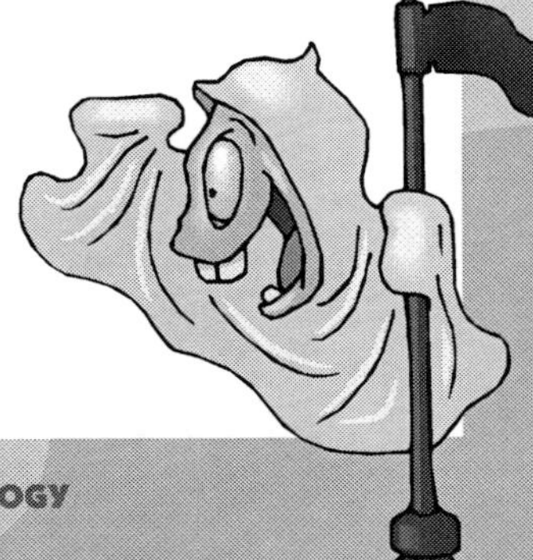

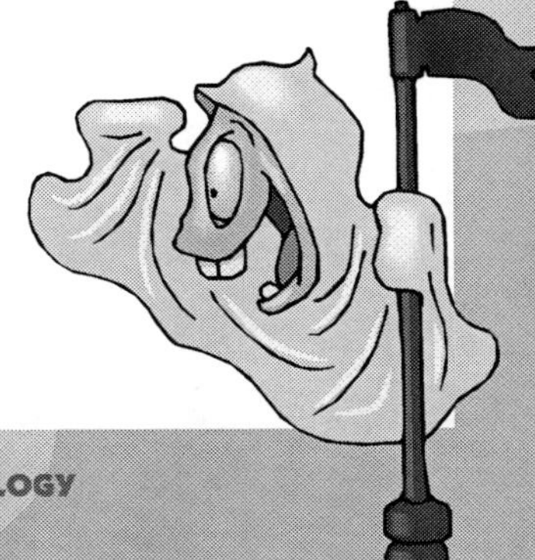

Thomas Keble School, Stroud

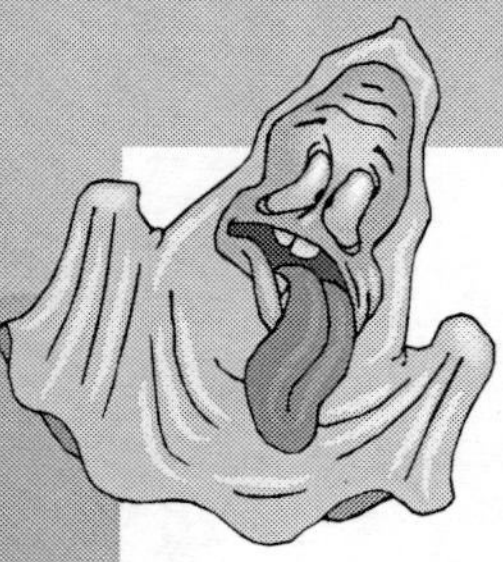

the London Dungeon

Congratulations Elizabeth! Your story wins you a fantastic family ticket to either the **York, London,** or **Edinburgh Dungeons**.

She Was Only Young When She Died

'It's haunted, this house,' said my brother. 'Someone died here.'

We were alone in the new house. I wasn't going to let him scare me.

Outside the grey sky glared at me through the window even though the atmosphere hung low and tight around me. My brother slipped upstairs, satisfied.

A sudden silence descended on the house. The trees kept swaying outside the window, yet their tap, tap, tapping had ceased.

Then I heard someone pacing the kitchen. Gradually the steady, even slapping of their bare feet on our tiled kitchen floor became more frantic.

Suddenly there was an almighty bang as a cupboard door was pushed, its hinges protesting. The panicked rattling of utensils was masked as I heard our cutlery drawer come crashing down.

At every sound I flinched, screwing my eyes tight shut. The sickening silence returned. I forced myself to creep towards the kitchen, my tongue like a dry slab of concrete in my mouth.

The kitchen was totally still. Nothing had changed. No mess, just our squeaky clean metallic kitchen. Empty.

Yet on the window, was a smeared print of an infant's hand and in the air hung the tepid remains of a child's terror.

Elizabeth Tilley (13)

Strangers

I guess it had been my fault Mr Nelson had put me in detention. Four years with a spotless record and one offence gets you in detention. I guess you're not in a very forgiving mood after someone's 'accidentally' poured paint in your morning coffee.

The evening was bleak and it grew darker by the minute. Walking through the park at this time of day was not a good idea. The trees loomed over me and through their swaying branches I could just about see that the moon had ventured out earlier than usual. I got the urge to look up, I don't know why, but when I did there was a girl in the bushes.

She was wide-eyed and fragile-looking. Very pale with bits of leaves in her hair as if she had been rolling around on the grass. There was nothing particularly striking about this girl but I had to go to talk to her. It was her eyes that got to me. I could tell that she was terrified, but there was more, the pleading look she gave, imploring me to come to help her.

'Hi, I'm Jake.' Before I knew it I was up to the bush trying to get her to come out. I climbed under the shrubbery and came up to face her. She had stepped back still scared, by now it seemed my body moved independent of me. I stepped closer. 'Are you OK?' On closer observation I could see that her dress, which had floral patterns and pink bows, was ripped and she was covered in grass stains.

'Help me,' she said. A lot of effort went into her keeping calm and not breaking down, though I could tell that she wanted to. She began to walk away and I couldn't help but follow her. I was drawn to her now and I 'had' to help her. She led me down the time-worn track, my instincts started to kick in and each step felt like I was betraying myself. Somehow she stopped at the edge of Robin's Cliff, a cliff that local birdwatchers called 'Eagle's Peak', because of the perfect view you got at that height.

She looked mournfully at me, then went back to staring off. 'Help me!' she moaned again, same sorrowful tone, not looking at me.

'Help you, how?' I needed to help her even though the bad feeling in my gut intensified.

'I don't want to be alone anymore.'

Like before my eyes looked up and I automatically followed her gaze. In-between the trees, the bushes and the rubble at the foot of the cliff, I could see a hand sticking out and beside it was a ripped piece of fabric with floral patterns and a pink bow. I would've gone to get help, my first instinct had been to save her after all. I changed my mind after, when her cold hands pushed me off Eagle's Peak.

No ... I changed my mind after she killed me ...

Jay-Dee Johnson (15)

Well done Jay-Dee. You win a superb reading and writing goodie bag which includes a selection of books and a **Staedtler Writing Set**!

RUNNER UP

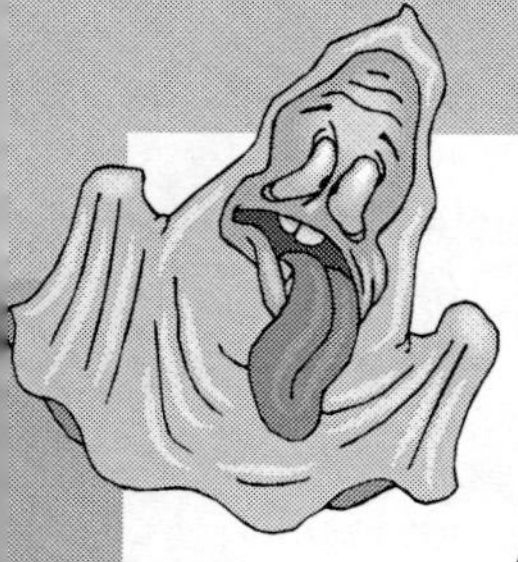

Happy Deathday To You

It was near midnight. The clock had chimed eleven some time ago. The only light was the moon shining eerily across our faces at Kathleen's sleepover party. As you could imagine it was a great time to tell ghost stories and the mysterious girl from Kathleen's drama club was telling the scariest story I'd ever heard.

'This occurs very rarely and happens to about one in a thousand girls. But you cannot deny it happens,' she started spookily. 'When your age corresponds to the date, the month and the time. To make this even more rare, there must be a full moon.'

'It must be really bad for it to be that rare,' interrupted a girl in my class.

'Oh trust me, it is.' At these words she continued. 'Strange things start happening. Their appearance changes to look like a monster. Loss of eye here, gain of leg there, up until the point where they become unrecognisable. They take on the exact features of a monster, such as skin colour, no reflection and so on. The worst part … they will have only one day to live. They will die silently, painlessly, no one will know the cause.'

The clock chimed twelve. There was an intake of breath. Kathleen was twelve. It was the twelfth of December. The moon ceaselessly shined ball-like. Kathleen laughed shakily, got up and stared into the mirror. Her face did not stare back.

Harriet Reed (12)

Congratulations Harriet! You win a superb reading and writing goodie bag which includes a selection of books and a **Staedtler Writing Set**. Well done!

STAEDTLER

The Living Room

One dark and spooky night when everything was covered in silence, I crept downstairs so that I didn't break the silence. When I reached the bottom of the stairs I peered round the corner to make sure that nothing was there ready to jump out on me. I crept down the hallway as quietly as I could. I finally reached the living room without making a noise or touching anything but the floor with my feet. Then suddenly I heard a scuttling noise coming from inside the room. It startled me so much that I jumped back in fright because it had just broken the silence that I had kept for so long. Luckily it was only a spider.

I squinted my eyes to look into the darkness of the room and there hanging from the curtain rail was what I thought was the outline of a body with a rope tied around its neck.

I quickly ran into the kitchen to try and find a flashlight. As I was feeling around the worktops, I felt something hard under my fingers. I paused. Was it a flashlight or was it something else? I felt around it a bit more and I then realised that it was indeed the flashlight that I had been searching for. I carefully picked it up making sure I didn't knock anything off.

Creeping back into the doorway of the living room … I stopped. The outline had gone.

Daniel Day (13)

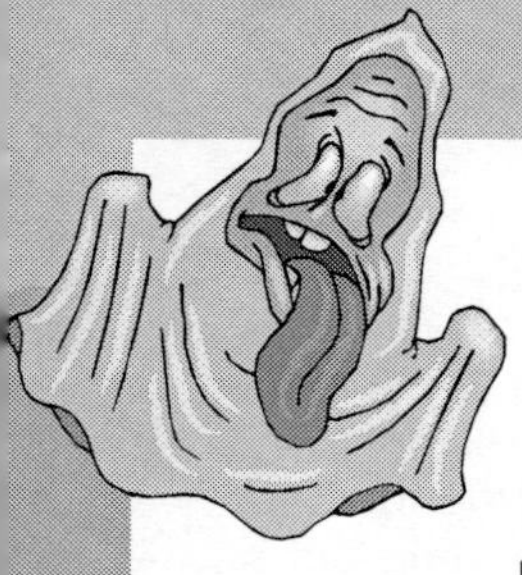

Is He Dead Or Alive?

One day in the middle of April there was a man called Mr Xavier. He was having an incredible amount of problems in his work. First, he had a problem with his business partner. His business partner, Mr Zemolion, was very selfish and thought he was the best. Mr Zemolion would also annoy Mr Xavier and keep all the money that Mr Xavier earned.

One day Mr Xavier could not bear staying with Mr Zemolion any longer so he knew what he had to do … get rid of him by murdering him.

The next night at 12 o'clock he crept into Mr Zemolion's house and stabbed him while he was sleeping. Mr Xavier managed to get out of Mr Zemolion's house unnoticed. He had finally got even with Mr Zemolion.

Though Mr Zemolion's body lay in his grave his soul wouldn't rest in peace until it took revenge on Mr Xavier. He flew into Mr Xavier's body and put him into embarrassing situations, with little knowledge that if he came in front of fire his soul would instantly fly out of Mr Xavier's body.

One day Mr Zemolion's soul decided that he should burn Mr Xavier's naked bottom by dipping it in a fire in front of a large crowd.

A few days later Mr Zemolion was all ready for this task and was about to burn Mr Xavier when Mr Zemolion's soul came popping out. Mr Zemolion's soul went to Hell and never came back.

Milaap Mehta (9)

The Dead Will Keep On Haunting

This story starts in the fifteenth century in a creaky mansion where people say the 'Duke of Devlin' was murdered. Later his murderer was hung in the Duke's mansion. It is said that they roam side by side through the mansion scaring off any intruders that enter.

There was one family who didn't know about this myth as they had just moved into the neighbourhood. They needed a new home and bought the mansion. The first week that they were there they said that the creaks they heard were natural and the shrieks were just the wind.

After a fortnight they were getting worried, but it all became clear when they went into town and saw an article in the local paper about the fools in the haunted house. They went around asking if the house really was haunted. The majority said it was, others said it was merely a myth. As they loved the house so much the only choice was to get the ghosts out of the house.

When they got back home the creaking of the walls and floorboards got worse and the shrieking now said, *'Get out of my house!'* Those words also appeared on the walls and continued to be repeated.

Now they could see the ghosts, so the father shouted, *'No, you get out of my house!'*

Suddenly the voices and words on the wall started to disappear and slowly the ghosts faded away, no one had ever asked them to leave before.

Tomos Norman (14)

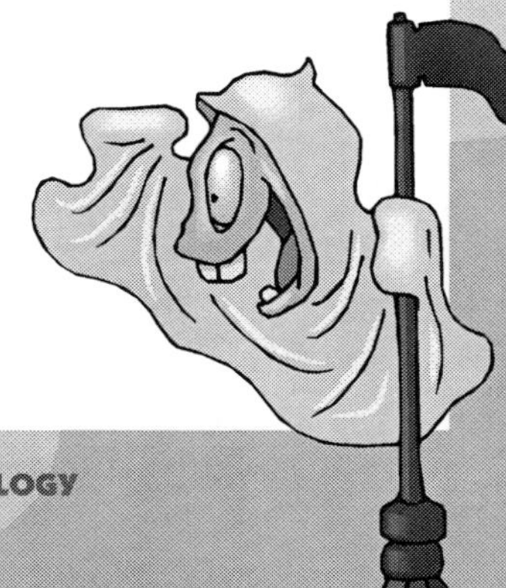

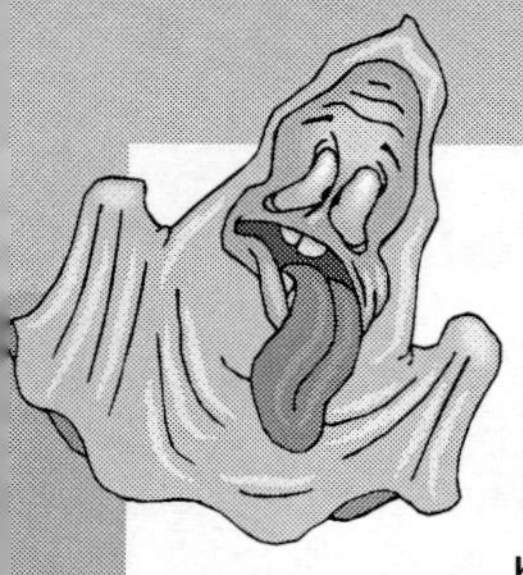

The Deerhound

A shrill howl came from the forest. Mia was terrified but also curious. *What could it be?* she thought to herself. It was the middle of the night but she had an urge to go out and find the source of the noise. She prided herself on being the bravest cat in the village.

She slipped downstairs and jumped swiftly through the cat flap into the night.

An owl hooted loudly, then silence fell. Mia walked to the edge of the forest. The howl came again, louder. Mia was so frightened she almost turned back but curiosity kept her going. The dim light of the moon disappeared as she stepped beneath the trees. Once again all was silent.

She moved quickly and quietly into the dark woods, being careful not to step on twigs or trip on tree roots. After walking for ten minutes the howl came again followed by a deep, echoing bark. She was getting closer, she could tell.

Suddenly, without warning, a huge ghostly deerhound bounded out of the bushes. It was silvery-grey and seemed to shimmer in the darkness. Mia didn't know whether she was dreaming. She only realised she wasn't when it let out a high-pitched howl disturbing the silence. Then she knew it was real.

The deerhound pounced and Mia tried to run, she was too slow!

Nobody knew why the ghostly deerhound was in the forest, but as the old saying goes, curiosity killed the cat.

Siobhan Paisley

Soul Suckers

There's a new girl in my class. Her name is Eliza. Her dad is an embalmer. I'm sleeping over at her house today, but I'm not scared. Really, I'm not.

I'm going up her front path. She's waving from her doorway. I'm going in. Here goes. *Phew!* It's like any old house. I'll calm down now.

'Hiya,' she says.

'Hi,' I say quietly.

We go up to her room and play there for ages. Eventually her dad calls us for tea. I am starving. I imagine what food they will have. I don't want to think.

When we get downstairs, I see a huge glass coffin with three tubes coming out. On the side it says *Soul Sucker.*

'Nooooo!' shouts Eliza as some cold hands grab me. They are ghost hands belonging to her dad and brother. They are ghosts.

Eliza suddenly changes to transparent. Her brother tries to cram me into the box.

'Ssstttoooppp!' Eliza's dad roars. He turns green, then yellow, then ...

I am in hospital. Eliza is here with her family, so is my mum.

'So sorry dear,' Eliza's dad says. He clasps Eliza's shoulder and she shudders elaborately.

'You fell down the stairs,' my mum says. 'Just going to get a Coke now,' she says and walks away.

Eliza's dad leans up to me as soon as my mum has gone. 'You better not tell anyone what happened,' he says.

Suddenly he goes transparent, then green, then yellow, then ...

Claire Langer (11)

The Haunted Palace

It was a dark, cold night and everyone was in their bed fast asleep apart from Courtney (the eldest princess) who was lying in her bed, wide awake. She lay there for ten minutes and then decided to go downstairs for a glass of water. The weather was bad outside. It was thundering loudly and Courtney was walking down the spiral stairs, quietly. She was getting really scared when she heard something smash. Someone was in the palace!

She eventually got a glass of water and then went to sit in the drawing room. She was sitting quietly when she heard small footsteps creeping up behind her. She didn't dare move. She then heard a squeaky voice say, 'Hello. My name's Dobby. I come from Harry Potter.'

The princess replied, 'You scared me!'

'I smashed the window by accident, to come to be your slave,' he said.

'Oh!' said the princess.

She went to bed and Dobby slept in the drawing room.

In the morning the queen said, 'What's that creature here for?'

'He's come for slavery,' said Courtney.

'He looks cute,' Sarah-Louise fussed.

'Yeah,' everyone said apart from the queen.

'Disgusting!' she said.

That night everyone went to bed including Dobby. There was another smash and this time Kirsty woke up. She went downstairs and grabbed a stick. The thing was coming closer. Kirsty whispered, 'This palace is haunted,' then Pinocchio appeared.

'I'm a real boy,' he said and his nose grew larger.

Kirsty, loudly, gave a big laugh!

Karen Ratcliffe (12)

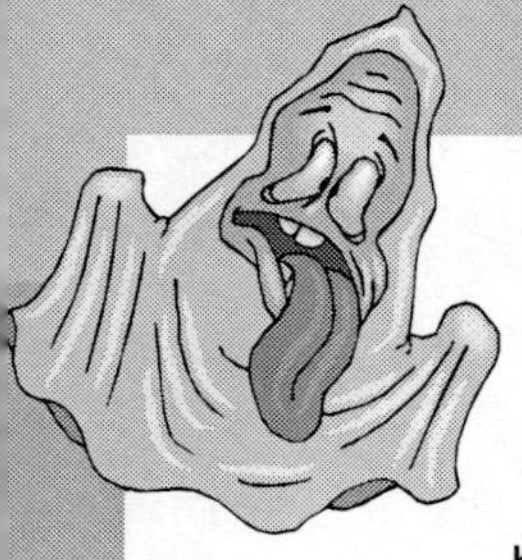

The Werewolf's Secret

The mist swirled between the tombstones in the graveyard of the old, abandoned church. As the old man walked his dog along the overgrown path he noticed flickering candlelight through the stained glass windows. A strange chill ran through his body and his dog whimpered. He decided to look through the windows, but the closer he got the more the dog panicked and pulled at its lead, so he turned for home. As he walked the wind blew the clouds apart and revealed a full moon.

Back at the church, a girl was waking to find herself tied to the altar. The only sounds she could hear were the howling wind and her own heartbeat. Suddenly she heard a swooping sound and a vampire flew through the stained glass window above the altar showering her with shattered glass.

In the moonlit churchyard the lid of a tomb was slowly being pushed to one side and a dishevelled man emerged. As he stood in the moonlight his body began to change shape. When he had completely transformed into a werewolf he tore down the church door and saw the vampire bending over the body of the girl. The vampire and werewolf launched themselves at one another and had a vicious fight. At the end of the fight the vampire lay dead. The werewolf picked up the dead girl and carried her back to his lair.

The girl's body was never found but her ghost haunts the graveyard to this day.

Matthew Dyne (12)

Sweet Dreams

The old familiar dream returned. First she was in the boatyard then she was surrounded by the dark. She was drowning in the blackness. A figure emerged from the inky darkness. It looked menacing with sharp teeth and long pointed fingers. It smiled and murmured, 'Your time has come!' She yelled but no one heard her.

Sara jumped in fear. Her clock read 7am. Breathing deeply and steadying herself she got dressed and went downstairs. Ten minutes later she was sipping on cocoa. The image of the creature was still fresh in her head. Deciding sleep was no longer possible and fed up with it, she headed out to the boatyard to calm her fears once and for all.

She arrived and was disgusted with the view. Half the river was covered in floating trash. 'How much longer can we do this?' she sighed. Work had already started. She kept to the edge as she knew she couldn't swim and shivered. Sara questioned why she was here, after all it was just a dream.

She heard a low growling; as she turned she was startled. A fork-lift started moving and painfully knocked her into the inky black river. Quickly looking around, she saw what she feared, the creature of her dreams. Looking closely she saw it was a scarecrow. Exhaling her last breath, she slightly relaxed, at least she would die in peace. An arm suddenly grabbed her and the scarecrow grinned, the darkness closed in all around her ...

Duncan Harkness (14)

The Haunted Mansion

Sam and Mike were driving home from an outrageous party. It was very icy and their car skidded into a tree. As they got out of their car, they realised that they had nowhere to go. So they searched the area for somewhere.

'*Sam, over here!*' shouted Mike,

'We have to stay here until morning,' Sam suggested. 'After you Mike!'

They knocked on the door and awaited a response. There was none. So they pushed the door open and saw a very old mansion. The stairs were broken and the pipes had rusted. There were rats scurrying around. 'We'll have to split up. Search for a room to stay in.'

Sam went upstairs. He opened the first door and he saw a pile of skeletons. He slammed the door.

Meanwhile ...

Mike opened a small latch and he saw nothing but a sign ... *Beware!* Before he could move, he woke up, strapped to a board. 'Who are you?' There was a person in white floating in the air.

'I am your worst nightmare!'

He started thinking about Sam.

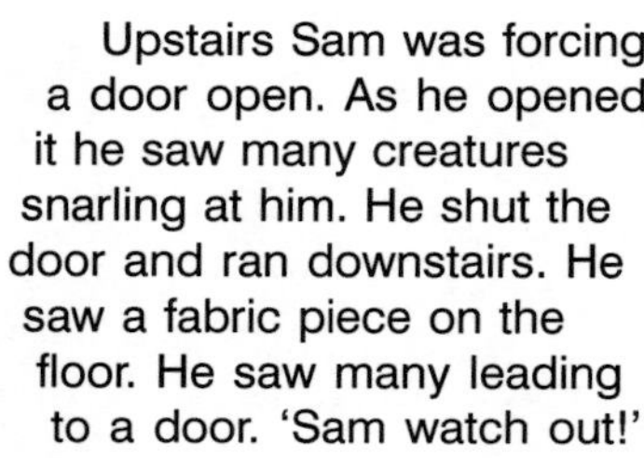

Upstairs Sam was forcing a door open. As he opened it he saw many creatures snarling at him. He shut the door and ran downstairs. He saw a fabric piece on the floor. He saw many leading to a door. 'Sam watch out!'

The ghost swung a sword at him but the sword got stuck in the door.

Mike got out of the ropes and they ran out as fast as light.

They ran ...

Jehpal Jhita (11)

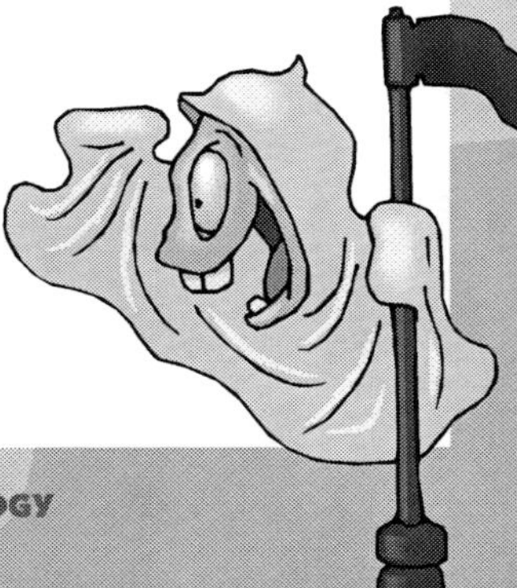

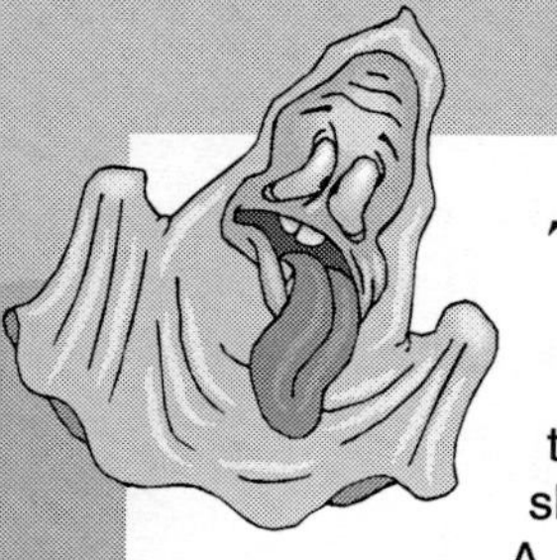

The Trial

The hall chilled as a swirling mist drifted through the open doorway. The air took on an icy sharpness and the bare marble floor turned to ice. A light frost appeared on the tapestries and wall hangings that could be seen only just through the tall, gleaming, white columns that were scattered around the room, stretching to an impossibly high, huge, domed ceiling.

Mist spread through the room slowly, edging its way carefully to the far end of the hall and maybe uncertainly, climbing the smooth walls. A face appeared in the mist, small in the large mass of white. It looked to be one with the mist; two parts of the same thing, a misty face, a cloudy face.

Defiant, slightly tilted eyes above a bold nose studied the room, taking in everything, confused somehow, as if not knowing where this was or even when this was, silently wondering if it were reality or dream.

The face glided forward to a painting hanging from perhaps ten feet above the floor. The painting showed a dark-haired young girl kneeling to a beautiful woman with a lily and sword carved crown entwined around her temples. The crown lay atop red-gold hair, arranged in curls to her shoulders. When looked at closely, the girl in the painting showed a startling resemblance to the face floating in the dense mist. Too much resemblance to be natural, unless …

The face jumped, if a floating head could be said to do that! The painting looked to be a trial of some sort but the pair in the painting were surrounded by finely dressed men and women, nobles and too many to be a trial for a small offence. They looked grim but satisfied. The beautiful woman looked angered. This could be a trial for kidnapping or even murder. The face appeared to remember something, something important.

Then the mist dissipated, the face fled, terrified whimpers echoed in the hallways, tears splashing on stone floors and sounds of weeping everywhere. The building was suddenly silent, nothing moved. Surely, nothing would move in an empty building?

Julia Harold (13)

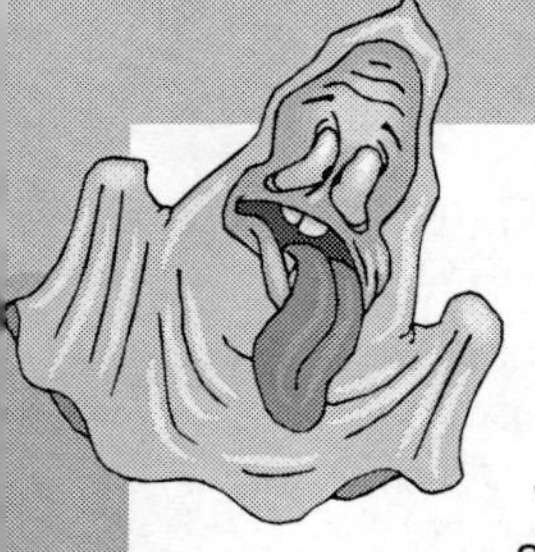

Mrs Harding's Ghost

It was early one sunny Tuesday morning when old Mrs Harding looked out of her living room window and saw a ghost. She was quite shocked and had to look again to make sure. There it was, a spooky woman in white with a deathly white face, standing in the doorway of the house opposite.

At first, Mrs Harding didn't know what to do. She didn't know the people who lived in that house, so she couldn't telephone them to warn them. She decided to enlist the help of her next-door neighbour, Mrs MacDonald.

The two old ladies bustled across the empty street towards the offending property and, after much debate, decided to ring the doorbell. 'Don't you think we'd better call the poli … ' began Mrs MacDonald. Too late. The door flew open and there it stood, the ghost.

They jumped and backed away in terror, but then the ghost spoke, 'Oh, I'm sorry!' it exclaimed. 'I'm afraid this face mask does make me look rather scary!'

After several cups of tea, much explanation and many apologies, the matter was finally resolved. The ghost (who was actually a nice young lady named Miss Phillips) had been answering her door when Mrs Harding saw her. The elderly friends were about to take their leave when, at the last moment, Miss Phillips' doorbell rang.

'Excuse me ladies, I must answer that,' she said with a sigh, as she passed through the kitchen table on her way to the hall.

Emily Ford (14)

Dead ... Or Alive?

Her fingers like a rake, hair hanging loosely, it looked like snakes. I was sure they hissed at me. I turned to head for the chapel door but it slammed shut in my face.

I turned to see this ghostly woman's hands out, as if practising magic, evil magic. Surely she hadn't closed the door? What if? No! that was silly. This woman, this thing could not be.

I turned to face her properly and found myself drawn to her eyes. There was something about them, they were filled with something. Like when someone smiles and you can tell they're happy, through their eyes. Well this woman just had to look at me and I was sure she was hurting inside. Cold, hate and emptiness filled her pupils. I walked towards her; I saw wrinkles of age on her weathered face.

What was she doing here? This was a chapel and she was sitting at the altar. I could have just thought she was praying but at 3am it was a strange thing for an old lady to do. I heard a creaking, I released all my thoughts and scattered my eyes around the room, then back to the wrinkled face in front of me. She just stared at me, through me. She seemed quite alive physically, but mentally, inside this woman was well and truly dead.

Chantelle Skett (14)

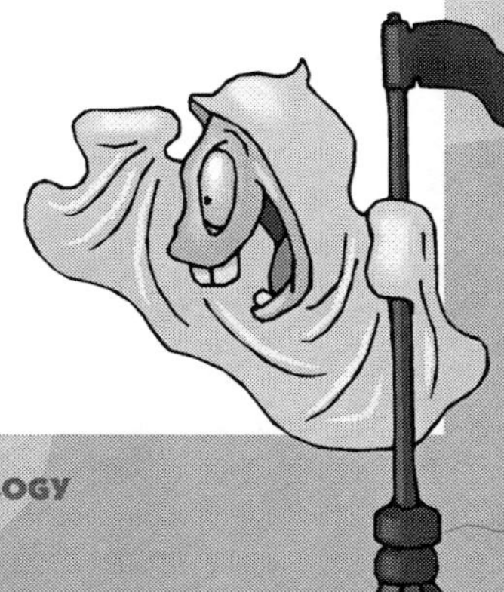

Misery Island

Wide gloomy eyes surrounded me. Hundreds, thousands of dark eyes. Then a series of screams. Head-banging screams. Torturing screams. These were screams like no other.

My heart was pounding hard, so hard I could feel the pulse vibrate through my body. My breath seemed to quicken. I dared not move, but I had to. I had to find out where I was and what I was doing here.

Last night I had fallen asleep in my warm, cosy bed. Now I've been woken up by loud, bellowing screams of pain. I felt a cold shiver down my spine. I clasped my hands tight together and scrunched my toes up, then silent tears flowed down my cheeks. Tears of pure fear.

I took one small, silent step and then out of nowhere six shadows circled me! I froze, too scared to move. They weren't shadows, they were ghosts! Six horrid, ancient ghosts circled me. They started to move around me. I felt my feet lift off the stony ground. I was floating in mid-air!

I closed my eyes as tight as I could and longed for home. I felt myself go through a series of turns; forwards, backwards, sidewards, not knowing where I was to end up. Then *thud!*

I kept my eyes shut for a moment or two and then slowly one by one, I opened both my eyes. I let out a sigh of relief. I found myself back in my room! The ghosts had saved me from Misery Island.

Racheal Rajah (13)

Ghost Dog

In a village called Spookwood. The village was haunted by a ghost dog. It grew dark at 2pm every day.

The new family in the village decided to go for a walk with their dog, they didn't believe the tales of the ghost dog. Mist came over the haunted field, the wind grew higher, they heard, 'Awooh!' They ran like the wind home.

In the morning, they walked across the field again and peered into a muddy burrow. *Jump!* Out of the hole stood a ghost dog, its teeth shone like bloody daggers. It bit a member of the family. Lucy knew about ghosts and poured water on the ghost. It died.

The village shouted with joy. From then on it became dark at 9pm and Lucy was known as the smartest girl in Spookwood.

Bethaney Alicia Nicolson (9)

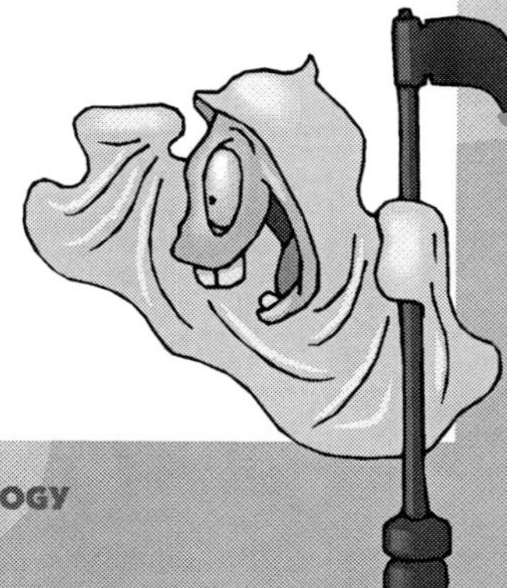

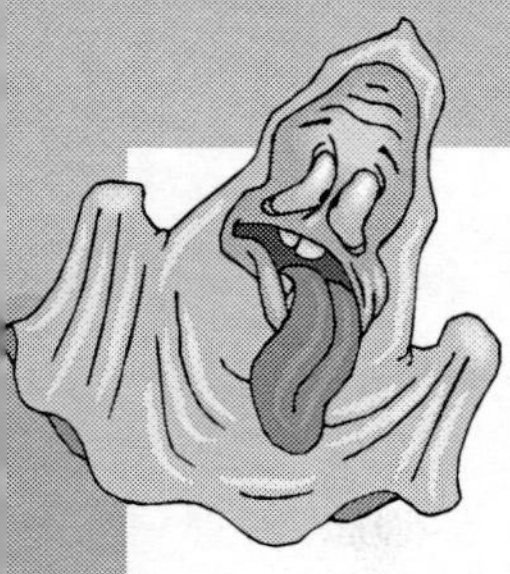

John's Ghost

All the food was ready for the funeral party to return. I was a little nervous, to think I was sitting in the very room he died in. The old house was warm, very dark, with a few small windows. It was creepy, almost scary. I didn't think that houses like this existed, it was so old-fashioned. The whole house was plastered in dust, it looked like it had never been cleaned.

Then suddenly a *tap, tap, tap* began on the old-fashioned latch on a door in the corner of the room, my heart jumped into my throat, I left the seat as soon as I heard it, I wished they'd come back now. The tapping went on and on. I wanted to run but I was frozen to the spot. At last I heard a car and footsteps and strangely the tapping stopped. I started to unwrap the food, everybody thanked me for all my help, it was a cold day and some warm food was welcome. I was still scared and must have been as white as a sheet.

I was just about to leave when the tapping started again. I jumped, everybody jumped and looked at the door.

John's son Dave said, 'That stupid cat, he can see you through a gap in the old door. He'll even open it sometimes.'

He opened the door and out came the cat. I think I would have died if it had have opened!

Georgina Tabberer-Mills (11)

The Schooner Hells Gate Ship

A long time ago there was a ship sailing across the Atlantic Ocean. The Schooner Hells Gate had a blood-thirsty crew of seven. They looked out at sea and saw the waves had gone down and the sea was flat. Captain Piofin; the cruellest person ever; had decided that he and his crew should go to bed. So they went to bed not daring to disobey the scariest person they had ever met.

Their beds were made of old sacks; but Captain Piofin had the most comfortable bed they had ever seen. Yet again they wouldn't dare to ask for a better bed because a person who had already asked, suddenly died. They jumped into their rotten sacks and as the last person fell asleep the waves crashed.

The crew jumped out of bed only to find themselves being thrown back in their beds by a huge wave. Captain Piofin shouted as loud as he could, to be heard over the waves. The crew died as they tried to get away. Captain Piofin drowned as the biggest wave came, the entire ship then sank to the bottom of the ocean.

Many years later the ship was discovered by a submarine. The captain asked a diving company to explore it. The next day, two divers swam to the wreck. They swam inside to find seven crew members holding daggers. The divers were never seen again.

So take my advice and stay clear of the Schooner Hells Gate wreck.

Jack Braithwaite (9)

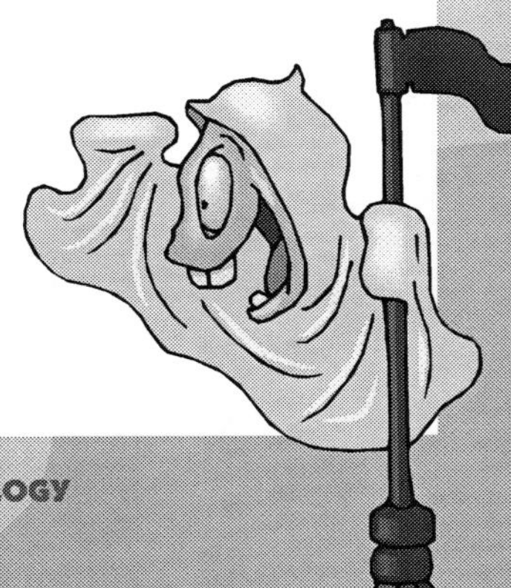

The Forgotten Pub

I inhaled the foul smell of smoke and alcohol. Beside me sat drunken pirates of the past ages, long before my time. The barman floated cautiously to the table to collect the used glasses.

Jon Page, who died of the plague many centuries before, now floated dangerously up to the rafters above me. Frederick Jones passed through my body making me shiver, he then headed for the bar for a drink after his long day working down in the mines in the past era. Johnson carried on buoyantly walking through the walls to go and haunt the inhabitants living in his house in this present day. Betty Canbon, who was beheaded years ago, now carried her head under her arm as she went.

'Surprised are you?' spoke one of the pirates with an accent to his voice. 'I don't suppose you've ever seen a pub full of ghosts before,' he said.

I said nothing in reply as I was too shocked by what I saw.

The bell for last orders rang, there was a mad rush for more beer. The punters finished their glasses and headed for home. Haunting fun was just about to start.

'Carrie, Carrie,' whispered Mum. 'You were having a nightmare dear,' she said.

I finally came back to the real world. I don't believe her, I thought I knew it was true. It was, wasn't it?

Rebecca Blake (13)

Horror In Savanna Woods

Once there lived a boy called Finn. He lived with his sister Anna. One day they went to Savanna Woods. It was very dark in the woods and although they had a torch, they couldn't see a thing. The next thing they knew they were lost.

'Finn?' squeaked Anna. But there was no answer. She looked everywhere for him. After a while she gave up looking and fell hopelessly to the ground. She looked up at the stars and started to cry.

'Hello Anna,' said a familiar voice. She spun round to see who it was. It was her old schoolmate, Candy. But not for long because suddenly, Candy turned into a strange-looking man. He started to tie her to a tree by wrapping leather bandages around her and the tree. She screamed loudly until she felt somebody hold her hand. It was Finn. He was also tied to the tree. They both closed their eyes while the strange man set fire to the bandages. They tried to escape but it was impossible. Anna began to cry again.

'Goodbye!' said the strange man, 'no one can help you now.'

The children heard his evil laughter as he walked off into the woods leaving them to die. Seconds later, the fire burnt through the bandages and the children were able to escape. They quickly put out the fire on their clothes and hugged each other with joy. Then they heard someone coming. Was it the strange man? No! It was their dad, who had come to fetch them for their tea.

Dana Dorricott (8)

Hallowe'en Scares

Chris was dressed up in his skeleton/vampire costume ready for trick or treating round his village. There had already been people coming to his house for the same reason.

When he went out, there were people everywhere. Chris knocked on a few doors and got a small selection of sweets and then walked down an alleyway into the next street. *It's cold down here,* Chris thought to himself. All of a sudden the lights went out and three figures loomed out of the darkness ahead. 'Who are you?' Chris asked.

The only answer he got was 'MRH!'

At this Chris stopped. He realised he was facing a zombie, a vampire and a werewolf! And they were after him! *'Help!'* Chris screamed and sprinted home. The chase was on! The three monsters went after Chris.

At Chris' house, his opened gate suddenly shut and wouldn't open! *Oh no!* Chris thought. *I'm going to get captured by those, those monsters!* Chris screamed again.

All of a sudden the lights came on and the monsters stopped and lifted their heads off! There were three familiar faces there. 'Did we scare you?' It was his older brother, Tom and his friends.

'Yes, you did!' Chris said and all four boys went inside for some hot chocolate and their sweets and chocolate from their trick or treating.

Christopher Duffy (10)

A True Ghost Story - Grandad Watching Over Us

When my dad was only eight and his brother Andrew was six, their grandad died and their nan was very upset so they went to stay with her for one night to keep her company.

It was very late when they arrived so my dad and Andrew went straight to bed. Their nan lived in the middle of nowhere in a very isolated house and it was very cold in that small room so their mum put the electric blanket on them. She kissed them goodnight and went downstairs, warning them to go straight to sleep.

Their nan and mum had a few drinks while they played cards and their mum was very surprised to hear noises coming from upstairs. She thought that she could hear running around and jumping off the bed upstairs. She was very cross that they weren't asleep, so she stormed upstairs to tell them off.

When she got upstairs she was shocked. They were fast asleep and the electric blanket was on fire. The flames were blazing above the two little boys. So she quickly opened the window and threw the bedcovers out, with the heated blanket. The boys woke up choking and screaming in pain from the burns on their legs. Any longer and they would have been killed by the smoke.

When they had calmed down and were all talking about it later, they realised that the ghost of their recently dead grandad must have been the one making all the noise upstairs. Who else could it have been that had saved the boys' lives? To this day my dad still bears the scar of the terrible burn he received on his right leg. Ask him and he'll show you.

Josie Pond (10)

The Haunted Football Ground

One night after a football match, a caretaker was cleaning the stands. He was tired and wanted to go home but before he could, he needed to finish cleaning. The floodlights were on so he could see. But then the lights started to flicker and then went off completely. This didn't scare him as he knew they needed new bulbs. Then they started to flash on and off, but he didn't think anything of it. The virtual scoreboard started to flash on and off too. He started to wonder then what was going on! Music started to play but then it started to skip tracks and sounded wrong. Sparks came out of the wires … suddenly everything stopped! Screams and howls came from the pitch. He hid behind the seats, shaking.

Silence came and so he decided to peer over the seat. But he couldn't see anything but blackness. *I'm not scared,* he thought to himself and so decided to investigate the pitch. He slowly walked forwards and stopped in the centre circle. The floodlights came on again, brighter than ever. He shielded his eyes. As his eyes adjusted to the light he looked up and saw a girl hanging in mid-air. She had a white dress, which was dripping wet and torn. Long, black, scraggly wet hair. A pale white face with blue lips and closed eyes. He gulped loudly and then her eyes opened …

David Booth (10)

The Spooky Roller Coaster

A few days ago we went to Alton Towers because I had won a competition for the whole family which included Mum, Dad and my sister Hannah.

When we got there it was a lovely warm sunny day and we were all excited, except Dad because he hates roller coasters. We got to go to the front of the line because we had our tickets already. When we got inside, we gazed at all the fun rides. I ran to the nearest roller coaster, Mum, Dad and Hannah ran after me. The first one we came to was the largest and scariest of them all. It was called 'The Black Hole' and we begged Mum and Dad to let us go on it. They gave in and we got on the last carriage.

The roller coaster started and Hannah and I were really scared. We went up and up and I could see for miles. Then I looked and we were at the top, then down we went. I could see a cave, then suddenly I was inside it. It went on for ages, then I said to Hannah, 'I'm scared!' She didn't answer. I closed my eyes and then opened them, I found myself at my grave. I screamed, closed my eyes again, then opened them, and I was back on the ride with my sister. When we got off I said, 'I never want to go on a roller coaster again.'

Clare Littler (10)

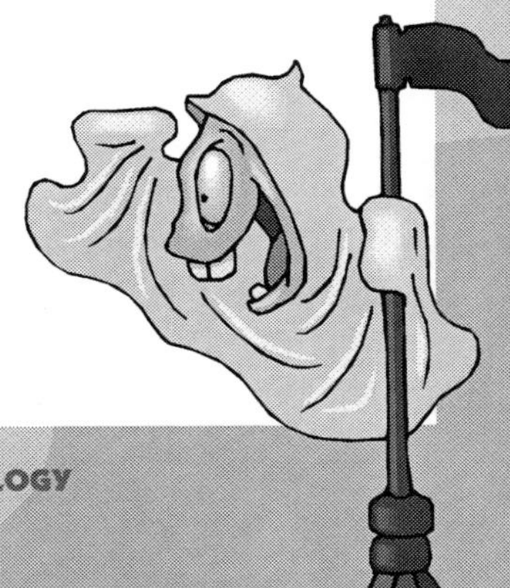

The Mystery

In a house not far from here lived a teenage girl who suffered a terrible fate. One morning she woke up to go to the bathroom. While she was there her worst nightmare popped out of the closet and into her bedroom.

When she went in, she screamed like a baboon. Her parents didn't come in for they were away. It was the witch of all … ugly faces!

Sam, for that was her name, plucked up her courage and said, 'Your lipstick is so out of place.'

The witch got really mad, sat Sam down and went to find her gruesome make-up box. When she got back she set to work on Sam. First she used slug slime lipgloss, earwig eyeshadow, maggot mascara, fag foundation, putrid powder and bleach blusher. Sam wriggled and kicked, slapped and spat. So the nightmare took out her sword and stabbed Sam in the spine. As she did, the make-up dissolved the dead body.

When her parents got back they searched and searched and called the police who sent out a search party but they found no trace of Sam. So all you girls out there, beware of the witch of all … ugly faces!

Jack Adie (10)

The Beast

It waits for you, waits for that one special moment when you are weak, alone and vulnerable. It knows when. It is an unwanted creature of the night and it can smell your fear, you know the end is near and so does the beast. It is taken by the irresistible stench of your crimson-coloured blood. Life force. It sets out to find you, searching from up in the midnight sky, following the smell of your fake innocence. It flies across the moonlit sky, its wings like that of a large bird, but its face ... its face, like that of something that is only seen in your worst nightmares. Its eyes black, they show no emotion, the beast has no remorse for its actions, this is how it lives, this is how it chooses to live. It is the hunter and you are the hunted. It is coming for you, coming for its next feed. Say goodbye now for soon you will feel the beast's cynical embrace.

Kayleigh Balmer (15)

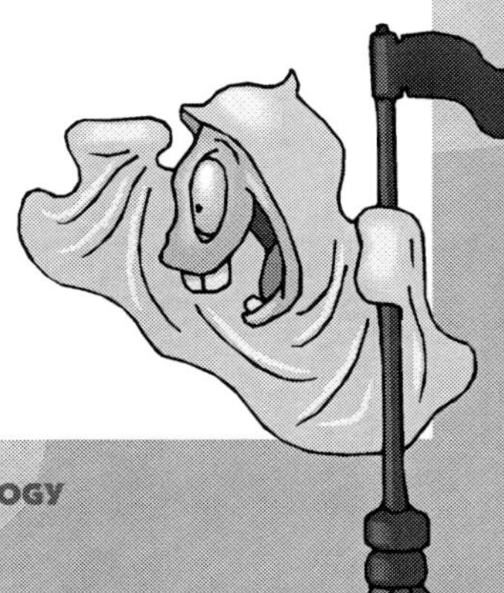

The Robbery In The Deserted Dark Ghost House

One dark, dismal, foggy evening there were two robbers walking past a large house. Their names were Jon and Jack. When they saw the house they thought to themselves, *let's rob that house!* So quietly they crept in through the window. When they were in the house they saw cobwebs all over the walls and in the corners of the rooms.

They also saw two big fireplaces. On one they saw diamond rings, necklaces and lots of earrings. They both picked up everything (including a lot of money). They stuffed their sacks completely full.

They put the sacks under their jackets and went to celebrate at the pub. As they were walking back, they heard a twig snap. They both looked around but nothing was there. So they carried on walking. By the time they got home it was twelve o'clock … midnight!

Jon and Jack got their swag out of the sacks and laid it on the table. As they laid it, the table tipped over. Jon and Jack jumped up into the air, but nothing was there. So they picked the table up and laid everything down again.

'Come on let's share this,' whispered Jack.

'Well, I'll have the diamond necklace then,' said Jon.

All of a sudden the lights started to flicker. Then the fire went out and the room became icy cold. They both felt a breeze on their necks and everything started to shake in the room.

They felt cobwebs brush their faces. All of a sudden

the door flung open and the lights and the fire both came back on. They saw that the diamond necklace was missing. They both ran out of the house screaming. They ran back to their own houses.

A few weeks later they both went into the pub and saw a painting of a lady with a diamond necklace around her neck. Jack and Jon looked at each other terrified. 'Who's that?' they asked the landlord.

'She's meant to be the ghost at the big house,' grinned the landlord.

Jon and Jack stared at each other and felt like blood was running down their spines.

Alex Hemming (10)

The Night Of The Living Mummy

One spooky night, two girls, Laura and Lauren met up with each other at the shopping mall. Instead of shopping, they decided to go for a walk and ended up in some woods. They had heard a rumour about a ghost but they said, 'Who believes in ghosts? We don't!' So off they went.

They weren't scared about the rumour as they both agreed people love the woods. But it was not long before they began to hear strange noises.

'What is it? What is it?' Lauren said.

'It's probably just a fox or a rabbit,' Laura said.

'What if it's a ghost?' Lauren said.

'Don't be silly,' Laura said. 'Ghosts don't exist - remember?'

Then the bush shook and began to open up. There in front of their eyes was a tomb. They stepped back shaking like leaves, as the tomb opened before their eyes. There stood a mummy just staring at them. They screamed and began to run. The mummy tried chasing them and its bandages started unwrapping. Then as they turned around again it had disappeared ...

Laura and Lauren never ever went there again!

Laura-Anne Wilkin (9)

Expect The Unexpected

'Girls we have no choice but to stay the night.'

'It looks a bit gloomy,' remarked Jayne.

'More magical,' sighed Ellie.

But the tall building that stood before us looked old and frail, but seemed to hold the key to many untold stories.

We tapped the iron door which echoed throughout the hallway. A moment later the door slowly creaked open. A croaky voice coughed and slowly said, 'What do you want?'

'The signpost has blown down and we are lost! Can we stay the night?'

She hesitated for a moment, but then welcomed us in. The lady introduced herself as Miss Jones. Her family and herself had lived in the old mansion for 9 decades, but her husband had sadly passed away. Just thinking of a ghost being in the same room, gave me shivers.

Miss Jones led us up the grand staircase to individual rooms with four-poster beds and silk sheets. It seemed that she was expecting visitors, or why had all the guest rooms been prepared when she lived alone?

The night was uneventful apart from Ellie and Jayne losing things. We thanked Miss Jones for her kind hospitality and after showing us directions, we drove off.

After half an hour, we ended up back at the house, we were lost! When Ellie spotted a man walking towards us, we asked him directions.

He said, 'Turn around in the house's drive where Miss Jones used to live, she won't mind, she's been dead for 10 years.'

Siobhan Harris (13)

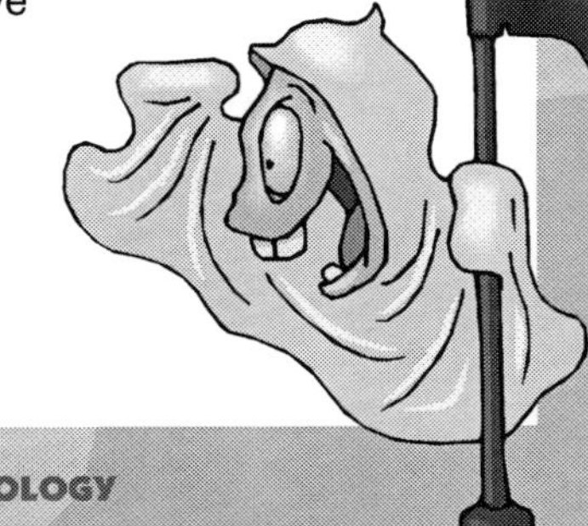

The Mystery Event

One early morning a fisherman was going down to the harbour to fish for some big fish for tea. So he started to fish. Then the sun was coming up and the fisherman saw a huge wave, but when he turned his head back again - the wave was gone.

The following hour the fisherman had still not caught anything! Suddenly the wave came again, and the wave disappeared quickly. Round about midday the wave came again and then he saw a shadow so he said to himself, 'I will wait another hour and get my net ready this time ...'

Sure enough an hour later he saw the wave crashing towards him. And this time he quickly cast his net towards the choppy sea. After a few minutes he felt a pulling on his net. Then a voice said, 'You're going next,' then a roar and a crash of a wave tried to pull the fisherman in. But the ghost fisherman got his fish knife out and stabbed the man in the stomach and pulled him in and he was never seen again ...

Jonathan Wilkes (10)

The Haunted House

One dark evening there were two robbers who decided to rob a haunted house. They did not know that it was haunted.

It was twelve minutes to eleven so they said, 'By a quarter to one in the morning we should have finished everything.'

After they had loaded everything into the truck, however, there was a problem with it. It wouldn't move. They tried pushing it as hard as they could but it still didn't move.

Later on they heard a voice, looked around, but there was no one there. The voice came again. This time it said, 'Put back the things that you've taken!'

They quickly put back the stuff that they had taken. Then when they had finished they wanted to go out but the door was locked.

Music started playing. Suddenly the music got louder. They were so desperate to get out they tried smashing the window, but it wouldn't break.

The sun rose. The glass broke. The music stopped and the door opened. As soon as they got out they ran as fast as they could.

'You were fools to go there!'

Those two never did anything bad again.

Tsitsi Dhliwayo (10)

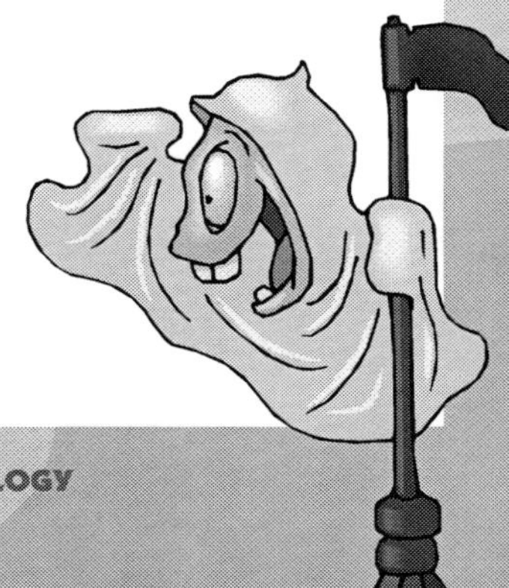

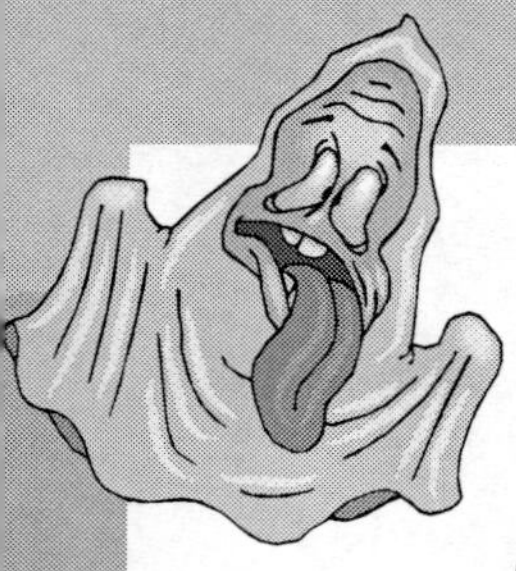

The Pet Cemetery

One cloudy day, a man called George Berger and his wife Rose were going to Africa to build a school so they could help the poor children. George had ordered a ferry to cross the sea to Africa, because they both thought trains and aeroplanes were too dangerous. Before they got on the ferry George and Rose went to collect their dog from the kennels. Their dog's name was Polo; they wanted to take Polo to Africa.

When they got on the ferry Polo was really excited so he was jumping around but then … Polo disappeared. He had fallen into the sea. Rose was screaming with sadness. George jumped into the sea to get Polo. When Polo was back on shore he wasn't breathing so they called for help but Polo didn't make it. They both agreed to bury Polo in Africa.

After a few hours they were finally in Africa. They stayed in a cottage with nobody around, just one next-door neighbour. George asked their next-door neighbour where they could bury their dog. He showed George a pet cemetery. The next-door neighbours warned George, 'Never bury anything on the burial ground by the cemetery.'

George went back to the cottage to tell Rose that she could bury Polo but he forgot to tell Rose about the burial ground. When Rose got back George asked her where she had buried Polo.

Rose said, 'This empty patch of ground.'

George trembled.

In the night Polo was staring at Rose. She woke up and started to panic. She pushed Polo away from her and started to run, but Polo chased her. George came in with an air rifle (he had found it in the yard) but Rose was already dead.

He dropped the air rifle and ran beside her so they could still live together in Heaven.

Owen Nuttall (11)

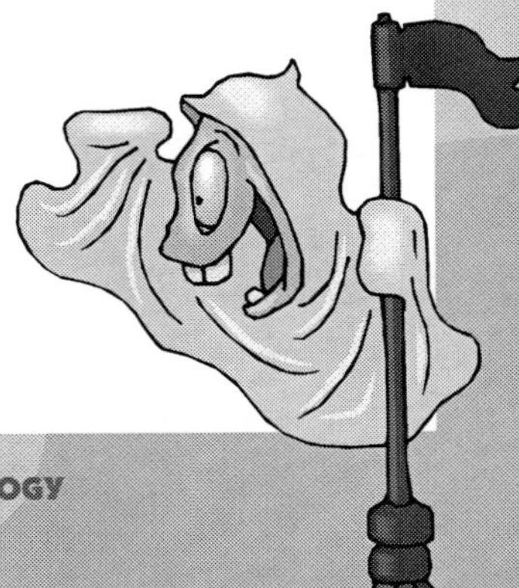

Cold

Darkness smothered the sky consuming everything into shadow. Mist surrounded the town as the day of Fawn's Moon drew near.

A time when tales were told
Of a story of old,
Many years ago
A girl did go,
To the forest one night
Planning a fright
Of a kiss
Of pure bliss
Climbed a tree
Did she
But she did fall
No one heard her call
This night after many moons
Her ghost still looms.

It was a dark night; Alex O'Brian was making his way home from school, the only route was through this forest. It was very cold, colder than usual. Mist had formed over the ground.

He walked, trying to be brave; he had heard the stories of Fawn. He heard a howl and twigs snapping behind him, a chill of terror ran through his veins. His head told him hide, but his heart made him run, run as fast as his legs would carry him, spindly branches clawed at his face.

Suddenly he stopped, looking around, he was lost, alone in the dark wood; he heard a soft voice whisper. A chilling hand touched his cheek. He turned to see a pair of cold eyes staring at him, the power pulling him in, he knew it was her …

Fawn.

He was pulled in, his lips touched hers and he knew it was the end, he felt the energy being drawn from him, it felt like time had stopped as he fell to the ground cold …

Amie Sandell (16)

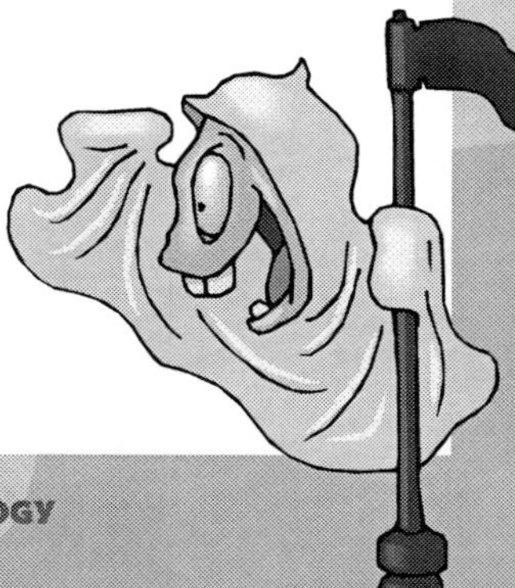

The Cornfield

One day the farmer, Matt, was washing up the dishes when he noticed that his cornfield had a hole in the middle. He ran outside. Why was there a hole in his cornfield? No one could cut it down, it was well protected.

When night fell Matt thought, *whoever cuts my corn down must do it at night*, so he grabbed his torch and went outside.

He couldn't see over the corn because the corn was more than a metre tall. Suddenly a great wind went past him, his torch flickered, then another wind went past, this time his torch went off. He began to shiver, he walked silently back but a cold smoky hand touched his shoulder. He ran up to his room as quick as he could, slammed the door shut.

When he looked outside though, a smoky figure was crawling up the corn.

Next day the corn that had been cut down had regrown ...

Simi Virdee (8)

My Worst Nightmare

One dark, miserable night in the deep woods was a cottage and there lived a little girl and a little boy. Their mother had passed away when they were young. The little girl was left in charge.

One afternoon the little boy was hungry so they went to find something to eat. The little boy saw a juicy red apple and tucked it up his sleeve. When the two children got home they sat down by the fire. The little boy took the apple out of his sleeve and took a big juicy bite out of it. The two children did not know that it was poisonous. The little boy fainted. The little girl felt his heart pounding, it was going down fast. He died, the little girl should have known better.

She was feeling very lonely so she went down to the secret room, where her and her brother used to play. She was sitting on a box when she saw a shadow, she hoped that it was her reflection, but it was moving. She became very scared, it was her mind playing tricks on her. She ran out of the room screaming her head off.

She woke up with a fright, it was all a dream.

Kelsey Gale (8)

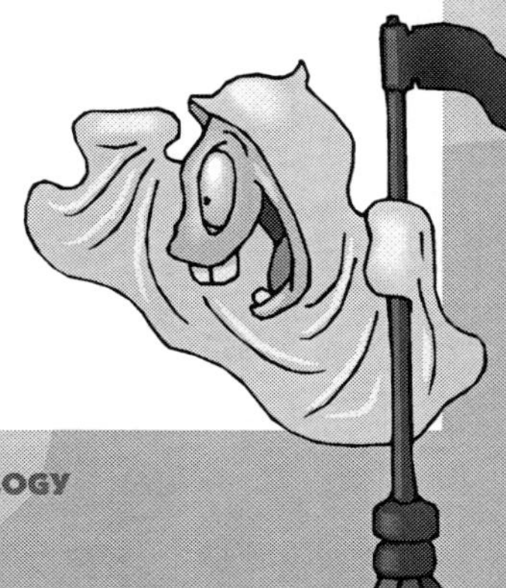

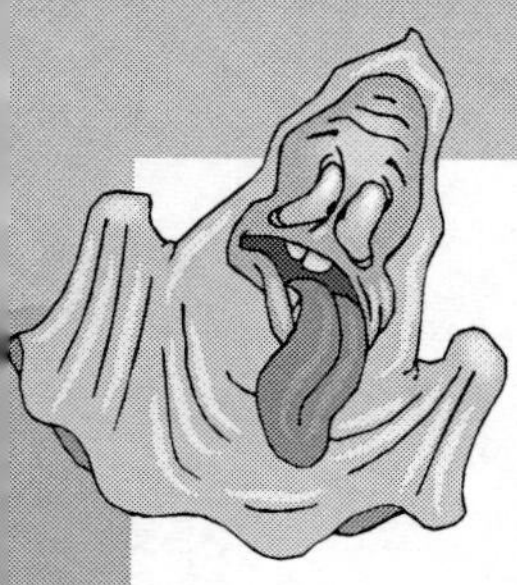

They Will Never Rest In Peace

The setting of this story is as most ghost stories, set on the 31st of October, Hallowe'en.

It was late and a pool of moonlight was shining on the house which just so happened to be the house of the naughty and cunning little twins who are this story's main characters.

'OK Mummy we'll be good tonight,' said the twins, George and Jeremy, as innocently and sweetly as they could.

But once they were out of sight the twins immediately got out the eggs. These just so happened to be mouldy eggs and were at least four years off their sell-by-date, that was the best bit about them.

They walked down a narrow, dark alleyway and then straight in front of them was their main target, the Gregory family. The twins looked through the window and instantly saw the family crying. A family member had passed away.

After looking through the window they stepped away from the big rusty house and together they threw the eggs. They soared through the air hitting the windows upstairs. That was when a figure suddenly loomed over them and then next second he said in a low tone of voice, 'You will never rest in peace.'

Five seconds later you could see two boys getting horribly slaughtered but obviously there was no one there to see it.

The only trace ever again found were the words engraved in blood at the crime scene, *'They will never rest in peace'.*

Matthew Kent (10)

The Ghost And The Ugly

It was Hallowe'en for Rosie and she was dressed up as a vampire. She walked past the crooked house like a castle but smaller. Rosie stopped and walked to the house.

'No,' bellowed a boy who was dressed up as a vampire.

'Why?' she asked back.

'Because people have gone in there but never came out.'

'Can you keep a secret?' she sniggered, 'they're fables!'

Rosie ran in.

Suddenly something touched her, a cold fingery touch, but then it pushed her into a portal. She entered a world she never dared to think about. It was ... the world of the ghost and the ugly!

She saw a lightning sword and she grabbed it. Suddenly there stood the ghost and the ugly. The ugly trapped her. She stood there as still as a coffin. Suddenly, as fast as a blink, she shot him in the heart and he turned into a pile of dust. Then she pointed to the ghost and struck him hard, there was nothing left.

Rosie saw the portal and jumped into it and popped out the other side to enjoy Hallowe'en.

Katie Davies (9)

Dead Nightmare

Once, in the town of ghostly ghouls and horrific beasts, dwelled a bloodthirsty killer ... The Killer Ghost.

It had returned.

The fearsome creature could not be controlled. It possessed no glory, only the thought of death and pain.

It is called the Ghost Creature from the Underworld and it is back to haunt people.

It is here to kill.

So, watch out ...

Tom Heathfield (9)

Pascale

Once, centuries ago in a mysterious, gloomy corner of the haunted island, I sat crying. A wispy man-like thing floated behind me. The cloud bounced off the moon. I screamed, petrified as I heard a snarl behind me. I daren't think what was there! I tottered around and almost fainted. It was the ghost of … a werewolf! It didn't seem to have noticed me. I held my breath. Suddenly I felt something. I shrieked in agony. Splashes of blood surrounded me. Then I remembered not to worry, for God was there and I must count my blessings.

Before I had even started (or so it seemed) I heard cackling. It said, 'Hold its nose to make it open its mouth.'

An ogre called for silence and prepared to step on me. With the thought of death in my heart I grabbed a tree root and hauled myself up. Then, suddenly I saw something. It was a young boy, about the same age as me.

But there was no time for that, for a pack of ghostly werewolves had surrounded me. I simply made a run for it.

The boy was running too. We were running towards a patch of daylight.

Suddenly … the haunted island was gone! We were in a grassy forest. I sat down and asked the boy what his name was. He said it was Darren. I told him I was Pascale.

And from that day on Darren and I have lived happily ever after.

Jennifer Baker (7)

The Underground Tunnel

Katie had to find her brothers. It was important. Oh where were they? Katie went into their room. They weren't there, she went into the living room. They weren't there. Then she thought, *of course, the backyard*.

She ran out the back door into the yard to see her brothers playing football. 'Come quick, I have something to show you,' Katie yelled.

'What is it? You look like you've seen a ghost,' laughed George, following her inside.

She took them up to her room and showed them the weird door she had found. She told them to open the door and look.

'Wow, let's follow it,' said Derek, when he saw the tunnel.

'No, we can't, it might be dangerous,' said Katie.

Eventually they all agreed to go and explore the tunnel. The tunnel led to an old house that hadn't been lived in for over a hundred years. They walked into the first room. It had broken chairs and bits of wood everywhere. They went up the stairs into what looked like a little girl's bedroom.

They were looking around when suddenly the door locked behind them. They shouted and screamed but no one could hear them. Instead, it is said that they never did get out and no one knew about the tunnel except them.

Hannah Jack (13)

The Chilling Tale

It was a cold, dark night. The full moon at its peak. I was too tired to notice such things as these, it's 'Mary make the breakfast, Mary clean the dishes, Mary wash the clothes'. The list is just endless. I do everything. Dad can't help me. He's too busy fulfilling stepmother and Hannah's wishes. Hannah's no use. She just jeers and makes it worse. Her mother is no better.

That night, the next thing I heard was the door creaking, and in the doorway stood, my mother. I thought I was seeing things. My mother died years ago. But she said, 'Do not be afraid, I am doing this for your own good.' Next thing I heard was a door creaking open, a scream, and then quiet. Another door opened, another scream, another silence.

Little did I know that my mother killed those two cold-hearted women, who had made my dad and I their personal slaves. Next thing I heard was Dad screaming. Oh no, not Dad too! Mum should have known that he was innocent, but Dad had just seen them.

They were two cold-hearted females and at this day in their graves. Dad and I moved to a new house. Just rebuilding those years lost. No one dares enter my house of terror, otherwise they will be slaves in their own home. My mother did a large favour for us. In our old house are two ghosts searching for slaves.

Maria Irvine (13)

A Boy Called Marvin

One hot summer's day the boys Steven, Dale and Barry were playing football in the park. They were having such a good time that they didn't realise that it was getting dark. But it was too dark to go the long way home. So they decided to take a short cut through the graveyard.

Whilst walking in the graveyard a boy approached them and they got chatting. The boy's name was Marvin Mantle. While the boys were chatting they started to hear strange noises, the boys got spooked out except Marvin who seemed calm and settled. The boys noticed that Marvin seemed to know his way around the graveyard pretty well, he told them the names of the people who were in the graves without seeming to look at the headstones. The boys were starting to get even more freaked out. Especially Dale who felt uneasy around Marvin. Then the boys said, 'We'd better be on our way.'

'I'll walk you,' said Marvin.

'OK then,' said Steven.

Barry was just walking along when Dale and Steven stopped stone cold.

Barry said, 'What's the matter?'

'Look ahead, that headstone says 'Marvin Mantle aged 10 died suspiciously 1899'.'

As the boys ran away all they could hear was the eerie laughter of Marvin.

Lauren McPhee (10)

Like Mother, Like Daughter

The rain pattered against the windowpane, everything was peaceful and calm, other than the thunder and lightning which haunted the sky. In the cosy household of the Smith family Melanie couldn't sleep, she was having terrible nightmares, the same one she had been having for days now. Before the accident she would have run into her mother's room and cuddled up with her, but that was not possible. She went to find her dad, who was sitting all alone staring into the fire, she tried to tell him how she felt, but he didn't want to listen.

At 8am Mel's alarm went off, she didn't want to get up, if her mum had still been there she would have had a cup of tea in bed. She didn't understand why her dad hadn't said good morning, so she crept out of bed, and went down the stairs. There were lots of people, many crying, she heard someone say, 'It's time to go now.' Everyone got into cars, she sat beside her dad, and took his hand.

They all entered a small church, she saw her mother's coffin and beside it a smaller one, with her name on it, she began to understand, why her dad didn't answer her, she too had died that night, but she hadn't been ready to leave, she needed to know her dad would be alright. Looking around at all his friends and family she knew he would be looked after. She could now leave.

Laura Bradford (10)

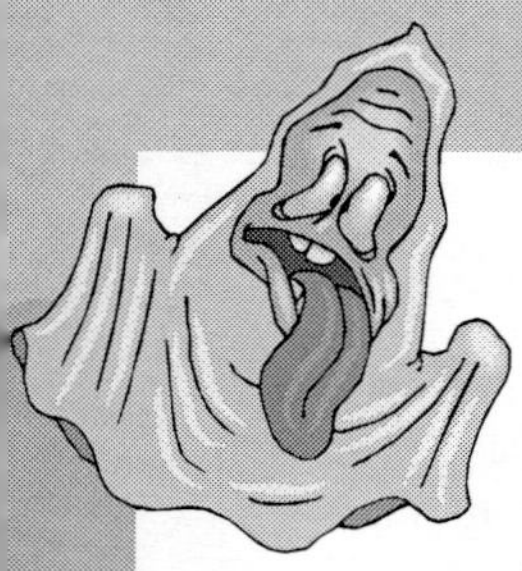

Beware!

There once was a little girl who played in the nearby field. But she doesn't anymore. It was a tragic moment for that girl. I shall tell you about her story, if you promise you won't scream …

One morning a little girl, Melissa, went to play in the field. She didn't know that underneath the field, lay a cemetery. No one knew this, except the man who lived alone in his cottage. The girl always went to this field even though there was a sign saying *No Trespassers!* She couldn't resist the flowers that bloomed there.

One cold evening she decided to go there. She didn't know that there was a surprise awaiting her. As she was walking towards the field, she could sense someone following her. She shouted, 'Who are you?' There was silence. She started to run towards the field in terror. She closed her eyes for a bit. When she opened her eyes she screamed in fright at what she saw. There was a ghost in front of her.

It said, 'Hello girl. I was waiting for you. Remember these?' It was all the flowers Melissa had picked up from the field. 'Because you picked my flowers, now I can take something from you and it is going to be your soul.'

Then the ground started to pull her down. What was left were the flowers she'd *picked!*

That's why, children out there, don't end up like Melissa. I did and became a ghost. So … boo!

Tariq Ajumal (11)

The Hand And The Hammer

One day there was a girl that used to walk her dog on Norton Glay Hills.

She went walking one night with her dog and she could hear whispering in her ear, saying, 'I will get you!'

She started to shiver and her shoes were icy.

A bolt of lightning came, a hand and a hammer were on the floor.

The hand started walking and ...

Two weeks later only her dog was found ... *dead!*

Mary Kate Bowers (11)

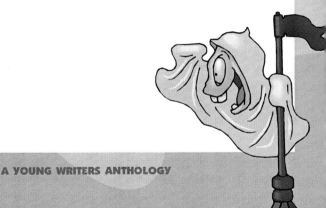

The Ghost That Haunts Christmas

It was Christmas 1982. Emma was going sledging with her best friend Ellie. They wrapped up warm in scarf, hat, gloves and coat. Emma wore the red jumper that Gran had knitted her for Christmas. It was so cosy. They set off down Rosemary Lane. It started to snow. Ellie shivered, 'It's so cold,' she whispered.

The sparkly wisps of snow floated gently to the ground. They eventually got to Wimbledon Hill. They plodded towards the top. 'I wonder when we'll be at the top?' panted Ellie. 'Ah, we're here now!' said Ellie joyfully.

They put their heavy wooden sledges down at the top of the bank. When Emma and Ellie were sitting themselves into their sledges a young girl appeared, she was very pale. She had Victorian-style clothes on. She waved her arms and shook her head. 'I think she wants to go first,' said Emma.

'Oh, let's let her,' said Ellie kindly. So they let the young pale girl go down the hill first. She slid down the slope and suddenly disappeared into the frozen pond. Emma and Ellie ran down the slope to see where she had gone. She had sunk through a gap in the ice and was nowhere to be found.

Emma and Ellie frantically ran to the nearest house to get help. When they had quickly told their story to the old crooked lady who had answered the door she went all pale and had to sit down. She was trembling badly while she explained that her sister had died the same way in that pond on this very same date almost eighty years ago. She was five years old.

'Could you possibly describe her please?'

'Yes she had dark brown hair in a bun and was wearing a long, navy coat with a long, black skirt showing underneath. She had black button up boots on and a red bonnet.'

'That was my sister Elizabeth. She must have been trying to warn you of the danger of sledging from that part of the hill,' she said. 'If she hadn't you surely would have gone through the thin ice and drowned the same way she did. She saved your lives.'

So, if you ever see a young girl, about five years old, sounding like this description near a hill when you are sledging, it may be the ghost of Elizabeth, the ghost that haunts at Christmas.

Chloe Charles (9)

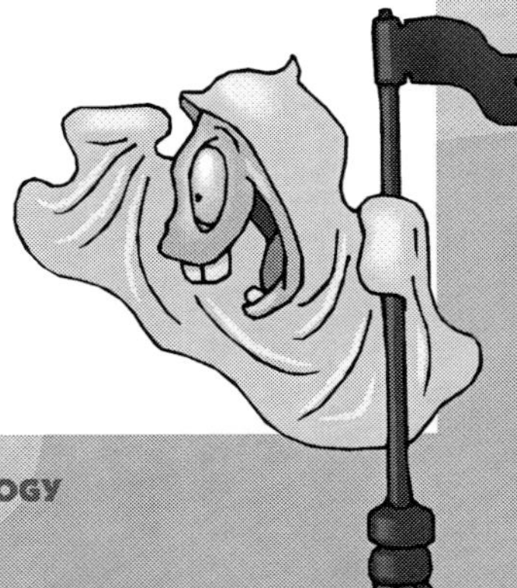

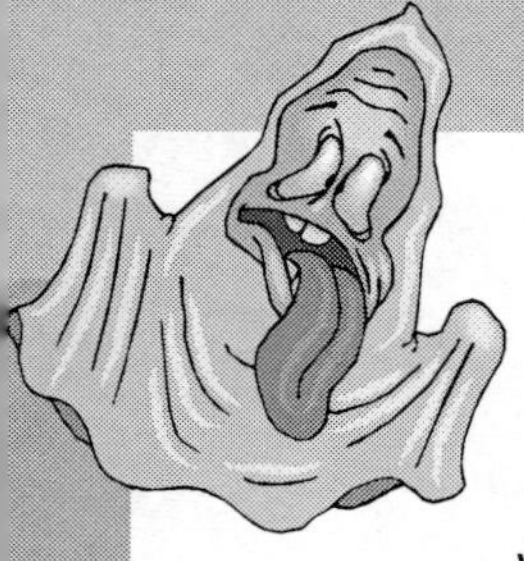

Didn't You Know?

Going to meet someone new can be freaky, especially if they are your great grandma's friends. They must be ancient, anyway, Great Grandma was looking after me and my brother, Stephan. She wanted us to meet her friend, Gontag. Scary name too. Great Grandma said they've been friends for years. I got more frightened as we drove up a steep cliff, I could see his house at the top. It looked old and creepy. Great Grandma parked the car outside next to an old dusty grey car, I assumed belonged to Gontag.

Great Grandma knocked on the dusty door, it looked like it was never opened. Then a tall scary man came to the door, I thought it was Gontag at first but no, it was his servant.

'Yes?' said the scary man.

'Hello, you must be Mr Slasher,' greeted my great grandma. 'I'm Betty.'

He nodded his head and let us in. The floorboard's creaked, not that you could see much of the floor.

'Visitors!' a voice bellowed.

We went into a room, it was all made out of stone, it was damp and smelly, there was slime oozing from the walls. There were bats hanging from the ceiling. Then in walked an old man, with a brown cloak over his head so nobody could see.

'Gontag,' laughed Betty.

'Get out!' screamed Gontag …

Now don't get your hopes up, this spooky story ends here, or else it would scare you half to death. Didn't you know?

April Smyth (10)

The Graveyard Terror!

It was a sunny day but I had a detention so I couldn't go out to play. It was dark when I left the school so I decided I would take a short cut through the graveyard. As I entered some of the tombstones began to move, so I began to run. Then out of nowhere a hand appeared from the ground, I went straight into a 6-foot hole. I screamed but no one could hear me. I sat up and looked around me for some way out. As I turned there appeared to be a dead body lying next to me, I screamed once again but my throat started to hurt.

I thought it might be a nightmare, but it wasn't, unfortunately. I sat there shaking, it seemed like I had been there for hours but it was only a couple of minutes before I heard voices, I leapt to my feet as the voices got closer. It was two men, there was something weird about them but I wasn't going to complain, they had saved me!

I got out and started heading for my house then another hand came out of the ground, it pulled me down, I was screaming but no one came, then I heard my mom so I screamed. I could see her looking around, she saw me. She ran over and pulled me out. We got home and she gave me a nice cup of tea, but now I have nightmares every night!

Nicole Quinn (12)

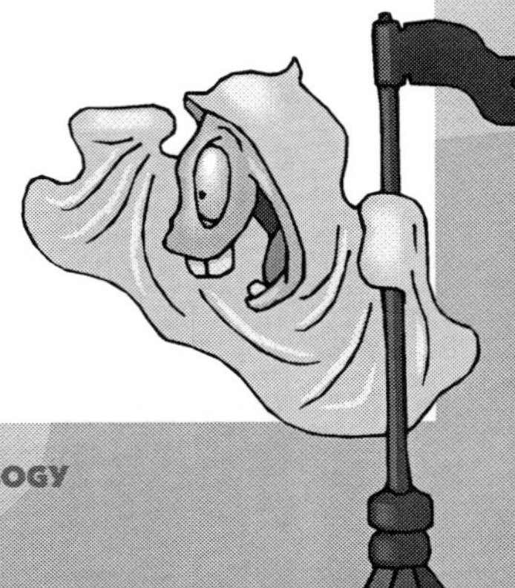

Ghost Story

She sprang bolt upright in her bed, gasping and flailing her arms desperately. Her nightclothes clung to the cold sweat that drenched her back and trickled down her throbbing neck. The dream had ended, yet the scent of lavender lingered. The sapphires that studded the child's pallid face shone with fear and tears as she stepped soundlessly into her bedroom slippers.

Years had elapsed since her vibrant mother had dropped dead.

'You poor man,' they cooed to her father, 'a widower at such a young age and with a little daughter to care for too!'

None of the neighbours though, had seen his sturdy hand trickling the fatal drops into her glass of red wine or shuddered at the satisfied grin that crept across his face as the unsuspecting woman sipped it appreciatively.

At the sitting room door, Myra paused. It was here that the incident had taken place years ago. As the door creaked open, a musty smell tickled her nostrils. Her stomach tightened and her left fist clenched. She fumbled for the light switch and finally hit it. The chandelier's myriad crystals illuminated every speck of dust and a scuttling spider. She drew back in horror at the sight of her father's portrait: slashed violently as though by the razor-sharp claws of a wild beast. Before she could flee, a sensation of something brushing against her shoulder froze her in her tracks. Presently, she caught a whiff of the overpowering perfume of lavender. 'Mum,' she whispered.

Anna Maria Zammit (15)

The Happy Family

It was dark and cold and I could feel my best friend Zoë, breathing down my neck. I looked around the house, a dripping tap, stairs with hardly any stairs, hard, wooden flooring covered in dust.

'Let's sleep down here,' I said, still a little amazed at the sight that had greeted us.

It wasn't long before Zoë was fast asleep. I myself, was wide awake, so I decided to have a wander round to see what Zoë had been so scared of. I pulled on my trainers and crept into the kitchen.

A cool wind swept past my knees and I saw the kitchen but this time it was brand new. I saw a family. A mother, a child, a father. Footsteps. Soldiers. They dragged the family out of the kitchen, through me, as if I wasn't there.

It was only then that I realised a bright light was shining behind me. I turned around, not wanting to see what was behind me. It was the family, but not the happy family I saw, they were thin, covered in bruises, whip marks. Suddenly I saw what they were holding, they were holding Zoë's head.

'You disturb us while we sleep, we disturb you,' they said in such an eerie voice that it sent chills down my spine.

They started to move towards me, but I couldn't move, I was rooted to the spot with fear. They grabbed me, covered my mouth, trapping my body, trapping my soul, trapping me forever.

Rebecca Piggott (12)

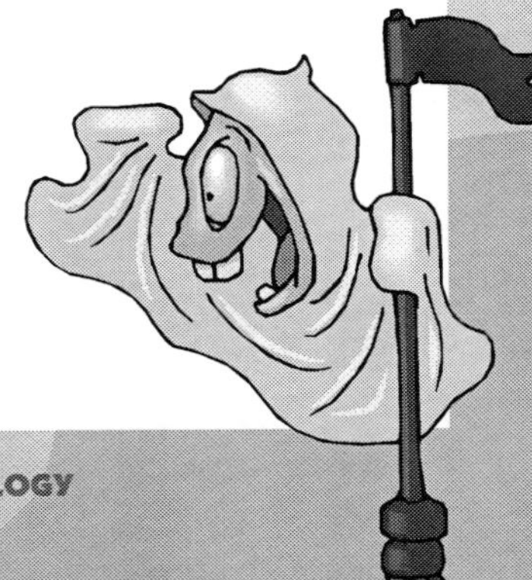

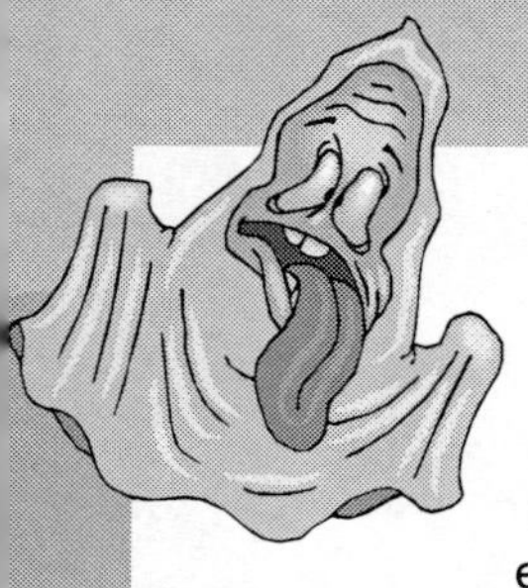

The Warning

It was the dawn of night and the shape of a girl was treading through the dusk. The dark grass under her feet squelched loudly in the silence and emptiness and soaked the bottoms of her trousers so they clung, wet and cold, to her ankles.

Then she stopped. Only the wind murmured around her, except ... somewhere in the darkening gloom something creaked, ominously. She shook her head and tried to smile to herself; she was being stupid again. Stupid. Silly. Out of the dimness she could see a shadow moving. She forced herself to walk steadily forwards. She had to get back. She had to get back. Gradually the shape became a swing. An old, deserted swing, hung on big rusty chains that squeaked as it slowly swung, alone and empty in the darkness.

But there was no wind.

She could hear laughing, the giggling of children echoing happily around her head, louder, louder. Her breath started coming in choking gasps and she was stumbling much too quickly. Then the high echoing whisper of a child, trickling quietly through the grass towards her ... 'Emily, I've got something to tell you, Emily, something important.'

A look of horrible recognition dawned on her face. 'No! No! No!'

'Emily ...'

She was running, stumbling, into the dark, desperately covering her face with her hands, tearing at her hair. In her head the words echoed urgently over and over ... 'Emily ... Emily ... Emily ...'

Only a scream punctured the dark, before there was silence forever.

Nina Kain McCondichie (12)

The Sharpened Ghoul

Do you want to know why I wear a bag on my head? Let me tell you.

I am an artist. Apparently in a small town called Dahlishia there had been lots of gruesome things happening, and I wanted to paint the village's feelings. I arrived and an old musty smell filled the air. It was silent. The cab drove off.

'Aarrgghh! Help!' There was a screech, like chalk on a blackboard and there was someone in one of the houses beckoning me in. So I went.

'Are you mad, have you not heard of the Sharpened Ghoul?'

I didn't answer.

'No ... well I'll tell ye the legend. Over 100 years ago there was an evil warrior who killed only innocent women and children. Now ye ghoul loved fingernails and grew them of a length of 13cm. The men of the village were so full of hatred for the Sharpened Ghoul, they wanted revenge. So they caught him and chopped of his hands and stuck his fingernails through his heart. After 100 years he rose and everyone in the village was disappearing ... now ye stay here tonight.'

And believe me, I did.

I was in my bed, when there was a bang. Someone came up the stairs, on the landing and burst into my room. *'Aarrgghh!' Screech.*

So now you know why I keep a bag on my head, so I can hide the scratch down my face. It was amazing that I survived, or did I?

Kate Newman (11)

Haunting At Hallowe'en

It was Hallowe'en and the children on Winterford Lane were having a Hallowe'en party. Pumpkins with scary faces and candles inside were outside houses.

Jessy, Tessa and Peter went into the dark wood at 9.15pm. They were going to the supposedly 'haunted house' in the middle of the wood. They had been walking for about 20 minutes when Peter said, 'You don't think it is haunted do you?'

'Don't be stupid,' laughed Tessa.

A crow called and Peter ran and hid behind a tree, Jessy jumped in front of him, 'Boo!'

'Argh!' exclaimed Peter.

'You big girl!' joked Tessa.

They were in the grounds of the old house. It was silent. They stood in a row. A twig snapped, it broke the silence. An evil laugh came from behind them, thundering hooves came through the mist, it passed them through grounds. It was the headless horseman ...

The three kids ran as fast as their legs could carry them. They eventually got home and Tessa burst into her house and shouted, out of breath, 'Mum, Mum!'

She ran into the living room, she wasn't there. *Where could she be?* she thought.

Tessa walked into the kitchen. 'Mum, there you are! I wondered where you had gone. Why are you wearing a black cape?'

Her mum turned round. It wasn't her mum.

The black cape spoke, 'I've been waiting for you.'

There it was again, that evil laugh.

Isabelle Mangan (12)

The Body On The Floor

It was the night of Hallowe'en. The wind was howling louder then I had ever heard it, there were forks of lightning coming from the sky. The clouds were as black as a cat. I was watching a film by myself. Suddenly the television switched off, there was a smashing sound coming from behind me.

I looked back and there was a vase on the floor with blood dripping from it. I decided to ring my friend to see if she wanted to come over. I started to dial the number ... Then I heard a scratching noise coming from down the phone line. A lump rose in my throat. I could feel a piercing breath on my neck. I tried to open the door, it was locked.

At that moment a scream came from upstairs. I went up, taking a knife. I didn't find anything. When I came back down, on the floor was a body. I had no idea who it was. It was covered in blood. I stood there looking at this mysterious body. The wind was blowing harder now.

The lights flickered and went out. I could hear footsteps behind me. I looked back and saw a shadow. I launched my knife at it and it fell to the ground. Right then the lights came on. I saw right in front of me the body of my friend. Had I just killed her? There was something else behind me. It raised an axe and ...

Sophie Chambers (12)

Fantasy ... Or Not?

The moon was full and floated above Earth in the starry sky. It lit up the dark country lanes and houses. Roni was sitting on her bed on the phone to Ernessa. Somehow, it didn't feel real. There was an eerie silence hanging between the two of them. Roni looked at the window at her reflection and saw fear. Her eyes wide but also, somehow, wilting from the light of the moon, her pale skin, like the snow on a mountain, and her lips were blood-red, but not like lipstick, like blood.

The silhouette of nothing crept towards her. She could sense the cold-hearted, bloodthirsty fingers, entwine themselves around her body. She stared and stared at her lips and slowly the red blood began to mix with fantasy and reality. She looked back at her eyes and it was as if she could see through her body and she dropped the phone, whirled round, and screamed at her own presence.

Strangely, then the feeling of the non-existent life around her dropped to nothing. She felt nothing. It was as if everything in the world had been sucked into the core of the Earth. Then the pain shot through her body.

Imogen Williams (13)

The Nightmare Before Christmas

When the night begins, children collapse onto their beds. All children are trapped in a vehement dream filled with joy, laughter and pleasure. The exuberance in their powerful minds was most optimum. But what happens when all that merriment fades away and when it perishes? Fear, darkness and melancholy all replace it and what appears in darkness? All children begin to shake in their beds and shiver. It becomes cold and a plague of depression sweeps through the air. The youthful minds are now constantly focused on the horror withheld in their visions. They are flustered and neurotic and suddenly their personal phobias are unleashed and entrapped. Nothing is able to rescue the victims except, leaving the child twisted and disoriented. This procedure of horror is repeated for hours on end, until happiness and laughter return.

The child awakens and is fulfilled with joy as they know their hero, who comes only once a year, has visited. They rush out of their beds, half-dressed, tumble down the stairs and their eyes broaden as the appearance of wrapping paper and a variety of colours is about. Throughout the whole day they celebrate and are merry. Though they forget that the day must end for the night to begin.

Sam Wood (13)

The Willow Tree

It was a cold summer's eve and dew hung in the air, intoxicating the living and incapacitating the dead.

However these were not the thoughts on a young boy's mind as he walked through the willow groves. Tom Spencer was walking from his grandmother's. He was halfway home when he noticed a shadow in the back of his mind's eye. This made Tom very unsettled, because when he turned around it was never there.

He decided to ignore this fragment of imagination, but however much he tried he knew he was being watched. The sun darkened, the birds stopped singing, the bees stopped buzzing and the squirrels scampered up their trees. Life itself seemed to disappear, his watch had stopped, how long was it since he'd left his grandmother's? Twenty minutes, an hour? It seemed like a lifetime.

Tom was absolutely terrified, he ran dodging through the willow grove until he lost sight of the person in the grey coat. After about 5 minutes he lost sight of the figure, however Tom was now lost, it was getting dark and beginning to rain, after a few minutes he was soaked through and of course very cold, so he decided to take shelter in a willow tree. At least he stayed out of the rain, but the tree was old and home to lots of creepy-crawlies. He scrambled out, searching blindly for signs of life.

The world was closing in around him. Blackness took him. The grey figure appeared.

'Don't go to sleep, don't go to sleep!'

He went to sleep and so did his guardian angel.

Robert Galazin (12)

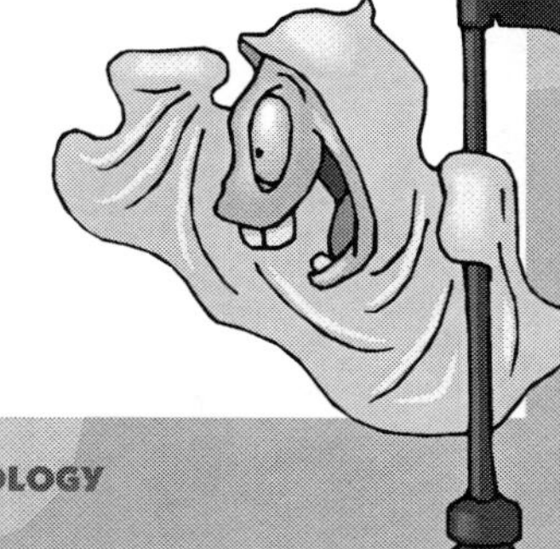

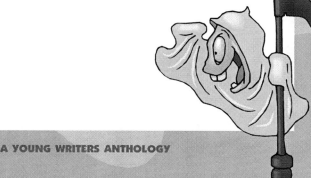

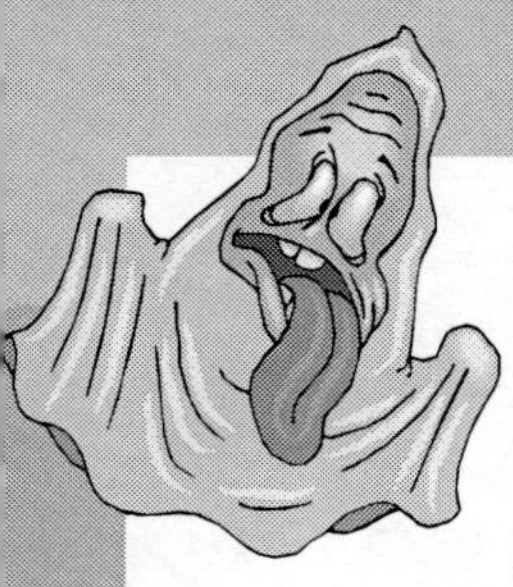

Dead Fun In The Sun

It was summer. We had gone to South Africa, looking for a break from busy school life. My parents were sightseeing and my brother was, well, I don't know where he was.

I lay back, enjoying the warmth. Children surfed, adults sunbathed and seagulls cawed.

I became uncomfortably hot and decided to have a swim in the sea. I dived in. The coldness made me gasp. It was too cold. Everyone else was enjoying themselves though, so I kept swimming.

Suddenly I heard a scream. I spun around. A surfboard was coming at me, too quickly. It hit me hard and I waited for the pain that would knock me out, but it never came.

Confused, I turned. The surfboarder had kept on surfing. He had gone through me like a ghost! The thought gave me massive goosebumps and I felt sick. I tried thinking of why it hadn't hit me, but couldn't think of a reason.

Suddenly the whole beach disappeared. The thirty-foot wave was over me before I could see it and everything turned black ...

I woke lying on the sand. The beach was full. I had survived! It was too much for one day though, I had to get out of there. I stood. Weird, I felt fine.

When I arrived home I heard footsteps behind me. It was my brother. He got his keys and walked through me ...

Oliver Coombe (12)

The Spirits Of The Deep Sea Floor

The door creaked open and the atmosphere was lifted as the sea breeze slammed the door shut. A rat scuttled under a broken floorboard, and the floor of dust broke like shattered glass. The spiderwebs hung everywhere and glistened in the light of the moon which shone through the open window.

The stairs stood swaying and the floorboards creaked upstairs. I moved for the stairs cautiously, making sure that I didn't step in something unworthy. I could feel a spirit around me, something didn't feel right.

I gradually walked upstairs towards the noise. Halfway up there was a step missing so I had to stretch to reach the next one. Once I got upstairs I realised that the noise was coming from the bedroom. I could see the light pouring out from under the door. I thought it must be a tramp that didn't have anywhere to sleep, but I could still feel a spirit in the air. I stopped and felt something go through me. I collapsed to the ground in a heap. My life flashed before my eyes and I was out cold.

When I woke up I just lay there for a moment, working out what dimension I was in. I could hear a ticking noise somewhere in the distance, so I dragged myself up and saw the light pouring out from under the door. I turned the brass door handle and pushed the door open. There they sat, the four mermaid spirits of the deep sea floor.

Katy Wagstaff (12)

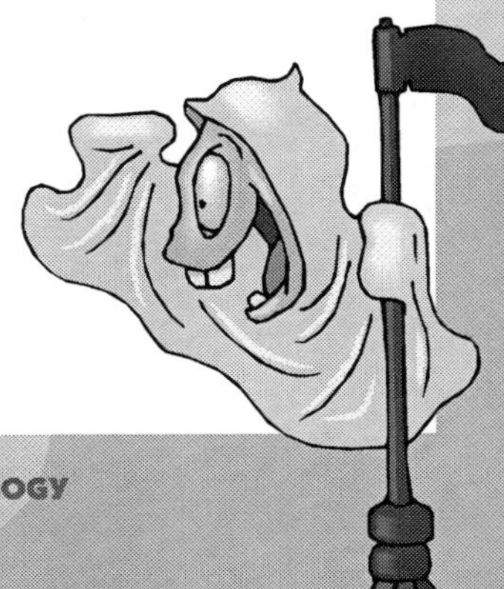

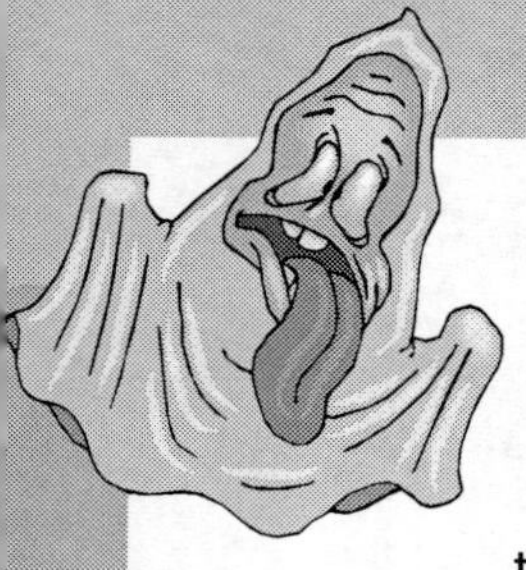

The Mediator

It was a warm summer's evening and all was quiet in the sleepy suburbs around my house. It was hot and stuffy in my bedroom and I had been tossing and turning under my duvet. I could not sleep so I rose and went and stood by my open window, my elbows resting on the sill. That was when it happened. I couldn't place it at first but it was like someone had flicked a switch. All the shadows seemed more menacing and the calm, pleasant atmosphere had been replaced by a silence that was more scary than any amount of noise.

I could hardly breathe, my heartbeat had increased and the tick, tick of my clock was echoing eerily around the room. The hair on the back of my neck stood up and I spun around, someone or something was watching me. I knew it. My curtains flapped in a sudden breeze and the wooden floorboards creaked even though I was standing still.

Then I saw it, a shape beginning to form in the middle of my room, spinning around growing as it did so. Now my heartbeat had stopped and my fear could be smelt around the room. I wanted to run but my feet were stuck to the floor. I wanted to scream but no sound would come out. Then the silver shape took form, a young woman screaming. My dead mother. That was when I found out I could summon the dead.

Alice Udale-Smith (13)

Seeing Is Believing

The chill wind sliced across the houses like a whetted knife. It was peaceful, the wind was silent. The supernatural seemed at rest. A heat haze shimmered and died as the sun set. For a second, it appeared to leave a shadow. Then that died too. I cautiously stepped through the twilight in the middle of the deserted street. The red brick houses loomed, enclosing me. A cat ran down the street. From what? A movement caught my eye. I whipped around. A shadow flitted. Where was it?

The blacked-out windows stared at me. My house was 200 yards down the road. It seemed like a mile. In the dark, the friendly street was monstrous. In the corner of my eye, I saw the shadow at a window. Was it real? Was it a person? There was no other movement. What caused it? I began running, I was slowing down. I couldn't run. I fell down, down to the hard tarmac. The shadow! It was in front of me, teasing me! I looked up slowly. It wasn't there. I just wanted to see it to know what it was and where it was! There was something there that shouldn't be! In my panic, it never occurred to me that I was imagining it. The darkness was oppressive, suffocating. The streetlights were no longer bright. The darkness was blinding. The silence filled my ears, like a roar! The shadow had caught me. It had grown. Would I die?

Suddenly, lamps lit the street. It was gone.

Keir Macdonald (13)

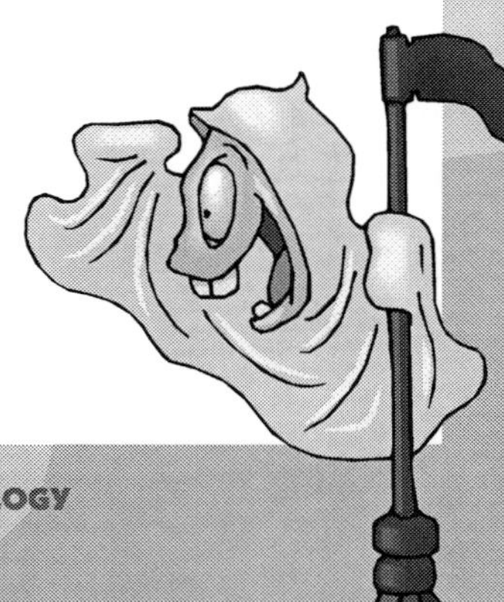

The Truth

It all starting on a camping trip. Ben was eleven, he had black hair and blue eyes. Romy also was eleven with black hair and blue eyes.

There was a knock at the door, it was Ben. 'Bye Mum, bye Dad,' Romy cried. No answer.

On the hill it was very windy.

'Shall we put up the tents?' asked Ben.

'Yeah.'

The tents were up and it was getting dark. They were wrapped up warm. There was a sudden *snap* as the guide rope snapped. The tent flew away.

'No, what are we going to do?' cried Romy.

'There's an old house across the hill, so get your stuff and we'll get going.'

The door creaked as they walked in. They dumped their stuff.

'It's dusty!' whispered Romy.

They walked up the stairs and into a large room.

'Go get your stuff.'

'Okay.'

They had fallen asleep. Ben suddenly awoke. 'Romy, where are you?' Ben shouted. He stood up. He heard a door open. He ran outside. He saw Romy, she was collapsed by leaves. He ran to her. He moved the leaves and he stood back. There were two gravestones. One said 'Romy Williams' and the other 'Ben

Gorvescone'. 'What? This can't be right, it's mine and Romy's graves.'

Ben found Romy standing outside.

In the cold and misty air, he caught sight of a group of people, dressed in black. A priest was reciting a prayer as they lowered two small coffins into freshly dug graves.

Kayleigh Luscott (11)

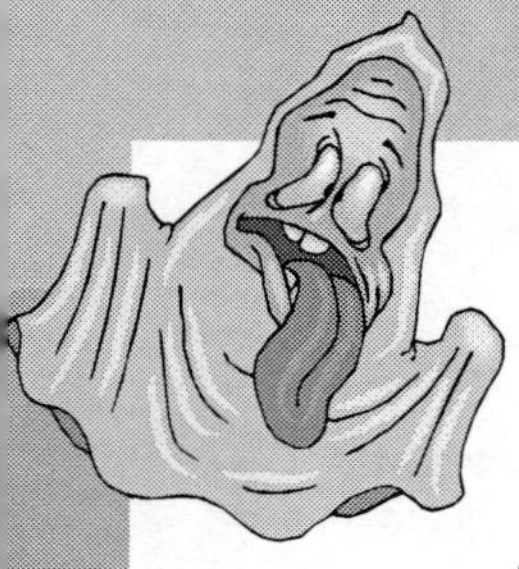

Deceived Reflections

The sun hung low in the tinted sky. Creamy clouds floated, pushed across the landscape by the breeze. Bees hummed in the distance. Lucy sank low into one of the old benches. The pleasant warmth covered her, the song of a bird lulled her to sleep.

Lucy woke to find bitter rain seeping through her jacket. Wind twisted through branches of contorted trees. Leaves circled Lucy's ankles, there was something wrong. A shiver rippled through Lucy as realisation sunk in. Malevolent tranquillity had spread itself over the park. Through the mist Lucy saw the moon, cradled in the arms of a deep, empty sky. The only sound was Lucy's voice, telling herself to run before the darkness engulfed her ...

Lucy squinted through the night, checking for a presence other than her own. She felt her body numb as she heard a haunted voice calling into the night. The voice of the shadow child pulled her towards the lake. Frozen fingers of fear crept around her heart as the eyes of the unknown, bored into the back of her head.

Lucy looked into the pearly water and saw her reflection ripple slowly. The hand of her reflection rose out from the water, its icy fingers entwining with her own.

Lucy looked closer and saw that it was not her reflection she saw, but that of a wicked girl.

The girl cackled evilly and pulled Lucy into the water. The soul of the girl was released, but Lucy's spirit remained in the lake.

Here's some advice: steer clear of the park ...

Laura Knight (13)

The Wanderer Of The Night

White as paper, cold as ice. Something was there, I heard it. And again. Where was it? What was it? Was it him? I didn't know.

All around me was mist, I couldn't even see my own hand. I was trapped, stuck, and he was coming. Closer and closer, I could feel it.

A girl no older than twelve. Transparent, a ghost from the past, from his time. She told me to run and not look back. 'Run,' she said. But I didn't listen, so now I would die.

For now I couldn't run, could hardly breathe. He was coming and I was trapped. Nowhere to run, nowhere to hide, alone. I was going to die alone and afraid.

Black, jet-black he was. He emerged from the mist and stopped my heart. A crooked smile and no eyes, just sockets where they should have been. Some say he did it to himself after someone killed his wife. That someone was my great grandfather and now he wanted revenge. He was going to kill me, this transparent wanderer of the night. I was dead and I knew it.

He drew closer and closer. I felt cold, I felt pain and I screamed. He held his ears and stumbled back. I screamed again with all my might. It was working, he was in pain and then he was gone, just dust on the ground. I saw a dim light in the distance and then I fainted.

Lucy Gardner (14)

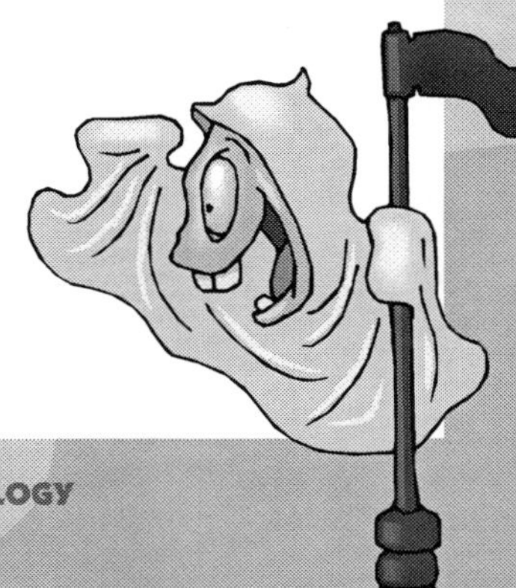

The Death Of John Dyer

It was winter 1996 and John Dyer was coming home from the butchers. He had purchased a lovely big chicken for him and his kids. He took his usual short cut down a dark alley and ahead of him he heard a scream. On hearing this, he ran to where he thought the scream came from, he saw a lady standing in front of him ...

It was winter 2005 and Harry Dyer was coming home from the butchers. He had purchased a lovely big chicken for him and his sister. He took his dead dad's usual short cut down a dark alley. Ahead of him he saw a lady being chased by what looked like a ghost. Harry followed them down the alley. When he had caught up with them, he told the lady to hide in the old toy shop, she did as she was told and hid behind one of the counters. Harry asked the ghost its name, the ghost replied, 'John Dyer.' Then Harry knew that that was his father.

Harry laid John to rest and reported the lady to the police for the murder of John Dyer, his one and only father.

Ben Maguire (10)

Beating Heart

'Hey! What's that little cottage doing in the middle of this wood?' asked Emma.

'I don't know, but I'm sure it would make a better house than these leaves we're sleeping on,' Sammy replied.

'Okay then, let's go and have a look,' Emma said, with an excited face.

The cottage had four rooms, a kitchen, a small sitting room and two bedrooms.

That night as the girls rested, Sammy heard a noise. It was like someone screaming. She got out of bed and went down the narrow corridor. As she got nearer to Emma's room she heard a boom. It got louder until finally she saw it. Emma was lying there on the wooden floor with her soft silk hair, drenched in blood.

Sammy saw, was it, could it be? Yes! It was Emma's heart still beating! Sammy screamed. She picked up Emma's heart. She saw a man dressed in black, dripping with blood. She ran for her life down the stairs, through the corridor, out of the woods, she saw her village. There was her house.

She opened the door. Both her and Emma's hearts were beating. The man followed her and said, 'I want the heart.'

Sammy dropped the heart and closed her eyes. She heard a lot of movement and opened her eyes, he was gone. Was it a dream or was it all true? Her hand was still dripping with blood - or could it have been the tomato ketchup from her chips!

Beth Hopkins (10)

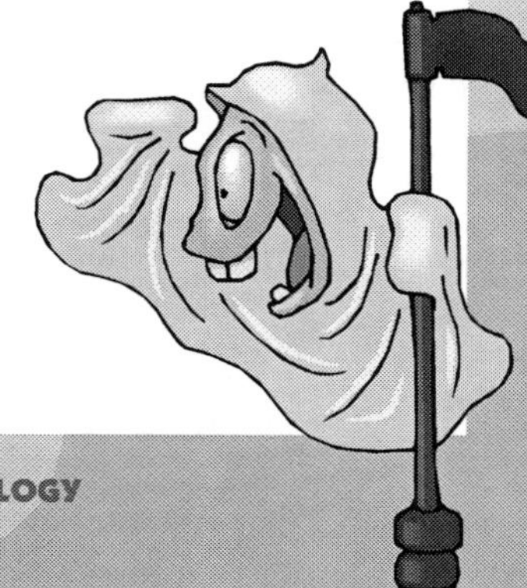

Where A River Can Take You

Daisy slammed the door shut. She sprinted down the road and stopped at an old lamp post to rest. Her gentle brown skin had turned ashen and her neatly plaited hair was all messy and frizzy. She walked cautiously down to the bank of the river and fell asleep instantly.

She woke, she was floating on a piece of driftwood. She swam to the side and on the horizon was a tall castle, three out of four towers had crumbled and fallen. Daisy couldn't resist. She walked slowly in.

The drawbridge crashed behind her. She wandered through a tall, echoey tunnel. Someone was following her. She found a bed in a small, damp and dark room and fell asleep.

She woke, she stood up and stretched her legs but as she did, she stood on something. She looked down. It was her body lying still on the floor with a knife in her back.

Charlotte Alsop (10)

One Ghost, Two Ghosts

Devon was a peaceful village, you could only hear the wind rustling through the trees and people walking to work. I don't really want to tell about the town, I want to tell you about the most stubborn boy I know (and I know a lot of boys). This story is kind of a legend, or maybe a myth.

Gary was his name, he wasn't superstitious like the rest of us. He broke mirrors, walked under ladders, stepped on cracks etc. I think he was a daredevil because no matter how we tried, he didn't believe there was a ghost in the woods that only came out on the 31st of October.

Well that silly boy went into the woods on the 31st of October. Suddenly the ghost came out of its hiding place. Gary tried to run but the ghost was too fast.

Now no one goes into the wood because instead of one miserable and lonely ghost there are two vicious and fierce ghosts! Who knows who will be their prey? You never know, it may be you!

Ha! Ha! Ha!

Kirsty Beacham (9)

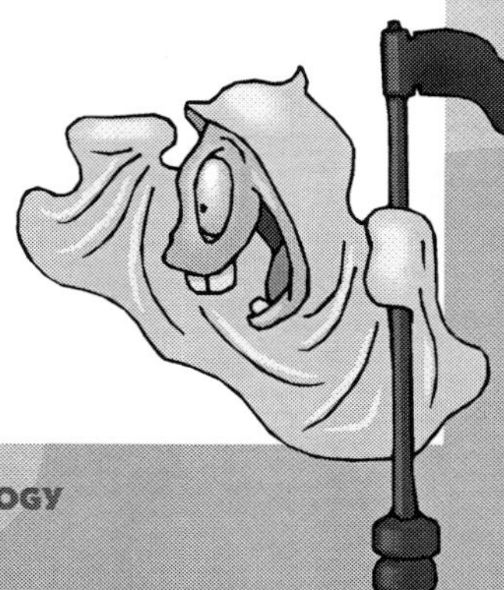

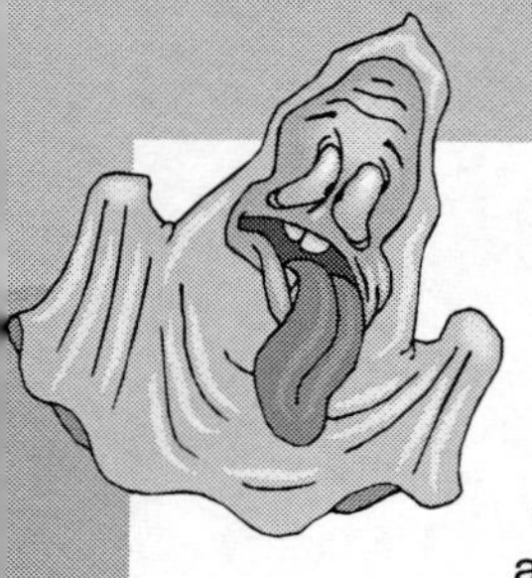

Frank's Heart

Frank was a lonely man, for his wife had died not long ago, she was doing her hobby, talking on the telephone. Suddenly the line went dead and from behind she was stabbed in the back. Since then Frank had always been cautious of using the phone, but at this moment he was on the phone and the door was unlocked.

While Frank was on the phone, the door opened. A skinny short man tiptoed into the room where Frank was. Frank hadn't noticed a thing. The robber took out a long, thin silver knife. The man crept up behind Frank. Suddenly the line went dead. Frank turned around and was stabbed straight in the heart.

A few days later, Frank's grandson came into the house and saw Frank just lying there. Frank's heart was sitting on his tummy, dead.

The boy picked up the heart and took it home. The boy wasn't really bothered about his grandad being dead.

Later that night, Frank's ghost walked across the street, climbed up his grandson's drainpipe, jumped into his room and said, 'Give me back my heart,' again and again. The boy woke with a start, went over to the wardrobe where Frank's heart was and threw it out of the window - Frank followed.

Ryadal Sturt Chapman (10)

The Mystery Hole

It was a cold miserable day. We were getting ready for bed. Simon came for a sleepover. That night we woke up and went to the kitchen and took a torch off the table.

We went outside, it was freezing cold. We went down to the wood at the end of the garden. We were walking nervously into the gloom of the forest. I asked Simon if he was cold, but there was no reply. I screamed, 'Simon, Simon, where are you?' I heard a little 'Help.' I ran back to where I had just come from.

It was almost pitch-black now. I tripped over a root of a tree. I skidded on the leaves and felt in front of me, a big black hole.

'Is that you Nick?' said Simon in a shaky voice.

'Yes!' I said, 'I'll go and get help.'

I came back with Mum and Dad and found the hole. I said, 'Simon!' but Simon had gone.

I never knew what happened to him and I've never been to that wood since.

Silas Orr (9)

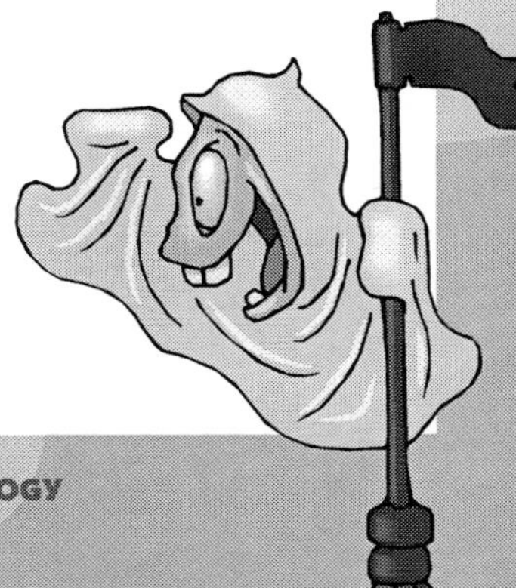

The Mansion In Faraway Wood

There it was, Tom had found the mansion in Faraway Wood. Tom opened the door and walked in. It was dark and gloomy. Then Tom heard a weird sound. It sounded like a ghost.

Tom stayed at Faraway Mansion for a few days and it got creepier and creepier over those few days. More noises started. It was very scary.

Tom was walking up the stairs one night to go to bed. Tom was startled by a noise so he turned round but it was only the door creaking.

Tom decided to leave Faraway Mansion after a few days. He walked out and found that it was pitch-black. Tom thought to himself, *I can make my way home.* So he set off into the night. After a while, Tom came to a door. He opened the door and he was back in Faraway Mansion!

Ella Blackwell (9)

A Nightmare Come True

Josh just stood there, in the middle of nowhere. He was troubled by the dream that had visited him every night last week. He just couldn't figure it out, although he could remember it clearly. There had been a plane flying through the mist and Josh was holding a walkie-talkie. The plane was going for a test run and *he* was supposed to guide it. Suddenly he saw a mountain looming out of the sky but he was slow to react and the plane plummeted to the ground in flames.

Josh stopped thinking about the dream and started to walk. He soon came to an abandoned airport. Over in the corner of the overgrown runway, Josh saw a plane! Then a man called to Josh from behind, he was carrying something small and black.

'Oi!' the man shouted. 'Can you guide my plane for me ... please?' he added quickly.

Josh was astonished but extremely eager. He snatched the apparent walkie-talkie and saluted. 'Let's go!' Josh called happily.

The man went to start the plane. As it left the ground, the plane vanished from view. The sky was full of mist. Josh saw glimpses of the plane but it was virtually invisible. Then he saw the mountain. He stared in horror as the plane smashed into the dark silhouette.

'No!' screamed Josh. But it was too late.

Josh knew he couldn't live with the guilt of his nightmare come true. And he didn't.

Emma Yapp (11)

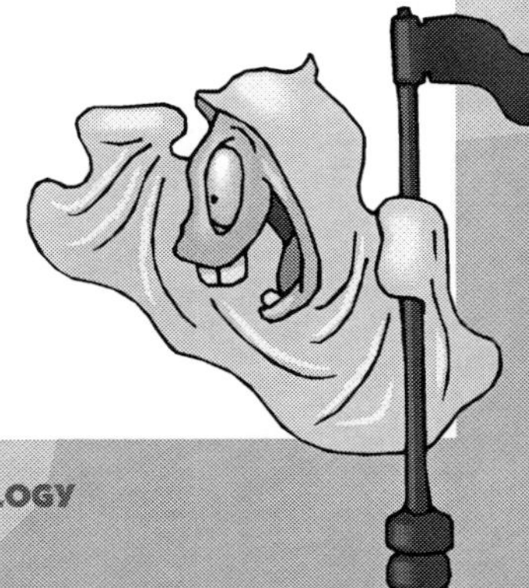

Silhouette

Stuart rolled over in his bed. He couldn't sleep, especially with there being no curtains covering the window. Standing, he got his telescope and looked out of the vast window. He looked up at the stars, it was a cloudless night. Suddenly, silently, the whole of the sky was blacked out. What was happening? Slowly the sky cleared itself again, Stuart realised it was only birds. He continued to look at the silent sky through his silent telescope, something was missing, but what? Sound.

It happened, there was a loud scream from outside. He ran out and saw a petrified woman. She just pointed behind him. Stuart looked round and saw nothing, just darkness. He looked back and saw a body of a woman on the blooded ground.

Stuart looked around and saw the thing; a silent silhouette. He ran onto the dark road from the silhouette. He looked behind him and saw darkness. He looked in front of him, he was running towards the silhouette. Immediately he turned round and ran to his car. He reached into his pocket and got his keys.

Stuart slipped into his car and started to drive his car quickly down the silent road. He weaved this way and that through roads, small and large. However the silhouette stayed behind the car whatever he did. Finally Stuart looked in the mirror and was hypnotised. When the silhouette stopped the hypnotism, he was driving forward, he was perched on the edge of a deep abyss ...

Alan Bowman (12)

The Follower In The Woods

It was a cold and misty dark day. I had finished school and was starting my daily routine to walk back home. But today it wasn't like the other normal days I have. It was sequestered and dark. Darker than normal. I had no choice, I had to make my daily trek along woodside paths and cobbled streets.

The buildings looked lifeless from the outside and I assumed there was no life inside. My hands immobilised at this point, the birds weren't singing merry tunes. All I could hear was the swaying of the trees.

But apart from my own footsteps, I thought I could hear someone else's! My heart was trying to beat but it couldn't. I slightly tipped my head to one side to see who it was. All I saw was a figure in the mist. You know that feeling when you have to walk slightly faster than normal? Well I had that melancholy feeling.

The trees were rocking from side to side rapidly. I had to do something, so I turned my head once again and the figure seemed to be gaining on me. I switched to a quicker pace, more like a jog. I kept turning my head but it was gaining on me, I didn't even know who it was, I then went into a sprint. But its arm touched my shoulder. I turned my head.

'Hi Tom, you've forgotten your books again.'

My heart sank. I was safe, that's all that mattered.

Danny Kohn (12)

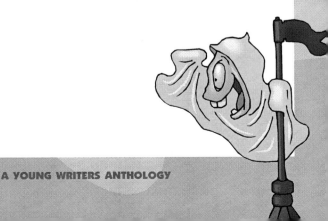

Mummy, We're Hungry!

Miss Methol starved her children to death. She locked them in their room. They died within a week. A three-year-old girl and a five-year-old boy. Some people say it wasn't her fault. She couldn't cope since her boyfriend left. Some people say she was just pure evil. Who knows? The one thing everyone knows though, is they came back ...

A few days after they'd died, an old man who lived next door, said that he'd heard children crying and screaming. No one took any notice of him though because he was old and mad. The following day however, the postman claimed to have seen the children scratching at the window. More and more sightings were reported and the town became a very unpopular place to live.

Miss Methol was tried for murder and prosecuted in court. She went to jail but she was mentally disturbed and disrupted the whole jail. She would scream for hours on end, clawing at her eyes, trying to get the terrible images of her dead, starved children out of her head. Some days though, she was quieter and just sat whimpering in the corner of her cell.

But then suddenly, three months after she had been put in prison, she was found dead, lying on the cell floor. The odd thing was though, she had no injuries and nobody was suspicious. Her sudden death was put down to guilt. But I think it was a little more than that. I don't think it was just guilt. I think the children really did come back ...

Annina L Dowman (12)

Bridget's Hot Milk

I lay in bed and watched the curtain blow in and out of the open window. We were staying in our favourite guest house in Banff, a beautiful Victorian house owned by Maureen and Lloyd. I couldn't sleep, it was after midnight and tomorrow was a big day. I was competing in the Scottish Karting Championships.

I got out of bed, deciding to go downstairs, hoping Maureen would still be up. I walked into Maureen's large kitchen, noticing for the first time an old-fashioned range with a fire burning in it. A bit strange for August!

'You must be Adam?'

I looked over my shoulder at a lovely old lady with white hair.

'My name's Bridget and I'm Maureen's mother. Sit down while I make you some hot milk.'

She placed a large mug on the table beside me and sat down opposite. We chatted easily, Bridget telling me all about her husband Hugh who died in the war. I told her how nervous I was about my race and that it was keeping me awake. Soon I felt much calmer, more confident and totally at ease.

The next thing I remember was Maureen kneeling beside me looking concerned. I noticed the empty mug lying in my lap. I stretched then reached over to put it on the table.

There was no table. I looked around. There was no Bridget. There was only Maureen, probably wondering why I was in her kitchen, sleeping in front of her shiny stainless steel oven, looking like I had just seen a ghost!

Adam Hutchison (13)

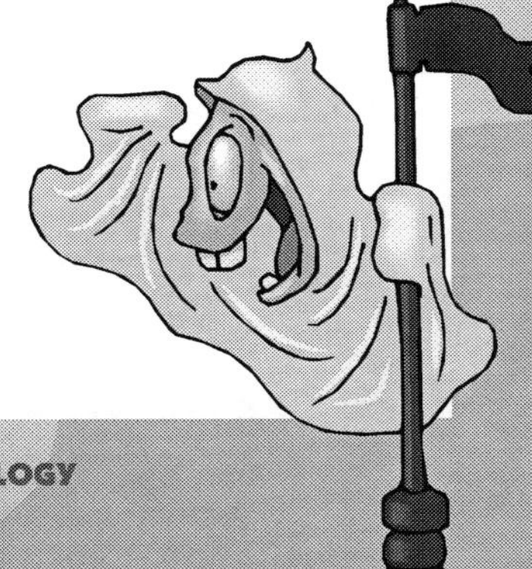

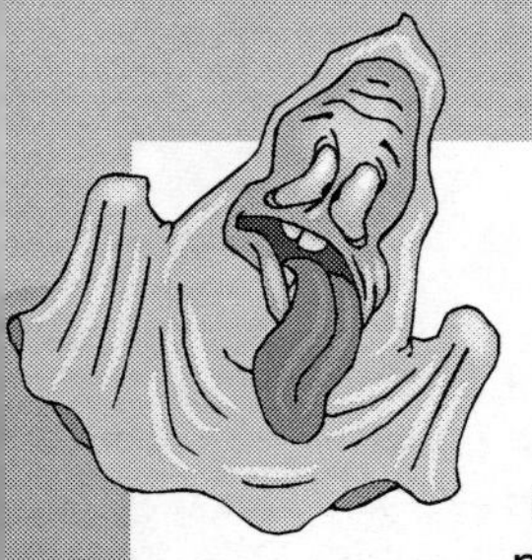

Haunted House Castle

The wind howled and screeched as Mike and Joanne ran home to their terrifying, old, ugly house. When they got in they found a crumpled-up note. It said, 'Come to my car outside to get back to your mum and dad.'

Mike and Joanne rushed outside. They leapt into the car which was very rusty. The car sped off at once. Mike looked into the front and was horror-stricken, there was no one there.

They arrived at a dark, ugly castle. There was a white figure saying, 'Go back!' Mike and Joanne held hands and went in. Immediately they were zoomed in two different directions.

Joanne was zoomed to the left and Mike was zoomed to the right. Joanne battled with a devil but lost. She was thrown in the dungeons. Mike battled a ghost and won.

He ran and got his family out. They all ran home, chased by that devil. They ran into their house and they locked the doors and windows. They sat far away from the door. They said, 'We'll always stay together from now on!'

Cara Dineen (9)

The Haunted Lighthouse

It was a cold winter's night and the waves were crashing against the rocks. I knew something was behind me. I looked, nothing was there, only the swaying trees in the background.

I carried on walking, getting faster and faster. Suddenly I stopped and there stood the old lighthouse. I was astonished with what I saw. The light was working, it hadn't been for years. I saw that the door was open so I ran inside.

I stopped. There stood a strange figure. It was an old man with a pipe, beard and a sailor's hat. I knew for sure it was a ghost. *'Argh,'* I shouted and ran.

'Get back here *now!'* he ordered.

The chase began ...

Teresa Shaw (9)

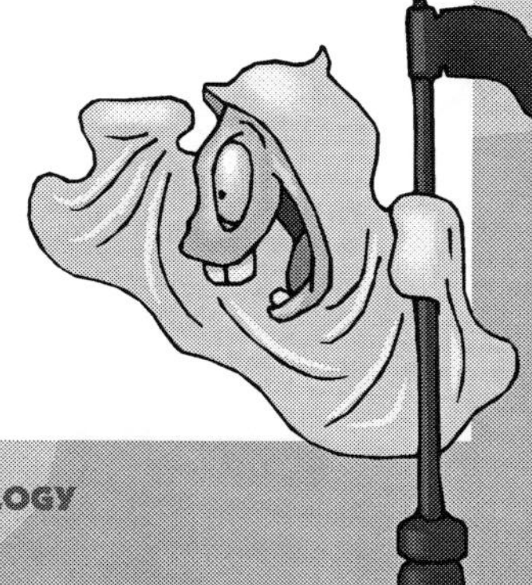

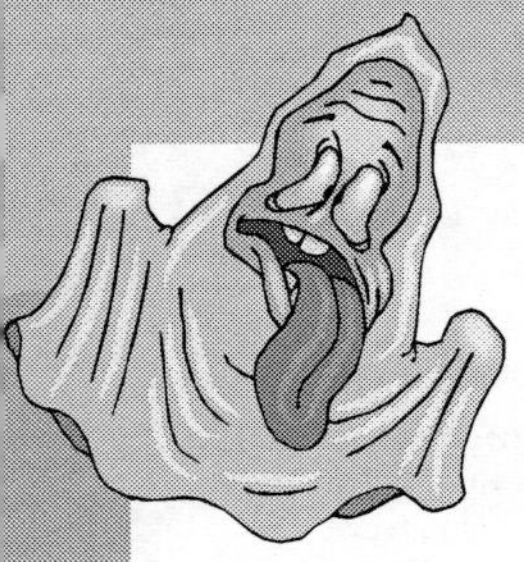

What Lies Down Beneath?

I'd always feared the attic, full of dusty boxes and dark, hidden corners. I knew something lived there.

I could hear the rattles and screams. Maybe it had a black hood and coat and its eyes and mouth drooped down just like a skeleton in a cloak. But what was it doing in my attic?

It was gloomy and slimy in the attic, the walls were covered with silky webs. I heard the sound of scuttling, maybe rats.

Then I heard it, 'I want to be alone.' I closed my eyes and opened them when the noise had stopped.

It was night-time when my mum climbed the attic ladder. Walking slowly she entered the attic. A scream came from a dusty trunk. She moved towards it.

'Alexander Patrick' was spelled on it.

Click, the lid opened, she found herself thrown against the wall and stabbed ten times.

'Mum!' I shouted in the morning. I heard her call my name from the attic. I rushed to find her.

There she lay, next to her a dagger with - 'Alexander Patrick' spelt on it.

Hania Steblyk (10)

The Unfinished Mystery

We reached the first floor of our new house and appeared outside a candlelit room with bloody footprints leading towards it. I could hear creaking noises and the sound of heavy breathing.

The door fell open, there, right before my eyes, was someone in a rocking chair with their back towards us. I looked down to find footprints trailing into a cupboard.

The wind cried, releasing a faint whistle. The hairs on my neck stood up and my fingers turned ice-cold. The candle flickered but stayed alight. My brother noticed the footprints and darted for the cupboard.

'You won't want to look in there,' the distinctive voice spoke. However, they only ignored him and gradually opened the door.

'Aarrgghh!' I loudly screamed.

I sprinted for the door but didn't get far as my dad held me back. They were all mad! Why weren't they running? Because if you're wondering what's in the cupboard, you'll be sorry I told you, as sitting on the shelves, acting innocently, were half eaten, blood ripped, revolting heads! Suddenly the chair swung around, showing the hidden figure. The man was covered in blood with bloodshot eyes and bits of meat hanging from his mouth. He smiled, showing his disgusting bits of food between his teeth.

'If I were you I'd flee from this building as fast as you can, for I am tempted to *eat you all!'* the horrid man frantically yelled.

'I'm turning this film off,' shrieked my mother.

'Absolutely!' my father wailed.

'It's ghastly,' proclaimed my brother.

'But ... it's the best film I've ever seen,' I unhappily cried.

Tanya Adams (13)

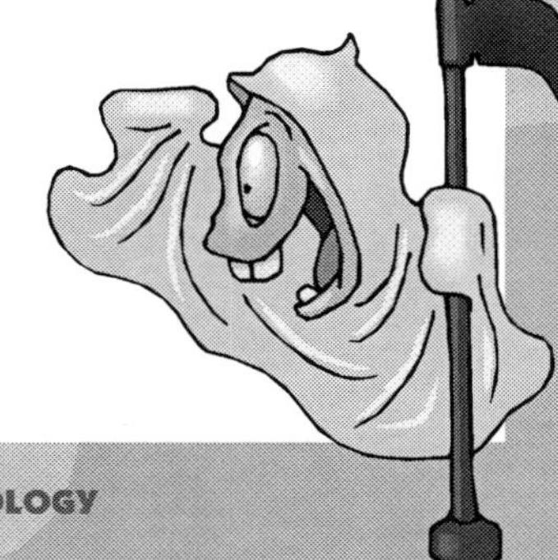

A New Life

He hid in the darkness of the cupboard. A floorboard creaked nearby causing him to hold his breath, praying for life. There was a cackle of glee and silence ... more floorboards creaked but further away now. A door slammed and he let out a long relieved sigh. She was gone, she was gone! But it couldn't be right, not after such a long chase. He frowned in puzzlement. She wasn't going ... the cupboard door flew open and she stood before him, the wind blowing her ripped robes wildly in all directions. She smiled triumphantly, revealing two black teeth. Raising her hand she reached out to him as if blind.

'No!' he cried, frightened. 'Stay away!' She didn't listen. This was what he had expected. He groped desperately in his pocket and felt a round, smooth object. He pulled the egg out. It gleamed reassuringly at him. He rubbed it revealing ornately carved words. *Wind and Rain, Cloud and Sun. A new life has just begun!* Colours swirled around him as he was pushed through a tunnel to an unknown place.

It seemed he was travelling miles per second. Time seemed to rush by like a leaf on a cold autumn day. He felt dizzy and somehow unaware of what was going on. He felt his memories changing, his body was too. What was happening? But before he could think further his feet struck solid Earth. Footsteps told him he wasn't alone. He looked up and realised his world was gone.

Julia Crane (11)

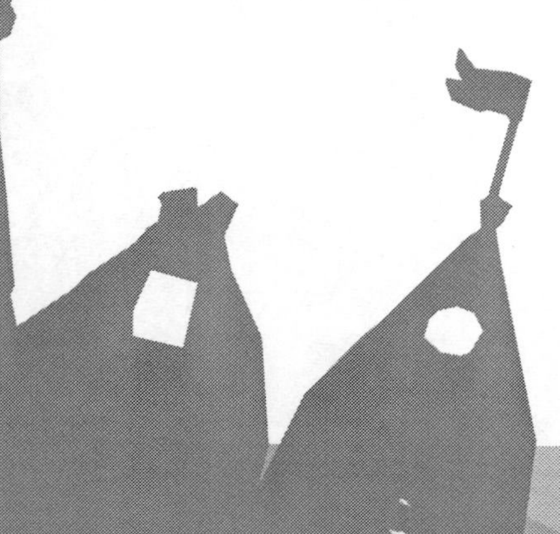

Senses Of The Mind

In a dark, gloomy street unlit and deserted, a girl walked sluggishly, step by step by step. She trod on the gravel and with each step came a harsh and painful crunch. Every step her adrenaline level got steadily higher, her heart pounding like the beat of an African tribal drum. What was she doing in this street where no one ventured? Then as if by some inhuman or sadistic force came a flash as bright as the sun which made the girl flinch.

The girl seemed to be drawn by some dark temptation to this light. As she neared her destination the eeriness of the entire situation seemed to get greater and as it mounted so did the tension. Suddenly there was an ear-piercing screech which sounded like it could have come from a banshee, the spirit who warns of death. There was a horrific stench in the air, like a rotting corpse. The smell drifted progressively to the girl's nose, when it reached her nostrils it made her shudder, the way in which it lured her was unlike any other. She could taste the foul stench, just what her appetite desired, like a starving person who would do anything for a morsel of food. She was drawn deliriously.

She reached the door, blood rushing. She rubbed her hand over the rough, coarse and long-forgotten door. She became possessed, hysterical and psychotic … was it a dream? A vision? An hallucination maybe or possibly a trick of the senses?

Oliver Hooper (13)

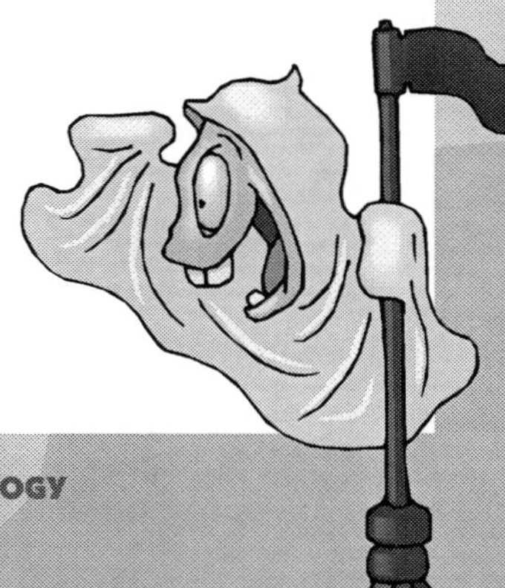

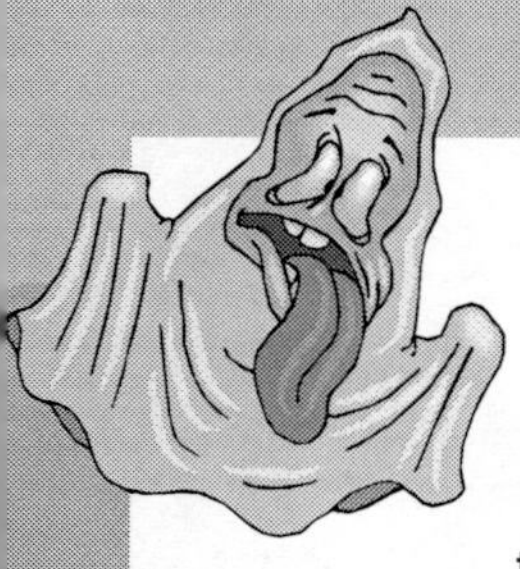

Grampa's Story

'My story starts at the river that runs deep inside Blackthorn forest,' Grampa told the little ones who respected him so much and looked up to him in every way. 'There have been stories of others who encountered it too, but I am the only one around to tell the tale.' At this the ancient house groaned as if urging him to continue.

'I had once been in the forest before but I had been with my comrades. It was much less jolly by yourself I can assure you. Rustling bushes frightened me and I was worried about what might be behind them.' He was grave and showed no signs of being comical. 'The water rippled and formed unusual shapes and I heard eerie sounds coming from all around.'

The younger ones were intent and gazing into the eyes of this brilliant storyteller.

'I stopped when I heard a voice ... nothing else happened so I cautiously moved on. I wasn't sure what I would find or if I would find anything when I turned the next corner.' He paused for a moment then blurted out, 'Then I saw it! I saw a ... a human child!'

The little ghosts gasped at this. Their mother came in at that moment and sighed. 'You should really stop scaring them with your silly tales. Anyway, everyone knows that there are no such things as humans!'

Eleanor Horn (14)

Shadow Ghoul

I was in my bedroom. The light was off, the door closed. Nobody was here but I didn't feel alone. In a dark corner, there was a figure, a small shadowy figure. I pulled my sheets up to my nose. But it was no good.

The shadow moved. It got closer … and closer … I could see empty eye sockets. I could smell the rot on his bones, the smell of … death. He was laughing. A loud eerie laugh. Soft at first, then louder and louder and … I tried to scream but a lump of fear was caught in my throat. It made my eyes water.

I could now hear his breath. It was rattling in my ears, loud, *loud, loud!* He got closer putting his disgusting hands on my shoulders. Shaking and shaking and shaking.

'Help!' But I was just in my bed, shouting at a little school jumper in the corner! And my annoying brother, Matt, was shaking my shoulders and telling me to be quiet or he'd get Mum in here.

Hannah Lloyd (10)

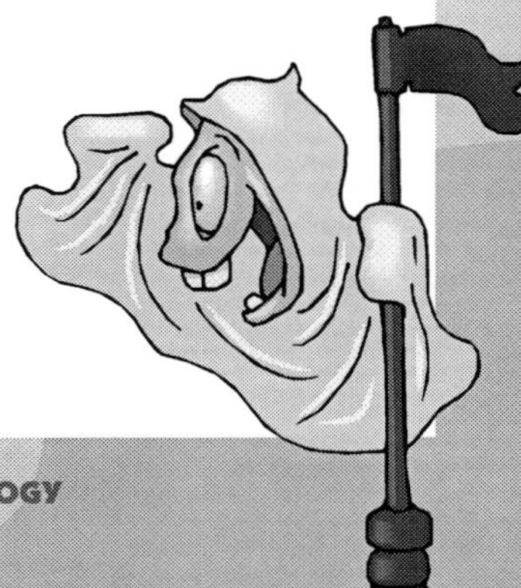

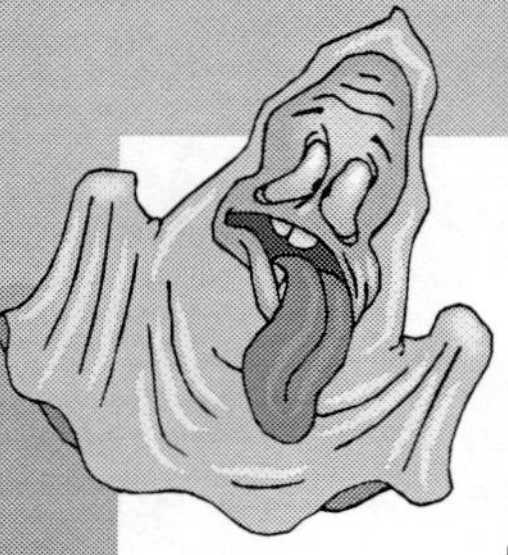

My Final Breath

It was behind me. I could feel it breathing on my neck, pointed teeth like fangs as sharp as pins, waiting to bite at the precise second. Its breath smelt like blood. I did not dare to move. It was the worst and last moment of my life. A giant chill ran down my spine. My body felt like it was nailed to the floor. It had taken control of my body. Now my heart was beating faster than the speed of sound. I was waiting. I tried to move thinking it was a dream but I knew it was reality. I was so scared. Soon I tried to move and my foot moved an inch and suddenly it happened. It bit me. I was dizzy and fainted. After a few days I died.

Mohit Tandon (11)

The Story Of Click-Click-Slide

Not a long time from now there lived a man named Click-Click-Slide. His face was very disfigured and he had no legs. Click-Click-Slide got around by digging his long nails into the ground and sliding his body along.

He got his name from the noise he made. If you were around the corner from him you would hear a *click-click-s-l-i-d-e* noise which would be enough to tell you to get as far away from the area as possible.

A student called Jane came home one evening to find a mysterious letter waiting for her. It said that her best friend, Carol, had been strangely murdered the night before. No one knew how she had been murdered or who had murdered her, but she was found in her kitchen covered in deadly scrapes.

The following day, after lectures, Jane came home and went into her kitchen. She was very upset and cried out, 'Why did Carol have to die so horribly?' Then she turned on the light ...

Looking up, Jane saw a horrible thing hanging from the light - it was Click-Click-Slide. She was petrified. The man said, 'You are next,' before jumping down and digging his nails into yet another victim.

The police eventually found Jane lying motionless on the kitchen floor, bleeding all over her body. There was no sign of Click-Click-Slide but that does not mean he is gone forever. You never know, he could be somewhere near you ...

Caitlin Lewis (9)

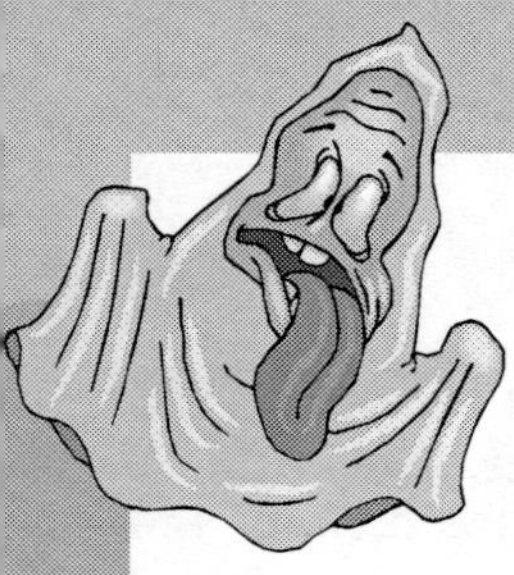

Ghost Story

A girl called Sally, who always got what she wanted, went to a toy shop to buy a new doll. When they got there Sally looked at all the different dolls, but she liked one specific doll. Sally's mum didn't like the doll, so she tried to make Sally pick a different doll, but Sally wouldn't budge. Then Sally saw the head of the doll move.

'Why do you like that doll?' asked Sally's mum.

'Because it moves!' exclaimed Sally.

Sally's mum let her buy the doll. She took it home and went straight to her room, putting her new doll on her bed. Soon after, Sally went to bed.

During the night she woke up and heard a voice, a strange voice, but not her mum's voice - it was a spooky voice... 'Sally, Sally, Sally! Sally, Sally, Sally!' Then the voice changed. It mysteriously said, 'Sally, I'm in your kitchen, Sally I'm in your lounge, Sally I'm on the stairs!'

Sally was so terrified that she hid under her blanket while the voice got gradually louder and louder.

'Sally, I'm on the 1st step, Sally, I'm on the 3rd step, Sally I'm on the 7th step, Sally I'm on the 10th step,' screamed the voice.

By now Sally's blood was curdling.

'Sally, I'm on your landing, Sally I'm in your bedroom, Sally I'm getting near you!' crept the voice.

The voice was haunting Sally.

'Sally, I'm going to kill you,' shrieked the voice.

Sally screamed but, by the time the scream came out, she was already dead.

Early the next morning, Sally's mum walked into Sally's room and screamed. She saw blood everywhere. She ran downstairs and dialled 999 but she heard a voice saying, 'Sally, Sally, Sally! Sally, Sally, Sally!'

She turned around and there the doll stood with a knife in its hand and suddenly ...

Leah Callander (10)

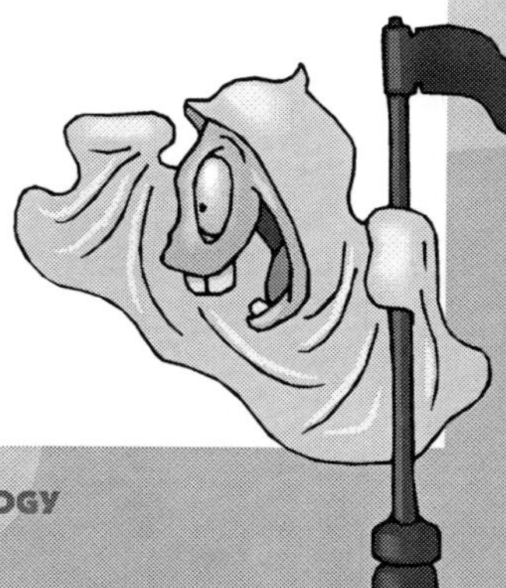

The Scream ...

She was alone.

'What was that?' she whispered to herself as she heard the front door shut with a bang. She was sure that the brats' parents wouldn't be back yet.

Hannah was a babysitter. She hated the job but really she was only doing it for the money. You see, she was looking to buy this really cool mobile that *everyone* had except her! It was so unfair!

The brats were horrible - they were spoilt and they were rude. Hannah babysat them every Tuesday night while their parents went out salsa dancing. It was strange, normally they got back around 10 o'clock, so if it was them they were quite early.

She quietly went upstairs just to check that Josh and Katie (AKA the brats) were in bed. Yes, they were fast asleep. She cautiously tiptoed down the stairs, wondering what the bang was. Luckily for Hannah she

had babysat there loads of times so she knew the house like the back of her hand.

The front door was wide open and the wind was gushing through the house yet she was sure she had closed the door properly. She heard the bang again. This time it wasn't like the door. She didn't know what it was. Hannah screamed.

'We're home,' called the parents. Yuck. What was that red liquid dripping down the walls? It was like blood! As soon as they saw it they screamed with horror. *Bang!* They screamed again. This time with pain.

Annabel Latham (11)

I'm Watching You

'Don't go Mum!'

But it was too late. Mum had died of AIDS, just like my dad. It was left to me to look after myself and Lewis. I don't know how I managed to cope, but I struggled through, though every day seemed to last a lifetime. We don't have much in our house, never have, never will now Mum and Dad have gone.

But it was my job to use the few resources we had to keep me and Lewis alive long enough to see the light at the end of the tunnel.

I used to imagine Mum was still there watching over me in the heavens of East Africa. She'd talk to me and give me advice when I didn't know what to do. She was an imaginary friend at the time, but it wasn't until later on I actually found out she wasn't as imaginary as I had first thought.

It started one night when I was tucking Lewis up into bed. I heard a faint voice whisper, 'Angie, you've done so well. You've made me proud.'

I knew that voice. In a split second the candles started to flicker, the beds shake and the room cool down. I could feel a presence in the room and the odds were on it being Mum.

A figure slowly emerged on the broken chair. It *was* Mum.

Just because someone is dead doesn't mean their spirit doesn't live on. That I have proved.

Zoë Ashton (11)

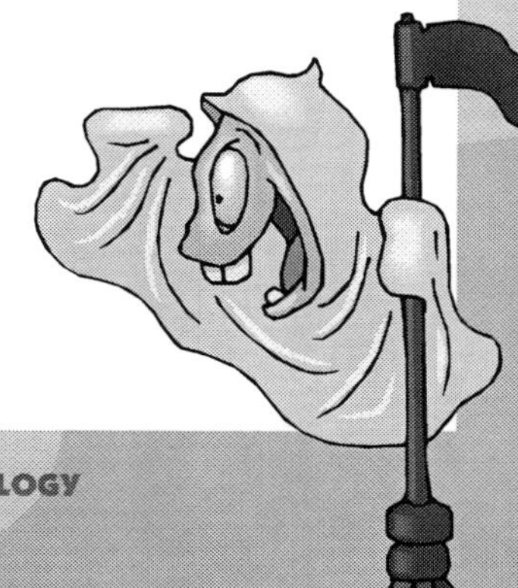

Attack Of The Vampire Squirrels

The squirrels darted about in all directions pouncing and bounding around the city, gnawing savagely at already chewed lamp posts and gigantic office blocks. The squirrels were extremely violent. They had wild, rugged hair which could kill a human with their dreadful pong, they never washed it. They had wide eyes that looked a million miles away; razor-sharp teeth dented and blunted that hung out like a pig's twirly tail as it flops. They had messy fur that had spots of hairless skin which were covered in deep cuts and huge bruises. Their hands were small, steel-like, with a grip better than an eagle. They had filthy feet that seemed covered in soot.

What used to be a pavement in the street with joyful people skipping happily down it without a care in the world, now was a series of burnt craters filled with mothers and children hiding to escape the fighting. The shops were full of squirming squirrels hopelessly trying to get the best spot to take over. They had broken windows and signs dangling above the doorway of the shop. Platforms floated to the ground but when it touched down everyone was massacred.

Alex Lyons (10)

Ghost Girl

Mysti was sitting in the warmth of her study working on a school project on the Celts, when a strange tapping noise came from outside that sent a shudder down her spine. The wind was howling and made the branches of the trees look like snatching hands.

Mysti got out of her chair with its comforting cushions and went to look outside to see what was making the strange noise. Suddenly she saw a girl with a dagger in her hand. The ghostly-looking girl had silver blood where her heart would have been, if the girl hadn't been dead. Mysti's view of the girl went foggy, when her sight came back the girl had disappeared. Mysti turned round to get on with her homework but stood shocked and scared as there was a blood message on the wall; *'Leave this house or die!'*

Mysti ran to her wardrobe and grabbed a travelling bag with all her clothes, books and homework, and scrambled out of the house. Mysti ran till she was out of breath. She looked around to find that she was in a strange place.

All around the place there were small mud-covered houses. She went up to one of the huts and tried to lean into it, but was disappointed to find that she'd fallen right through the wall of the hut. She got up and walked around then all of a sudden she saw the ghost girl. Mysti screamed. Then she was cold dead.

Annabel Wilson & Nicola-Jayne Guy (12)
Avonbourne School, Bournemouth

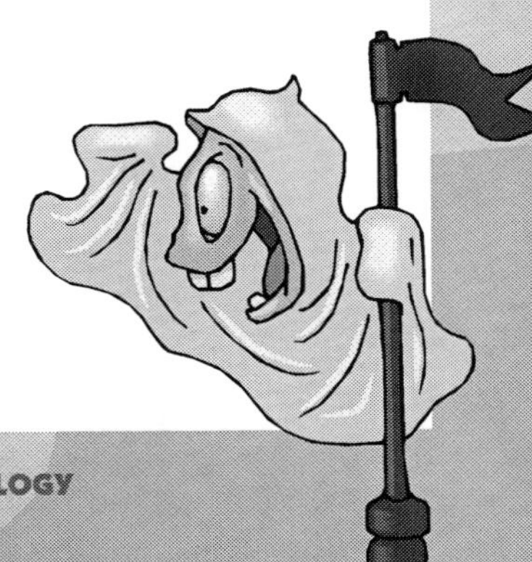

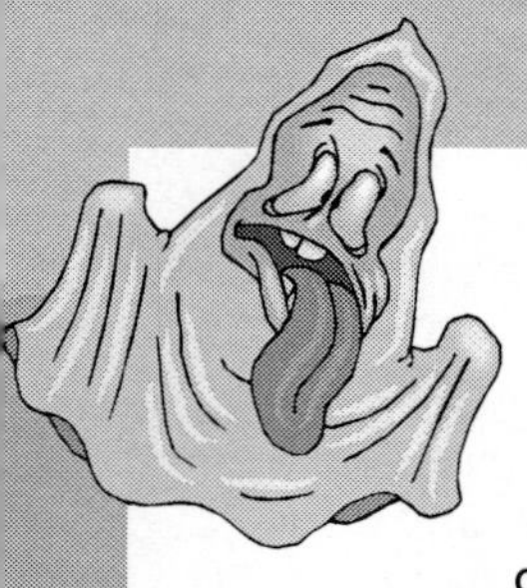

Following Eyes

I was running. As I ran, windows on walls seemed to sweep past me, patterns and colours were vivid and seemed illuminated to me. I had to get away; I could hear my heart pounding in my ears. My blood velocity was getting advanced. I could even feel it sinuous through my veins as I ran.

The chimera that I had just experienced was still in my head. A wraith-like stature. The image wouldn't leave my head, even if I tried avoiding it.

I was just walking. Walking down a dense alleyway. Of course I was frightened. My hand had been in my pocket, gripping hard on my mobile phone, lest I needed to whip it out. Then as I finally reached the opening of the alleyway, the whole area, which I stood upon, seemed to ignite. I turned, expecting a brood with torches, or even starting to burn something, but then I saw it. The eerie finger. It seemed to me a natural individual at first, but then I looked closer and my eyes widened in alarm. I could see the wall, the wall through the spectre. The figure softly smiled. I backed away, turned then ran. Why stay and wait for the worst?

I ran around the bend, turning every so often, searching for the apparition. There was no one, except for the huddled groups of people, talking and warning themselves as they huddled closer together.

I stopped, panting heavily. Finally. I had escaped my delusion.

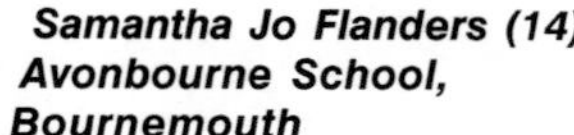

Samantha Jo Flanders (14)
Avonbourne School,
Bournemouth

Revenge

The blizzard that refused to settle raged on throughout the glacial night. Ghostly whispers rippled across the icy air as I slowly pressed my swollen face against the window.

A deathly whisper echoed repeatedly inside me; every whisper robbed me of strength, my power, my confidence. Pain flowed through my body, my hands shaking from the memory of that fateful day. It was her fault. She turned on me, betrayed me, tore out my soul. Her innocent face did not stop the swipe of the deadly knife.

I could feel her presence amongst the icy surroundings. Memories rushed through my mind, my conscience repeatedly telling me I was wrong.

I committed a crime, a crime which could never be forgiven, nor forgotten. I am sure most of you have heard of Betty Ryan, the woman who was murdered brutally by a mysterious assassin. No one ever found out who that assassin was. No one except for one person. Me. Then someone else realised the truth. It was her. If she didn't find out then now she would not be dead. She had promised revenge against me.

The lights flashed. The door closed with a thunderous slam! The window smashed and the cold air slit my tender throat. I screamed, the pain cutting through my insides, and in a rush, I could remember the screams of her, the one who swore revenge.

Now, you may guess, I have been cast into Hell where I belong. I have taken her life and now she has finally taken mine. She got her revenge after all.

Rebecca Tsang (14)
Avonbourne School, Bournemouth

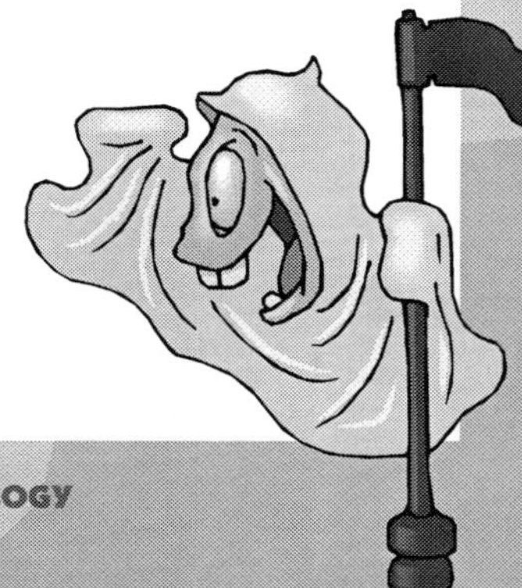

Reaper

The curve of his cracked scythe against the boy's cold skin. Within his body, bound by fear, he felt his taut tendons pull at his pulsing veins. The mournful requiem took safety in his mind, the final barricade having been torn down, ignoring the blazing firestorm. He would not look at the crimson eyes, the mottled bone, the ragged robes he was swathed in. Nor would he face the reality of losing all sanity, the eternal darkness that formed his life, the metal held firmly by his quivering skin. As death enveloped him, he still turned from the facts and cast his mind into an abyss of lies. It was like a drug, dragging him from the excruciating pain dealt by the Grim Reaper, taking him from the scarlet spatter trickling down his neck.

The inferno that had been content to crackle in the hellhole now leapt forth and engulfed his legs. Still he felt neither heat or burn as the lies sang the requiem. Knowing his last drops of sanity had long since fled, the Reaper drew back his scythe. The boy did not feel the cool swipe of death, nor did he realise his head lolled on the floor. He noticed none of this for he was already dead inside.

Claiming what was rightfully his, the Reaper tore the boy's soul from his convulsing body. At long last the boy was yanked back to the reality of his young death, to the soul wrenched from his body and gripped in the bony fingers of the Reaper.

Kirsty Brooks (13)
Avonbourne School, Bournemouth

Finger And Chips

James and his father were very happy until a tragic accident happened ... his mother *died!*

After the tragic death of his wife Mr Jones treated James as a slave. James agreed and heavy heartedly did all the chores demanded by his grieving father. James lived in a Victorian mansion which neighboured the cemetery where his mother was buried.

James was an eleven-year-old boy with blond hair and blue eyes. His face was pale. His father on the other hand had brown hair and black eyes and was bony with a stern face.

One evening, Mr Jones had had enough of James' cooking and asked his hard-working son to go to the fish and chip shop and buy a large portion of chips. James put his coat on and made for the door. He'd had enough of the slave treatment. He realised it was time for revenge. He had a devious plan up his sleeve.

He ran to the cemetery and fetched the spade from the shed. He carried the spade to his mother's grave. He put all his effort in and dug the grave and sliced off the ten delicate fingers and wrapped them in a bag. He refilled the grave. He hurried to the fish and chip shop and bought a large portion. He hastily ran home and as he did this he slipped the ten fingers in the chips. James gave the portion of chips to his father and ran upstairs to bed. Next morning he found his father *dead!*

Gowtam Rajasegaran (9)
Bancroft's Preparatory School, Woodford Green

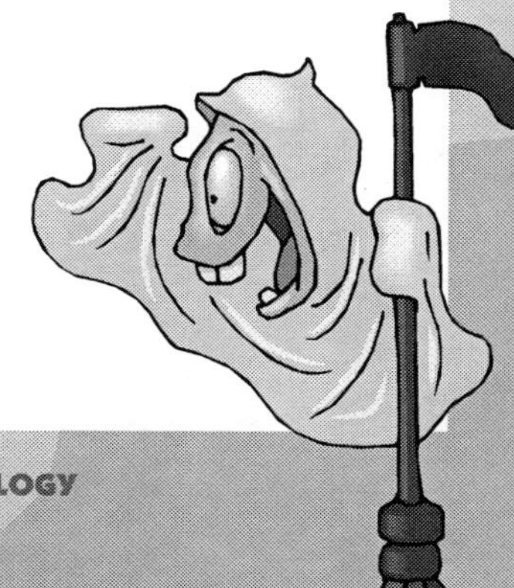

Ghostmania

It started as a normal school day as my friend and I walked home after school together. As we passed an old, rickety, abandoned house, I stopped walking, somehow this house caught my attention, the window was open and a cat sat at the window sill eyeing my friend and I. Soon after, my friend was walking towards the door and beckoned to me to follow her, so I did. As we opened the rather old creaky door I paused, it was said that whoever entered this house never came back out again.

As I turned towards the door to run back out, the door shut, I tried to open it but it would not budge. I turned around to face my friend but she wasn't there, I was alone, all alone. The hairs at the back of my head stood up as something moved behind me I turned but I saw nothing. Questions ran through my head, *where on earth is my friend? Will I ever get out of this house? And if I do get out of this house what will happen to my friend?*

Suddenly I heard a cry. *'Help!'* the voice cried.

I thought I would die of shock. I feared for my life at that very moment. The voice came out of what seemed to be a kitchen, it took courage to enter the room, I was so scared I was shaking as I turned open the door handle. I opened the door, I saw … *a ghost!*

Hazel Ijomah (10)
Bancroft's Preparatory School, Woodford Green

The Reaper Of Fear

It was a dark and windy day. But I was still out playing football with my friends. I kicked the ball too far and it landed in an abandoned house's front garden. Just as I went to get it, the wind blew it into the house through an open door. I went inside to look for the ball. To my dismay, the door slammed shut behind me. I tried to open it, but it would not budge. I was petrified! I kept searching for a way out.

There were scary paintings hanging crookedly on the wall. I spotted a rickety staircase, and at the top of the staircase was my ball. I was shocked, how did it get there? I did not care how it got there. I just wanted it back. I took my first step, it seemed all right. I continued, when suddenly, the staircase collapsed under me. I fell into a dark, dingy room. I seemed to have landed safely.

I heard something, a gust of air. An icy cold shiver ran down my spine! I heard it again! It was louder this time. My heart was pounding, I was numb all over!

Suddenly, I saw my ball again. It was floating in the air. And out of the darkness a cloak appeared to be encircling my ball. It came towards me. It swung its ghostly arm in a circle around its shrouded head and out came a gleaming scythe. He dug it into me. I silently ...

Omar Ali (9)
Bancroft's Preparatory School, Woodford Green

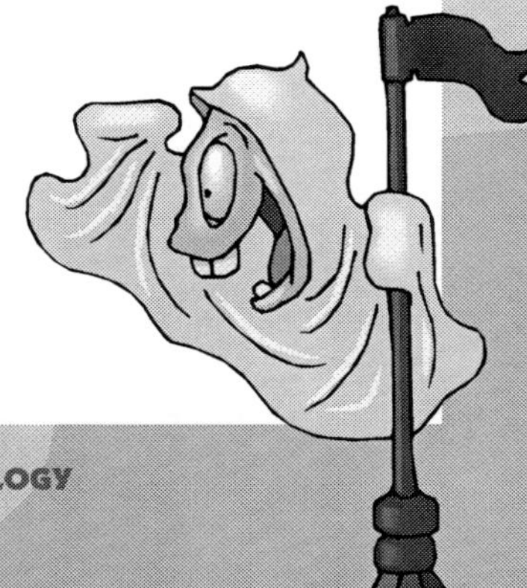

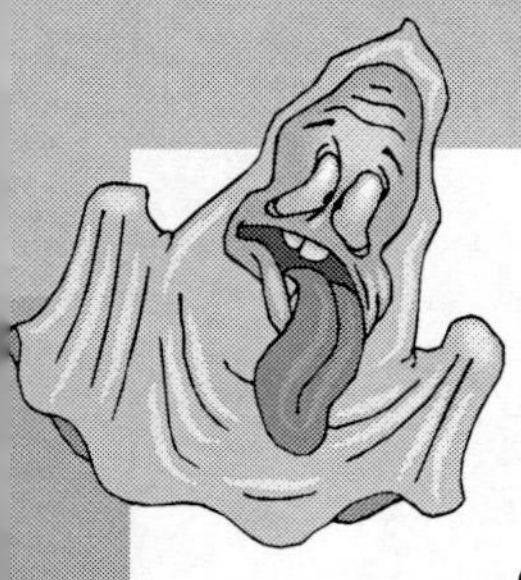

Mirror, Mirror On The Wall

The whistling wind flew through the dark night. My mysterious friend, Jake, and I were camping out in my back garden for the night. The tent was extremely big with only a few breathing holes. You could hear nothing except us munching our mouth-watering midnight feast. I was so excited, the hairs on the back of my neck tingled with excitement. We could not believe that our parents had actually let us stay out here by ourselves. We pulled our comfy covers over our shivering bodies away from the chill of the night.

'Can I go to the loo?' asked Jake.

'Sure but watch out for the bogeyman,' I said cheerfully. I couldn't stop giggling to myself after that.

But where was Jake? It was too quiet for my liking. Suddenly I heard a noise from the bathroom. I slowly slid out of the tent to investigate.

The rain ran down my sweaty spine and the hail hit my head stinging my skull. The piercing wind ran through my racing heart. All of a sudden a figure appeared in the bathroom. As I came closer I realised that the figure was Jake and he was chanting some sort of voodoo. I was frozen to the spot, I could not move. A ghost appeared from out of the mirror looking like it was sucking the life out of him. Then a sudden sickening surge of panic ran through my body as it turned towards me. Would I escape?

Rory Strycharczyk (10)
Bancroft's Preparatory School,
Woodford Green

Mystery At Oakland Drive

One dark, moonless night Alex set off for Madeleine's party at 5 Oakland Drive. Little did she know, she was about to have an evening like no other! Alex had only just moved into the area but at school Madeleine had invited her to her birthday party.

When Alex arrived, she couldn't believe her eyes. Was this boarded-up and abandoned house really Madeleine's home? The ivy had grown all over the windows and, barely visible in the overgrown garden, stood a statue, the cracked head of which was lying in the long grass.

As she walked up the unstable, crumbling, stone staircase, she noticed that the rotten oak door was slightly ajar. Despite her apprehension, the sound of Britney Spears egged her on. She cautiously entered through the door, which suddenly slammed behind her. The music stopped. By now, Alex was convinced it was a trick. Yet there was no evidence of a party.

Just as Alex was about to give up all hope, she spotted a pale-faced girl wearing a Victorian blue satin dress. Out of the darkness a clock chimed. Numerous swirling silver figures ascended from the floor. Terrified, Alex fainted.

Waking, Alex gasped. The pale girl had no feet! She must be a ghost!

The girl whispered, 'You don't belong.'

Alex ran home, without a backward glance.

The next day, unable to believe what had happened, Alex returned to Oakland Drive. She saw that number 5 was in fact number 50 - the zero had dropped off - and when she looked up, *the house was gone!*

Philippa Chilvers Woolley (10)
Bancroft's Preparatory School, Woodford Green

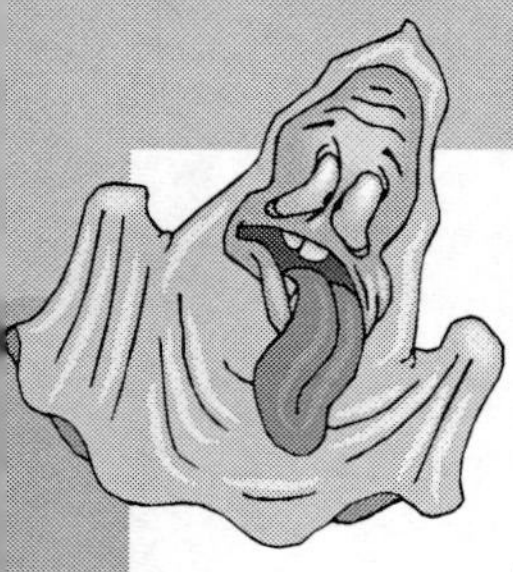

Memories

When Brad was eight years old at Cub camp, he was in the middle of the woods with only a tiny lantern for light, and a little bit of help from the moon. The boys were sharing the scariest ghost stories they had ever heard. These stories were about 'The woodsman' and 'The man in the woods'. The night was full of adventures although bedtime was looming. Before Brad could say goodnight everyone was asleep and he was left alone.

All of a sudden Brad heard a noise coming from the darker part of the woods. He heard the crackling autumn leaves. The noise got louder and louder. Then from out of the darkness came a figure. The figure moved closer. Brad screamed, he woke everyone up, but the figure was gone and had taken their only lantern with him. Everyone was left in the dark with the moon shining on their backs wondering what was going to happen to them all.

It was many years since Cub camp and Brad had forgotten about the man or ghost he'd seen in the woods.

During his Sunday hike in the woods he was listening to all the sounds. The footsteps he heard in the autumn leaves led him to believe he was not alone. Then he thought it was good someone else was strolling in the woods. His mind remembered Cub camp and he started to tremble with fear.

No one could help Brad this time from the mystery figure ...

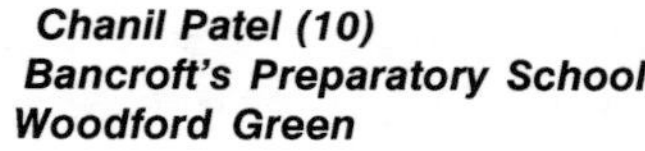

Chanil Patel (10)
Bancroft's Preparatory School,
Woodford Green

Invisible Murder

It was a cold and wintry night. I had been a long-distance driver for many years, loneliness and tiredness were no new words to how I always felt. Tonight was no different, I had a couple of drinks, maybe one too many.

As I journeyed home the road seemed much darker, longer and more winding. I had taken this route before but this night seemed different. Maybe it was the Guinness.

It was no time to think about myself, there was a bump in the road. It was sudden, loud and hard. I staggered towards the object. What was it? Rolling it over, the picture in my blurry eyes was the face of my journalist friend's daughter. This was his favourite daughter. How could I be so careless? If only I questioned myself later.

The journey to my friend's house was quick. A list of questions and answers flooded my thoughts. The rap on the front door was loud. The way he looked at me I felt he knew my thoughts. Mumbling an explanation I opened the back of the lorry only to notice that the object, which I thought was his daughter, was gone!

I felt stupid, mystified but relieved. Muttering a quick apology I drove away, confused. Did I kill the girl or not?

A week had passed when my friend called to say his daughter had been killed. My friend's heart was broken. I was not sure if what had happened was an invisible murder.

Ethan Avril (10)
Bancroft's Preparatory School, Woodford Green

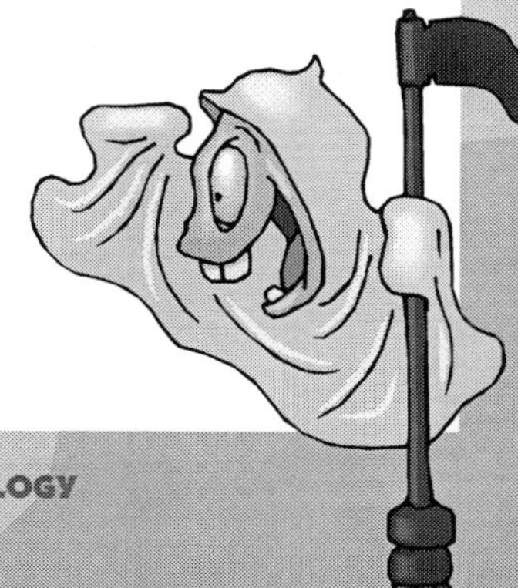

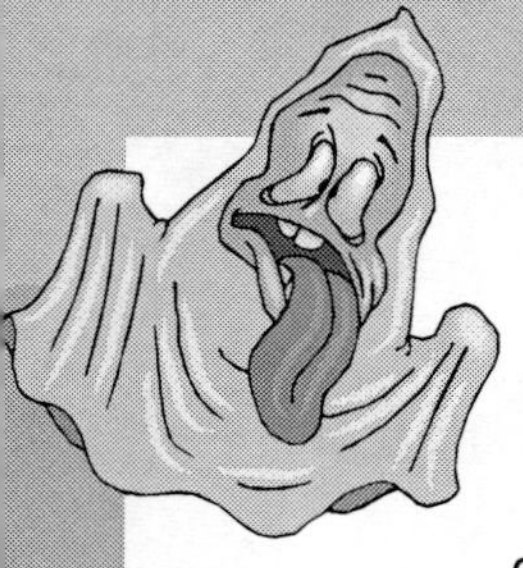

The Death Game!

We had just moved in and I knew the house was creepy. The first occurrence was not of interest but yet was unusual. I was playing in the garden when I heard a scream. I thought it was my next-door neighbour so I went to take a look, but no one was in. I left it at that.

Two days later, I heard another scream. How could this be? I went into the house. It had the appearance of a medieval building. Where could the scream have come from? I heard another one. It sounded louder as if it came from upstairs. I heard a creaking noise. What was this?

I went into a bedroom and on the mirror in blood was written *'Die in the washroom!'* What did this mean? I presumed the washroom meant the bathroom.

I went to take a look, in blood this time was *written 'Redeem a soul in the garde robe'*. I had been doing Medieval history at school so I knew that it meant the lavatory. I went to the next room, which was the lavatory. On the toilet lid was written *'Beloved knows naught'*, which I knew meant, 'You do not know what you have got until it is gone'.

I heard another scream, it sounded like Mum. It came from the basement. I flew straight down the stairs. There in the half-light, on the cold floor, lay Mum, dead on the floor. I was next, argh!

Tim Knott (10)
Bancroft's Preparatory School, Woodford Green

The Station Master

One winter's night I was playing around at the deserted train station, when the rubbish bags that were stacked up in the corner fell over. The tyres that leant up against the wall rolled down the hill. I ignored it, it was probably just the wind. Suddenly it got too scary for me when I heard a voice. It wasn't a normal voice it was eerie and deep. It said, 'I must tidy the station before the next train comes.'

'But, but, but who?'

'No buts young boy, I don't like children so scram!'

I was scared stiff and refused to move but I at last had the courage to turn round slowly. I was amazed to see a whistle floating in mid-air. I managed to stutter, 'Who are you?'

'I said go and stop bothering me.'

'All right, I agree, but who are you?'

'I'm the station master, if you really want to know my story then listen ...

It was 130 years ago early in the morning. I was behind on all my duties, I was sweeping the platform ready for the next train to arrive at the station when I slipped and fell onto the track. I was struggling up when I heard the whistle of the 07.15 coming. It happened so quickly. Nobody else was hurt only me. All I wanted to do was finish cleaning the station platform ready for the royal train to arrive. I never did get to meet Her Majesty.'

Katherine Booth (9)
Bancroft's Preparatory School, Woodford Green

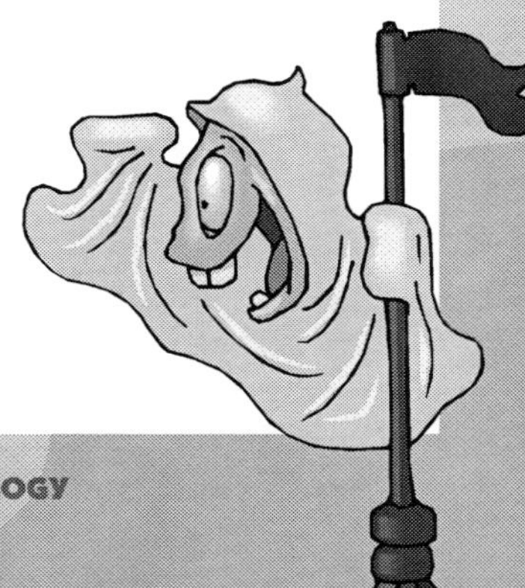

Seeing Is Believing

The other day I was reading the story of King Arthur - the part where only he can pull the sword from the stone. Soon after, I found a door in my new house that only I could open.

I couldn't see what was inside because of my eyesight. I was going to have an operation. The doctors said that there was a chance it might work. Until then I spent most of my time reading books in Braille.

I wanted to explore my house but it wasn't easy. I had to feel my way round. The door was in the attic. My father said it had been nailed shut but when I tripped and fell against the handle, the door creaked open. I was inside.

I could feel heavy drops of water falling all around me. A strange smell filled my nostrils and I tasted something metallic on my lips. Blood!

When you're blind your other senses have to work much harder. My ears were straining and then I heard a voice whisper, 'Thank you for coming. We've waited so long stuck in this chimney.'

Suddenly I could see. In front of me were two boys of about eleven - pale and skinny, and dressed in rags. They had soot in their hair and on their faces. I'd read about Victorian chimney sweeps and the climbing boys who worked for them.

'Please help us,' they moaned.

But as I watched, their faces became just skulls then they faded from my sight.

Richie Layburn (10)
Bancroft's Preparatory School, Woodford Green

I'm Not Afraid Of Ghosts Anymore

I've always been afraid of ghosts, because in books, they always look so terrifying. They're really spooky, with great big eyes and they hover and moan.

One night, I heard a strange low scream. I felt very scared and worried. Suddenly, a ghost flew into my room. It told me it was going to take me to a land of ghosts and spirits! I saw lots of colours whizzing by, I was travelling fast. Then I saw hundreds of figures. *They were all ghosts!* I was shaking with fright. They were all laughing and making horrible faces. In the distance, I saw a little ghost, who was beckoning to me. I went over and he whispered in my ear, 'We are only scary if you believe we are.' I said to myself over and over again, *I am not afraid of ghosts, I am not afraid of ghosts.*

Suddenly, everything was different. It was a great big party. The ghosts were smiling, singing and dancing. They explained that it made them sad to think people were afraid of them and if people were just friendly towards them, they wouldn't look frightening to them. Booboo, the ghost that took me from my room, said he would take me back, he was so kind and looked after me well. Now, when I hear a noise in my house, I'm never afraid, because I know that it's just Booboo having fun.

Rhianna Saharoy (8)
Bancroft's Preparatory School, Woodford Green

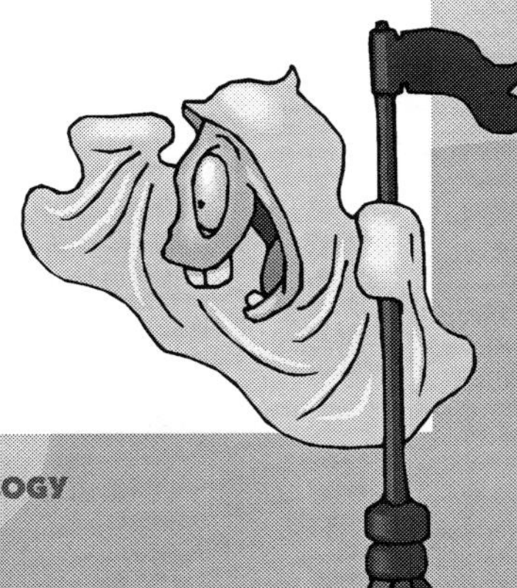

The Mummy Princess

We finally arrived in Egypt. I was so excited my eyes popped out with anticipation.

That night we had the pleasure of visiting the oldest pyramid in Egypt.

As we entered this fascinating and marvellous structure, I felt like a boiled egg in the intense humidity. Everything seemed strange as if it were all familiar.

All of a sudden I was alone. A shiver ran down my spine. I could smell the aromatic oils of the pharaohs. I heard a thunder of people roaring, trampling everywhere. I could feel damp blankets like bandages floating past me. Where was I? Was I alone? I had lost my sight? All was black yet I could feel the ancient and mysterious memories.

I tried to scream, when I looked around there was an Egyptian girl, staring back at me wrapped in damp bandages. As I stared at her I saw the rest of my class and the curator was explaining the mummified princess, whom I had seen, seemed to come alive and only be seen by girls aged ten (the age she was when she died) and girls with the first letter of her name (her name was Princess Simola). That was me! My pupils dilated with fear, as the curator winked, 'The princess is believed to visit those who believe in her!'

It has been a wonderful yet frightening experience. Who would believe me, but then when I opened out my hand, a beautiful brooch lightened my palm, it was the princess' … !

Simran Kaur-Singh (10)
Bancroft's Preparatory School, Woodford Green

The Haunted Hall

I went for a walk with my dog in the forest and we came across an enormous ruined building. It looked burnt out and had large arched windows. It had large pointing towers to each side of the building. As we walked around it I saw white figures at one of the windows. It was a tall man and a woman sitting with a baby in her arms. My dog all of a sudden started to bark, I think he was as frightened as I was. We started to run towards a bridge and turned to look back, the figures were right behind us.

We were very tired by now, but still ran until we came to a main road and looked behind us, the figures had gone. I was tempted to go back into the house and as we did my dog quivered with fright. When I looked up I could see that there were no floors so how could I have seen real people at the window? It was very dull and there were no paintings on the walls and no lights apart from one candle. Then there were spooky noises and the candle went out. We ran!

A couple of years later there was an open day for the refurbishment of the hall, I was looking around and I saw a painting on the wall and to my surprise it was a picture of the figures I saw - painted over one hundred and fifty years ago.

Oliver Marsh (10)
Bancroft's Preparatory School, Woodford Green

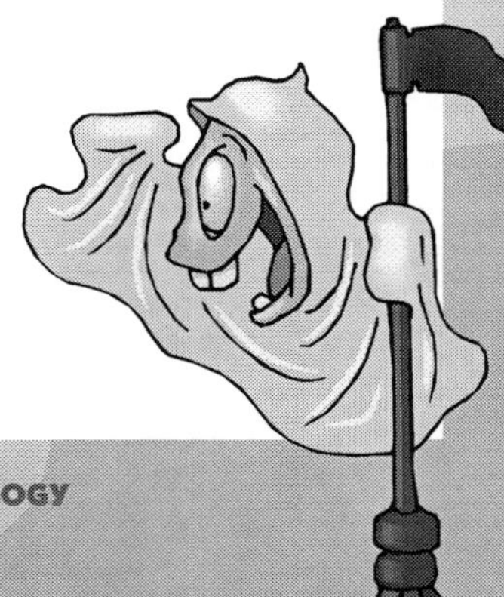

The Ghost Who Hid In The Cupboard

Once a boy called Peter had a dream about a ghost and ever since he was scared of them. His parents wanted him to go to bed early one night and that was the night he dreamt this dream. He screamed until his dad carried him into his bedroom and put him into his bed. He finally calmed down and went to sleep.

In the middle of the night he woke with a fright. He could hear the windows rattling and the door shaking. He hid under the covers but that just made it worse. He didn't cry but decided to be a big boy and go downstairs and see if anything was there. He opened the door silently. He couldn't see anything nor hear anything but he knew someone was in the house.

After a while he gave up looking and started to climb the stairs back to his room again. Out of the corner of his eye he saw a white thing hiding in the cupboard. It looked like a white cloth. He went to take a look and to his amazement it was a ghost, the night he had been dreading was here!

He ran back upstairs as fast as a hare, went into his room and locked the door. He still didn't cry. He could hear the ghost banging against the door. Suddenly the banging on the door had faded! 'Yes it has gone,' he whispered.

Had it been a spooky dream, or had it not?

Leah Fisher (10)
Bancroft's Preparatory School, Woodford Green

It

Tap! Tap! The same sound every night. Ever since we moved here. *Tap! Tap! Tap!* There it is again coming from under the floor.

A week ago we moved here to the small countryside village of Norton Marsh. I don't like the name, it sounds mushy. I think the village is spooky. By day the village looks like any other sunny Midland village, but by night our 'palace' as Dad calls it is covered by a deep mist. Every night I don't sleep, the dark rings under my eyes getting deeper and darker. Mum always comments. I deny sleeplessness.

'It' (as I had named it) taps again. *Tap! Tap!* Oh my god it's louder than ever before. I can't talk to anyone, they would not believe me, they can't hear what I can. *Tap! Tap! Tap!* It's louder. A noise like no other. It's shriller. Hang on just a sec, it's under the floor and over there is a ... a loose board. Oh, should I feel worried or excited? I think I'll be worried, maybe 'it' could come up through the floorboards! Eek!

I climb slowly out of bed and tiptoe across the creaky floorboards, past the ginormous wardrobe and the tiny window with no curtains. This and my bed are the only things in my dark, dank room. I bend down and pull up the loose board. There 'it' is. 'It' swoops out and just floats, then an icy blast hits me. I die.

Lucy Gatrell (9)
Bancroft's Preparatory School, Woodford Green

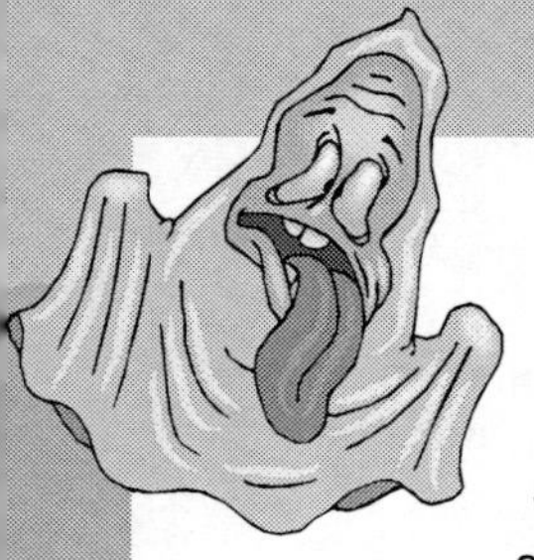

Mystery Deliverer

We had only just moved in but already I had received a letter. It was on the doorstep just waiting to be picked up. An anonymous letter saying 'Meet me in the room under the steps at midnight'. It was written in an old spidery hand. Strange, nobody knew I was moving here except for my family and the owners of the house and nobody around here knew my name. The house was an old rickety house with missing windows, no electricity and a number of strange noises coming from each spooky room.

The clock struck twelve; I waited breathlessly in the basement to see what would happen next. A great flash appeared before my eyes and floating before me was a ghost. I gasped and dropped my candle in surprise.

'What is your name?' it wailed at me.

'Mi-Mi Angel,' I stammered. 'Who a-are y-you?'

'I'm King Arthur.'

'Why are you here?' I asked, getting more suspicious by the minute. The ghost explained it had escaped from Avalon.

'What's Avalon?' I questioned.

'Avalon,' it replied, 'is an island where people who are half alive and half dead exist.'

Wait a minute, I thought, *this is probably one of Valentine's pranks. He has been studying King Arthur at school. That weasel of a little brother.* 'Alright Valentine you've had your fun but now it's time to take off the sheet and come upstairs, OK.' There was a moment of silence between us so I came forward to take his hand. *'Argh!'*

Chloé Michaud (10)
Bancroft's Preparatory School, Woodford Green

The Ghost Story

It was the month of November in 1950. I was staying at my grandmother's house for a week to look after her. She was a weak, frail woman who hardly spoke to me. She stayed in her bed day and night just staring blankly. I hated her house so much. It stood alone on a hill in the middle of a field. It was a very gloomy, cold house. It felt damp, dismal and empty.

One lonely night a storm broke out. The wind howled outside. The rain lashed against the windows. The thunder roared like a lion. The windows suddenly flew open and the power switched off at a shocking speed. It was pitch-black. I couldn't see a thing! I hate the dark; I was frozen to the spot. What should I do now? Then I thought of the candles.

With trembling hands I tried to light the match, when another almighty gust of wind blew open the window and blew out the flame. I lit it again and to my absolute horror I could see a strange shadow on the wall of a ghastly creature. It seemed to be beckoning me towards the door. Then suddenly ... *slam!* The door shut tight behind it. By the light of the candle I made my way over to the door with this dreadful feeling inside me that something sinister and wicked was waiting for me. *It was a ghost!*

Nadia Abraham (10)
Bancroft's Preparatory School, Woodford Green

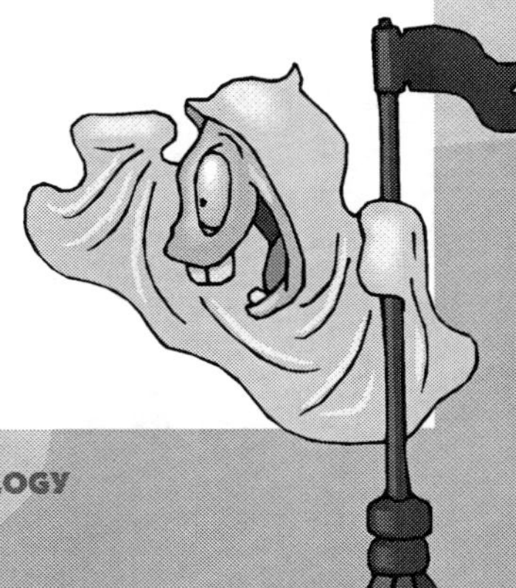

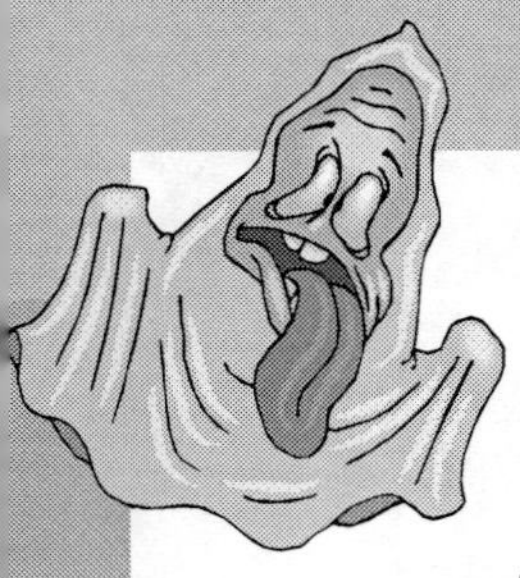

The Floating Daggers

One windy night I woke up and my stomach was aching with hunger. So I crept down the cold, dark staircase. I was in the middle of chomping on a slice of bread when there was a loud *crash!* It was the chandelier in the living room. I dashed into the living room to see what had happened to the priceless chandelier. It lay shattered on the floor, the glass covering the wooden ground. I was too terrified to enter the room.

I spotted something resting, and it looked to me like a large knife. It moved and I thought my mind was playing tricks on me. Then with no warning the knife raised slowly into the air. My stomach leapt out of my mouth. I stood there motionless. It shot towards me and I ran like I had never run before. I sprinted upstairs and almost died of terror when I saw it was already there. I stumbled down the staircase to find not only the first knife, but another knife. You would think by now I would have called for help, which is true; I tried, but no words came out. Both blades lunged toward me. The first dagger missed me by an inch. The second, however, caught me on my ear. I jumped into the living room. The glass dug into me like needles. I could make out more knives! Each one charged forward at me. I waited for death, but they disappeared with a loud *crack!*

Philip Simpson (10)
Bancroft's Preparatory School, Woodford Green

The Witch's Grave

It was a day like any other except it was a full moon on Hallowe'en. I was with my friends, we were trick or treating. We lived in a road where the most horrible people lived. We decided we would play a dare. The first dare was to go into the old haunted house on the hill where the farm man used to live.

I was very foolish and went in. My friends shut me in for a joke, then the door was jammed. I was stuck for the night. People say there is the grave of the farm man's wife in the old house. People say, she was a witch!

The night was my last and I knew it would be.

Suddenly the ghost of an old haggard witch floated towards me and to my surprise, she hugged me. I thought*, she is not a witch she is a kind loving person.* To my dismay, she was sucking out my guts and my liver.

I began to turn thinner, lighter and paler until I too became a ghost. I realised the witch was no longer a ghost, she was alive once more. She used her magic to open the door. I was left to hover in the air. Suddenly the name on the gravestone read my name, 'Ruby Smith'. I was sucked down and down into the grave.

... Never to be seen again ...

Elizabeth Willoughby (10)
Bancroft's Preparatory School, Woodford Green

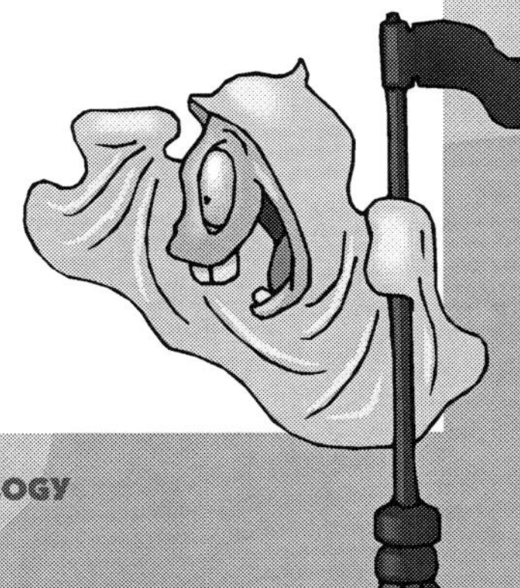

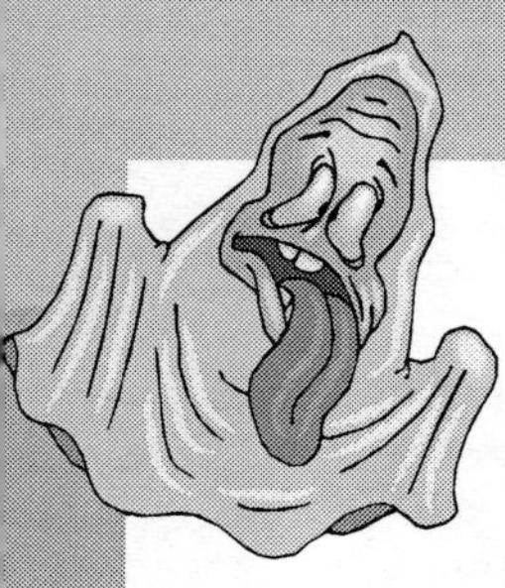

Poor Dolly

'Hello Luke … it's Phoebe … I'm running late … do you think they can hold the table? Well, I'll only be thirty minutes; I just want a bath. Okay, phone me back when you know.'

I hung up and rushed upstairs. I twisted a tap, and let the water gush out. Then I uncorked a bottle and poured in the remains of the bath salts. I dashed to the cupboard to retrieve some more.

It was only when I leant over the tub, that I noticed a strange, shadowy object at the bottom of the water.

When I had drawn it out of the bath, I realised what it was - the head of a porcelain doll.

I recognised it from the collection that I kept on the shelf next to the bathroom door. I must have knocked it in my hurry.

There were holes where eyes had been, making its gaze uncanny. Its lips were shining, but it was an eerie shine, with none of the warmth of a sunrise.

For a while I just stood there, with the face in my cupped hands. I was brought back down to earth when I heard the telephone. 'Oh hell!' I breathed. 'I'll bet it's Luke with bad news!'

But it wasn't Luke - it was uncontrollable sobbing.

'Hello?' I asked. 'Is someone there?' It was then that I realised who was sobbing.

'Isabel, is that you? What's wrong?'

After a little more coaxing, she answered: 'It's Dorothy! She's dead! She's drowned!'

Linnet Kaymer (10)
Bancroft's Preparatory School, Woodford Green

The Rising Of The Ghost

It was a dry winter's evening. The sun was setting. I was playing cricket in my back garden. I was batting. I hit the cricket ball a bit too high. Amazingly the cricket ball was floating in the air. Suddenly the stitching of the cricket ball cracked open. A white gas-like material gradually wafted through the still air. It formed the shape of a hot air balloon and was the size of a pumpkin. Two dark black dots appeared and were staring straight at me. The gas below the dots gradually became transparent. I now realised that it was a ghost. It also made a low-pitched and dull noise, which vibrated my body. I was so scared that I ran into my house and locked the door.

The ghost came through the door with ease. I ran to my parents to tell them what had happened. They didn't believe me at all. My parents sent me to bed.

At about one o'clock in the morning, there was a deafening noise. It was exactly the same noise the ghost had made. I was so frightened that I hid under the covers. My heart was thumping fast. I was shivering with fear. I tried to scream but no voice came out. I slowly started to feel lighter. I gradually rose from the bed covers. My body was beginning to turn white. I couldn't see my hands or legs at all as they seemed to have disappeared. I was becoming a ...

Krishna Aswani (10)
Bancroft's Preparatory School, Woodford Green

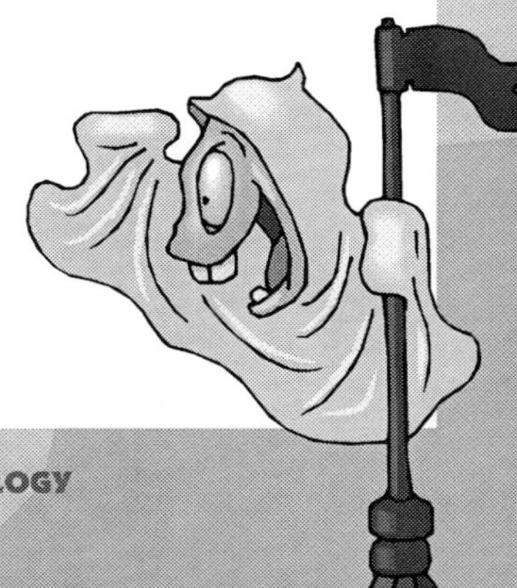

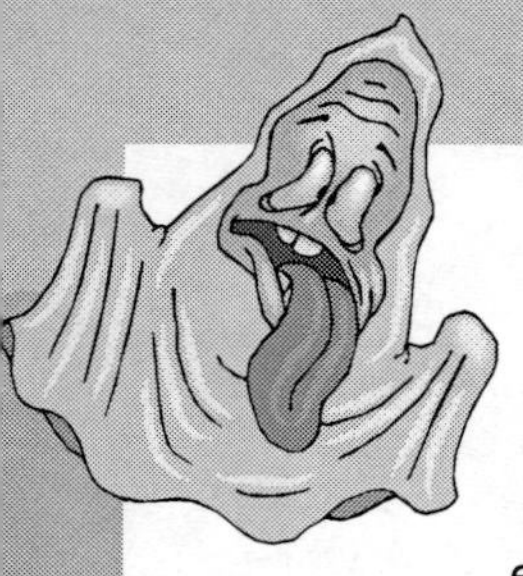

The Mysterious House

Craasshh! It was the day we were moving house and Dad had put 4 boxes on top of each other that had just fallen down. There was a lot of excitement going through our house because our new house was so much bigger. Strangely we got it very cheap, even cheaper than our old house.

When we arrived we saw how gigantic the place was. I immediately started running into the house but Mum called, 'Fred can you come and meet our neighbour?'

I reluctantly went and greeted the neighbour who was called Mrs Lee.

She said, 'I'm sure you're aware why you got your house so cheap?'

'Luck,' my mum said.

'You got it cheap because everyone who has lived there has died in some mysterious way.'

My mum said, 'That's utter nonsense,' but I could see she was shocked.

I went to sleep in a new bed having nightmares of people being killed by a ghost.

The next morning I woke early. Dad was busy in the study. While I was having breakfast some strange noise came from the study. My mum and I went to look what had happened. The study was a mess with all the pages of books torn and the chair upturned. I went to look at the computer which said, 'Now it's your turn to disappear' ...

Miren Radia (10)
Bancroft's Preparatory School, Woodford Green

The Creepy Tunnel

It was a bright summer's day with the sun shining, I was playing in the park and I was running over a hill when I fell into it, a deep, dark, murky pit. It seemed like someone had just bored a hole down through the hill.

As I woke up from the fall I saw a long tunnel lit by lanterns which made the tunnel glow orange. As I was walking along, in front of me was a big, gloomy, deserted house. I walked in past the door, it creaked back and forth from the wind of the tunnel.

Inside it was as gloomy as it looked from the outside; there were stone gargoyles everywhere. As I walked past them I heard a whispering sound, I quickly turned around and the gargoyles were moving around, I was so scared. Then the whisper turned into a voice and said, 'Why are you down here? This is ghost property.'

Then in front of me the whole house just collapsed and I was inside! I fell into another pit; I must have been three floors down from the park I thought. Then a lot of small ghosts formed a circle around me, each one of them was plain white and had a different face to all the rest. The ghosts were attracted to something else I was not sure of, it made like a screeching sound, it came from a room, I looked inside, it was a giant ghost - noooo!

Matthew J Tann (10)
Bancroft's Preparatory School, Woodford Green

The Ghost Of The Emerald Box

When I arrived at my granny's cottage it was late so she sent me straight to bed. There was one strange thing about my granny, she was never sad.

I heard her ascending the stairs and the creak of her bedroom door. I couldn't stop thinking of her emerald-green box; she always had it, covered in pictures. *Thump,* what was that? I knew it was the box. *Thump,* it was louder, I had to find out ...

I waited for as long as I could resist, I crept over the creaky floorboards to her room. My hand on the doorknob, I pushed. I saw her snoring silhouette against the duvet covers.

I crept over the rug, hoping that it would muffle the sound of the floorboards and slowly reached for the box, I grabbed it. My plan was to take it back to my room, but I couldn't resist. I opened it, it was empty, but then a face stared up at me. It screamed. I stared at it in horror and then turned to my granny, she seemed not to have heard it. Perhaps only I could hear it.

It slithered out of the case. I was in so much shock. Something flashed. I opened my mouth to scream but nothing came out. I fainted.

When I awoke my granny was looking over me, it was strange, I felt no worry in the world, as if all the sadness had been sucked out of me!

Harriet Bartlett (11)
Bancroft's Preparatory School, Woodford Green

Mr Jones

The moonlight cast shadows against the pale face of the already dead Mr Jones' son. Lying on his father's gravestone, blood had poured from his heart where the wound had been opened with a dagger.

I rang my colleagues at the police station telling them to come as soon as possible. I put my gloves on and looked at the dead body in more detail. The iron smell was drifting around my nose. I could hear the police siren nearby and soon after four tall men came out of the police car.

I ran up to them and pointed at the body. My legs were shaking as I saw them taking the dagger out of the dead body slowly. My heart was pounding quickly and I could feel the sweat run off my forehead. Finally the dagger was pulled out.

The coroner had now taken the body away and I started to talk to a tall figure. He started to talk to me about how the man was killed. I then realised by the details he told me that this man was the ghost of the dead body. I backed away slowly and ran.

Kush Sikka (10)
Bancroft's Preparatory School, Woodford Green

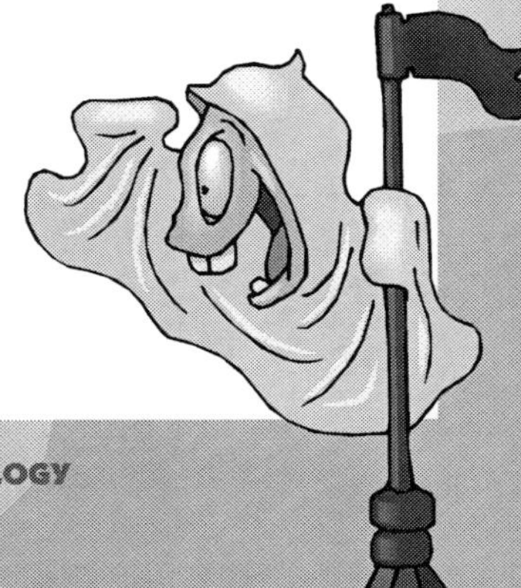

49586746

'Dad, when will we reach our new home?' Prill and Colin were asking their dad, for it had been several hours since they left their old house. They soon arrived in their new home.

As they walked in a dark, eerie house caught their attention. They noted the house and were going to have a look at it soon.

The school bell rang and the children seated themselves. Next to Colin sat a boy who was secretive and next to Prill sat a girl who was noisy.

At playtime Colin and Prill met up with the children. The boy's name was Oliver and the girl's name was Rosie. All four of them seemed inquisitive about the house.

The next day was the weekend and they met up outside the house. They looked at the house and were certain it was haunted.

It was filled with insects and cobwebs dangled above their heads. The musty smell of mould lay on to the door that carried on clinging open and shut like a hungry mouth. The ivy was prickly and bushy. They soon entered the house.

Nothing lay in the house apart from a dial that they soon reached and saw a code, it read: '49586746'. The children pressed the numbers and a door opened.

Inside lay a skeleton was lying on top of a treasure chest. They were speechless. All four ran out of the house as fast as they could. They were soon home, tucked up in bed keeping their secret bottled up inside.

Mihira Patten (10)
Bancroft's Preparatory School, Woodford Green

The Haunted House

Abigail fell and screamed!

'Be quiet!' I whispered. Honestly, I had never been so scared in my life. We had decided to visit the haunted house at the top of the crooked road outside our village. Everyone had warned us never to venture out there, but in the end we couldn't resist and we just had to see what the fuss was about. I wish I had given the idea some serious thought, because right now I wanted to be home, having hot chocolate and a muffin.

Abigail pulled herself up, muddy, wet and moaning.

'Oh for goodness sake, it was your idea too!' I said, unsympathetically.

We scrambled up the steep hill towards the house. As we got nearer, we could see smoke gushing from the chimney. Was there someone inside? We were getting nervous and excited too, the fear starting to disappear.

Approaching the house, we crept to a window and peered in. Amazingly we saw a little girl sitting on a sofa reading a book.

We began to relax and decided there wasn't anything frightening.

Then we heard a strange noise from within, and as we stared hard again, we saw that instead of the girl there appeared to be a white, smoky cloak floating around the room.

We didn't stop to look, but rapidly sped all the way home, out of breath, our clothes torn and muddy.

Looking at each other in disbelief we whispered, 'Was that really a ghost?'

Serena Mayor (10)
Bancroft's Preparatory School, Woodford Green

The Deadly Force

It all started last week. I was out on the beach when a strange-looking man walked up to me.

'Oh, de sea is nigh and one of us peoples shall disappear. I warn thee to stay away from dis beach until de curse is abroken,' the man said in a croaky voice.

I shivered. The man slowly walked away, limping, as if he had done something to his leg. A strong breeze suddenly made me change my mind to go back home from Cotton Beach.

That night, something strange happened. That night a voice called to me. A ghostly voice. A dead voice. 'Ggggooo ttoooo tthhee bbeeaacch,' it said repeatedly. A force made my body drag myself out of my house and down towards the beach. I slumped on the soft sand and lay down. Soon I heard more voices. Dead and ghostly. A hard wind gathered around me. Too strong for me to remain on the ground. It threw me up in the air and hurled me into the deep, dark sea. Just before I started drowning I caught a glimpse of the people who had been talking. Ghosts.

The next morning I woke up and went to the local shop. I asked for some milk. The shopkeeper wasn't listening. He couldn't see me or hear me. Then I realised. Last night I had drowned. It was just like the old man had said. Now I was dead. Alone, in the land of ghosts.

Ciara Murphy (9)
Bancroft's Preparatory School, Woodford Green

Death's Shadow

There it was again, that deep breathing. It was driving me crazy. I opened my eyes, the sight was frightening. A shadowy figure towered over me. Its eyes were glowing red. I reached out my hand and it vanished. I calmed down, my eyes felt droopy. I fell into a warm and comfortable sleep, or so I thought.

My house was burning. It was an inferno. I heard screaming, it was enough to make your hair stand on end. I coughed and coughed and then fainted.

I was in bed; thank goodness it was just a dream. I thought about the dream all day until I got home. My house was just ashes! I searched for any surviving objects; I found nothing but a picture of the shadowy figure. I arranged to go to a hotel.

At the hotel I decided to calm myself after the shock. I had a shower then went into my bed and closed my eyes. I heard deep breathing. Suddenly it stopped and I fell asleep. In my dream I was on a building; I fell off. When I was tumbling down I looked up and saw the shadowy figure.

Adán Mordcovich (11)
Bancroft's Preparatory School, Woodford Green

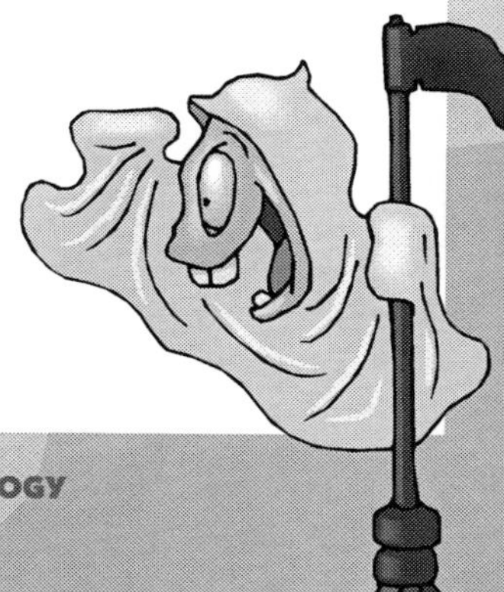

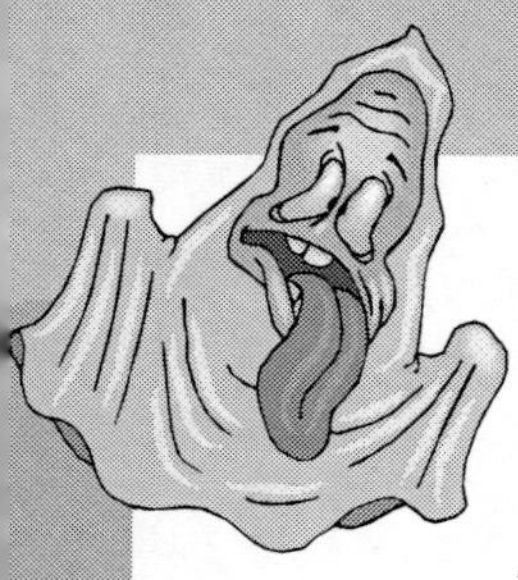

In The Forest

I trudged through the undergrowth of the dark old forest. The leaves crunched as I stepped on them. I kept on walking, with the fear of being followed.

I carried on my path and then timed a stop. There was no noise. Was someone following me? Was it a ghost? While I was walking, I looked down and saw a shadow pursuing me at every abrupt turn. What was this thing? I was getting frightened. I glanced down again at the shadow, too afraid to look at this person who was chasing me, and saw he had sharp grey claws. I was terrified. *Will he harm me?* I thought. Blood rushed through me with the force of Niagara Falls. The hairs on my neck were as erect as the Eiffel Tower. My heartbeat was similar to a drum's beat ricocheting through me.

With the thought of him harming me, I was nor concentrating on what was ahead of me and I tripped over a stone. The shadow drew nearer and I knew I had to face him. Trembling with fear I stared at the figure. When I looked, the figure that I thought was a ghost, was a curious gardener and the sharp claws were actually a rake.

After a quick chat with the gardener and a hot cup of tea, I stepped back into the darkness. The church bell struck 12 …

Neville Jacob (10)
Bancroft's Preparatory School, Woodford Green

One Saturday Afternoon

One Saturday afternoon, my sister Elizabeth and I were making cakes. Elizabeth asked me to go into the basement to find our mum's old cookery book. There ahead of me I saw a white flash. I wasn't worried, I just turned around and got the cookery book and walked towards the door. Just before I reached the door, I saw the flash again and after the flash had gone I saw a tall white figure with long brown hair and eyes that stared at you. I stared at the figure for a minute and ran out of the door, up the stairs and into my kitchen. I didn't tell Elizabeth that I'd seen the strange white figure because my sister would have thought that I was telling a lie.

While the cakes were in the oven I went down to the basement to try and investigate more about the figure. I opened the door and there it stood in the corner. The figure came towards me. It started muttering to me in a strange sort of way. I thought the figure was saying something bad so I ran to a corner, got a sharp object and went over to the white figure and stabbed it in the belly. The figure didn't scream or try to fight with me, it just kept on speaking in a strange way. I ran upstairs to tell my sister there was a ghost in our basement, but for some strange reason I was speechless.

Anna Harman (11)
Bancroft's Preparatory School, Woodford Green

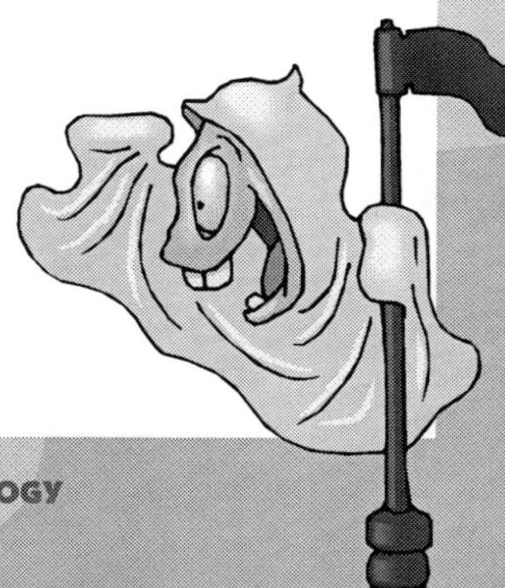

It Changed Her Life Forever

The Cubs got off the coach after a long outing. They were tired and weary. All they wanted to do was sleep, so they all went to their tents and changed into their pyjamas. It was a bit early to go to sleep so they decided to tell ghost stories. Emma told them one about a poor boy who was dragged away from his family in the dead of night and was never seen again. They were all scared stiff after this story and as it was dark they had to go to sleep, which they found very hard.

Hannah was the only one awake when she saw silhouettes outside. They looked nothing like humans so she started to get really worried. There were weird sounds coming from the gloomy trees behind her tent. The hairs on her arms and back were sticking up and a shiver went down her spine. The sounds eventually died out and the silhouettes were gone, so finally she went to sleep.

The next morning she told her friends all about the previous night but they didn't believer her, they said it was probably the leaves rustling and the trees making the silhouettes. She didn't think so, so she decided to investigate. Slowly she walked into the trees. The leaves crunched underneath her feet. Suddenly there was a sound behind her and a hand clasped over her mouth. She was being dragged away through the gloomy trees. She tried to cry for help but no one heard.

Emily Nickerson (11)
Bancroft's Preparatory School,
Woodford Green

Soul Picture

I propped myself in the stiff chair and rested my feet on a matching footstool. A flashback of my childhood memory swept over me. I had a vision of dear, dear Stacey standing on the doorstep in her new school uniform wishing me goodbye, only never to return.

My last memory of her urged me to go to the cupboard and take out the forbidden picture of my long-deceased sister. I rustled through some old documents and stumbled upon a dusty photograph tinted with a rusty gold frame. I braced myself for the moment to come and fixed my eyes on the photo of my 8-year-old Stacey.

Except it wasn't Stacey. But it had to be! It was, but it was the spitting image of me. Stacey had been killed in a car crash along with my mother decades ago, yet her spirit had carried on living in the picture. I checked the others to see if the same thing was happening, but there was nothing. Stacey when she was born, when she was four and so on, but why the one picture? It would remain a mystery ...

Next day I came home from work and checked the photo daringly. My eyes, disobeying me, looked at the photo and to my surprise her hair was tied up in a ponytail whereas yesterday it was down. Her flowing brown hair swayed a little and her eyes leapt to life. They moved like a pendulum, watching my every move ...

Gheed Mahir (11)
Bancroft's Preparatory School, Woodford Green

Noises From The Other Side

The siren echoed through my mind. The sound seemed to be going on for hours. Not fearing at all, I crept over to the alarm and typed in the code. The noise slowly faded away and soon it had completely gone. I heard a loud swishing sound coming from upstairs. There must have been someone in the house. As if floating, I walked up the spiralling stairs. My feet could not be heard. Looking up, I realised that it was just a fan.

Curiously, I started to look around each and every room in the house, for I had only been there once. When in the living room, I saw a television remote floating in thin air. Then the TV suddenly turned on! I went into the kitchen and found that the tap was dripping. I went up to it and put my hand straight through the cool, refreshing water.

Moving on into the master bedroom, I came face to face with a mirror. I had no reflection. I touched the mirror in surprise, but still nothing was there. I carried on staring and I saw a floating calculator out of the corner of my eye. Suddenly I realised that I was the ghost and that the floating objects were being held by humans that I could not see.

Alison Harvey (11)
Bancroft's Preparatory School, Woodford Green

The Mind Twister

The echo of my footsteps increased in volume. The figure stayed in my confused mind. Whatever I did it wouldn't leave me alone. All I could remember was when I was a little baby and every night it looked over my cot. Its blank face with no features and emotions, looked like it stared into my eyes. This figure haunted me until the time I could speak. Now it has just come back.

I have just been living on my own for a few days and all of a sudden I feel like my fears have conquered my entire body. All these years I have thought that maybe I could have a peaceful life, but I was wrong. Lying in bed I strained my ears trying not to listen to anything. The voices around me whispered, 'You'll be on your deathbed, you'll be on your deathbed.' These few words kept repeating in the air. I wondered why this mysterious person kept following me around everywhere. I thought that maybe it was because I had done something wrong in the past, but I couldn't remember. The fear of going crazy was a thought in my mind, but my brain felt like it was going to burst. I started to feel very irritated like my mind had run out of space and my questions were queuing up and waiting for their turn. I ran, trying to get free but something or someone kept pulling me back. Suddenly ...

Fiona Mo (10)
Bancroft's Preparatory School, Woodford Green

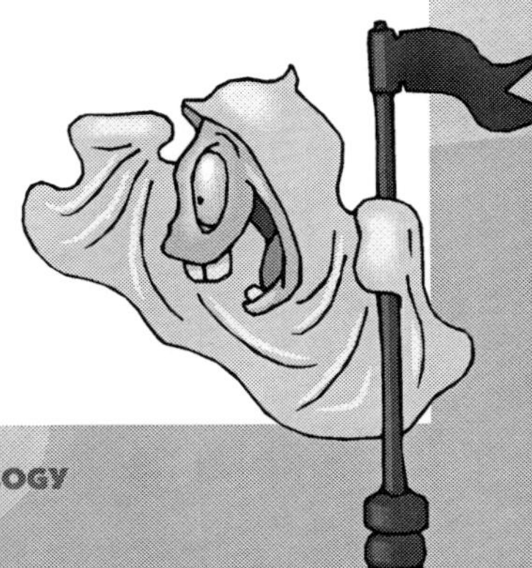

The Ghost Journey

It all happened a few years ago when I was trudging through the forest to get to my grandmother's house. Darkness was approaching the sky like a thick velvet blanket. Soon only the stars shed any light.

Later, looming in front of me, was a great jagged rock I longed to sit on it to rest my aching legs. All I wanted was to get to my grandmother's house. I closed my eyes and thought of a lovely warm fire, a delicious meal and a drink to quench my thirst.

As I snapped out of my daydreaming, something caught my eye. It was a colossal, pitch-black figure with blood-red eyes and razor-sharp teeth. Next to it was a half eaten animal.

My first reaction was to run and that's just what I did, I ran though the ghost-like trees that were waiting to grab me. I was panting and I had a deep, blood-filled scrape on my arm, but I still ran.

When I arrived at my grandmother's house she asked me how my journey was.

'Fine,' I answered, 'just fine.'

But the thought of the ghost still lurked in my mind.

Kavidha Clare (10)
Bancroft's Preparatory School, Woodford Green

My Graveyard

My journey from school took me though the churchyard and past an open grave. I ignored all the other ivy-smothered graves, but this one caught my attention. Something told me not to go near it, so I just left it there and ran home. I expected there would be a funeral later, but I soon forgot about it.

Later that night my mum sent me out to buy some bread for the next day. It was stormy outside and the moonlight cast shadows over the great trees that loomed above. From in-between the towering buildings, a small voice emerged. 'Come, come, come to me.'

The voice seemed to hypnotise me and, before I knew it, I was making my way towards the churchyard. The lightning struck and lit up the writing on the grave I had seen earlier. 'Edward Blake'. That was my name! I wanted to cry or wake up. Something! I needed to escape. I fled, but as I reached the gate an insistent force drew me back. I was being pushed towards the grave - closer and closer and then I fell.

I landed with a thump and the sides of the grave rose up and enclosed me in fear. I was plunged into darkness and everything disappeared into thin air. My senses evaporated, leaving me discarded from the world. I tried to dig myself out. The truth was confirmed.

Calum Lomas (10)
Bancroft's Preparatory School, Woodford Green

The Ghost Encounter

It all seems so silly really. Ghosts don't exist, but I swear I had an experience with one, a long time ago.

A swishing sound and another, then nothing. That was not normal, it doesn't happen like that.

Suddenly a hazy figure let itself into my room. I stared at it. It seemed like a shadow. My senses broke down and I was panicking I knew it. I tried to reply to it with the most disgusting word I knew. I couldn't speak. My mouth was failing me. Even my mind was buzzing, it would not work.

I was terrified. My legs were shaking wildly, uncontrollably, wildly. My face was as white as snow. A shiver ran down my spine. I felt cold all over. The shock and terror overcame my effort to be calm.

My heartbeat felt as loud as an earthquake. It was astonishing that the ghost could not hear it. Suddenly the ghost seemed to make a shadow out of me. The shadow joined to the ghost in an eerie way. It hit the ghost then spun round till it disappeared inside the ghost. I felt a sharp pain on my chest, then it all went black, then I fainted.

My mum and dad never knew because they'd say, 'You dreamt it,' but it was real I know, it haunted me, not them.

There, silly isn't it? I must have dreamt it but I'll never know for sure.

Arjun Popat (10)
Bancroft's Preparatory School, Woodford Green

The Boy From Hell

I am thinking this because it is all I can think. It is forty years to the day of my disappearance ...

I left for school in my bright red Vauxhall. When I arrived I parked just outside Ilford County High School. Before I reached the gates, a strange-looking boy (speckled face and wore glasses), said in an intelligent, stunted way, 'Follow me I want to show you something.'

I followed him, he looked a good four years younger than me, around thirteen, maybe fourteen, wouldn't say any older. He didn't look dangerous, I was fifteen minutes early for school, so I went. He led me to St James' Church a hundred or so feet away. He led me behind the church to the graveyard. Now I got a bit worried because why would somebody lead someone to a graveyard? I was into horror films and books and they involved graveyards. Though, like in all the films, I just carried on and didn't say anything.

Then the boy shrieked with laughter, then chanted a weird Latin sentence again and again. I knew something was wrong so I ran, but there was a figure chasing me then I fell over. Something went inside me like it was tearing out my heart. I then vanished and I am now trapped in a glass prison along with other victims from 'that boy'. It is a mental torture. No way to die, you can't talk, no feelings and your body doesn't need food.

Tom Markovitch (11)
Bancroft's Preparatory School, Woodford Green

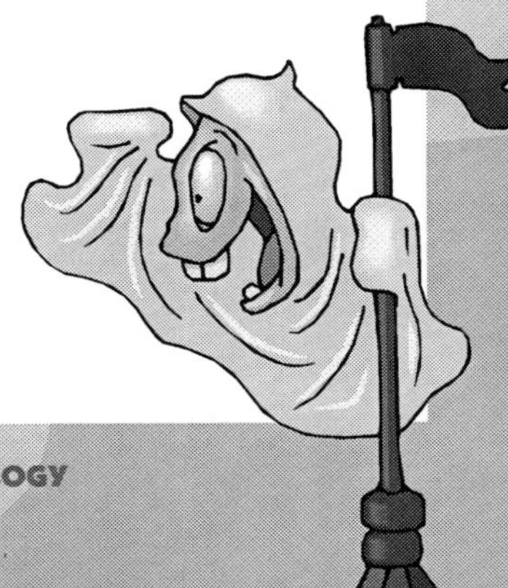

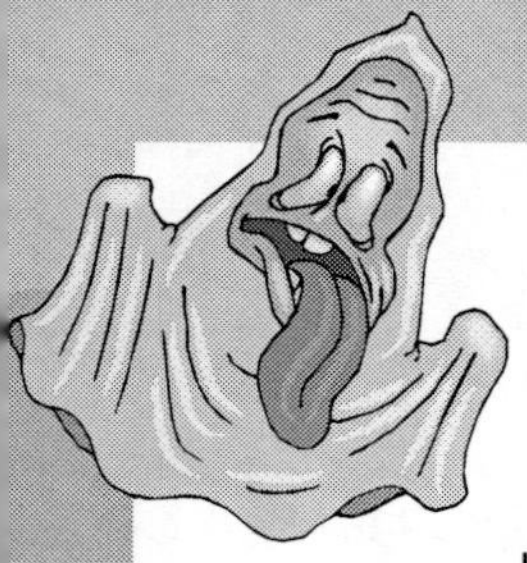

The Mansion

I was walking down a steep road, coming home from school. I passed many houses and soon came to the white, abandoned mansion. It had been on sale for about five years. I found the house very nice. Many people disagreed. People judged the house by the person who lived inside, the person who lived inside the house committed suicide because he believed a ghost was haunting him. I found this very silly.

I took a minute and stopped to look at the mansion. How I wished to go and investigate the interior. Nobody thought the mansion was any good to look at.

Then I thought to myself, *maybe this is my chance of seeing the interior.* Nobody's watching and Mum's not expecting me till 5.30. I climbed over the rusty gate guarding the mansion and climbed down. I ran to the door so nobody could spot me.

I twisted the chipped, wooden handle gently. I pushed really hard and to my surprise the door opened quite easily. Everything was neatly set out as if someone was already living there. I took a look around and spotted an emerald-green vase with a strange-shaped china lid. I handled the vase gently and lifted the lid. A gush of wind pushed me to the ground and a strange figure hovered in front of me. Suddenly I felt droopy; I felt I was put under a spell, by a ghost.

Salisha Amin (10)
Bancroft's Preparatory School, Woodford Green

The Footless Man

I looked up and approaching from the mist I saw a dark and slender figure. I was sure I had seen it before, but where?

As the figure emerged from the mist, I could see him more clearly. The figure was unhealthily pale; his eyes were electric-blue, I was sure I saw sparks fly from them. I looked up and down his sickly thin body; he looked like a beggar from what I could see. He was wearing a worn out tail coat with holes all over and ragged trousers. I looked further down, he didn't have any shoes; wait, that must be because he had no feet! He was hovering.

I screamed and ran, weaving in and out from all the gravestones. As I looked back I saw him grin with a wild look on his face. What was I thinking of, spending the late hours of night in a graveyard?

Finally I reached home, unsure if the footless man had followed me. I slammed the front door with sweat running down my back.

'What's wrong dear?' my mother asked.

I was thankful that she was there. I was terrified.

My mother turned around, I was expecting the sweet, comforting face of my mother; instead I saw the face of the footless man; pale face, electric-blue eyes, the face expressionless.

Lydia Katsis (11)
Bancroft's Preparatory School, Woodford Green

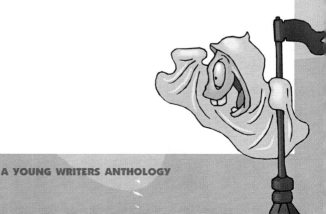

Back From The Dead

(My story is set some time around the end of the Second World War on a small island off the shores of Jersey in an isolated house surrounded by ghostly mists. It's about a mother named Grace and her two children, George and Lucy. The story starts with Grace advertising a position for a gardener and a housekeeper.)

Grace hires two servants, a gardener and a housekeeper. The children take to the servants quite well. Lucy is always boasting that she keeps seeing ghosts to her mother. Grace is a Christian and does not believe in the supernatural, so she keeps telling her children off for making up such ridiculous stories.

A few weeks go by and Grace notices that there is something not quite right in the house, especially since the servants have moved in.

Grace goes snooping into the servants' quarters when they are out and finds a photo of the two servants taken 100 years ago. She is astounded as now she knows that they are truly ghosts, but what are they doing here? She questions them and they tell her that she is dead and her children also, she committed suicide when her husband left for the war because she was so depressed. The ghosts have come to ask her and her children to leave as the owners are scared to live in the property.

Grace initially doesn't believe the housekeeper, but adds two and two together and finally agrees to go and rest with her two children and to have peace and harmony.

Neha Agarwala (11)
Bancroft's Preparatory School, Woodford Green

The Premonition

It was the coldest night for many years and I was lying asleep in my bed. I was having a really peculiar dream when suddenly a single bolt of lightning woke me up. I don't know how it woke me as there was no thunder but I felt the shock.

The boy let out a shrill, piercing scream trying to attract someone's attention, but no one heard him and the boy continued to be chased by the gang. I watched in amazement as I remembered my dream. *No,* I thought, *dreams can't be real.* But then as he came to the edge of the cliff I realised that my dream was becoming reality. I got up and ran. I ran as fast as I could but he had gone. I stood alone at the end of the cliff looking over the edge at something that would haunt me forever.

Fifty years have passed since that day and the tragedy still haunts me.

Ever since then I have never returned to the cliff, but just yesterday I had the urge to revisit the scene of that haunting sight. When I looked over the cliff I saw exactly what I saw fifty years ago. A boy, but not any boy, it was a boy that I knew, whose arms were flailing, who was screaming and was now desperately trying not to get washed away by the tide.

Aaron Naisbitt (11)
Bancroft's Preparatory School, Woodford Green

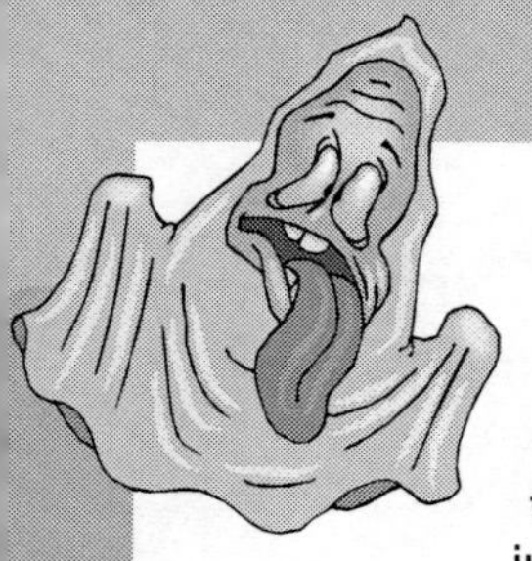

Murder Is Not The Answer

We had just moved here and the little village was quiet and cosy. Not many people had lived there since the terrible disaster in the prison. It was just off the village where a graveyard lay next to the prison. Nobody went there. It was too dangerous. But one dark night I crept out hoping that I wouldn't be seen. The prison towered above me. The gargoyles leaned right out at me. The windows were all cracked and broken. I stepped inside. It was dark. I was standing in the middle of the floor shaking. The beds were all tattered and torn.

A silhouette shot past me, as fast as lightning. I was scared. I tried following it. It had chains on its wrists. It was taking me somewhere. But where? After a while the sun was coming up and I had to get home before my mum and dad woke up.

On my way home I saw a poster saying, *Wanted, A Murderer Has Escaped.* Underneath was a picture of the same figure I had seen just then. I wiped off a piece of dirt from the bottom of the poster. This said the date. It went back quite a long way. It went back to March 7th 1972.

I ran home as fast as I could and now I was scared. Horrified!

Emily Goodier (11)
Bancroft's Preparatory School, Woodford Green

Ghost Story

It was Hallowe'en at Oakdeen School. Mr Harvey's class was really bored. Instead of learning about ghosts or creepy monsters, they were learning about ancient Rome.

'Please Mr Harvey, can we please learn about something fun for Hallowe'en?'

'No, all that stuff about monsters, isn't real anyway!' he shouted.

That night the children went home depressed. Mr Harvey went home, had his dinner and did his marking. Later he went to the graveyard because it was the 9th anniversary of his mother's death. The tombstone was a statue of an angel holding a cross. Mr Harvey was rather fond of it. He was sitting on a wet bench, when an old man passed by. You couldn't see his face because it was covered by his coat and it was dark. Suddenly Mr Harvey looked at his watch, jumped up and ran home as it was almost 9 o'clock.

On the way home he saw the man again. He was walking towards Mr Harvey. He nudged him into a dark alleyway. Mr Harvey fell to the floor. When he looked around he saw lots of ghosts standing in front of him.

'Kids, go away, I don't have time for silly games,' he said getting up. He realised that they were too tall to be children. All the monsters jumped onto him. 'Argh!' he cried.

Mr Harvey teaches the ghosts nowadays and he never forgets Hallowe'en.

Sanjna Dhaliwal (10)
Bancroft's Preparatory School, Woodford Green

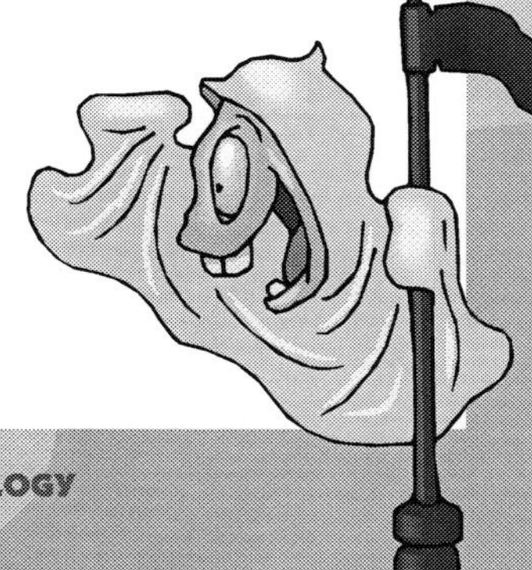

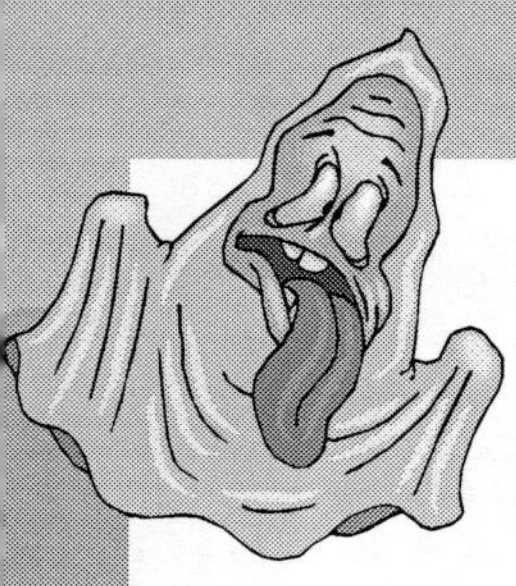

Ghost Phone

100 years ago Vera Haill was murdered. Three years ago she came back, in a modern way. Here's how it happened.

For generations and generations my family had lived in this old rickety house. Why, I don't know. It is full of evil corners. It feels like anything could jump out at you at any second. I have nightmares every night about the house. And monsters.

One particular night I woke hearing the phone ring. Why would someone be phoning at this time of night? I looked at my clock, 01.23. No one was answering the phone so I went downstairs to get it. I picked up the phone. 'Hello,' said an elderly woman in a friendly voice. *'Get out of my house and stay out!'* She hung up.

Then my mum came out and poked her head out of the bedroom. 'Get into bed. What are you doing on the phone?' she asked.

'Didn't you hear it?' I said. 'The phone call?'

Mum said, 'Stop telling lies and get to bed.'

The next night it happened again and carried on for a fortnight. I hadn't told anyone because they would think I was lying. No one else had heard the phone call. I was the only one. That night another phone call but this time I felt strange as if someone took something very important away from me, my soul. Then I fainted.

I woke up and saw an old woman peering over me. Goodbye life. I knew I was dead.

Anne Millar-Durrant (10)
Bancroft's Preparatory School, Woodford Green

The Legend

The local inhabitants of Blackwood have always known and feared the legend of Cefn Fforest.

The large red beast would roam the outskirts of Cefn forest and often lured itself into the shops and houses. It was hardly ever seen in the daytime, but at night the beast would awaken. He would prowl up and own the streets, his red fur would glow and his eyes gleam.

Warriors would travel far and wide to try and kill the beast, but would never return.

Long ago a warrior named Gethin Llewelyn travelled from Cardiff to try and defeat the beast, but had to find its dwelling first.

Gethin carried all of his apparatus into the forest. He lingered under a negligible bush, when he heard a minor sound. It got louder, until the beast appeared in front of his very own eyes.

The beast lashed out at him and scraped Gethin's face with his claws. Gethin's face began to bleed rapidly. He gouged the beast's eyes out with his sword and thrust the sword into its stomach. The beast fell to the ground.

Gethin returned alive and the inhabitants of Blackwood lived in peace for evermore.

Samantha Flynn Aklawi (13)
Blackwood Comprehensive School, Caerphilly

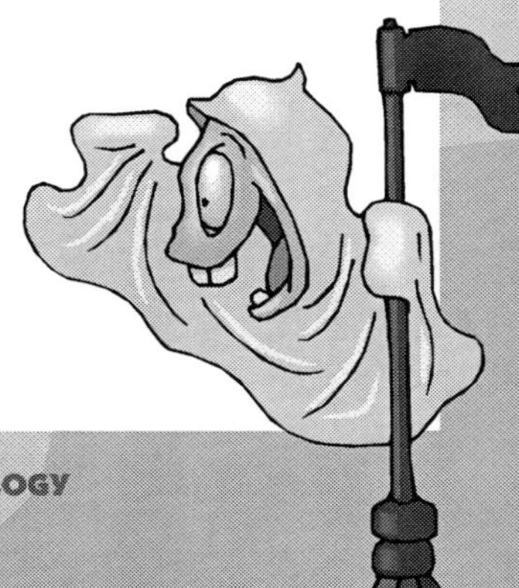

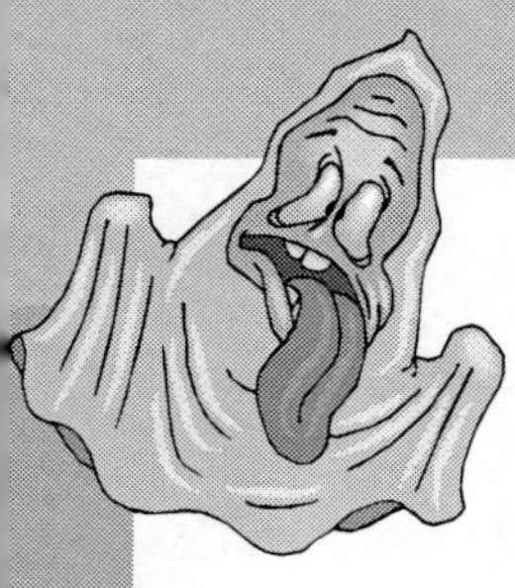

The Ghost Of Sir Joseph Clays

The inhabitants of Blackwood have always known and feared the ghost of Cefn Fforest.

It all began on 1st June 1874 when a battle took place in Sir Phoenix Logan's fortress which has now been turned into the show field. Sir Joseph Clays, an ex-convict who had been accused of murder and sentenced in 1850 to twenty-four years in prison, was released to find his wife, Corretta, dead and his son taken to another country. With no one left, Sir Joseph sought the wisdom of the magical enchantress, Cassandra.

Cassandra told Sir Joseph that, while he was imprisoned, Sir Phoenix Logan of New Tredegar, stabbed Corretta in the back and left her to die. On hearing this Sir Joseph mounted his horse, Pride, and galloped to Sir Phoenix's mansion. When he arrived at this destination, he jumped off Pride and entered through the grand doors of the mansion to discover Sir Phoenix stood in the hallway, beaming with delight. Their eyes locked onto each other and they stared for what seemed like an eternity, when suddenly they drew their swords in unison. Still glaring at each other they crept closer and closer together until their noses almost touched. Without warning, Sir Phoenix swiftly plummeted his sword into Sir Joseph's chest and sharply wrenched it out. Bleeding to death, Sir Joseph managed to mutter, 'Some day, my death will be avenged!'

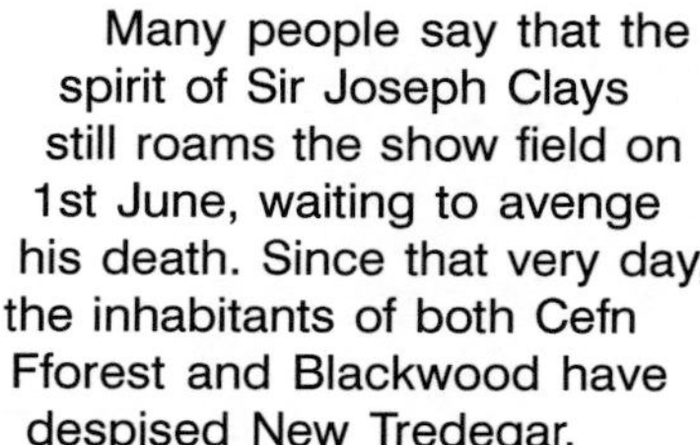

Many people say that the spirit of Sir Joseph Clays still roams the show field on 1st June, waiting to avenge his death. Since that very day, the inhabitants of both Cefn Fforest and Blackwood have despised New Tredegar.

Charlotte Vaughan (13)
Blackwood Comprehensive School, Caerphilly

Mini Legend

Rome had been the main power of the world for centuries. However, civil war meant that her awesome might was crumbling. The armies of Caesar were being withdrawn all over the Empire. Eventually, only one brigade remained outside of the capital.

Captain Luca Julii was in command of the garrison at Massilia in the south of Gaul. His force had been here for fifty years and were highly experienced. With Rome disarming, an army of 5,000 Gaulic warriors marched on Massilia, garrisoned by 600 men. Barett Mauli, commander of the Gauls, was determined to fight his way to Rome, but he also wanted his wife, Paelli, back at his side. For him, victory had a double meaning.

The alarm was sounded in the early hours of the morning, when Mauli's army was sighted on a nearby hill. The gates were rammed open and while the Gaulic army engaged in fierce combat with Roman legionnaires, Mauli went in search of Paelli. He found her in a tent. As he led her out, an arrow pierced his heart. His wife mourned him at a hero's funeral. Captain Julii allowed her to go free.

To this day, Maulli's death and defeat has set examples to many generals. (Although brave, his foolishness cost him his life and Gaul was lost.)

Rome never recovered though, and a few centuries later its empire disappeared forever.

Thomas Darling (13)
Blackwood Comprehensive School, Caerphilly

The Haunted Village of Cefn Forest

The local inhabitants of Blackwood have always known and feared the legend of Cefn forest.

Many years ago in the 1600s, a cruel social worker named Logan 'looked after' orphans, despite the fact he hated children. His only reason for his job was that he loved the wage he was paid. The children were treated terribly, they were starved and worked until their hands bled. The eldest child, Alonwey had been offered a job down at the local bakers. Logan was raging with anger because if Alonwey left, his salary would decrease. As Alonwey tried to walk out, Logan pulled out a knife and drove it deep into her chest. As he watched her die, he knew that he would pay dearly for this, with his job and maybe his life.

He buried Alonwey's corpse in his garden and didn't tell the government, so automatically he collected his weekly wage for looking after her. Late at night, he swore he could hear her laughing at him. With guilt he went to all of the children's beds late at night and killed them all.

A week later he opened a cupboard where he had stashed the bodies, expecting them to be alive and laughing at him, but they were all dead. He carried on his 'scheme' for collecting money for one month, until the laughing became unbearable. He took a drill to his temple, in an attempt to drown out the laughing.

It was a further two weeks until the government discovered him and the 12 dead children, but they never discovered the thirteenth ...

Hannah Luther (14)
Blackwood Comprehensive School, Caerphilly

Abandoned

The local inhabitants of Blackwood have always known and feared the legend of New Tredegar.

It all started long ago in the town of Blackwood when a baby was born into a rough background. His parents couldn't afford to keep it and for some reason didn't hesitate to abandon it.

Through some miracle the baby survived and grew up to make a living. From when he was dropped off to when he made his living, he had good luck, but his luck changed.

One night the man with no name was just about to nod off, but he was not alone, a strange old woman stood next to him.

She explained what had happened to his parents and that she had fed and clothed him. She told him his real name ... 'David'. It was a lot for him to take in. He didn't understand and then her news was about to get worse. She announced that she was magic and that they had a deal, she would give him success in life if only he ... She stopped and said that he must work this out for himself. But he could not remember, then she turned nasty and cursed him into half man, half ogre and the only way the spell could be broken was by doing his part of the deal.

To this day he still wanders the darkest corners of the darkest streets, trying, trying to remember.

Andrew Richardson (14)
Blackwood Comprehensive School, Caerphilly

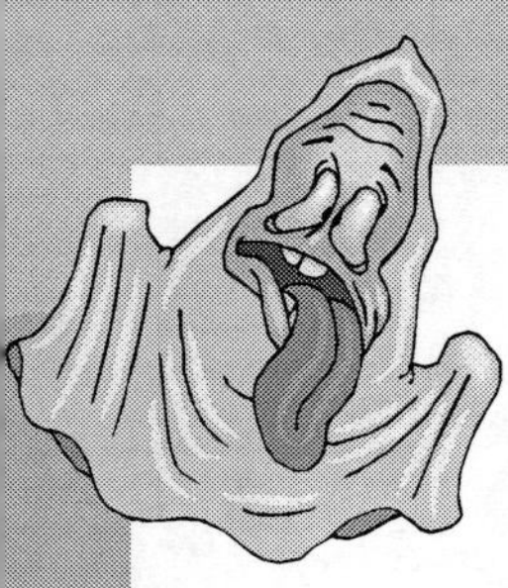

The Wolfen

In a time of strife and war the mighty Roman Empire was conquering the world, but in the valley of the Sirhowy the Cymraldol tribe were fighting them for every inch of ground.

The battle had been waging for many years with many men on each side being killed, for the control of the valley.

At a time when the two sides were once again gearing up for battle, five mighty warriors of the Cymraldol took part in a terrifying ceremony. The high priest of Lunar sacrificed those warriors in return for help against their enemy. The cry went up and the battle began.

As the hours went on the Cymraldol were forced back and back until they had reached the town of Cefn Fforest.

The world was pitched into darkness. The moon rose and down from the sky came five wolfen - half man, half wolf - these mighty warriors of Lunar defended the town for days, massacring every charge sent against them and when the Romans finally retreated these warriors became statues guarding the entrances to the town.

But, whenever the town is under threat, these warriors will fight again. And since that day no one has ever conquered Cefn Fforest.

Jacob Matthews (13)
Blackwood Comprehensive School, Caerphilly

Valley's Legend

The local inhabitants of Blackwood have always known and feared the legend of Cefn Fforest ...

The rich and prosperous Blackwood people lived in wealth and were always depriving Cefn Fforest folk, who lived a life of poverty and despair. The ancient valley's woodland was covered in mythical creatures and demons.

Dai Thomas was fed up of the inequality and set out to defeat the people of Blackwood and take back Cefn Fforest's council funding. However, first he had to cross the black wood that separated the towns.

He set off on his quest and entered the wood. It was dark and gloomy, and he was being watched. With a shriek, arrived the fearsome hound of Bloomfield. With an almighty roar it pounced on Dai.

Bravely he drew out his sword and with a massive swoop he killed the famous beast. Little did he know that the wolf had the money that Cefn Fforest needed in his den. He searched long and hard for an exit to the wood, but he was lost.

Suddenly a giant dragon descended on him and he was killed instantly by the dragon's fire. If he had listened to the hound Cefn Fforest would be rich once more.

The legend has been passed on through generations but still Cefn Fforest is poor thanks to Dai.

Luke Jones (13)
Blackwood Comprehensive School, Caerphilly

The Legend Of Cefn Fforest

A long time ago when magic and gods still existed, there was a beautiful forest, but this was no ordinary forest, it held the temple which led to the underworld. The temple was guarded by three shadows who were dead soldiers which worshipped Hades brought back from the dead as ghosts, but were more powerful and stronger than any ghost known. Anyone who wandered into the temple of Cefn Fforest looking for treasure or quicker routes to different places all perished under the power of the creatures living there. But what no one knew was that the great god Hades controlled the Underworld. Hades was planning to take over the upper world with his minions.

Exactly one month later a bell rang from the lookout towers near the edge of the forest leading to Blackwood. This meant someone or something was attacking.

Black smoke was rising from the lookout towers, trees were ablaze and arrows were spraying from the forest like bullets. The grass was turning red with people's blood.

All the villagers were planning an attack to put the army from Hell back to rest. They ran with spears, swords and metal bars, as a group of villagers went to the temple and closed the gateway to the underworld. The demons turned into dust as the gateway closed and the temple was hidden from sight.

But what nobody knew was that Hades was angry and once again building an army to take over the upper world and create destruction and horror across the land ...

Alex Wood (14)
Blackwood Comprehensive School, Caerphilly

The Legend Of Blackwood

The local inhabitants of Blackwood have always known and feared the legend of Cefn Fforest.

The dragon of the show field has killed many, but the first death was a mystery.

A king had just been crowned, after 20 years of waiting to get the crown off his father. The new king, King Gerald, was celebrating and rejoicing until daybreak, and after the celebrations ended, King Gerald of Cefn Fforest decided to walk around part of his kingdom, the show field.

Not knowing of the terrible fate that would await him, King Gerald walked freely around whilst being watched by the horrid dragon behind a large tree. King Gerald was startled as he heard a noise from just behind him, he squinted his eyes and he could vaguely see this monster walking towards him.

Quickly, knowing he should do something, King Gerald slowly walked back, hoping this dragon wouldn't see him, but it was too late as already this monster jumped in front of the only gate leading out of this dreaded place, and so King Gerald did the only thing left, drew his sword.

The king tried to battle the dragon, but he knew he had no chance, the dragon dodged every sword swing thrown at him and in return, his eyes grew bright, and he let out a massive roar followed by a mass of fire.

The look of fright grew large in the king's eyes, and in one moment he had gone.

Kirsty Trainer (13)
Blackwood Comprehensive School, Caerphilly

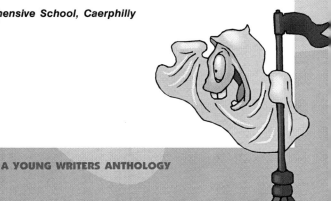

The Legend Of Blackwood

The local inhabitants of Blackwood have always known and feared the legend of Cefn Fforest.

It all began in Blackwood a long time ago where there lived two different types of people who didn't agree on anything. The people of Blackwood were rich and wealthy, whereas the people of Cefn Fforest were made much less wealthy. They had been at war for many years as the leader of Cefn Fforest, Sir Geraint, believed that Lord Dylan of Blackwood had taken over areas of his land.

The people of Blackwood were fed up of fighting and Lord Dylan ordered a meeting with Sir Geraint at his castle.

The two sat down to dinner and were joined by Lord Dylan's daughter Cerian. Instantly the two fell in love. Lord Dylan sensed tension between the two, and sent Cerian to the dungeons.

Lord Dylan was a ruthless, heartless man who didn't believe in his daughter's happiness. Sir Geraint protested and went to look for Cerian, but the Lord took his sword and challenged Geraint to the death. He told him that whoever won the battle, would rule Blackwood and Cefn Fforest. It was a harsh battle.

Eventually Lord Dylan fell to the floor and Sir Geraint stabbed Dylan in the heart. Sir Geraint had been victorious. He freed Cerian and ruled Blackwood. The people of Cefn Fforest were finally treated equally.

Carys Williams (13)
Blackwood Comprehensive School, Caerphilly

Innocent Blood

Me and my twin sister Trudy have just had one of our secret meetings under the stairs. There's a cupboard where we like to sit. We went through reasons why Mum and Dad shouldn't have bought this new house. I'll tell you a few.

The cellar's really creepy and I swear I saw a rat. I bet this place is haunted. The bathroom is rank, it looks like it hasn't been washed for a millennium. It's got cockroaches too. And in mine and Trudy's bedroom there are even spiders on the ceiling. I wish we could live somewhere else.

It's bedtime but I can't sleep. I'm tossing and turning this way and that but my pillow still feels like a large, flat rock. I see a shadow pass over the wall. It may be my imagination.

I hear a whisper, I must be hearing things. I hear a laugh.

'What's so funny Trudy?' I ask.

There is no answer. All is still.

As the sun slowly starts to rise I see bloodstains on Trudy's sheets, but no Trudy. In her place is a long, jagged knife. What could have happened? I swing my head round. On the wall is a message in blood that strikes fear. It says *'You're Next'.* I see a shadow pass over the wall. It must be my imagination. I hear a whisper. I must be hearing things. I feel a knife digging into my throat and blood gushing out like a scarlet fountain. I do not hear the laugh. I shall never hear laughter again.

Laurel Stone (8)
Bradley CE Primary School, Ashbourne

The Empty House

I was sitting on my sofa in the living room with my dog Misty at my feet, while my mum and dad were in the kitchen cooking our tea.

Suddenly the power went off. I couldn't see. I thought it was just a power cut, therefore I shouted, 'Mum! Dad!' There was no reply.

I couldn't feel Misty at my feet anymore. I saw a black shadow that looked like Misty outside in my garden. But it wasn't quite right. I knew it wasn't. She always barked when she was outside and there was no barking. I was all alone.

Suddenly I heard a voice saying, 'They have … ' Then it stopped, the voice had stopped.

Suddenly the lights sprang back on. Misty was definitely not at my feet.

Again I shouted, 'Mum? Dad? Misty?'

There was still no reply. I saw some of Misty's hair at my feet and then I heard the same voice saying, 'They have died … ' After hearing those words I felt myself falling down and down. The last thing I saw was a dark hole with the walls cramped up beside me. I could just see a narrow slit of light. It was closing in. I heard a voice, 'You are dying, like your mum and dad did.'

I heard a scraping sound and the light disappeared. I was left alone in total darkness.

Rebecca Hart (9)
Bradley CE Primary School, Ashbourne

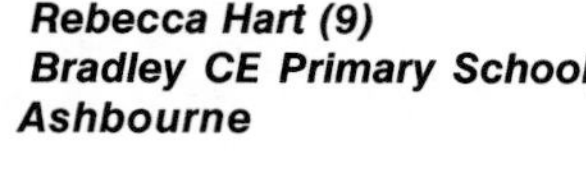

The Haunted Funeral Director's House

The funeral director pulled open the door of the carriage and pulled out a massive black coffin.

'John, come and help me carry this coffin into the house,' shouted Edward, the funeral director.

It was tipping it down with rain and getting dark. They carried the coffin out of the rain, down into the dark, misty cellar. *Clonk!*

'Phew, that was heavy,' moaned John.

'I'm off to bed,' said Edward, pulling off his wet top hat.

'Right then, I'll go to bed too,' replied John.

Ting, chimed the clock. It was one o'clock. Everyone was sleeping until John woke up - *creak, thud! What was that?* he thought. It sounded like a door opening in the cellar but it couldn't be. He could hear Edward snoring. *Tap, tap!* He could hear the sound of footsteps getting closer. John was terrified.

A shadow slid under the door. John hid under his cover and shivered. The door handle turned and with a creak the door was opened. John peeped out of his cover and was scared to death. There, in front of him, was the figure of the man from the coffin. He walked up to John and leaned over him. John tried to scrabble away but the dead man grabbed him. He wrapped his cold, withered hands around John's neck and squeezed hard 'til John stopped breathing. The dead man bit open John's neck and sucked the blood 'til none remained in John's body, then walked slowly back to his black coffin and closed the lid, but left a trail of red sparkling blood behind him.

Rebecca Woodward (10)
Bradley CE Primary School, Ashbourne

The Spooky House

I was at my friend Amy's house. We were sitting on the bed playing board games and watching TV. Amy's mum came up the stairs to turn the light out. After she had gone to bed we heard something creaking on the wooden floorboards and the door slowly crept open - *creak, creak, creak!*

There in the dark was a pair of yellow gleaming eyes. We saw a shadow creeping by the window and we screamed, 'Help! Help!'

Amy's mum was fast asleep so she couldn't hear us.

A while after Amy's mum came in and turned the light on but the eyes had gone. Amy's mum told us to go to sleep and switched the light off.

Soon after the eyes appeared again. We didn't just see one pair of eyes, we saw a whole load. Then we heard Amy's mum scream, so we went out of the bedroom and we searched everywhere but she had disappeared. We noticed some of the ghosts had gone too. As we looked up the stairs we saw a ghost with a knife and that was the last thing we ever saw.

Abi Mason (9)
Bradley CE Primary School, Ashbourne

The Ghostly House

I was coming back from a party with my friends. It was pitch-black. Our car started to stutter, then it stopped dead.

'We'll have to find a place to stay,' I shouted.

'OK,' shouted Oli.

We stumbled on.

'I can see a place ahead,' I said.

We tried the door. It flew open, so we walked inside.

'Hello,' I wailed. 'I don't think anyone's here.'

We tried the phone, but the line was dead. I started to panic, the atmosphere in the room made the hairs on the back of my neck stand up.

'This place gives me the creeps,' I muttered.

Jack went to the toilet. 'Argh!' he screamed. 'You guys come and look at this.'

We ran upstairs. There, lying next to the toilet, was a dead body. I took a look into one of the bedrooms. Lying there were thousands of knives. It sent a shiver down my spine.

'Get out of my house,' shouted a voice.

We ran downstairs and tried the door. It was jammed. We felt something was looking at us. Me and Jack turned round. Oli was gone.

'Get out of my house,' the voice croaked.

I looked for somewhere to escape but when I turned around Jack was gone. 'Jack, Oli, where are you?'

I raced upstairs and hid under a duvet. 'I know you're in there,' said the voice.

I could hear it whispering. It was getting closer and clos ...

Alex Monro-Jones (9)
Bradley CE Primary School, Ashbourne

The Mystery Room

It was an ordinary day at Crescent Bay Primary School. Timothy and Alex, identical twins, hung their coats and hats up on their pegs as usual. They started to walk away to their classroom, but something made them turn around immediately. They could hear a scratching sound. It seemed to be coming from the boiler room. They assumed it must be mice, so they turned back around and headed to their classroom. Mrs Honey, their teacher, greeted them in and took the register. Paul, their best friend, wasn't there. Where could he be? They assumed he was ill and forgot about him.

Later that day, they went to get their coats and hats from their pegs. They picked up their coats, but their hats were gone. Suddenly Alex turned around. Se saw a deep, dark red puddle coming from under the boiler room door. Could it be blood? Timothy ran to the door, the red liquid splattered up his legs. He slowly turned the dusty handle. As it opened, the liquid spread further across the floor. Timothy and Alex crept inside. A dark shadow crept past them. *Bang!* Someone had closed the door they were locked in.

In the distance Alex could hear faint laughter. Who was it? Timothy felt around, trying to find a light switch. Something grabbed his head.

'Alex, is that you?' whispered a voice.

'Yes, Paul is that you? Are you OK?' he replied.

No one answered. The lights began to flicker. Something crawled up Timothy's leg. He looked down. On the floor he could see his and Alex's hats. They seemed to be covered in blood. He could also see skulls and knives with sharp, shiny blades, also covered in deep red dripping blood. He shrieked in horror. Alex shrieked too. Then suddenly the door opened. It was Mrs Honey. 'What's all of the racket about?' she asked.

Timothy looked around him. Everything had disappeared. They explained to Mrs Honey what had happened, but she didn't believe them. Then Paul walked around the corner. He had been to the dentist.

What was the mystery of the boiler room? Who was crying for Alex?

Maisie Forton (11)
Bradley CE Primary School, Ashbourne

Singing Steps

Jess was so excited. It was her birthday tomorrow and she was getting a special surprise present.

That night Jess woke to the howling of restless trees, the rustling of the unknown. But … downstairs, something much worse lurked in the shadows. What was it? The odour of death hung heavily in the air as she heard the chanting whispers of a voice. 'I'm on the first step. I'm on the second step. I'm on the third step.' Each time the voice got closer and closer. 'I'm on the fourth step. I'm on the fifth step. I'm on the sixth step. I'm on the seventh step. I'm on the eighth step. I'm on the ninth step. I'm on the tenth step. I'm at the door … at the door. I'm gonna get you!'

Silence echoed around the abandoned room. Nothing happened … *bang!* The door slammed shut.

The next morning, when Jess' mum and dad woke there was a knock at the door. When Jess' mum opened the door, a huge box wrapped in pink paper with a bow on the top lay at the door.

'Jess,' called her mum, 'your present's here.'

Mum opened Jess' bedroom door and there was her neatly made bed with not a single crease. But, when Jess' mum pulled back the cover, instead of Jess lay a dagger smeared from top to toe with … *blood!*

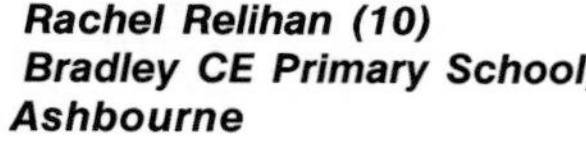

Rachel Relihan (10)
Bradley CE Primary School, Ashbourne

Lewis

One day Lewis was walking home from school with his ball and it was getting dark. He kicked it over a fence. He went to get it and he saw a big mansion. He went in, no one was there so he decided to sleep there because he was tired.

He saw the door open but no one was there, there was an echoing noise in the air.

'It's my mansion Lewis.'

Lewis got his bed covers and scrambled up.

Then it said it again, 'It's my mansion!' even louder this time.

Lewis hid under the covers and then he said, 'Get out!'

Lewis tried to run home but the spirit had locked all the windows and doors, and then chased Lewis around the house.

Lewis hid in the corner of the darkest room. He could hear someone playing music. Suddenly someone crept up behind him ...

Lewis Pickering (8)
Bradley CE Primary School, Ashbourne

The Haunted House

One night in 1945 the gruesome murder of Sir William Crocker took place in a big, old haunted house.

One sunny day in 1975 four children were playing football on the small pitch with the spooky house next to the pitch. The haunted house had tall spiked towers and huge turrets with dead horses on the top.

The next day the football went over the haunted house's fence. One of the boys called Liam Crocker caught his T-shirt on one of the spikes and ripped it. They eventually got over after a long struggle. They could see the ball. Sam England gave Liam his jumper. Daniel Isaac ran and got the ball, kicked it and it hit the wall and then bounced back through the windows of the house.

John yelled, 'You've done it now!'

'Who's going to fetch the ball now then?' said Liam.

Sam said, 'We could all go,' thinking very carefully.

The door creaked open and the four boys walked nervously in. Just as Daniel stepped into the house, the door slammed behind him. *Bang!* They all jumped. There was a long corridor that split left to right. Sam and Liam took right and Daniel and John took left. The hall was covered in pictures of Sir William Crocker. The man in all the pictures had the same surname as Liam.

Sam said, 'Maybe he's related to you?'

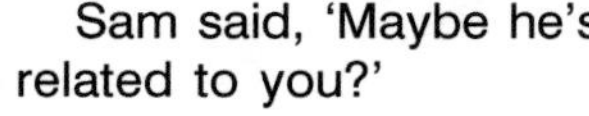

Sam and Liam walked down the corridor. A person came out of a single passage and started following Sam and Liam down the steps into a dark dungeon at the bottom of the house. There were hundreds of dead people hanging from the ceilings and walls, thousands of rats climbing up the walls. Urgh!

The boys realised that they were being followed so they ran away to find Daniel and John. As they were running, Sam cut his leg and Liam didn't notice. Daniel and John had found the football and called Sam and Liam, so they all ran out and over the fence back to Sam's house to tell his mum that they were back.

The next day the boys found out that Sir William Crocker was Liam's grandad. Sir William Crocker had been murdered by his wife.

Kelly Jenkins & Silas Lovejoy (10)
Bridestowe Primary School, Okehampton

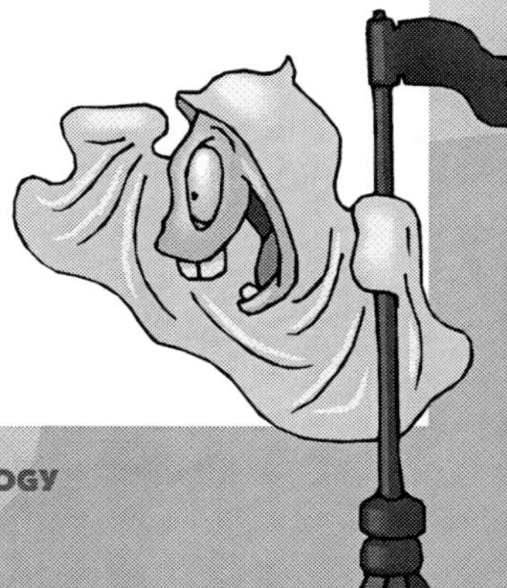

A Ghost Hunt In The Village

Sabrina was tired so took a nap. She saw them, they were all surrounding her. Opening her mouth to shout, the words didn't come out, then they disappeared. Just then she realised she wasn't alone. They were in that strange village; Ben, Ann, Jude, Safina, Marina and herself, all six of them.

Suddenly they heard voices that sounded like rumblings of thunder. They quickly turned, what they saw dumbstruck them; a figure that looked like a man with one big eye on his forehead, three arms, two legs, three feet, flaming blue and red. They began to run, but saw ten more of them, they took another path that unfortunately led to the forest but when they realised it was too late.

They had landed in the middle of the 'Land of Ghosts' - invisible ghosts.

Jude felt someone tapping him. He turned but saw nobody, he kept turning round and round. Safina felt pulls at her hair and all of a sudden, she went up, going higher with each look she took at the ground. Ben started spinning on the spot until his legs hurt and head ached. Ann's eyes were popping from their sockets. Marina felt her intestines fighting within her. Ben and Safina started laughing, then something happened - all the ghosts appeared at the same time, the kids stopped all their acts. The chase began again, then they were surrounded by ghosts, they kept coming closer to them until there was just an inch space between them. All the kids screamed in fright.

Sabrina woke with a start. Suddenly the ghosts appeared again and then disappeared.

Mercy Bello (16)
Demonstration Secondary School, Nigeria

Ghosts Of The Hall

It was 1944 and the hall was pitch-black. The smell of rubble and dust that could choke anything seemed to swarm the air. The walls were as cold as the Arctic and felt rough. The silence was deafening, filling the boys with fear. They could taste fear everywhere. They entered the darkened hall.

The boys could remember when the hall was full of joy and laughter, eating their lunch with their friends, but then the bad memories, when it happened.

60 years later ...

Two men were walking by the monument that stood in the schoolyard. When they saw the school hall, they bowed their heads in remembrance. Then they saw something in the hall. Thoughts were going through their heads. What could it be? The men went to investigate the situation. The hall was different, a cold chill filled the air and a strong feeling ran in the men's heads. They were thinking, *run,* but something inside said no. Then they saw the glow again. Was it a trick or was it real? They went closer and closer not knowing what was round the next corner, then something grabbed the men. The men turned round but it was only a brush which had fallen on the men. They walked on. Suddenly they heard a voice. 'Was that Tom playing tricks on us?' Then they saw a brooch that read, 'This belongs to Tom McKenzie, 9 years old'.

'It is Tom.'

'It can't be he died 60 years ago ... '

Andrew Smith (10)
Frenchay CE Primary School, Bristol

No Bell

One morning three girls were skipping in the playground when they heard that something had gone wrong. Their names were Kelly, Chloe and Jessica. Chloe looked at the time. 'Hey, shouldn't we have been called in?' she asked.

'Gosh, we are late aren't we?' replied Kelly.

'Yeah, but it will be more fun,' laughed Jessica. Both girls growled at her. 'Don't look at me,' she said slowly going down away from them. 'In fact, let's go and explore,' she said reluctantly. Jessica didn't like being growled at.

They all rushed off to see what was happening. It was quiet, too quiet. They all crept down the hall. All they could hear was *drip, drop, drip, drop.* The noise was coming from behind them.

'Isn't that noise coming from behind us?' asked Jessica timidly.

'Yeah it is,' replied Kelly in a terrified voice.

Kelly, Chloe and Jessica all stopped and stayed as still as possible.

'Urgh, what's that slobber on my shoulder?' asked Chloe fearfully. Chloe turned around and looked up. 'Argh!' *Bang, crash!* and she fainted.

'Chloe!' shouted Jess. Jess turned round to see why Chloe fainted. 'I think, I-I-I know now … run!' she shouted.

'What about Chloe?' asked Kelly.

'Just run,' replied Jess in a bumpy voice.

The monster went round the corner dragging Chloe behind. Kelly looked behind over her shoulder still running with Jess and stopped, nearly falling over.

'Jess!' shouted Kelly. 'Chloe has been dragged by a monster.'

They turned round and ran after the monster. When they got round the corner they saw the head teacher's door closing. They crept to the door to see what was in there. What they saw was the head teacher.

Where was Chloe?

Beth Downes (9)
Frenchay CE Primary School, Bristol

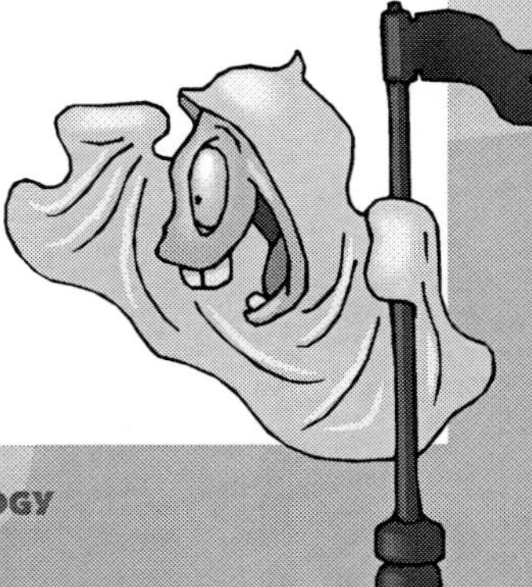

What Was She?

It was a cold, dark night; the howling of the wolves awoke me from my sleep. I crept into the bedroom across the hall. I was petrified. I could see shadows lurking around, up and down the corridors. Now I was really scared. I could feel things touching my shoulders. I had to touch the walls to find my way around. They were as cold as the grave. I went into another girl's bedroom. I woke her.

She was freezing. Now it was just me and her in this creepy castle. We were both scared, The smell of rotten bones drifted along the corridors and the smell of decay wafted around us. The taste of fear and terror leapt into our mouths, we were really scared.

Her name was Jessica and my name was Amy. We were 10 and the reason we were in Whipstaff Castle was because of a dare. I had been dared to stay here for two days. We wondered what would happen in this suspicious castle.

We went walking around the castle. Jess whispered, 'Do you think we'll be OK?'

'Of course,' replied Amy in a hushed tone.

'Boo!'

'Argh!' we screamed, running down the corridors.

'What was that?' I said, still running for my life.

'I don't know,' shouted Jessica.

'I can see an open door,' I said.

'Well let's go inside then.'

As we entered into the darkened room, we saw a gaunt, pale figure of a spirit drifting into the room. Jess screamed, 'Argh!'

The deafening sound brought me to the floor.

My mum awoke me and I asked her, 'What happened?'

'I found you in that awful castle again. What have I told you?'

'Where's Jess?' I asked.

'Who's Jess?' my mum said.

'But she couldn't have been the ghost could she ... ?'

Amy Hillier (9)
Frenchay CE Primary School, Bristol

Untitled

The inky-black night surrounded me as I stared at the old park. I could hear something under the slide. I crept over to the slide, my heart started pounding in my chest. The air tasted bitter as I licked my lips. The air smelt old and rotten as if something old was there under the slide. As I crept closer it got stronger. I turned to run but a voice said, 'Oi, get over 'ere, you ruined my sleep.'

I found the courage and ran!

Mitch Clark (9)
Frenchay CE Primary School, Bristol

The Graveyard

The moon was casting a gloomy glow on the gravestones. I touched the cold metal gate. I could see the gravestones in the gloom of the moonlight. I could smell the fire coming from the graveyard. I pushed the cold metal gate. I could see a fire. I did not know what to do. I could hear people talking. I did not know what they were saying.

One of the men saw me and said, 'Oi you little boy, you should not be here.'

I could smell burning flames but it was then that something strange happened. Everything went quiet. All I could hear was the wind blowing. The fire had gone and with it all of the people.

Aimee Ceccarelli (9)
Frenchay CE Primary School, Bristol

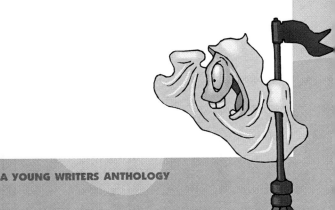

The Ghost Of Grove High School

I was 14 at the time and was only in Grade 9, but that was the day that changed my life ...

It was dark. The corridor was bare and the most irritating sound of creaking hinges echoed continuously through the sets of corridors.

A musky, pungent smell seemed to hang around me making me feel quite faint. I could taste dust on my tongue.

Suddenly, a sour strike of fear struck across my tongue like a bolt of lightning. I spat it out forgetting that the janitor Jeff was behind me.

I quickened my pace. I stopped at the sixth form corridor. It was silent. As I brushed my hand on the radiator I remembered it was on.

As I shook my scalded hand I felt a tap on my shoulder. I turned around quickly but there was no one there. I turned to the door of the corridor and as I looked through the shattered glass I saw the pale, gaunt figure of Mr Whitby, the founder and first headmaster of Grove High. I was rooted to the floor. A shiver went down my spine. I wanted to run away screaming, but I daren't move a muscle. He saw me, he came towards me reaching out and I fell to the floor, literally paralysed with terror.

Amie Cook (9)
Frenchay CE Primary School, Bristol

The Castle

I heard the howling wind which sounded like a wolf. The full moon shone down as if it were looking for hidden treasure. I was standing in the courtyard. I smelt mould that was hundreds of years old. I reached out and touched the hard, wooden door handle. I could taste the fear going down my spine freezing my senses.

I walked in and I took a few tentative steps around. A shape came up from a trapdoor. I thought I was daydreaming but I wasn't and I thought I saw somebody move. I didn't have time to look. I heard an owl howling like mad.

I went up the stairs and I saw animals on the ground. There were eyes in the paintings and they were staring at me. I stood still. I was frozen. The shape followed me but I didn't know what it was. I ran straight down the stairs. Someone was following me. Who was it? Was the castle haunted? I didn't stop to find out ...

Jim Green (8)
Frenchay CE Primary School, Bristol

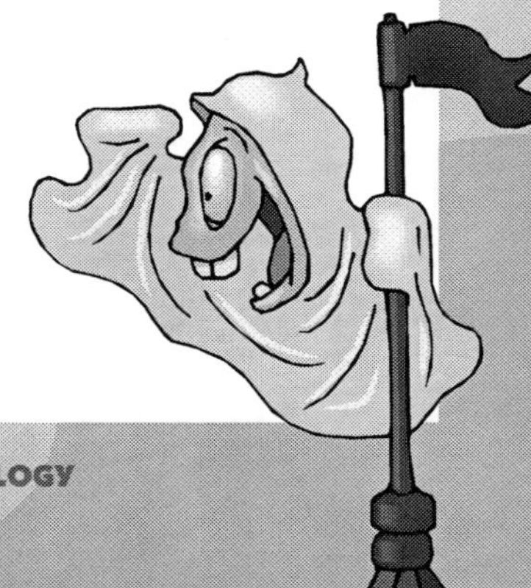

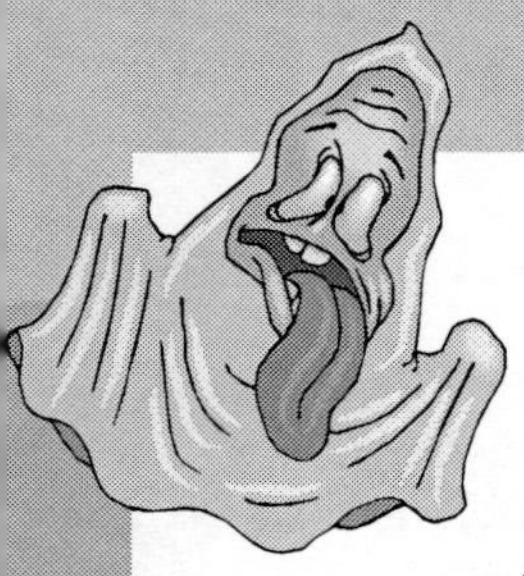

One Creepy, Dark Night

One creepy, dark night I walked through the graveyard on the way back from my friend's house. I saw the mist creeping over the dark, lonely graves and the clouds slowly covering the moon.

I felt the wind brush against my shoulders as it swept past making the trees sway violently. I could feel the rough fingertips of the trees' branches.

The smell of rotting bones made me shiver. As I walked down the path I felt someone tap me on the shoulder. I whipped round, there was nobody there, or was there? Fear enveloped my body. Was it a ghost from one of the graves?

I heard a noise behind me. I turned round and stared in horror. There in front of me was my great great grandfather who had died 88 years ago. I watched as he sank into his grave sending the mist swirling around above him.

I heard a creaking coming from the church door. I looked at the door and saw a ghost float out and then another and another. After a while lots of ghosts were floating out of the church, then behind them all came a vampire.

I screamed, which was a bad thing to do. Some neighbours walking by ran into the church. I ran and hid behind a gravestone. All I heard next was a scream. I looked up, there was nobody there. I never went back to that church alone and I never saw my neighbours again, but I think I've seen their ghosts …

Ella Hayden (9)
Frenchay CE Primary School, Bristol

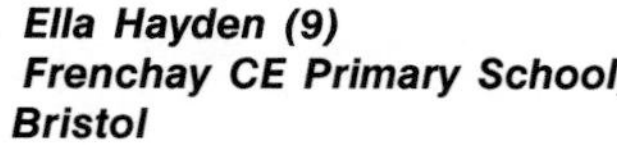

I Wish I'd Known - A Graveyard Tale

The creaking gates closed behind me with a loud bang. I was trapped with the dead and it was as if they were calling me.

I walked forward and it was as if a force was manipulating me to go forth and touch the cold grave. I jumped with fright when I saw that carved on that very grave was my name. It said that I'd died today. I hoped someone else had the same name as me but I couldn't be sure.

Then suddenly I could see a faint white light in the distance. What could it be? Where was it coming from? I ran forwards to go and find out, rushing past all the graves. Every time I got closer, the white thing moved further away. I started to feel dizzy and it was as if the whole graveyard was caving in on me. I was trapped. Then suddenly I could run no more. I fell to the ground, dead.

I woke up in the same graveyard but another world. Everything had changed. The white thing had been the light at the end of my road.

So that's my story. Having read this, I hope you will listen when your mum tells you that it's dangerous to go on your own into graveyards. You now know why.

Lily Grant (8)
Frenchay CE Primary School, Bristol

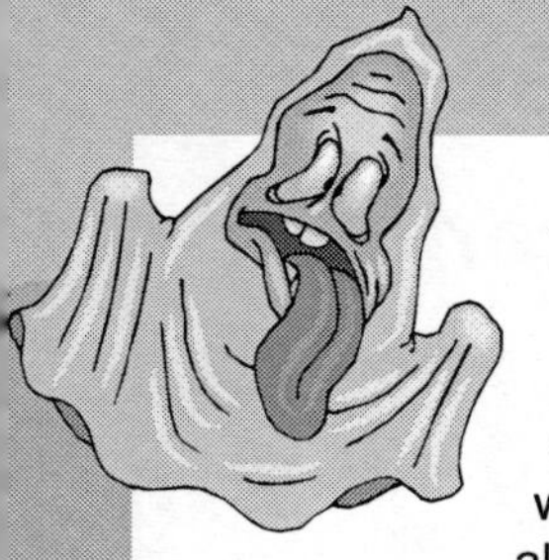

The Abandoned Theatre

The creaking of the door as the wind blew it open and closed, the sound of the steps as I walked further to the stage. The rank smell of food all rotten and the seats smelt like old people. The rusty curtain rails were all crusty and brown. I imagined the scene - people watching 'Romeo and Juliet' in all sorts of costumes,

Sucking in all the dusty cold air, chewing the top of my jumper as I rubbed my hand across the old dusty stage, it had splinters almost everywhere. I climbed the stairs on the cold, dusty stage and felt the curtains all dusty and rough. I sat on a chair and that's when I heard something - I heard crying like the crying of Romeo for Juliet, the sound of clapping and cheering and the flickering of William Shakespeare's feather pen. I heard a loud shriek, 'Argh!'

I said, 'Hello! Who's there?' I looked behind me, there was a cloudy white puff of smoke. 'Are you a ghost?'

'Well yes, I am.'

'Who are you? Who's there? Jess, I'm not playing games.'

'I'm William Shakespeare!'

We played a game of ghost chess although I kept on knocking over all the pieces because I couldn't see them.

I told him that he should go before he scared somebody else. I told him I would be back. I went back on my bike in the dark and stormy night, my bike all rusty and screechy.

Chloé Evans (9)
Frenchay CE Primary School, Bristol

Sleepy Hollow

One stormy night the wind was howling and the rain was crashing on roofs and on the ground. The lightning and thunder were striking at the treetops and the howling of wolves sounded in the distance.

I could see the grass swaying from side to side and I could see scurrying rodents rushing away from something or someone, then I saw its greeny-yellowy eyes. It was someone wearing a pumpkin head like the one from Hallowe'en with sharp, jagged teeth and evil, slit eyes. It was riding a black horse. It took off its mask. Well that's what I thought it was, he had no head.

I could feel the ground shaking under me. I couldn't move. I wanted to run away but I had to investigate the headless horseman.

I could smell the blood from his sword. I could smell the horseman's clothes and armour. I could smell the garlic from the villagers and the fire from the torches.

I could taste the bitter taste of fear and blood.

I couldn't sleep. I wanted to find out if it was real or fake. I went out that rainy night prepared with a torch, mask and garlic. I went into the forest to look for the horseman. Suddenly I heard footsteps. I hid in the bushes. I heard laughing and I saw the horseman taking off his pumpkin head, but Jamie was under the mask so I jumped out and said, 'Got you Jim and Jamie.'

Jim said, 'April fools,' and then we had a sleepover.

Andre Miller (9)
Frenchay CE Primary School, Bristol

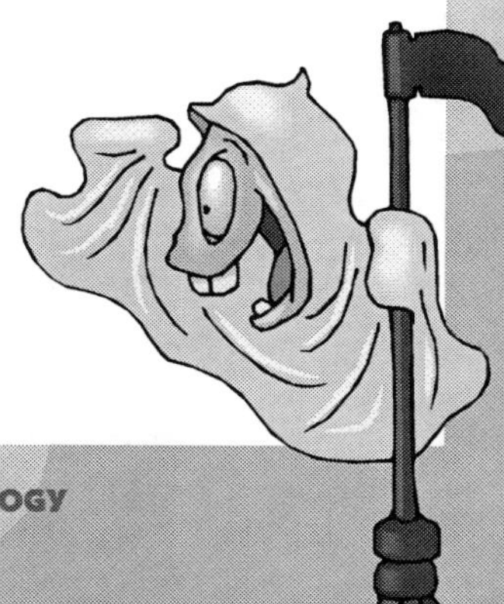

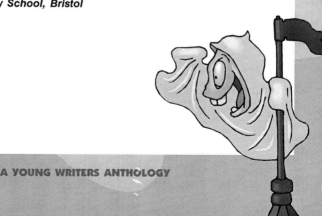

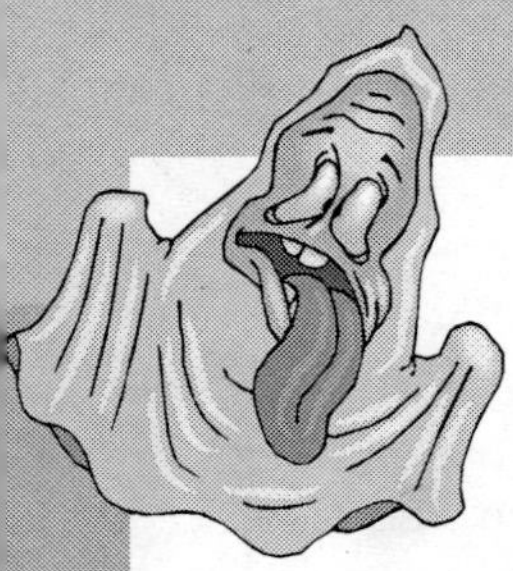

Scary Bedroom

The scary, dark night was defeating the lights as it drifted over my bed, then I heard a creaking sound coming from the cupboard. I quickly pulled the bed covers over my head. I curled up waiting for morning but the sound came back again. I jumped out of my bed. I saw nothing but darkness. Where was my flashlight? I reached out. I felt something, it was just my nightdress. Then I reached further, I felt, I felt my flashlight. I picked up my flashlight. I saw a dark shadow in the corner.

It seemed much darker than the rest of the room. I slowly put on my flashlight. I ignored the shadow and touched the cupboard. The door was cold. I heard the sound again. Then I smelt a recognisable smell. I opened the cupboard. It was my *hamster!*

Rosie Cronin (8)
Frenchay CE Primary School, Bristol

Graveyard Horror

I saw an iron gate swinging back and forth as I entered the dark, wet graveyard. There was no sound apart from the heavy wind rushing past my face. I felt the cold gravestone. The letters carved into my hand. I could taste salty tears running down my face. I could smell my mum's hair swaying either side of my head.

I remembered my mum. Suddenly the gates closed and the wind went away. I felt alone, very alone. I lay where my mum lay.

I could hear my mum's soft, loving voice, then it stopped. I ran to the gate, it was still closed and was too high to climb.

I remembered what my dad had given me. It was a tiny compass. I checked my pocket, it wasn't there. I ran to the church. The door was open. I stayed in there until morning. I realised it was just the caretaker locking the gate, so I ran to tell all my mates about it. But still, I never went back there.

Georgia Maxwell (9)
Frenchay CE Primary School, Bristol

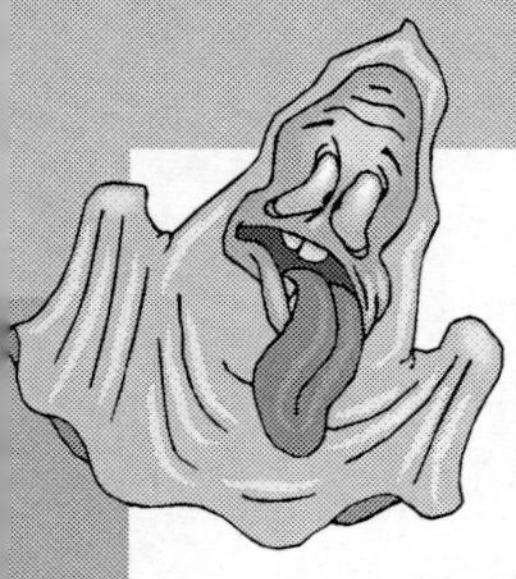

The Mystery Canyon

The howling wind cut through the eerie darkness that covered the Grand Canyon at night. In nearby Arizona everything was peaceful and everyone who lived there was unaware of the next day's happenings.

Chuck Stromberg woke up the next morning and said, 'Ahh, the weekend, my favourite two days of the week.' Chuck was twelve years old and lived in Fifth Avenue, Phoenix, Arizona. Chuck liked going to the canyon with his best friends Alan Abernackle and Tom Baker.

When they visited the canyon one day they saw something monstrously huge slithering through a gap in the canyon wall.

'What was that thing?' awed Chuck.

'I dunno, it might have been a mutant snake,' said Alan, with excitement in his voice.

'No, probably not,' said Tom, 'but whatever it was I don't like the look of it,' he said, in a worried tone.

'Us neither,' said Chuck and Alan in unison. So they trudged off home.

When Chuck got home his mum said, 'Why are you home so early?' in a surprised tone.

'No reason, I just wanted to,' he said.

That night all three boys lay awake in their beds thinking about what they had seen that day.

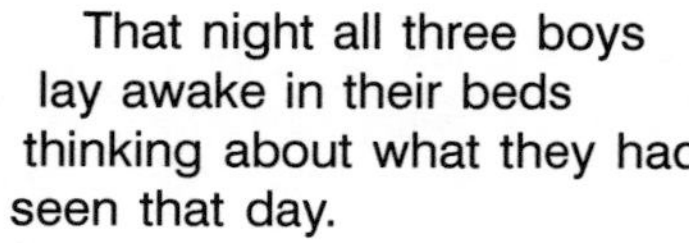

The next day they met up at the canyon again and decided on one thing - not to tell their parents. Alan borrowed his dad's camcorder to video the creature they had seen. They watched at the same spot where they had seen it the day before, but it did not show up again. So they moved on to a large cave where they had never been to before but could not find it there either.

They decided to head back on home knowing that no one would believe them until they had the evidence. Chuck said to Alan and Tom, 'This will be our secret until we can prove it to the others.'

The mystery continues ...

Daniel Kembery (9)
Frenchay CE Primary School, Bristol

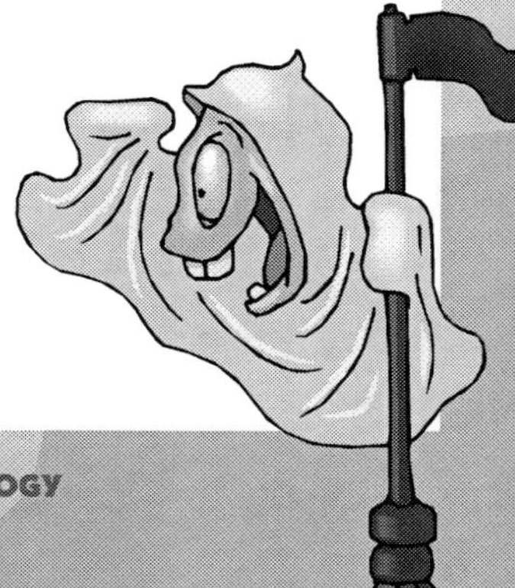

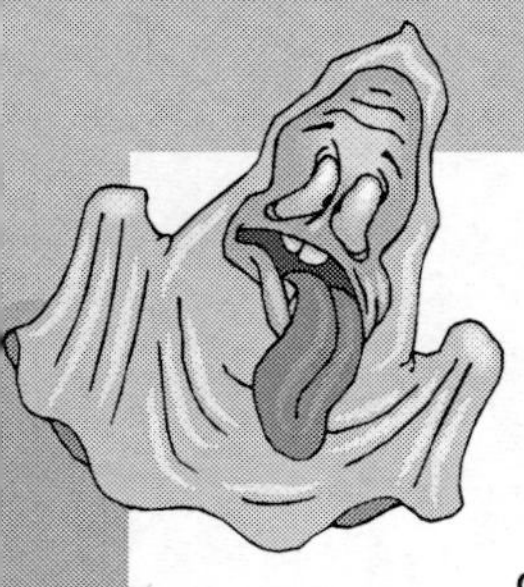

The Ghost Game

Two boys called Jack and Jake were walking to the Game Shop. After they had bought a game and gone home, Jack made himself a snack and dropped the knife. It fell into his pocket. He looked for it but could not find it.

'Come on,' called Jake.

Jack ran into the room. They clicked on the start button.

'What happened?' said Jake.

'We have been teleported into the game.'

'What's that?'

'It looks like a giant ant run.'

The knife fell out of the boy's pocket. He threw it at the ant.

'We're on level 2.'

'That's a giant spider, kill it.'

The spider fainted.

'Level 3!'

'Watch for its poison.'

Jake threw his shoe at it, the spider ate the shoe and died.

'Level 4.'

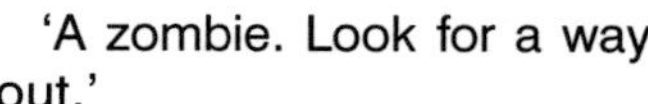

'A zombie. Look for a way out.'

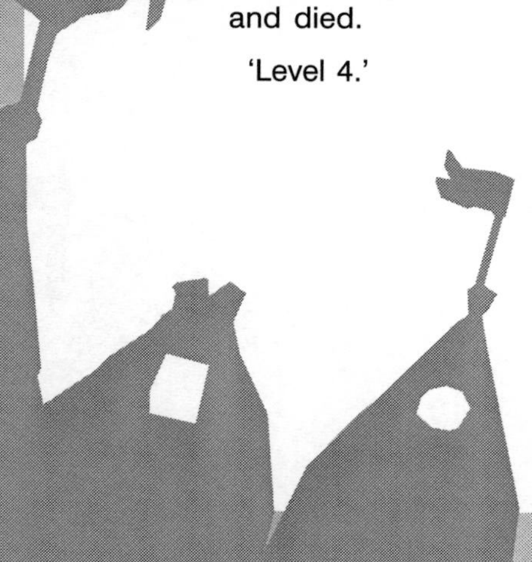

'Punch it.'

But it did not hurt the zombie.

'Try the knife.'

The zombie died.

'All the lights have gone off,' said Jack.

'It's a power cut.'

Zap!

'We're out of the game.'

The boys sold the game back to the shop.

Jamie Ali (9)
Frenchay CE Primary School, Bristol

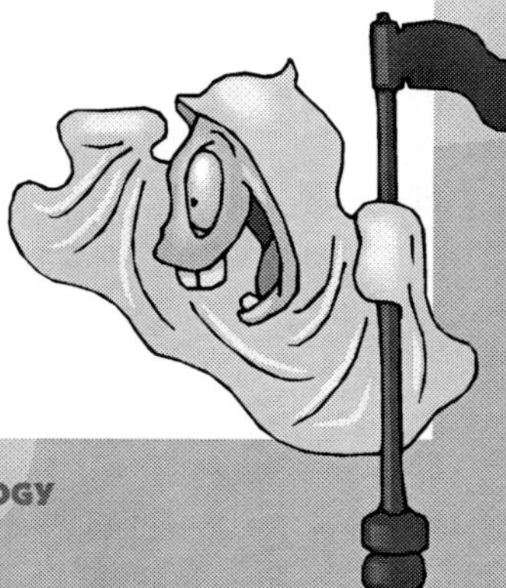

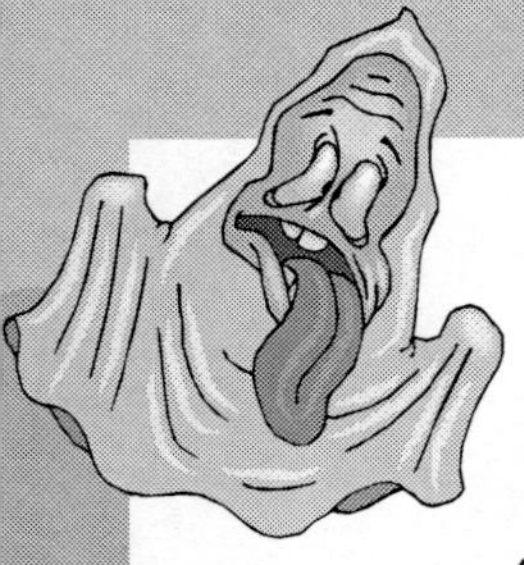

Vampire Graveyard

The moon was casting a weak glow on my grandfather's gravestone. Gloom stopped the shine. I stared in horror. I touched the slimy purple gates to open the ghostly graveyard. After touching the gates it felt sticky. The graves smelt like old blood.

The mist tasted like rotten apples. I thought I was going to be sick. Owls sang and hooted a nasty, spooky song. I screamed as if I were in Hell.

I heard something coming from behind. I turned around and ran further into the graveyard. I saw something but I couldn't see clearly because of the darkness. I put my hands in my pocket to get my flashlight. I switched it on. I saw something with fangs, a white face and a cape. I ran and ran. The thing I saw changed into a bat, then flew down and bit me.

I rolled down on the grass and bumped into a tree. Then I died. I then found an army of the things I'd already seen. They all bit me. I found myself somewhere and there was fire all around me …

Karim Mostafa (9)
Frenchay CE Primary School, Bristol

Mr Frill

18 years have passed since the murder of Mr Frill in the haunted house on Spooky Hill. It was said a flesh-eating, hideous, reeking, giant monster killed him but no one knows that for sure. There were no clues to his murder and his wife was killed earlier in the year so she knew nothing about it.

One day my friend and I could not stop thinking about it so we knew we had to go up there. When we got up to the unusual, old and ghostly house we were petrified. We glanced at the shattered windows and thought of what was to be discovered inside …

Inside it was mysterious, blank and gloomy. We glanced in the corners and saw old, dusty cobwebs. Upstairs was identical as downstairs but all of a sudden we heard a giant thump from downstairs. We rushed down as quickly as we could. My heart was throbbing with fear. The door was narrow and we knew someone was in the house. I then stepped on a mouldy piece of wood and unexpectedly we both fell through the floorboards. It was really dim. All of a sudden a light came towards us. We backed up into the corner and it got closer and closer until we saw a face …

It was Mr Frill. We asked him why he was down here. He said, 'After my wife died I couldn't live my life so I just locked myself away from everyone.' We convinced him to come out of the darkness and live his life like a normal person.

The next day when we woke Mr Frills' house was a big, beautiful house with tons of flowers and bricks. I don't know how he did it overnight but he did. After that Mr Frill lived his life as a normal person.

Paul McCrory (11)
Lagan College, Belfast

A Scary Story

17 Creaky Road had been empty for as long as I can remember. The story behind the house was that a man had killed his wife and buried her under the big tree in the garden. Some people say that she still haunts the house and can sometimes be heard crying at 8 o'clock, which is the time her husband killed her. My mates and I didn't believe in ghosts, well not until that night last year. Let me tell you what happened.

One day in December, just before Christmas, me, Chris, Johnny and Peter were in my house talking about what we were going to get from Santa. It had been snowing all day and the street was covered in a thick layer of snow. We went out to play in the snow and somehow ended up in Creaky Road, which was about three streets from my house.

The one thing that number 17 had that no other house had was a big back garden and we just had to go in because the snow looked so good - no footprints, just a big blanket of white. We weren't a bit scared, even though we had heard the stories about the house, sure we didn't believe in ghosts.

We climbed over the fence and looked around. It was very dark, the only light came from the moon reflecting on the snow. The back of the house was just like the front, all the windows were boarded up and we had to admit it was a bit spooky.

'Isn't that the tree where he buried his wife?' Peter said.

'Yeah, so they say,' I said. 'Come on, let's build a snowman.'

'I don't want to build a snowman,' said Chris. 'Let's play hide-and-seek instead.'

Johnny was 'it' first and started counting. We all hid. I was behind the shed and suddenly I had a very strange feeling like someone was watching me. I was glad when Johnny found me first.

Suddenly a cloud covered the moon and it went very dark. There was a loud cry and me and Johnny looked at each other nervously.

'Peter, Chris is that you?' I shouted.

There was no reply. Something grabbed my leg. I let out a scream and closed my eyes.

'What's the matter with you?' I heard. I opened my eyes and Chris, Peter and Johnny were standing laughing at me.

'You look like you have seen a ghost,' Peter said.

I laughed nervously. 'I think we better head home, what time is it?' I said.

'It's 8 o'clock,' Chris said, and just as he did we could hear someone crying. It seemed to be coming from near the big tree ...

Michael Moynagh (11)
Lagan College, Belfast

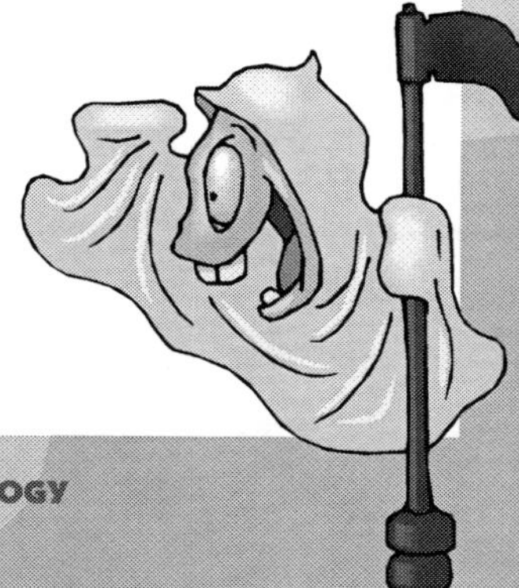

The Ghost Child Of The Cliffs

Holly, Zoe, Stephanie, Karla and Rachel were the best of friends. It was Hallowe'en, they were having a sleepover and were telling ghost stories. They had turned the lights down and had lit a pumpkin. It was Rachel's turn to tell a story, she began …

'This is the story of the ghost child of the cliffs. It all started nearly 50 years ago, five girls were walking on the cliff that was 500 feet above the sea. They were daring each other to go right to the edge of the cliff. It was Sally's turn, she was a small, quiet girl who was afraid to go to the edge of the cliff. The girls who were with her were older and teased her as she began to cry. Stephanie teased that she would show her how to stand at the edge because only babies were afraid. Stephanie hurried to the edge laughing. The others stood in horror as they saw her trip on her lace and fall backwards over the edge of the cliff.

Everybody was screaming and crying. Two of the girls approached the edge of the cliff almost afraid to look over. There was no sign of Stephanie in the water or on the rocks below. For a few minutes nobody knew what to do next. Sally and one of the girls ran for help.

It was 10 minutes before any help came. Divers looked for Stephanie's body but it was never found. The friends never went to the cliffs again.

It is said from people that walk along the cliff, that they can hear a girl's voice laughing and turning slowly into a scream of terror!'

Holly, Zoe, Stephanie and Karla could not settle to go to sleep after that story. They decided not to tell ghost stories anymore!

Zoe Nelson (12)
Lagan College, Belfast

Murder By Ghost

One night in November, Janet was entering her dormitory at Queens University. She was walking through the main building when suddenly she felt that someone was watching her. She turned around but no one was there.

The next day when Janet woke up there were no people in her dormitory and she got a bigger shock when she went down for her breakfast, not one person was there. Janet started feeling freaked out and when she walked towards the door she felt a presence in the room.

Janet started screaming, 'Stop it, leave me alone! Why are you doing this?' But there was no reply. Janet became very, very nervous at this point and started walking again, trying to get out when she heard a scream.

Janet was running, running fast, trying to get away from the presence. Just when Janet thought that she was safe she heard someone call her name, but in a chilling sort of way. She kept looking behind her and when she turned back around, a spirit was standing watching her. Janet screamed, 'Please don't hurt me!' but there was no reply.

Janet tried to walk away but the spirit refused and shouted, 'How dare thee, thee shall not pass.'

Janet did not listen and tried to pass. *Bzzzzzzz!* Janet fell to the ground, it was murder by ghost. There was blood everywhere, up the walls, windows and ali over the ground.

When daybreak came, Janet's mutilated body was discovered by Betty, the foreign exchange student.

The police service investigated it but could not work out who murdered Janet and now her soul roams *Queens University, Belfast.*

James Andrew Harper (12)
Lagan College, Belfast

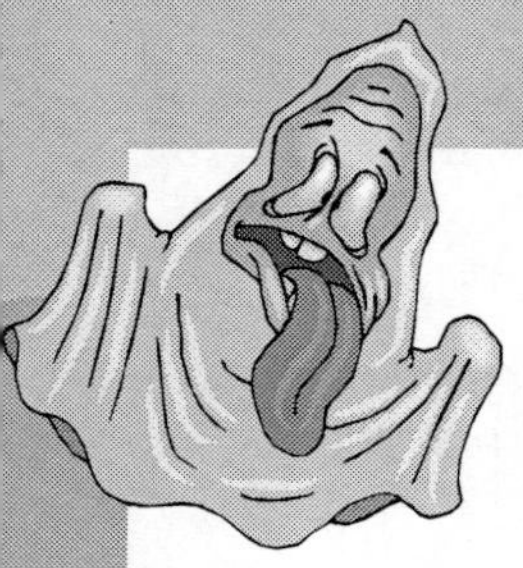

The Haunted House

One day when my mum went out, I heard this weird noise coming from what I thought was the roof space, so I decided to go and investigate.

When I got upstairs everything was quiet, I couldn't even hear the floorboards creak. Before I could get the ladders down ... *slam,* my mum had returned so I went downstairs and pretended to look busy.

That night lying in bed, I heard the noise again. This time I had a really big fright. I saw this man coming up the stairs wearing a black cape and a black hat. I was terrified. I screamed and my mum came running into the room. She thought I was dreaming and told me to try and go back to sleep.

The next day I couldn't get the man out of my head and dreaded going back to bed that night. I got to sleep quickly but woke in the middle of the night again and saw the man coming up the stairs. Although I was really scared, I didn't scream and the man came into my room. When I looked closer at him I discovered he had no head and when I let out another scream he disappeared again.

I asked my mum to take me to the newspaper library because I wanted to look back at old papers to see if I could find any other things about ghosts.

Looking through them, I couldn't believe the story I came across. It was from 15 years ago. It was about a man who was murdered on the building site of where my house was now built. This man had had his head chopped off and they never found the person who did it. Now I realised that the man I saw at night must be the ghost of the man who was killed years ago.

That night I went to bed and waited and waited to see if the ghost would arrive. It got really cold in the room and then I saw the man coming in with the cape on again. I started saying how I knew what had happened and suddenly I felt the room getting warm again. The man had gone.

When I got up the next morning I found a piece of paper on the ground with the name and address of a man on it. The note said, 'Take to police'. Because I was only a young boy I knew the police would not believe my story so I typed out a page and printed it off saying that this name might help them solve a murder from years ago.

That night the man did not come, nor the next night, nor the one after that.

A month later I was sitting watching the TV with my mum when the first thing on the news was the story of how a man had been found guilty of a murder committed 15 years ago. As I watched I was surprised to see that the man was the one whose name had been written on the piece of paper I'd found in my bedroom.

That night in bed I saw the man come into my room and this time he had a face. He smiled at me and then disappeared.

The next morning I found a piece of paper on the floor that said, 'Thank you, at last justice is done and I'm free to go to the afterlife'.

That was the last time I saw the ghost and I realised it had not been there to scare me but had wanted help to make sure that justice was done.

Philip Burns (12)
Lagan College, Belfast

A Fright At Night

A few years ago there was a young girl named Susan and she was about nine years old. She was staying over at a place called Cabra Towers with a youth group she went to on a Friday night.

One cold and wet night everyone was in their dorms sleeping silently. Every so often you could hear the wind blowing.

That night, Susan was awoken suddenly by a loud *bang!* She did not know what it was so she got out of bed to see if her friend had heard it too. She climbed up onto the top bunk where her friend was sleeping. Her friend had woken up and was sitting bolt upright with fear. They both sat up on the top bunk, quivering. They could hear footsteps walking along the hall. The footsteps were coming closer and closer. The two girls quickly hid under the blanket. They heard the door open slowly and the door then closed again quickly. The footsteps slowly faded away. The girls were relieved and in no time they had fallen asleep.

In the morning the girls told their friends what they'd heard and what had happened. When the girls told their leader she said that she had just gone round to see if everyone was asleep. The girls were happy that they did not have to worry about it again.

Julia Orr (12)
Lagan College, Belfast

The Strange Thing At The Station

One day my grandpa and I went to his work. He worked in a bus station on the Falls Road. The bus station used to be used as an old army camp. He showed me his bus and gave me a ride in it. I sat at the back. I then got moved to the front when passengers got on. When we dropped off the last person we drove back to the station.

Grandpa brought me to the staffroom where all the men dressed like my grandpa were sitting. I had a few things to eat and soon everyone left. When we left, my grandpa had to lock up the gates, so we walked past all the buses, all coloured red and blue. Grandpa then put the key in the lock and locked it. We both glanced in to see if the staff were out. Grandpa looked to the back of the station and saw a strange man walking slowly with a rifle held on his back and big boots. He was dressed in an Australian soldier's uniform. We were scared to death as he turned to look at us. Then I remembered that my grandpa told me about it being an army camp. Now I knew he was right.

We ran to get into an old black taxi. My grandpa then worried in case he should tell the caretakers that go up every night to clean up. He didn't in case it scared them and the buses wouldn't be clean. He then said, 'Don't tell your mother about that, okay?'

I didn't.

Conor McKenna (12)
Lagan College, Belfast

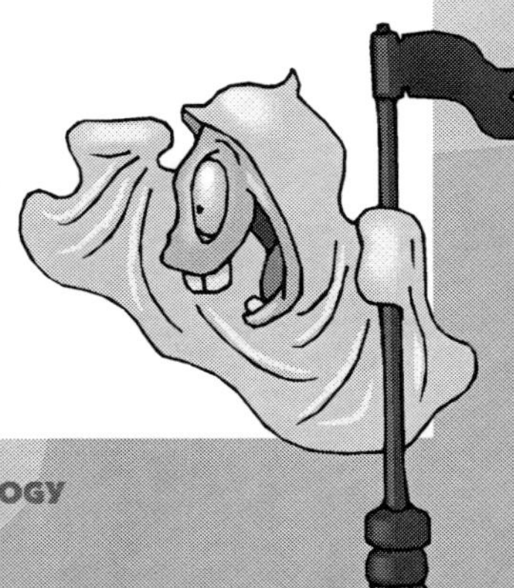

The Gypsy Ghosts

One cold, misty night there was nothing to be heard, not even a squeak from a mouse.

A young girl called Naomi was locked in her chamber bedroom. All of a sudden, she heard a drip, drip sound. Was it blood or just a leaking tap? Naomi tried to escape but was too scared to open the creaking door. She shivered behind the cold, open window; she did not want to open the door for she knew that death would be there. She cried and cried for many hours. Naomi fell to the floor with fear, she did not notice that she had fallen through a trapdoor and it had taken her to the land of gypsy ghosts.

Naomi did not know where to turn; all she could hear was the sound of tambourines and singing and she was surrounded by eerie, dancing gypsy ghosts.

Naomi screamed, *'Help! Get me out of here.'* However, nobody could hear her apart from the ghosts who were surrounding her.

'Who said that?' screeched the queen gypsy. 'Get her out of here, she does not belong here.'

Naomi screamed as she was extremely frightened. She was so scared, she thought she might die, but then thought to herself, *how can you meet death twice in a row?* Naomi realised she was already dead and that explained it all.

The drip was her blood and there was no sound because there was no one else there.

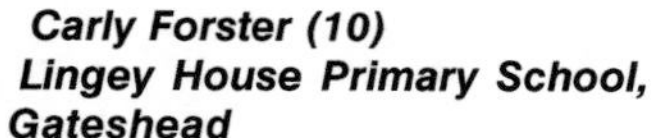

Carly Forster (10)
Lingey House Primary School,
Gateshead

The Dilemma

'You should rest, you have been too stressed after your brother's funeral, I mean it!' commanded the doctor.

I was left alone in a gigantic room, with wired paintings on the roof. I stared at the huge windows in front of my bed, which looked like the eyes of an enormous monster.

The door flew open and my heart skipped a beat. It was only my older brother, Karl.

'What's up baby sister? Feeling better?' he asked.

'Yes,' I replied. 'Do you remember when Mother told us that we had magical powers and we were destined to vanquish the ghost?' I asked Karl.

'Yes and we will defeat him,' he replied.

'Not until you die!' said a deep voice from the window.

The window broke into pieces and the chandelier fell down from the ceiling. We ran to our uncle's study.

'It has started,' I shouted.

'I know, we should hurry,' replied my uncle.

We started saying the spells, when a huge hole appeared in the door.

'If you leave, you die!' said the ghost.

'Help!' It was the gardener in the other room.

The walls were closing in and there was nowhere to run to, while my brother was being pulled towards the hole. We were in a dilemma, but we knew blood is thicker than water. We held Karl with our powers until the hole disappeared.

I then learnt that family is more important in life.

Dorothy Aluoch Suleh (15)
Loreto Convent, Nairobi

Recurring Nightmare

I went on, running into the woods, past the trees, then I fell.

Darkness couldn't hide that it was Woodville cemetery. I had to leave, bullies or no bullies. I bent down to tie my laces and on looking up, I nearly fainted. There, white as snow, was a ghost, floating towards me!

Naturally, I turned and ran, to no avail because it appeared before me again. I froze, speechless, terrified, hoping I'd arise from this nightmare, but then it started talking, crying. I couldn't tell because of fear. It also looked familiar. Maybe I was going crazy, how often can you see all this in a lifetime! A familiar ghost? I was going crazy. Then it hit me, Alex! I turned again and ran, but my chest was pounding and my feet felt like lead, oh no!

Then I saw the gates, maybe I'd make it, but to my horror, the ghost appeared in front of them! There was no escape …

Then I began running, through 'Alex', through the cemetery gates and I was out, unscathed. I had to sit down and catch my breath, this was too much for me.

I was in my own world when I felt a hand on my shoulder. Why didn't I go home immediately?

The bullies were back, with the real Alex. Out of the frying pan into the fire for me. Alex and I were herded like sheep into Woodville cemetery, my nightmare was beginning all over again.

Jacqueline Onyango (17)
Loreto Convent, Nairobi

Gone At Ten

It was a cold, shivering night and the whistling wind brushed through my ears. The moon was ripe and full of light. It cast shadows of the leaves that fell from the trees. The trees had been swaying from side to side in unison like a choir, having something to say.

One could make out everything outside, even the shadow of the smallest branch could be seen.

All of a sudden, everything stopped. It was dead quiet except for the sound of the dog that made the atmosphere more scary. It seemed as though life was dead and the hound, as if to warn me of danger.

Nearly five hours had gone by, my brother could not be seen. The cemetery was very quiet. I started thinking about the ghost stories we used to be told in camp. I remembered one about an old lady who would come every Hallowe'en to take the soul of a young boy of ten years. My brother had just turned ten a week ago! Amidst my thoughts, I heard some cries.

'Help! Help!'

Isn't that my brother's voice? I thought. In a flash, a bright light appeared from a distance and the voice could be heard no more.

I ran to where the light was but it disappeared as soon as I arrived. I called out a few more times but to no avail. I was left in total confusion, not knowing what was ever to become of my brother.

Mary Keah (17)
Loreto Convent, Nairobi

The Final Encounter

The night was cold and still. From my peaceful sleep, my eyes jerked open at the sudden sound of howling wolves, their greatest attraction being the full moon that was shining that night.

Deciding to look outside my window was the biggest mistake I ever made. I saw one strange wolf looking up at me, yet right through me at the same time. A sudden shiver was sent right up my spine and my blood froze in its channels.

The howling continued for another short period which I hardly noticed for my eyes were on the wolf, now jumping onto the roof near my window. I now realised why people die of shock. My legs refused to move, my arms clung to the windowpane.

I watched as it stood right in front of me with the moonlight highlighting its most impeccable features. It shook its head in outrage and I could see fury in its dark eyes as it began to change its features slowly. The other wolves from the woods came one by one and sat on the patio watching their 'god'.

Its head took the form of a giant frog and all the hairs on its body fell off. It was staring straight at me.

A sudden wind blew and when I looked at my arms, small hairs were growing visibly at an alarming rate. I only remember my body growing numb and falling into a deep sleep.

Cheryl Onguru (17)
Loreto Convent, Nairobi

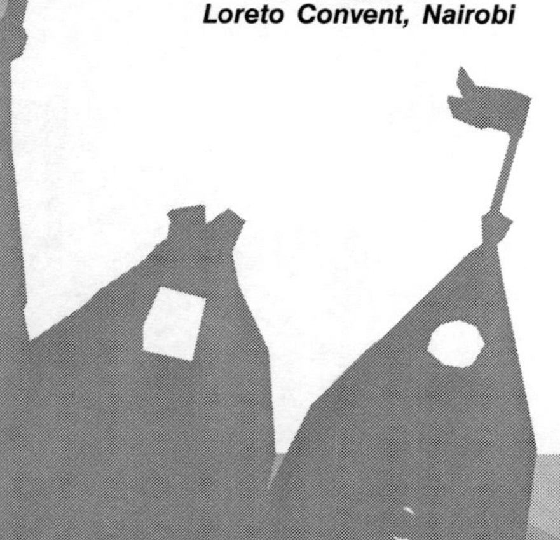

Ghosts In The Graveyard

'For the last time Mo, there's no such thing as a ghost,' I spat out to my best friend, who had been ranting and raving about ghosts for almost thirty minutes.

'Fine, then I guess you won't have a problem with taking a ride through the old graveyard,' he retorted, in a taunting voice.

'No, I won't! In fact, I am going to enjoy it,' I replied sarcastically. Little did I know I would be haunted by those very words for the rest of my life.

As we rode home, we were so engrossed in our conversation that we were oblivious to the sudden weather change. As we took a left turn into the graveyard, I knew that something was not right.

The moon was full and glowing as though on fire, giving the graveyard an eerie atmosphere. I knew then that death awaited both or at least one of us.

The whole place had an electric charge that kept me in a trance though Mo kept going. I watched as he dived in slow motion into one of the open old graves and a satisfied groan erupted from within the grave. I could hear myself scream and yet it was as though no sound came out. I closed my eyes tightly shut and when I reopened them I was in my own room.

No one knows what happened to Mo or how I got home, but I can clearly say that I lost my best friend to ghosts in the graveyard.

Melekte Petros (18)
Loreto Convent, Nairobi

Adventure In The Wood

Emmy and I arrived at the Martins' for a holiday and took the disowned path to our holiday adventures, 'the forest'. Supper wasn't ready yet. Usually the woods are a great spot for picking wild flowers.

'Emmy, look!' I gleefully said.

'What?' she retorted.

I ran forward to pick some. I then called Emmy again. 'Emmy? Come on.'

I turned just in time to see her in pain. Some dark figured creature was tightly grasping her neck and was grinning. Then, just what I thought would never happen, happened ... the creature spoke!

'What are you doing in my territory, my sanctuary?' it screeched out.

'We ... we ... we ... didn't mean to disturb you,' I said, shaking.

'Without notice it grabbed my shoulder. A sharp pain went down my spine. I couldn't move a muscle, let alone scream. 'We're sorry, please let us go,' I blurted out. My pleas fell on deaf ears.

Meanwhile, it dragged us down into a cave. My feet felt hot. The cave got darker and darker as we continued. I couldn't see a thing. It dropped us mercilessly on the rocky floor with a thud.

A bright light flashed before us and we saw large tables joined together and chairs arranged on the sides. On each chair was a skeleton holding cutlery in each bony hand and a napkin tied around its neck as if ready for a scrumptious meal.

The skeletons turned around and looked at us.

Waking up, I saw myself in my bedroom, shocked and sweating.

Sarah Itambo (17)
Loreto Convent, Nairobi

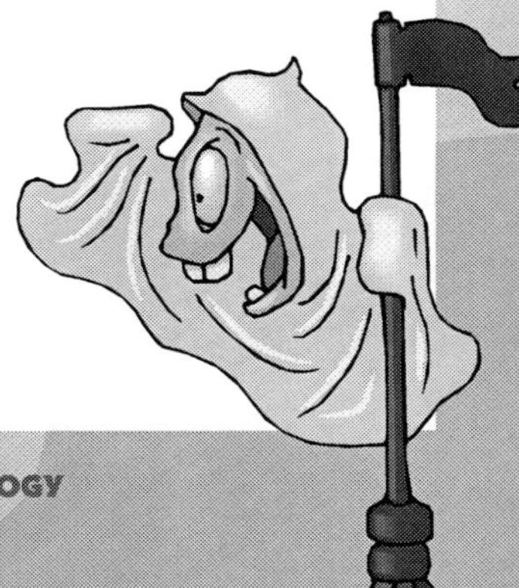

Underground Horror

'Let's watch 'Buffy The Vampire Slayer', I suggested, turning on the video.

'Okay!' Cindy called from the living room. 'Where are you?' she asked, seated on the couch with her legs placed on the table.

'I'm here!' I called coming from the kitchen, holding a tray packed with popcorn and milkshakes.

It was the late evening, the day before Hallowe'en when we were given a mid-term break from school, but something strange happened that changed my life forever.

'An earthquake!' Cindy yelled, searching frantically around the room for something to grasp on. The ground shook fiercely, making it crack into two. I crawled towards Cindy and held her hand firmly. We remained as silent as the grave, only our eyes were moving around in case we spotted any strange shadows.

After the earthquake, it was like the world was spinning, thus it made me feel dizzy. I could see zombies, skeletons, mummies, you name it, could be seen roaming around like hungry, wild dogs.

'Welcome to the Underworld!' boomed a voice, which seemed to come from the leader. His face was covered completely with a hood.

'What did you do with Cindy?' I asked angrily, after realising that she did not accompany me.

'Nothing!' he boomed, laughing. 'She is alright,' he assured, stretching his hand.

He showed me around his kingdom. Lastly, he took me to a cage firmly held by a chain, covered by flames of fire. Noises were heard everywhere to scare off intruders.

'Cindy!' I yelled, after I saw her in that cage, with her clothes torn. She was bleeding furiously and I blamed myself.

The leader of the 'Immortals' told me that I could set Cindy free if I took part in the Olympics held that day.

'I'm coming to save you!' I yelled as I was led by the guards to a big field where the games were supposed to be held. The audience were seated facing the field.

The contest was challenging so I lost all the rounds. The creatures were unruly, they mocked me, they booed, they persisted so the leader gave me a chance to go down and take part in the braincracking quiz. I knew I could beat them, even though most of them were the ones who contributed to civilisation, urbanisation etc.

After that they assured me that they would take care of Cindy for me. I entered inside the hole they led me to and off I went.

I sat on my bed pondering my next move. I felt that I'd let Cindy down. We just came to have a sleepover that turned out to be tragic. *What will I say?* I wondered. *I know I can beat them for sure but can I wait till next year? Tomorrow is school* I thought, untying my hair.

'Alexis!' the secretary called.

I passed by Cindy's parents, who looked at me hoping that I would utter a word.

'Let's go,' the policeman told me at the secretary's desk. He led me to the policeman ahead. My school mates stared at me in amazement as I was being led to the waiting police car. I could see a hallucination of Cindy nodding her head. I could feel that I was doing a good deed. I knew that one day we would reunite, on the day of the quiz in 'Horrorland'.

Ruth Orek (16)
Loreto Convent, Nairobi

The Ghost Who Lived

Fred was hungrier than a ravenous tiger but since his office was in the middle of nowhere, there were no restaurants.

Fred couldn't believe it, there was a Chinese restaurant where there wasn't one before. Seeing a light he drove up to the speaker box and ordered beef with onions.

'Proceed to the next window,' it responded, so he did.

The food floated out of the window, landing on the seat next to him. He found this strange, but forgot about it since he didn't have to pay because there was no one at the window. Fred said to himself, 'A ghost? No way! There are no such things!'

Fred got out of the car and opened the restaurant door.

'Why didn't you go straight home?'

Fred stopped, frozen like water dripping at the North Pole. A strange translucent man floating in front of him whispered, 'What do you want?'

Fred asked, 'Where'd this restaurant come from?'

'Sorry, I can't tell you.'

'Fair enough, do you need help?' asked Fred.

'You can reattach my skull, that's in the fridge, to my body,' replied the ghost.

'OK,' said Fred proudly. Fred opened the fridge. It stank! He took out the skull and attached it to the skeleton. *Bang!* There was a handsome man standing in front of him.

Fred and the ex-ghost ran the restaurant well together. Fred usually closed the restaurant when he liked, because he would sneak some beef with onions!

Drew Wardle (13)
Morna International College, Ibiza

The Little Ghost

It was a wonderful day in the little town that was far away from any big town, in the middle of nowhere.

My mom and I were sitting in the car and were driving to a house even further away from anybody. We were moving because my mother wanted to live at a place where she could work all alone and no one would disturb her. I had to come with her since my father had passed away.

As we finally stopped in front of a very big house I wondered why such a beautiful house was sold so cheap to us. It was an old house that was supposed to have stayed there empty for five years.

We got out of the car and walked towards the door. A little girl opened it.

'Who are you?' said Mom as we entered.

The girl showed us all the rooms in the house and even told me where the best room would be for me. That was odd. She also said that on the left side of the room the bed stands the best and in front of one of the windows the desk would stand quite well.

After that I looked out of the window and when I turned back to the girl, she had disappeared. Where had she gone? What had happened to her? Maybe she's with my mother.

I went down and looked for her, no sign of that little pigtailed girl in a pink dress.

Two days later we went to the little town to thank the seller that he had sent a girl to open the door for us, but he said he did not send anyone. We told him what the girl looked like and you won't believe this, but it was the girl that had lived there five years ago.

Bettina Ruehl (15)
Morna International College, Ibiza

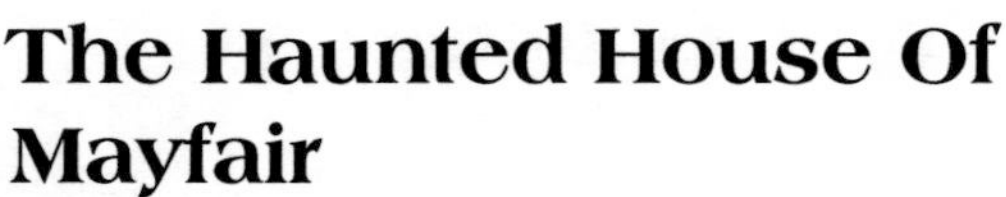

The Haunted House Of Mayfair

Number 33 Berkeley Square in Mayfair was once London's most haunted house. It was haunted by three men so evil that Hell spat them back out. No one dared to even walk past the house because of its terrifying reputation, except three men, Sean, Eddy and David.

They were sitting at the Winchester pub down the road from the house waiting for the torrential rain to blow over when Sean came up with an idea.

'Hey guys, there's this house down the road that is said to be haunted, the last one to run out the house screaming like a little girl will get to ask that hot babe Keira out, are you in?' asked Sean.

'We're in!' they both said.

'OK, we'll sleep there tomorrow!' said Sean.

'Fine, I don't believe in ghosts anyway!' said Eddy.

'We'll see about that!' answered David.

Tomorrow evening came quickly, Sean, Eddy and David were all ready with their sleeping bags and everything they needed. They walked inside, the three of them standing there looking around. *Bang!* the door slammed behind them.

'I get upstairs bed!' shouted Eddy.

'Be quiet,' whispered Sean, 'we're not allowed to be here you know!'

'I'll sleep down here in the bed next to the kitchen,' said David.

'I'll sleep on the couch,' Sean replied.

They were all so close to getting to sleep when suddenly a scream came from upstairs. Sean raced to Eddy to see what had happened while David was getting a knife from the kitchen. After Sean had seen what had happened he raced back down the stairs onto the street and ran for his life.

'Sean, wait!' shouted David but he didn't wait at all.

David carried on up the stairs to find Eddy's lifeless body lying on the floor with the fear still frozen to his face, his eyes were staring into space and there was a cigar still alight in his hand. With his fear he jumped out of the window and landed on the spike of the railings.

Sean had come back with a policeman but it was too late, they found David on the railings with blood dripping on the pavement.

Sean had won the dare and had a chance to ask the hot babe Keira out but he couldn't, he felt too guilty.

The next day the police found Sean dead, he'd shot himself with the rifle above the Winchester pub's bar. So they all ended up without Keira.

Zak Day (13)
Morna International College, Ibiza

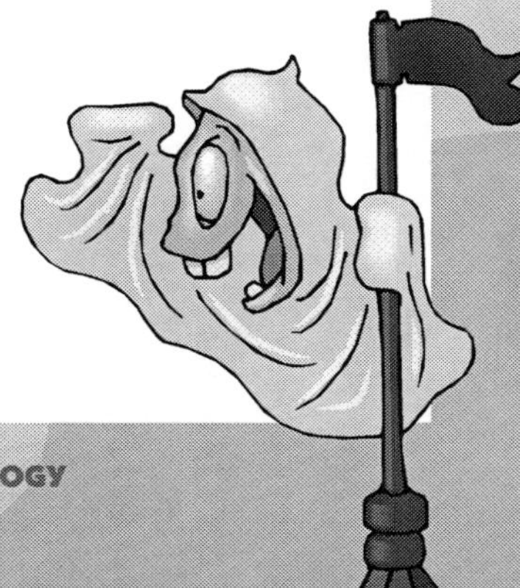

Hallowe'en Resurrection

I'm Amanda and I have a younger sister Amy. We have two close friends Nathan and Chloe. We were having a party at Chloe's house.

At the party, a strange man suddenly entered. We weren't worried and continued dancing. Since Chloe is not shy, she went up to the man and offered him a dance. The next thing we heard was a loud scream. When we got there, she was lying in a pool of blood. I had a sleepless night thinking of Chloe.

The next day, we went to school but it wasn't better. Amy went to get some snacks but when I got there, she was *dead!* What was happening? Things were getting too strange.

Mr Rodney (Nathan's dad) came over to our house. I went to get him some fruit juice but when I got back Mr Rodney was dead. My dad decided to explain everything to me.

He told me that Mr Rodney, himself and Mr Tony invested a large sum of money in a business. When the business was flourishing, they plotted to kill Mr Tony (the man who was haunting us).

I decided to fight the man myself. On my way to his grave, he appeared and tried to stab me but I took to my heels. He was so scary with maggots all over his body. He used his gross, rotten hands and tried to strangle me to death, I screamed.

I suddenly awoke in bed, it was just a dream. A horrible nightmare!

Selambi Belinda Mayikue
Our Lady of Lourdes Secondary School, Cameroon

Haunted Museum

I have always loved to visit museums. Thanks to God I have left Alaska for Atlanta where my next-door neighbour informed me he'd got one on Blackout Street. Yet he says blacks are not allowed there, but I have decided to go, black or white.

It was 11.30pm when I rushed down the street. There, the museum stood so big and tall. It was surprising no guards were around while lights were on. I got in. Lord! it was big. The statues looked so real and alive. 'I doubt what that guy meant about blacks not allowed,' I said aloud.

'He meant this.'

Someone hit me hard on the back. I turned towards the door but it was closed. I heard sounds of, 'Ouch! Klooo! Tack!' God, this museum *was* haunted.

Suddenly I heard a bell. It signified midnight. I closed my eyes but saw visions of a ghost floating in the air. My vision became a reality as I opened my eyes. The museum, no not museum, the ghostly haunted house was filled with horrible creatures. They were all coming for me. 'Help!' I screamed.

'Maggie!'

I looked up. There stood my next-door neighbour.

'Pull the rope,' he said.

I did. He pulled me up and we ran for dear life.

'Goodnight Maggie,' he said when we reached my apartment. I did not think the night was good at all. I never thought of going to the museum again!

Margaret Bih Wallang (15)
Our Lady of Lourdes Secondary School, Cameroon

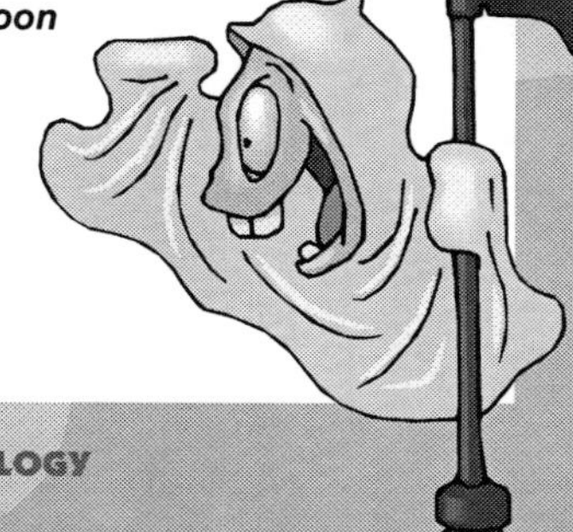

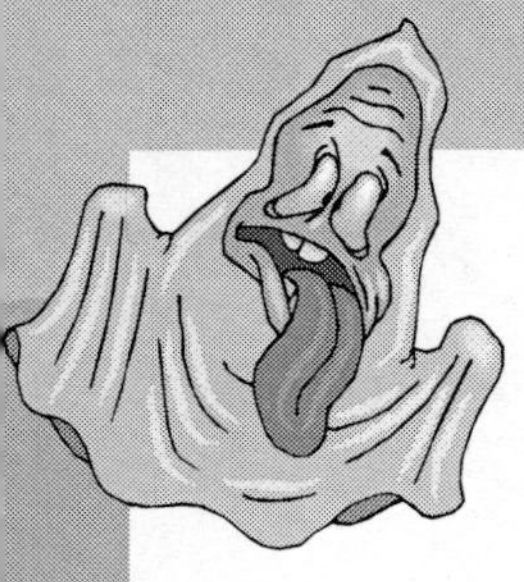

Pinchfield (Vampire Street)

'Mother, I am going to Lily's house,' I yelled. My mother is a little deaf so you have to yell sometimes.

'Alright you can go but be back soon.' She did not know that I was not going to Lily's house but to Pinchfield.

We had just moved to Crestview recently. My friends told me Pinchfield was the most dangerous area in Crestview. It was full of vampires. I did not believe it. I decided to see for myself.

I bolted through the door into the street. I started to run and dead leaves crunched under my feet. I was soon at Pinchfield.

It was deserted. There was only an empty house and a dim street light. Suddenly, I felt warm breath on my neck. Turning, I saw a pair of glowing eyes and teeth. This horrible apparition grabbed my arm with one rotten hand. I tried to pull away but failed. It was a vampire.

It bit my neck and started sucking my blood. Within seconds, I was surrounded by vampires. I tried to fight, my strength was failing me. I screamed and their teeth sank into my bones. I kicked wildly and pulled myself up and staggered to the light. One vampire grabbed me and started strangling me. I choked and I felt life leaving me. I screamed and woke up.

All this while I had been dreaming and sweating all over. I heaved a sigh of relief and went back to my precious sleep.

Sandra Leke-Tambo (13)
Our Lady of Lourdes Secondary School, Cameroon

The Alsatian Sensation

A couple of years ago, something happened that made me wonder if ghosts really existed.

I saw a small shack across the river and didn't really pay much attention to it; I was just doing my business when I saw something out of the corner of my eye. At first it didn't dawn on me what I was seeing, since we were almost in the middle of nowhere, but I realised it looked like a dog hiding in some grass.

This was somebody's pet. It looked like an Alsatian. Now this wasn't too hard to believe. But for some reason I got a strange feeling when I saw this dog. I zipped up and just stood there for a few minutes and this dog just stood there staring right back, very calmly. He was right in front of the shack.

I decided to go and tell my mate to go and look, when he grabbed my arm and went, 'Ssshh,' real seriously. He was listening for something.

I tried to listen but couldn't hear anything, but then we both heard a sound that made my blood run cold. It was seriously creepy, and sounded like it was coming from the shack, the closer we got to the shack the louder and more vicious it got. We finally reached the shack and we caught the look on each other's faces that was enough to tell us to get the hell out of there ... we *never* fished there again ...

Callum Hough (12)
St Chad's Catholic High School, Runcorn

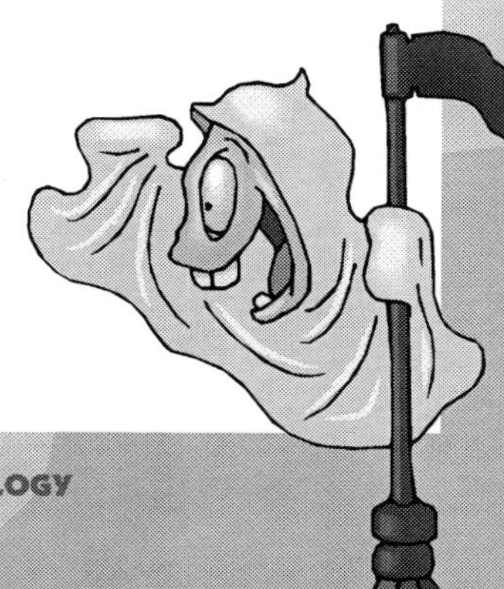

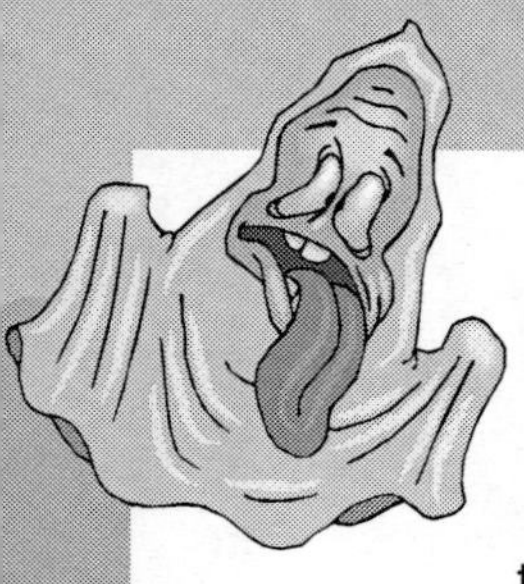

The Night Receptionist

Toni, Danielle and Louise approached the school. Toni had left her book there and was going to collect it. It had started to pour and the thunder grumbled.

They ran inside the building with its glowing lights. When they got to the reception a pale man, with dark eyes, queried shakily, 'Can I help you?'

'Who are you?' questioned Louise.

'I,' he said in a low voice, 'am the night receptionist.'

That moment the lights went out.

'Aargh!' they screamed.

'Don't worry, I have a lamp,' said the receptionist, holding it next to his face.

'You're here for a book?'

'Yes,' Toni answered.

'It's in there.' He pointed his long finger at a wooden door.

They walked through it and looked around.

'There!' Danielle collected it. 'Let's get out of here, it gives me the creeps!'

As Louise went to step out of the room, the door slammed shut and refused to open.

Later, when they'd given up all hope, Toni heard voices around the room. She scanned it to see who it was. Instead of finding a person, she noticed a door ajar.

'Hey, a door,' she beckoned. The girls looked through the door and walked down some stairs, into a basement.

In front, stood a gravestone reading ...

James Green
16th July 1941-1971

They ran from the basement, an evil laugh echoing around them.

When they returned, they asked their teacher about the night receptionist. 'We've not had a night receptionist since 1971, he was murdered in the basement.'

Esther Sargeant (11)
St Chad's Catholic High School, Runcorn

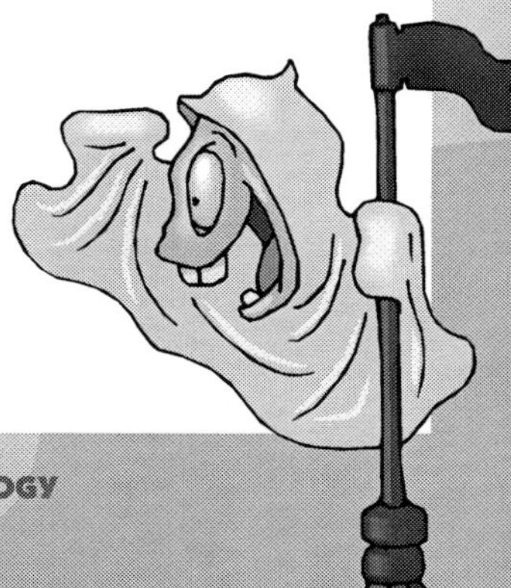

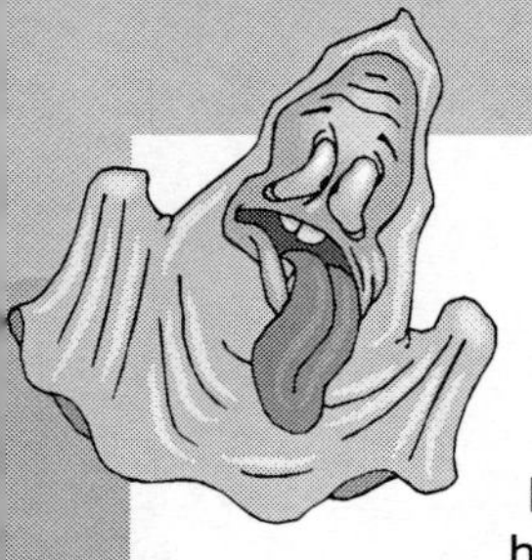

The Ghost Of Boxington

It was 11th December 2005; this was a special day in Boxington. It was the 100th anniversary of Boxington Rovers FC. The town were going to have the biggest party they had ever had, it was going to be held at the graveyard where the first ever team was buried.

At around 1.15am the townspeople heard strange noises. It wasn't any of the town, then suddenly *bang!* the 15 graves fell down and their ghosts came out. The town fled in fear. Then a little boy and girl both aged about 6 were standing in front of the ghosts and told the ghosts the bad news. 'They are planning to knock down the football ground,' said the boy.

It was 7am and the ghosts were at the football ground. There was a misty fog in the sky, the bulldozers were getting ready to knock down the ground. The ghosts said to each other, 'Are we going to let this happen?'

'No!' said one of the ghosts.

Then they flew so fast the fog split in half, they went through the glass of the office where the planners were standing. The planners were so frightened that they fell down and hit their heads on the floor. While they were knocked out the ghosts told them that they would never build on this ground unless to improve the ground.

At 8am the planners told the bulldozers to 'go home, the ground stays'.

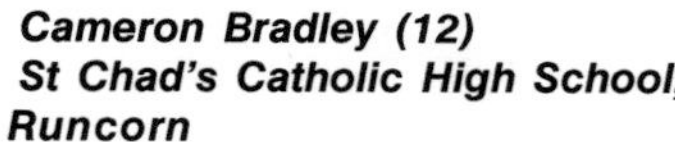

Cameron Bradley (12)
St Chad's Catholic High School, Runcorn

The Lady In The Attic

Ben and Lucy arrived at their uncle Alf's, while their parents were away. The house was large and Victorian with many rooms, situated on the edge of Exmoor.

One day while their uncle was at the village, Ben and Lucy decided to explore the house. Whilst in the attic they found old boxes, being curious they looked inside. The contents had been lovingly preserved. They carefully unwrapped them and discovered diaries and drawings of a woman with a distinguishing birthmark like a strawberry, just below her left eye.

The name on the diaries read: 'Rose Coombe', (the same surname as Uncle Alf).

When Uncle Alf returned the pair quizzed him. He acted a little strange and shrugged his shoulders ... 'Er, there's a mystery behind her and her death ...' mumbled Alf.

They soon received an invitation to their cousin's party.

On the night of the party Alf had to send the two in a taxi to the party. On the way the taxi broke down. As the rain was pouring the driver left them and went to find help. Engulfed in darkness they waited for what seemed an age when they suddenly saw lights. The car pulled up and they caught a glimpse of a familiar face. She offered them a lift and they gladly took it.

Later on Alf and the taxi driver arrived wondering where the pair had go to. They explained and described the woman.

'That's like my Rose!'

The children gasped, 'The lady in the attic!'

Rebecca Cornes (12)
St Chad's Catholic High School, Runcorn

Phone Call From The Dead

A few years ago Jack (Julia's husband) had died in an accident at work. His arm and leg were chopped off; they replaced them with gold as he asked before he passed away. Jack was buried in their garden.

Julia was very poor and could barely afford food. Julia's idea was excellent. She went into her garden, went to Jack's grave and dug up his body. There they were, the golden arm and golden leg. She snatched them from his body, put the mud in the grave, then ran to her house. Julia decided to make jewellery from the gold. Soon the money started to come.

It was a stormy night in December, the wind was howling, the rain was beating down and the trees were swaying violently. Julia was lying in bed. The phone rang. 'Hello?' Julia answered, 'hello, is anybody there?'

'You betrayed me,' said somebody with a husky voice.

A few minutes later Julia heard somebody come in the house, all the doors were locked. She thought she was going mad. Then she saw a figure at the door. She went under the covers to try and hide, wishing and wishing it would go away but it didn't. Then the covers came up, a face she recognised came closer, it was Jack.

One week later Julia moved house. When she was driving away she noticed that in the storm the phone line had fallen onto Jack's grave …

Amy Murphy (11)
St Chad's Catholic High School, Runcorn

Ghost Boy

It was a dark and eerie night. The wind howled and the rain thumped heavily against the windows.

Little Billy crept downstairs and pointed his torch in all directions; he could see nothing but was sure something was going bump in the night. Billy lived in a huge mansion and was used to maids and butlers tottering about. But not at night.

He stumbled into the kitchen where he saw a maid sweeping the floor and washing up. 'Excuse me,' whispered Billy, 'why are you working so late, and how did you get in?' But the maid carried on working and gracefully glided across the floor, almost ghost-like. Billy helped himself to a glass of water and went back upstairs.

As he walked along the landing he decided to check on his little sister but her cot was empty. He proceeded to walk and entered his parents' bedroom. That was empty too!

He ran into all the rooms of the house, switching on the lights and screaming for his family, but no one replied.

Billy sat down in the lounge and cried for hours until morning. Suddenly the door opened and in walked a family of four. They gathered in the lounge and completely ignored Billy.

Then the young girl spoke. 'Apparently in 1851 a boy lived here and then one day mysteriously vanished only to be found dead weeks later. The boy was called Billy and he still haunts this house to this day ...'

Stephanie Darlington (12)
St Chad's Catholic High School, Runcorn

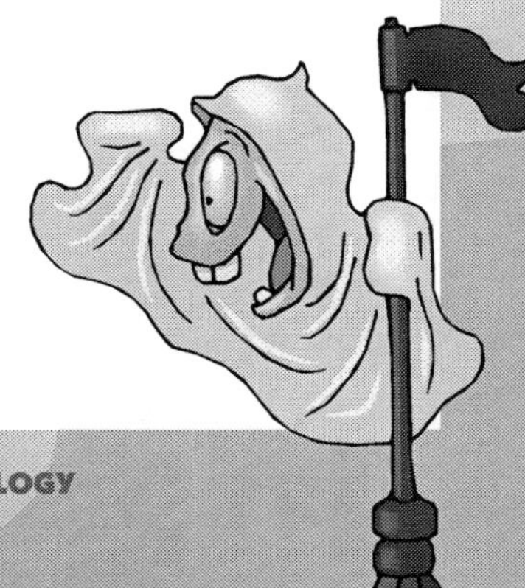

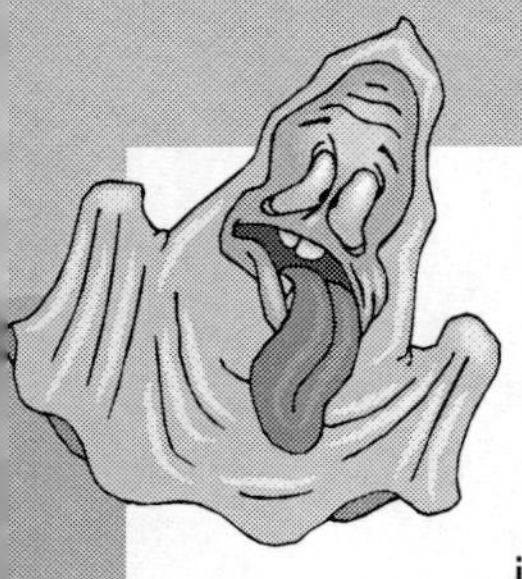

The Walking Dead

We had been travelling for hours, I was tired, fed up and hungry. It was getting late. We had enjoyed a full day at the beach but still had quite a journey to go, so my dad decided to take the next turn in search of food.

Within about five minutes we had found a little village. It looked a bit foggy and deserted but there was a suitable restaurant. When we entered there was a strong smell of lavender violets. My four-year-old brother ran to the rusted bell and rang it several times before anyone addressed us.

A woman with daunting eyes spoke wearily. 'Yes?'

We got out of there as fast as we could with our food (which didn't look very pleasant.)

The fog seemed to smother the car with its greedy arms. Suddenly from behind, vicious, bloodthirsty hands rocked the car from side to side. Frantically my dad reversed into those cannibals and told us to run to the nearby church.

Inside a vicar stood with his hood shielding his eyes. He spoke in a deep understanding voice, 'Your souls are safe now.'

My family gave a big sigh of relief, but we spoke too soon. He muttered under his breath, 'But not your bodies!' and opened the door to the walking dead!

'Noooooo!'

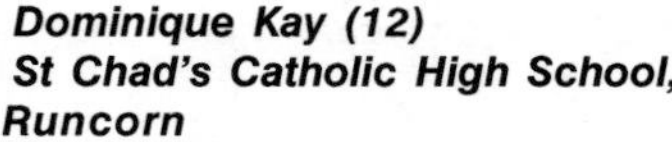

Dominique Kay (12)
St Chad's Catholic High School, Runcorn

Death Church

It was the beginning of the spring holiday for Tommy, Sarah, Marlon and Tilly so they decided to meet on top of Beverley Hills. The very next day they met up on top of the biggest hill there.

When everyone was there Tommy and Sarah decided to go to the church on the other side of the river, Marlon and Tilly went too. When they reached the door of the church they suddenly heard a man scream, 'Help!' so they went in to look, but there was no one there. Just then the wind blew and someone or something came out from nowhere and seemed to have no head, it was walking towards them.

'Argh! It's a ghost!' and they ran away.

The next day Tommy and Sarah went to see if they were dreaming it. When they got there they saw the ghost and it was looking at them then it disappeared and they never saw the ghost again.

Marie Chapman (12)
St Chad's Catholic High School, Runcorn

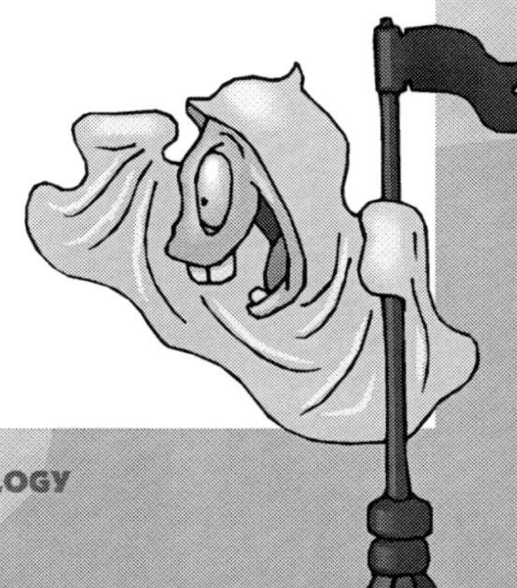

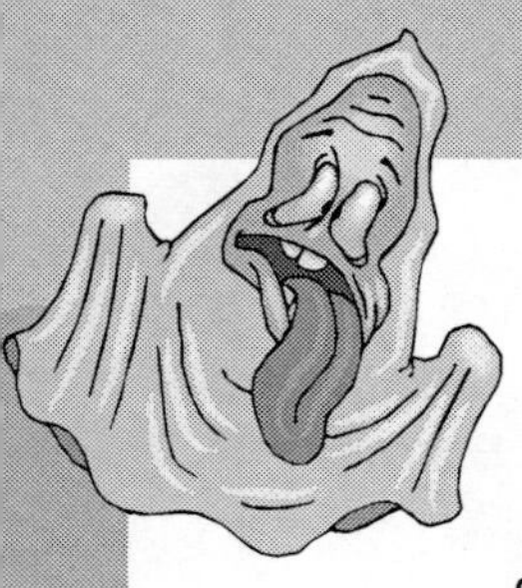

Boat Race

Even though it was a dark, cold, misty night Alicia still snuck out of the window and down the drainpipe. She ran up the road and round the corner where she met Angela, Owen and Anthony.

'You're late! What took you so long?' shouted Angela.

'Ssshhh sorry, come on let's go!' Alicia responded.

As soon as they got to the park Owen took out 4 bottles of vodka to celebrate sneaking out.

'I say we go to the lake,' said Anthony.

Angela and Owen smiled and nodded so Alicia just followed them.

'Hey look, there's a man fixing a boat, let's go and check it out,' Alicia whispered.

The boat looked small with painted pink sides and in bold, black fancy writing said, 'Mary Rose'.

With a pale white face Owen muttered, 'I thought that boat sunk 30 years ago?'

They starred in terror.

'What are you kids looking at?' yelled an old, wet, muddy man.

Alicia ran over to take a look. 'She's a beauty,' she smiled.

Angela, Owen and Anthony ran over.

'Yep but this old boat needs fixing up if I want to win that boat race today so I better get a move on!' he said and walked away.

When everyone had gone home Alicia did some research and discovered that the boat race hadn't been running for years because a boat called 'Mary Rose' had sunk and the owner had drowned, but hadn't Alicia met him?

Did I see his ghost?'

Sarah Townson (11)
St Chad's Catholic High School, Runcorn

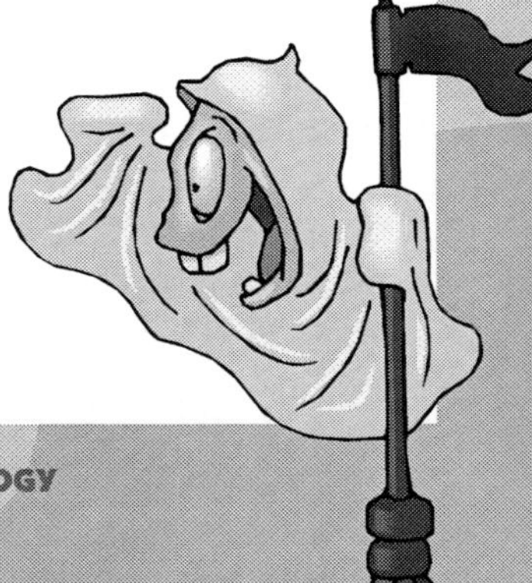

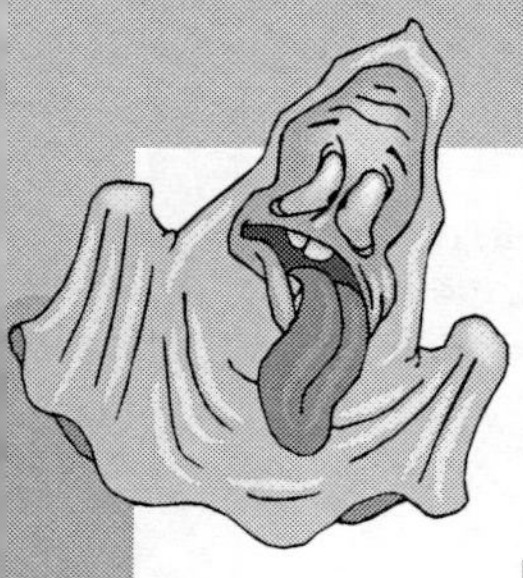

Help Us - The True Story!

About 10 years ago my nan and grandad bought an old pub called 'The Blarney Stone', it dated back to the 1600s when Oliver Cromwell lived.

We moved in, and for a few weeks everything was fine until one week strange things started to happen. First of all, the lights would start flashing and then suddenly switch off. Then all the beer kegs would switch off one by one. Then in the middle of the night we would see strange cats walking through the room. Then we would get trapped in our bedrooms and all the alarms in the house would go off. In the morning we would wake up wishing everything would be okay.

We had only been living there a month and already we were getting freaked out and we had not yet discovered everything ...

We decided to get a physic in to try and tell us something. The day of the physic's visit arrived, we invited her in and she said she could sense something but she would have to walk around. She walked around the building for about an hour, then eventually she came back to us. The expression on her face could just about tell us everything.

She slowly began to tell us everything, there were 5 or 6 spirits. But 1 of them was causing most of the trouble. It was his house, he wanted us to leave. She explained to us that he was just under 6ft. He also wore a uniform. He was killed in the war and had returned to visit his family.

Eventually things seemed to get back to normal but we would never forget ...

Laura Baxter (11)
St Chad's Catholic High School, Runcorn

Last Chat

Adam slammed his bedroom door. 'I'm 14! Don't tell me what to do!' he shouted to his mother. He turned his light off and lay down. He was thinking about running away. If he did he wouldn't get to see his grandad. Adam fell asleep faster than usual.

Adam woke in the middle of the night. On his clock it said 4.15. It was going off and his lamp was on. It was strange because his alarm could only go off on the hour. His grandad was sitting on the bed. 'Oh hello Grandad, why're you 'ere?' Adam sat up.

'Just comin' to visit you. I'm going on a bit of a holiday and won't get to see you.'

'Okay. Oh. I made this for you. The G's for Grandad.'

It was a little pendant with a thin metal chain through the top.

'Well thanks son. You promise me you won't run away?'

'How did ... ?'

'I knew. I just came to say bye. I know you're having a hard time; everyone does. It'll change. Do what you think's right. I love you. Night son.'

'Night Grandad. I love you.' Adam fell back asleep. As his grandad disappeared his lamp blew.

Adam woke the next morning; he felt peaceful. His mum came into the room. She looked as if she'd been crying.

'Your grandad died this morning. About quarter past four. I'm so sorry.' She hugged him.

Adam went to see his grandad; he was wearing the necklace.

Niamh Wenham (12)
St Chad's Catholic High School, Runcorn

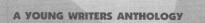

Hollywood Hotel

What's the spookiest thing that's happened to you? Well I know my spookiest happening was my night at Hollywood Hotel.

I got the tickets off my friend Lauren for my birthday. On the Saturday morning she picked me up at 10am and off we went. When we arrived at the hotel we got showed to our rooms straight away, it was a very empty place.

It was when we got into our room that the scary thing began. We were tired so we decided to have a nap. I was sleeping and I felt something shake me. I woke up and there stood at the side of my bed was a little boy. He looked ghostly and pale. All of a sudden he whispered, 'My name is Tom, get out of here, this place is dangerous, you don't want to mess with the people in here, they are all evil.'

'How did you get in here?' I shouted. 'Get out!'

I screamed and woke Lauren, but as she woke the boy disappeared. I told her all about it and we decided to leave Hollywood Hotel.

When we arrived home I told my mum about what happened, she was shocked and said, 'Nobody has slept or worked there for over 200 years because a little boy named Tom was hung there!' I screamed and began to cry and when I looked to the doorway I saw a little boy waving at me. It was Tom!

Chloe Williams (12)

St Chad's Catholic High School, Runcorn

Ghost Child

Some years ago a man bought a 'fixer-upper' house and after several hours work, decided to eat a cold supper, sleep there, and continue early the next day.

As he was lying in bed, thinking about what to do the next day he heard the wailing of a small child. Sitting up in his sleeping bag he looked across the room towards the staircase and saw the figure of a small child, hardly more than an infant, descending the stairs, crying. He called out to it, but it ignored him, and passed in front of him and went into the living room.

As he rushed into the room he saw the figure, still crying, pass through the wall next to the fireplace. The wailing sound continued, and then died away. Severely shaken, the man went to sleep, but rose early the next morning and attacked the wall where he had seen the phantom leave the room.

Imagine his surprise and horror when he found the skeleton of a young child inside the wall! He promptly called the police, who removed the skeleton, and after the necessary paperwork he and the two officers held a token funeral service at the local graveyard.

That night the man waited expectantly, but saw nothing. However, just as he was beginning to fall asleep, he heard the faint sound of laughter. No visions, just the sound of a child laughing. And from that time until today, he has heard nothing else.

Lauren Monks (12)
St Chad's Catholic High School, Runcorn

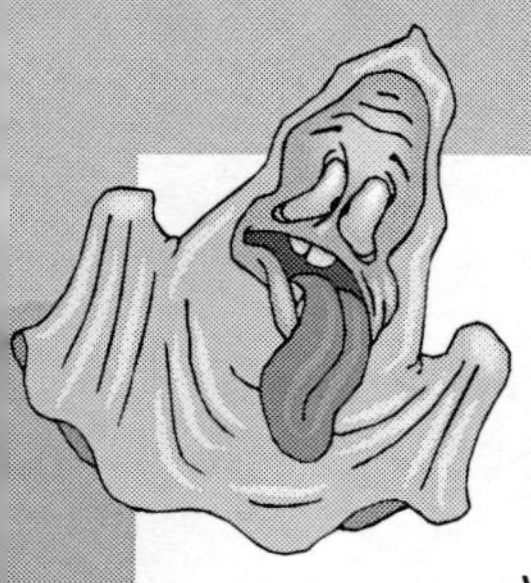

A Crack In The Brickwork

Alex walked into his new room and looked out the window at the garden. The garden was very plain and he glimpsed a shed underneath the window. *I wonder if the people before us left anything in there?* he thought and raced outside. It was empty and Alex was very disappointed, he loved finding junk that he could mess around with. Suddenly, he was lying in pain on the cold, wooden floor.

He stood up, looked around to see if he'd slipped on something and spotted a thin section of floor, which was polished. It led from the back of the shed to the door as if someone wanted to get out quickly. He opened the door and noticed something else. The handle on the inside of the door was clean and well oiled whereas the outside handle was rusty and looked untouched. He thought this was all very mysterious and intended to figure out what was going on for he liked to know exactly what was happening.

The next day he woke up with a brainwave as if his mind had been working on the problem all night. There was probably a secret door at the back of the shed. Alex squinted through the gap between the solid shed and the wall; he didn't like what he saw. There was a gigantic crack as tall as himself and almost as wide. The crack was behind the polished floor.

A figure emerged from the crack. No more Alex …

Yuning Zhou (11)
St Leonards School, Fife

Sheets

'Wake up, it's time to get up,' said my mother on a rainy Thursday morning. As usual it was time to get ready for school, but today was different. My stomach was queasy and I had pains in my left leg. Mother told me to stay home today.

'OK darling, Dad's at work and I just have to pop out to do some errands. Alright? I won't be gone long, if you need anything you know your dad's number at work and I'll have my phone switched on too. Do you want any medicine before I go?'

'If I need anything, I know where the medicine cupboard is.'

'We moved it because when we were unpacking, we didn't have enough space, so it's the ...' she started going on about where it was but I wasn't really listening. My head was aching and I felt my vision fading.

After she left, I took a nap on the couch and made myself a hot chocolate.

When I woke up, I felt twice as ill as I did before. I could hardly see anything, my head felt it was going to fall off, and my stomach was just about to deteriorate inside me. I went looking for the medicine cupboard, in the hope of finding anything that would cure the pain inside of me, even if it was only for a while. I came across a cupboard I had never seen before, it was black and blue, I was sure I had never seen it there before. I tried to open it. It was quite stiff. I finally was able to jam it open. I stood there, my mouth open, my headache getting worse as the seconds slowly passed. I just stared at these things in front of me. I don't know whether it was my eyes playing tricks on me, but I saw sheets, lots of them, stacked up to look like a dead body, with bloodstains to look like eyes and ears.

That's when I blacked out. Mother said she found me lying on the kitchen floor with a bottle of aspirin in my hand and I still had a ripped piece of white sheet in my hand!

Lynsey Underwood (12)
St Leonards School, Fife

Watch Out!

Ring! Ring! Ring! Ring! James oozed out of his bed like a slug. He wasn't looking forward to school exams. *If only I could miss them somehow,* he thought, then sniggering after a few thoughts. Reluctantly he dressed himself, and freshened up.

'I can help you,' said the voice of his brother.

'You aren't going to scare me Tommy, I can see you!'

'Are you sure … bro?'

Fear struck into his heart.

'James wait!' called a voice, the voice of Mark, their friend, known for his smile even when told his homework.

James stopped.

'Hi James, hi Tommy. Are you ready for the test today you two?'

'Yes …' they chanted in time.

'Man, you two are identical twins, you even speak the same way, and … you're both so white, did you catch the fever?' questioned Mark.

The twins laughed, smiled and laughed. Mark's smile faded away.

'Now, today I'm sure you all know there is an exam. Now remember to answer in full sentences …' the teacher droned.

'James, Tommy, Mark, get out a pencil and eraser.'

'Why? We're not doing the test,' they spoke, like robots, programmed in the same way.

'Whatever do you me …'

The class stood up in shock as the teacher fell to the ground, with a chilling thud. *Whoosh!* The wind blew hard. Outside was the most dreaded thing you could ever see. The three boys laughed, smiled and laughed again.

Kenneth Reid (12)
St Leonards School, Fife

Stranglers Wood

It was that time of year again, when the snowdrops would appear and completely cover the ground of Stranglers Wood. This was not the only thing that would appear, something much more than sweet-scented flowers, something else would also make an appearance.

Jamie and his dog, Scooby, often played in the wood and until recently, had no idea of why it had been renamed from Rosemary Wood to the strange Stranglers Wood, it was during one of their walks that he understood why.

Scooby ran ahead but failed to return, after ten minutes Jamie went off the path to look for him. He found him scratching at the bark of a yew tree. Scooby looked beyond Jamie and started to bark frantically at something. When Jamie looked round he saw white shadows coming towards them. Turning rapidly he tripped over Scooby and fell against the yew tree knocking himself out. He was awakened by Scooby licking his face. Looking up he saw that Scooby had something in his mouth, it was a red scarf.

On returning home Jamie told the story to his mother and that was when the tale unfolded of Stranglers Wood. Four years ago three teenage girls had gone missing after a day in the woods and apparently appeared at the same yew tree every year at the same time as the snowdrops, perhaps they were hoping someone would find the red scarf and this would lead to their killer being caught.

Connor Blackburn (13)
St Leonards School, Fife

The Ghosts Of The Knights Of Camelot

Jack's parents were in debt, so Jack looked in the newspaper for a job and saw an advert saying, 'Boy needed for experiments'. Jack rushed to the building and a man told him he would be testing a time machine. The man put him back ten years after the deaths of the knights of Camelot.

Jack was dumped in the great hall and saw in the distance a giant door with the words 'The Round Table' carved into the door. Jack looked through the keyhole and saw in the very thirteen chairs the ghosts of the knights of The Round Table and King Arthur, there was one spare chair, the chair of Sir Lancelot.

Jack went in and the ghosts were plotting to stop him haunting and send Lancelot to the Underworld. Arthur said, 'If we had one more knight we could have our unstoppable team once more.' That was when they realised that Jack was standing before them, so they asked Jack to take Lancelot's place at The Round Table.

'What's in it for me?' said Jack.

King Arthur said, 'I will give you many riches.'

Jack took the place of Lancelot and they sent Lancelot to the Underworld with a blow from each knight, then a final blow from King Arthur with his sword Excalibur.

Jack received his riches and was never in debt again.

Matthew Pugh (10)
St Mary's Bryanston Square CE Primary School, London

Death Is But A Dream

I walked slowly towards the park bench, pausing now and then, rubbing my palms against my jeans. It was dark. I sat on the grimy bench. I saw the full moon between the leaves of the trees, red leaves. Rain started falling and dripped off them. It looked to me like blood running down curled, clammy hands.

I could not believe what I had seen. My sister, Coral, lying on the floor, her eyes shiny. I was an expert at reviving people at the hospital. I could tell from a distance that she was not dead. I ran to her and switched on every light in the kitchen. I sat down on the floor next to her, got out my first-aid kit and fixed an air pack to her mouth. It filled and drained slowly. I gasped with relief.

I saw someone had laid a rose on her chest and another had cut her throat. She must have put up a fight against a strong person because she had a black eye, cut lips and her new jeans were ripped.

I tore my eyes away from her, got out my mobile and called 999, like you always should in a big emergency. I asked for the ambulance and the police. Then I put the phone down.

Out of the corner of my eye I could see muddy footprints and yellow eyes watching ... waiting.

I woke up ... *just a dream* ... I thought.

India Hill (9)
St Mary's Bryanston Square CE Primary School, London

My Story

It was a dark, cold night and there was no one to be seen, the trees waved in the thick black air. Tommy was out on his bike unaware of who he was with, the white ghost. Tommy sped down the street as the white ghost followed his purple gleaming bike. The tyres shrieked as the bike turned the corner. All of a sudden the bike stopped, the tyre had burst, Tommy didn't know what to do, he was surrounded by voices, he heard whispers in the moonlight. Tommy fell to the ground, the ghost was above him, the voices had stopped, there was now something much scarier, a flock of white ghosts.

Tommy got up and ran down the street as fast as he could. His legs were getting heavy, his mouth was dry, he was exhausted. But no one was there to give him water and there was not an athlete willing to carry him home to his bed, he was all alone.

Tommy turned around and there was a massive crowd of walking piranhas. Tommy ran like mad as the piranhas chomped the air behind him.

Tommy was petrified; the voices came back, the whispers, Tommy's head spun like the propeller on a helicopter. Tommy was shaking.

Tommy woke up, he was in hospital. He could see faces, familiar faces, his mum, his dad, his friends.

'It's alright now you're safe in hospital, you just had a nasty fall.'

Amelia Dimoldenberg (11)
St Mary's Bryanston Square CE Primary School, London

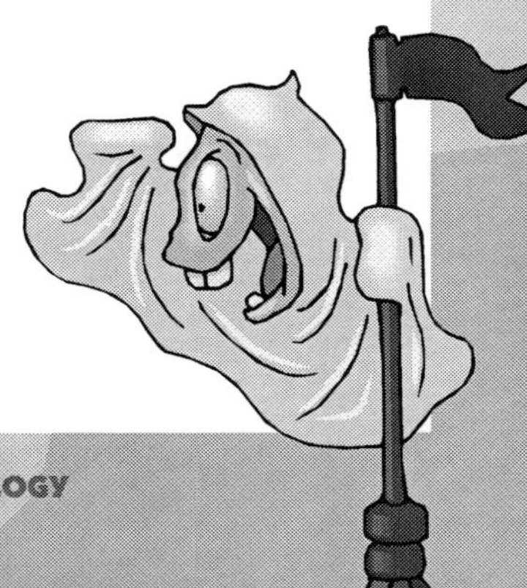

Don't Walk Through The Cemetery!

Have you ever wondered how ghosts come into Hallowe'en? Well, now you're going to find out, whether you like it or not!

'Lisa are you coming?' called Jennifer.

'Hold your horses,' answered Lisa.

Jennifer and Lisa are both 12 years old, but Jennifer, Jenny, for short, always acted older.

They were going to their best friend's Hallowe'en party. Jenny as a witch, Lisa as a ghost, she looked like one too!

'Here I am!' cried Lisa.

'Finally! Bye Mum!' called Jenny.

'By love!' Mum called.

They set out into the night, before long they were at the party. And it was ... *rubbish!*

The music was rubbish, the food was rubbish and most importantly the *boys* were rubbish!

'I'm out of here, this party is the pits,' moaned Jenny.

'No, no stay please, it might get better,' begged Lisa.

'Whatever, it's irritating having *you* as a twin. I don't care what you do, I'm going!'

Jenny set off home but had a strange feeling she was being followed. She turned around expecting to see Lisa but there was nothing there, or was there? What was that glow?

'Revenge,' said a hoarse whisper.

Scared, Jenny began to run, the glow followed her. She ran through a cemetery, she stumbled and fell.

'Revenge, revenge,' said the voice.

Quickly Jenny turned around to see a knife stabbing her in the heart.

The same thing happens every year. No one ever found the bodies. Or have they?

Nicole Jones (11)
St Teresa's Catholic Junior School, Liverpool

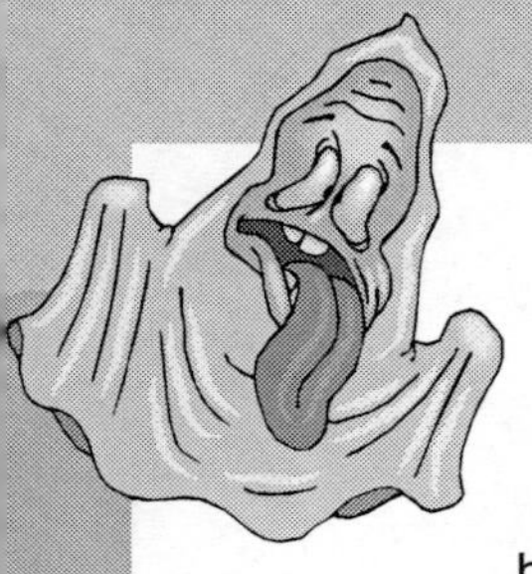

Ghostly Terror

One gloomy night Ryan was playing out with his mates, they decided to go to McDonald's. Ryan lived the furthest away, so on their way back he was the last to go home. On his way he could feel breath down the back of his neck, he turned round but no one was there. What was following him wasn't ordinary, it wasn't a human being … it was a ghost!

The ghost followed Ryan into the house, up the stairs and into his room. The ghost waited until Ryan was asleep. Then he went downstairs into the kitchen and picked up a butcher's knife. The ghost took it upstairs and dropped it on his head. *Slice,* it went right through his head. The ghost left the house.

28 years later the house became empty.

A year after that the Jones' moved in.

They were only there for 3 weeks when Jamie started getting suspicious. He was hearing creaks, bangs and things were moving around.

One night Jamie sat on his bed, the wardrobe was creaking, with curiosity he flung open the door. Jamie with shock and horror fainted and collapsed to the floor. His mum heard the thump and ran up the stairs. She saw Jamie lying on the floor as white as a ghost. With the sighting of this she had a heart attack and also died.

The police thought it was murder, but only you and I know what really happened.

The end - or is it … ?

Jamie Jones (11)
St Teresa's Catholic Junior School, Liverpool

The Haunted Cabin

The winds howled and rain poured down, but still Jordan ran and ran, the more she ran the faster the footsteps behind her became. She could run no more, so she decided to stop. In the corner of her eye she saw a cabin. It was very old and rotten.

She walked over and went in. She stopped, she had heard someone or something. Jordan presumed it was the trees whistling in the background. So Jordan carried on, it was someone talking to another person.

Jordan was walking and she knocked into a girl. Jordan asked if she was the person talking.

The girl said, 'Yes.'

'Who were you talking to?' asked Jordan.

'Myself,' answered the girl.

'What is your name?' asked Jordan.

'Sarah,' said the girl.

'How old are you?' asked Jordan.

'Ten,' said Sarah.

'I am ten and my name is Jordan,' said Jordan.

Jordan and Sarah were walking around with each other and Jordan found a mirror, when Sarah was standing next to her there was no reflection of Sarah in the mirror.

Jordan looked at her and screamed, she ran to the door and when she opened the door she knocked into a man. The man said to Jordan, 'I was the person who was running after you to tell you not to go into the cabin because it's haunted.' He took her safely home and she never went into the woods again.

Stephanie Macilwee (9)
St Teresa's Catholic Junior School, Liverpool

The Cemetery!

One dark night, Joe and his friends were running about around the cemetery pretending that the Grey Lady was behind them.

'Argh!' screamed Sarah.

'Really funny Sarah,' said Catherine. So they all stopped for a rest.

'I don't know why you say that because the Grey Lady could be real.'

'Come off it Joe!' said Thomas.

'Well you won't be saying that when you see her.'

'See who?' said a voice coming from behind them. They all looked round to see.

'Run!' they all said. They ran as fast as they could huffing and puffing all the way home.

When Joe got home he said, 'Mum?'

'What Joe?' said his mum.

'I saw a ghost.'

'Don't be saying that!' said his mum.

'But …'

'No buts, just get your pyjamas on, get a wash, brush your teeth and go to sleep.'

After Joe had done that he got into bed but he couldn't sleep. All night Joe was thinking about her.

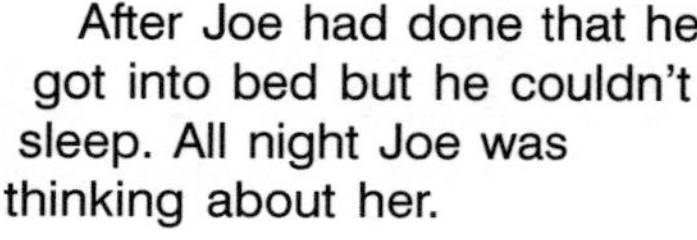

The next day Joe's mum went to a priest to ask if he could bless the house. He did. After that Joe did not see any ghosts at all. But he was still having problems outside of his house. He was getting followed by a ghost. The ghost that was following him had a plan, a plan on killing him. On some photographs Joe's parents saw white and grey around him.

Then Joe was found dead in the cemetery ...

Shannon Boswell (9)
St Teresa's Catholic Junior School, Liverpool

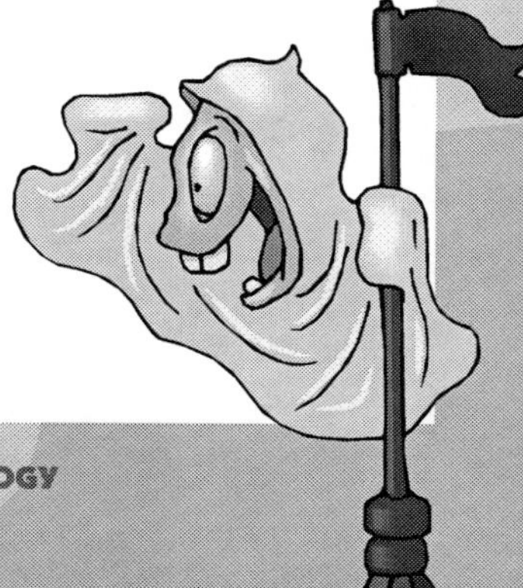

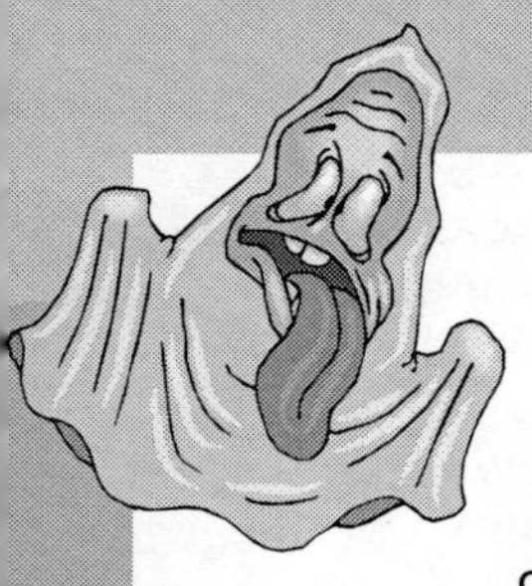

The Hand

It was late at night and Chloe was just going to bed, when she heard a knock at the door. She ignored it, then she heard it again, so she got out of bed and opened the door. There wasn't anyone there, but what she didn't know was a little hand crawled in, so she went back up to bed. Then she heard the TV.

She thought it was her brother, then she realised her brother was in bed and it couldn't have been her mum or dad because they'd died in a car crash. So she went down but there was nobody there so she went back up, then she heard the taps running.

Now she was getting scared. Then she heard *tap, tap* on the tiles, now she heard *tap, tap* on the wooden floor. She heard squeaky floorboards go then she heard the door opening. Something was coming up the stairs. Then it went in her brother's room, she shouted, 'Billy!'

He couldn't hear because he must have been in a deep sleep so she woke him up and told him something was in his room. They looked round the room but could not find it. So they looked in her room, her brother found it and that was the end of him because Billy was eaten by the hand!

Chloe moved out of the house, but did she escape the hand?

Lauren Broomfield (9)
St Teresa's Catholic Junior School, Liverpool

Peter Malone

It all started back in the 1800s when Peter Malone was sitting in his cottage alone. Later that night a mysterious figure opened the front door with a razor-sharp axe, it was freezing cold and windy. It went into the living room and with a swing of the axe Peter Malone was on the floor, dead ...

The house lay empty for years.

204 years later, Roy and Margaret Smith moved into that same cottage. Later that night the Smiths were enjoying Saturday night TV when suddenly the TV turned off. They went over to investigate but the power was still on. Roy and Margaret ignored the TV incident and went to put some of their luggage in the attic.

As they were putting some away they started to get a bit scared because it was very dark and the light switch was nowhere to be seen. Then there was lots of banging, next they could hear a loud voice saying, 'Get out of my house!'

Roy and Margaret ran downstairs trying to get out of the house but the door was completely locked.

The voice started chanting, 'I'm Peter Malone, I will kill you, I'm Peter Malone, kill.'

Suddenly lots of ghosts started coming through the wall with Peter Malone in front.

Suddenly a massive ghost with a special axe, which can kill ghosts, started killing the ghosts, when he had killed them all, he vanished. Roy and Margaret just ran away and never returned.

Mark Seddon (9)
St Teresa's Catholic Junior School, Liverpool

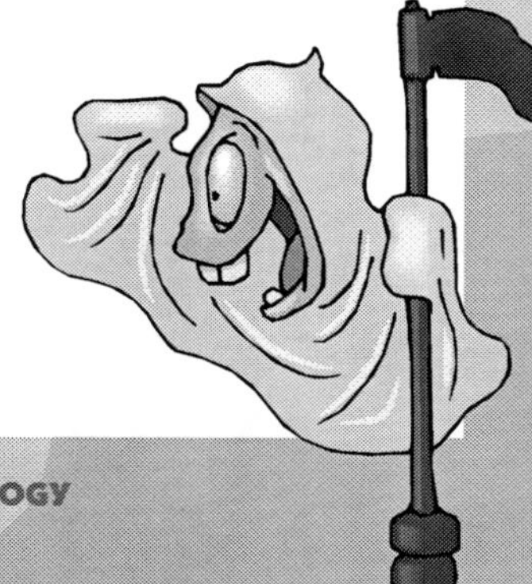

The Master's Hand

A note came floating through the window so I went to the forest as the note said to. A tree started burning and collapsed, I ran from the flames into the cave. A man approached and he reached out, his hand glowed and burned. When his hand made contact with my forehead, it was scarred and scolded.

The legacy is complete ...

I wrote the note of the legacy today. I had an eye on the boy for a while. So I followed it through. I met him in the same cave as me and my master; I performed a sacrifice as I fell to the ground.

The legacy is complete ...

Mike Kent (11)
The Cotswold School, Bourton-on-the-Water

Ghost Story

It was Wednesday the 3rd of December 1993 when something strange and mysterious happened, I can't remember much because I was mainly unconscious but I do remember it vaguely. Here is the story ...

It was a windy night and all the streets were bare like a deserted village, like no one ever lived there. It was like all the people had had their souls drained along with their emotions. I thought to myself, *this is London, the capital of England. Why are there no children running around or animals?* There was no noise, everything was silent ...

Then suddenly I felt cold air on the back of my neck like someone was breathing on my neck, which sent a shiver down my spine. I turned round but there was nothing but the breeze in the air. Then a rustling noise came from a bush. Out came a blackbird that was as black as the sky. It flew up to the bright moon and turned its head and I could have sworn it winked at me. It then swerved and landed on the wall next to me before vanishing. It left a gold eagle necklace which was hanging around its neck. And from this day on I have never seen the blackbird ever. And to this day it remains a mystery ...

Charlotte West (12)
The Cotswold School, Bourton-on-the-Water

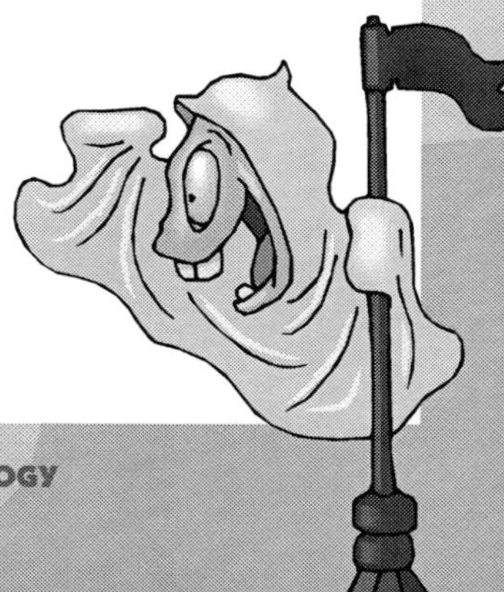

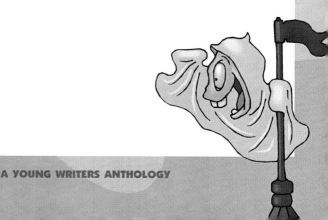

Scottish Ghosts

One dark night, windy, cold and with an almighty thunderstorm, Angus decided to lock the castle up and retire to bed early as the night before he was woken early by a small boat crashing into the rocks below his window. When he investigated it he found no bodies but a trail of blood leading to the grounds of the castle.

Crash! Bang! went the cups and plates in the kitchen.

Angus woke up startled, he raced towards the noise. When he got there, nothing! He searched other rooms and found nothing.

This went on for days and days, with not an idea of what was happening and making the noises.

Angus decided to sit in one of the rooms downstairs to see if he could find out what the noises were.

Midnight, 1am, 2am, 3am, nothing but then a strange smell, everything was freezing, plates, pot, pans went flying across the room. Knives just missed his head, he ran and ran, chairs, books came flying towards him wherever he went. Then it suddenly stopped.

It was daylight, sunny but cold. Angus awoke in his bed, safe and sound for one thing he could see, a man walking in the hallway, dressed in water-damaged, rotting clothes, he approached him.

'Hey who are you?'

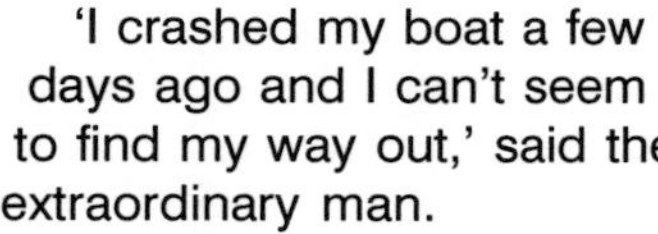

'I crashed my boat a few days ago and I can't seem to find my way out,' said the extraordinary man.

They both walked past a very large mirror, Angus was shaken and scared the stranger had *no* reflection and a large open injury on the back of his head.

'*A ghost*,' screamed Angus. Angus followed him glancing in the mirror as he passed. 'No! No! my reflection, it's gone,' said a very worried Angus.

'Oh,' said the stranger, 'didn't you realise dead people don't have reflections.'

'But ... but ...'

'Yes,' said the stranger, 'that night I crashed my boat, I shot you to keep you quiet, you're dead also,' said the stranger.

'No! No!' Angus cried ...

Gemma Mortiboys (12)
The Cotswold School, Bourton-on-the-Water

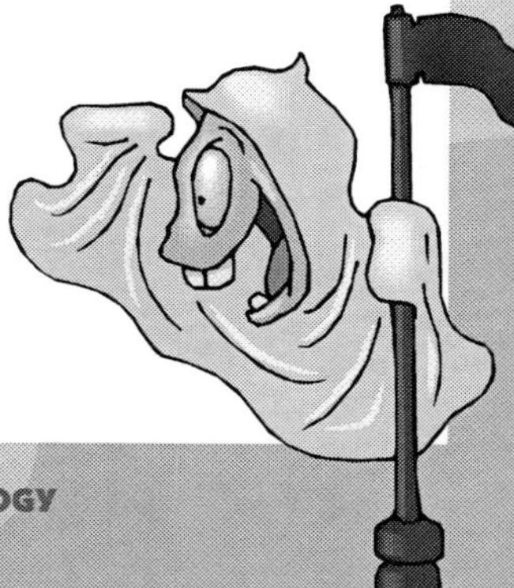

The Graveyard Chase

It was Friday the 13th and Chrissie was getting ready to go out for a night on the town. While she was getting ready she heard a knock at the door.

'Who is it?'

There was no answer. She shouted again. There was still no answer.

She walked towards the door. The floorboards were creaking. She felt a cold shiver down the back of her spine. The hairs on the back of her neck stood up.

She started shouting, 'Hello?' She paused. 'Hello?' Nothing.

Then there was another knock but it was claws on the window. The door was falling, it was collapsing, the door was going to fall on the vase her mum gave her before she passed away, her mum had died about 4 months ago. Chrissie ran to get it, but it was too late, the vase got smashed.

There was thick red blood oozing on the carpet. There was a ball of fog outside. There was something out there and it wasn't human, it was some kind of monster, what is it going to do to me?

A gust of wind shot past her, it had disappeared. *What if it came back?* she thought. I know someone died in this house but they weren't a monster, were they?

I can't stay in this house, I have to go somewhere where that thing won't find me! The graveyard, Chrissie ran over there as fast as she could ...

Sasha McPhilimey (12)
The Cotswold School, Bourton-on-the-Water

The Horror Love Story

There was a woman who lived alone, nobody to talk to, nobody to tell the secret of never being loved ...

Nobody knew her name as she had no friends or family, her dream was to be loved. The lady lived in a nice cottage in the country but still had no friends. She did have a secret obsession, and that was Antonio Denero. He was the hottest man alive but yet he was unloved just like the lady in the cottage.

One day Antonio was drawn to the little cottage and he saw the lady, and felt like someone was tying a knot in his stomach. So he knocked on the door and asked the lady to dinner, but only if she cooked at her house.

The big date came. The lady made dinner and was ready to eat but death was upon that night. There was only one person who knew who was killed and why she was alone ...

Kirstie Smith (12)
The Cotswold School, Bourton-on-the-Water

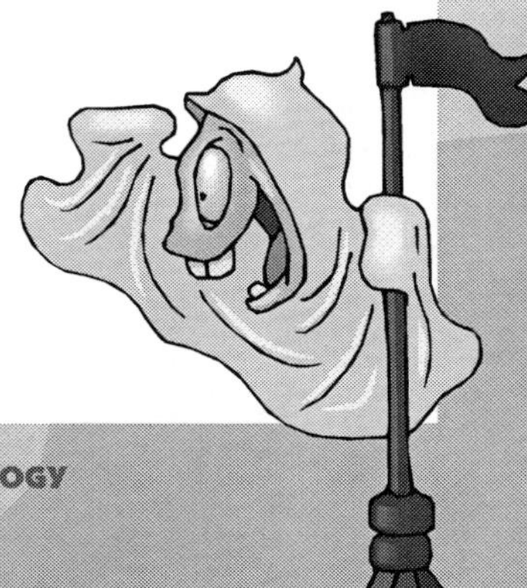

The Old Haunted Mansion

It was a cold, wintry night - so cold that the air seemed to bite. The new family that was moving in to the old, haunted, derelict mansion pulled up outside the gate in their posh car, with the removal van close behind.

They slowly staggered out of the car, stood and looked. The family firmly opened the creaky gate and followed each other up the path one by one. As they reached the front door, the door slowly creaked open.

The family walked inside and the door soon slammed shut behind them. They split up and went to a room. The mother went to the kitchen, the father went to the cellar and the two kids stayed together and went to the bedroom.

The mother pushed open the door and entered the kitchen. 'Argh!' she screamed.

She saw words being written on the wall by blood and a sharp, pointy dagger was floating in the air.

On the wall the words said, 'This mansion is haunted! Beware!'

The father came rushing in. 'What's the matter?' he said.

'Look at the wall.'

'Oh my God!' said Father.

The family walked out of the kitchen to get their luggage from the car, they went to open the door, it wouldn't open ...

Emma Stewart (12)
The Cotswold School, Bourton-on-the-Water

The Silent Scream

The creaking doors, Catherine was scared, she felt a whispering, creepy thing following her. It was coming up behind her.

Catherine always woke up at 12pm. She got quite freaked out about it one night. She went downstairs to get a drink. When she was walking down the stairs someone said, 'It is only me ...'

Catherine was really petrified. It was a ghost! She ran but he grabbed her, she screamed but no one could hear her. She went back to bed with lots of strange questions in her head. When she woke up in the morning, she just thought it was a dream but oh no, it wasn't a dream as exactly the same thing happened the next night.

Catherine saw the ghost, she saw its face. Its face was old and wrinkly and the ghost had blue eyes, one earring and a very big nose. It said, 'My name is Frank.' It then grabbed Catherine and smacked her over the head. She let out a great big scream but again nobody could see it because it was under her long brown, silky hair.

She also was wondering why her head didn't bleed, it was so strange that nobody knew anything or heard anything. She would never go downstairs again in her life!

Becky Berry (13)
The Cotswold School, Bourton-on-the-Water

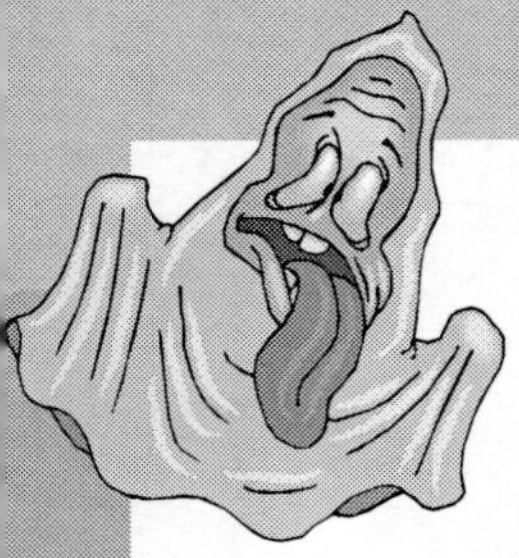

Echoed Screams

Her screams echoed as the enormous buffalo came racing towards her. She was having a nice slow walk at midday in the dark and spooky woods. Outside it was nice and sunny but as soon as you stood deep into the woods ...

Bang! The lights went off! It was here, first time in the spooky woods. No one else around except animals, trees that wailed as the wind blew.

Suddenly she heard a bashing noise come from behind her. Petrified she turned and, 'Argh ...' It was there, the bashing noise, she knew what it was now. But she wished she didn't, she saw the shadow come from behind her. She ran and the word, 'Er,' came from her horrified, stuttering mouth ...

Hannah Berry (13)
The Cotswold School, Bourton-on-the-Water

The Ghost Mansion

She walked slowly up the bumpy, uneven road. She heard footsteps in the wind, was it her or was it real? She was almost there.

The moon was shining bright in the dark, plain sky. She approached the big wooden door. She knocked ...

Suddenly the door opened slowly and creakily. She stepped inside. The door closed behind her, she ran back to the door. It was locked. There was no escape ...

She went forwards into the cobwebby room. Footsteps went across the floor in front of her, leaving footprints in the dust. What was it? Her tummy started to churn. She walked up the stairs and walked into a room. There lying on a bed was a woman lying in her own blood. The blood and the woman were still warm ...

Isabel Harper (11)
The Cotswold School, Bourton-on-the-Water

Ghosts From The Cinema

It was Saturday morning and 11-year-old Jack was still in bed, but not for long.

'Jack!' yelled his younger brother, Sam. 'Come and watch me open my presents! Please!'

'Go away *nooow*!' Jack replied.

'Mum said you've got to come *nooow*!'

'I don't *caaare*!'

'You can't play with my presents then!' Sam yelled right into Jack's ear. And with that Jack jumped out of bed, almost onto Sam and chased him down the stairs. It was Sam's 6th birthday, you see. And every birthday he went to the cinema, Jack's nightmare.

All of Sam's presents had finally been opened and they were getting ready to go to the ... cinema! Jack tried explaining to his mum that he was ill and couldn't go but she wasn't fooled. They got in the car and drove to the cinema. They soon arrived, got their tickets and found their seats. They were watching 'The Haunted Mansion' about lots of creepy ghost and ghouls in a huge house. Jack hated watching ghost films because he didn't believe in ghosts.

The following week was Jack's 12th birthday and he had chosen to go to visit an old castle. They had arrived at the castle and had entered through the big wooden door. They walked slowly along the hallway, the place seemed abandoned. Jack stood still, the hairs on the back of his neck suddenly stood on end. Mum, Dad and Sam had seemed to have disappeared.

Jack felt a tap on his shoulder ...

Madeleine Pegrum (12)
The Cotswold School, Bourton-on-the-Water

A Lover's Death Wish

Meeting down the valley with another man, was a betrayal against the will of my boyfriend. As the mysterious stranger appeared an unnoticed shadow followed close behind. It was my boyfriend! I was mortified, no, I was paralysed as a glance of daggers came towards me from my loving boyfriend. 'Shocked to see me? Don't worry Mandy I know you're seeing someone else.'

I didn't dare to deny it.

'Shall we walk home?'

With a nervous look on my face I replied with a meek yes.

As we walked home I was trembling, what would he do? He acted calm, he smiled as people passed. As I got home the door was open, I saw a sharp butcher's knife with an enlightening blade. I sat down being very cautious about what I was doing. I saw him pick up the knife, I started to scream as he came towards me. 'What are you doing with that?' I stammered. 'Argh.'

The knife was sliced right through me. I could hear the evil bellow of his voice. The blood was draining my weak body leaving me weaker. The stained T-shirt was absorbing blood and drying my veins. I could feel my heart slowing down getting quieter and quieter. My eyes began to get heavier as I staggered up the steps to the gates of death for eternity.

Kelly Welch (12)
The Cotswold School, Bourton-on-the-Water

Freaky Sleepover

Hi, my name's Jess but you can call me Midget, that's what everybody calls me at school. I live here at The Sands in Shipton-under-Wychwood with my mum, dad, 6-year-old brother, 3-year-old sister and 2-day-old sister.

I'm about to tell you about the time I had one of the biggest scares in my life, but before I do, if you don't like scary stories put the book down now.

It all started on Friday 6th March after school when I was walking with my best friend, Bryony. She was coming to sleepover at my house. We were just walking out the school gates when suddenly a shadow appeared in front of us.

'Whoa, what was that?' screamed Bryony as she jumped backwards at the same time.

'I don't know … but whatever it was I bet it's haunting one of us.'

It was 5pm and we were just walking through the door at my house when suddenly we saw the shadow again and it tripped Bryony over. 'Ow … it's the shadow again … I think it's haunting me,' stuttered Bryony.

'Are you OK? Does your head hurt?' I asked in a suspicious way.

'No … I feel really sick.' She wobbled around as she tried to get up.

'Right, let's get you inside, you can have some Disprin and a drink,' I said whilst looking around outside.

It was now 9pm and were just getting into our pyjamas when we heard a *thud!* at the window. I went over to the window and opened the curtains and the window.

The shadow jumped in without me noticing it and as I turned around it punched me in my left eye and again I fell to the floor and as I hit the floor there was a big bang.

My mum and dad ran upstairs to see what was going on. They opened the door. As they stepped into the room all they saw was Bryony kneeling by me crying. They rushed towards me. My mum screamed and as she did I started to wake up. My eyes fluttered and as I gradually started to move my mum knelt down beside me and kissed me all over. I sat up and as I did I shouted, 'Look, it's the shadow over there, no over there,' and then I fainted.

My dad got up and ran round the room trying to catch the shadow.

'Come here you little sh … you little sh … shadow.' He jumped and launched himself onto the shadow. 'I've got him!' bellowed Dad.

The shadow was wriggling all over the place and as it did it soon became clear who it was …

'Gemma,' me and Bryony said together in a confused voice. 'What on earth are you doing under well, what looks like an invisible cloak or cape or something.'

'I was trying to scare you, because you kept taking Bryony away from me today,' she said in an annoyed and grumpy voice.

'What … she's sleeping at my house tonight.'

'Oh … sorry … I thought …'

'It doesn't matter Gem just don't do it again.'

'No please don't I almost had a heart attack trying to catch you,' said Dad all red in the face and out of breath.

We all laughed.

So there you have it, that was the biggest scare of my life, I hope you enjoyed it!

Jessica Smith (12)
The Cotswold School, Bourton-on-the-Water

The Haunted Castle

The young princess was walking home late one night. It was very cold and the wind was whistling through the trees. She saw a castle that she had never noticed before. She walked towards it and was sure she heard screaming. The door was open so she crept in. She went up the creaking staircase. The castle felt creepy and smelt damp. The princess was feeling scared and frightened of what she might find.

The screams were coming from the bedroom at the back of the castle. She tripped on one of the broken floorboards and tore her long, flowing dress. As she got up, the bedroom door flung open and she was surrounded by thousands of bats. They flew around her making her dizzy.

She looked towards the window, the light from the moon shone in. She saw a ghost of a child come towards her. All she could think of was how to get out of there. She ran as fast as she could, never looking back.

Rebecca Webley (13)
The Cotswold School, Bourton-on-the-Water

The Ghost That Haunted The Boys!

'Shut up dorky!' yelled the boy, he was punching a boy who was a lot younger than him, and the boy managed to get away and ran off home.

All three boys were thirteen years old, their names were Brian, John and Mike. There was this boy who was called Alex. He was only eight and a half and they liked to pick on him.

One day when Brian was on his own he was hanging around his haunted house, he went back home and told John and Mike. Then they all went over to the haunted house. They were standing outside the door, when Mike pushed open the door there came an eerie sound from the door. All three walked in together they went upstairs first, they heard a little creaking that kept on going.

Suddenly, 'Argh!' They all went screaming down the stairs and outside, the thing which made them scream was a man who had been hung by a piece of rope. The boys stopped picking on Alex. But who knows what the creaking was?

Kirby Clayton (12)
The Cotswold School, Bourton-on-the-Water

The Haunted House

It was a dull day and Scott was moving into his new house. He didn't want to move. The house was tall and thin with trees each side. His friends said houses that are tall are haunted but Scott didn't believe them.

Scott was quite tall with blond hair, blue eyes and everybody fancied him. He went up to his room. His dad got the telly and sofa out of the van and went and watched the football with a beer in one hand and a fag in the other, and left the removal people to unload the things.

Scott went up to his room and started to unpack. Then he heard this howling noise. He thought it was his dad shouting because they had scored, but then he heard it again. He went to look around and saw this shadow. He was fat with green glowing eyes or that's what he thought they were. He got scared then looked around and it was gone ...

That night Scott was woken up by the branches screeching on the window. Everybody was asleep. Just then he heard the same noise just as before but after he heard knocking on the walls. He got a torch and looked around. There it was again in the same place. The shadow started to move towards him. He gasped and let out a big scream. His dad came but Scott was gone ...

The next day Scott woke up. Was it a dream or was it really a shadow?

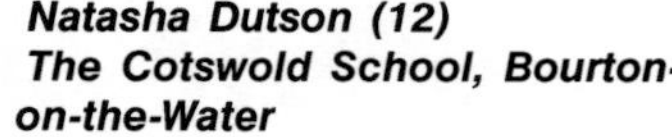

Natasha Dutson (12)
The Cotswold School, Bourton-on-the-Water

Wolf Kill

Panting, screaming. *Mustn't go back,* that's all that went through my head that night.

I was lost in the Midnight Forest. I had climbed a tree shouting, screaming, trying to get my father to hear me. Then there he was under that tree I was sitting in. I screamed. He heard me, I couldn't figure why he didn't look up at me.

The wolf must have heard me as well, it came chasing. Then there was my father, face to face with that bloodthirsty wolf. *Don't hurt him.* The wolf pounced, my father just dodged out of the way. I was very worried about my father. Then, then the dreadful thing happened.

The wolf was circling my father, I was praying, 'Don't take my father's life away.'

The wolf pounced ...

Joanne Drinkwater (11)
The Cotswold School, Bourton-on-the-Water

The Mad Vicar

It all started in the morning of the 5th of December in a small village called Corby Glen. It was a Sunday, I was walking through the village to the church. The church was the other end of the village; we did not have a car. Everyone we needed was in the village.

We got in the church and heard a funny noise. We were the first ones there and the vicar was always late.

'I know you're there, come here people of the dead and we will kill everyone and we will rule the world, *ha, ha, ha!'*

I could just make out what this person was saying, 'That is the vicar's voice,' I said. 'Vicar is that you?'

'Yes it is me. I'm just praying,' he said.

After church I went to Jim's house (my friend). I had to go through the cemetery. I have no fear of the cemetery. Jim's house is a tip. His family doesn't put anything away but Jim's such a good friend. 'I better go home now it's getting dark,' I said after a while.

'Stay for tea,' he said.

'OK,' I replied.

After tea I went home with Jim but we only got to the cemetery. I stopped. It was the vicar he was calling out, 'People of the dead come to the surface, I will give you land in exchange for helping me take over the world. Now rise! It's your last chance.'

Bang!

'Where am I?' I called out. It looked like Hell. I was in a cage. The cage was huge. It held everyone in the world. *'Help!'* I cried out. I thought of an idea how to get the world back to normal.

I found Mum and Dad and told them my plan. It was to kill the vicar and the dead would go back underground where we could control them. To get out of the cage we bent the bars. We managed to kill the vicar, we strangled him and the dead went back underground with him and the world returned to normal.

After a while we got a new vicar and no one ever spoke of it again, but I will never forget it.

Alex Jeffries (11)
The Cotswold School, Bourton-on-the-Water

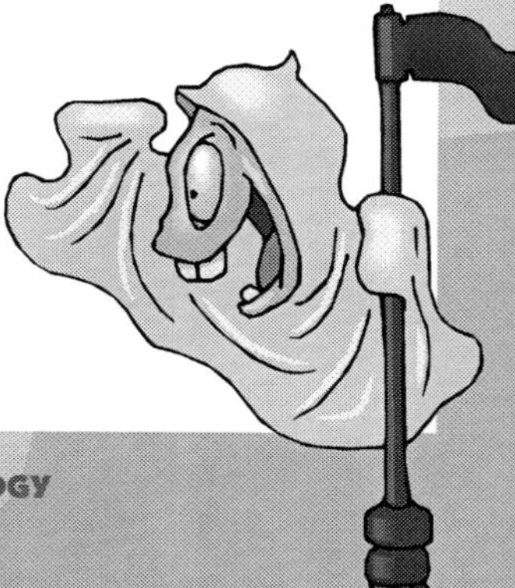

You Can Run But You Can't Hide

In 1913 a 28-year-old woman was slaughtered by her husband. After 30 years in Hell the woman rose up and started to lash at the chains with one of the 13 knives.

Her destiny was to kill her husband the way he'd killed her. The woman ran to her old house and knocked on the door. When a man answered the door the woman grabbed him and asked where her husband was, his name was Josh. The man said, 'East end of the town, the name of the house is Green Villa.' So the woman ran down the street. When she got to Green Villa she knocked on the door, then she slit her own wrists.

A man answered the door dripping with blood, there was no one there so he went back inside and the woman had opened the window. She grabbed him and said, 'Are you Josh?'

The man Peters said, 'Why do you want to know?'

'Because I am your wife, Hannah Peters.'

The man answered, 'Yes.'

So Hannah knocked him out and took him to where he had stabbed her 13 times with 13 different knives. She chained him up and put every knife that he stabbed her with in the same places he'd stabbed her. Then she dissolved into ash.

If you go to Green Villa you can still see blood on the door and walls.

Joseph Dodds (12)
The Cotswold School, Bourton-on-the-Water

Phantom Manor

Charlie is an ordinary guy who works as a staff manager in a game shop. He does his usual things in the day. A good citizen really. Until he, his wife and 10-year-old son Matthew moved into a mysterious mansion on the other side of town. The house was very dark and gloomy, with looming trees over the drive and a massive window shaped as a skull that illuminated when lightning struck. Every night there were spooky noises downstairs. Glasses smashing, mysterious whistles and creaks in the hallway. The mansion was a three-storey building, with a tall tower climbing up high from the attic. There was a notice on the door which read:

Danger! Do not cross!

Every time Charlie read it, it sent a chill down his spine.

As he trudged towards his bedroom, he noticed the door was ajar, and no one had been in the house. He reluctantly stepped towards the door, reached out and pushed it open, to find ...

... There was a big thump as Charlie hit the floor. Whatever he had seen, he was freaked terribly. As the creature floated in the air, it flew past Charlie and slammed the door shut. It carried on downstairs, through the hallway, and into the bathroom.

Charlie woke up five hours later, dangling from the banister upstairs, along with two decapitated bodies next to him. Charlie didn't want to look down for two reasons. One, he was scared of heights, and two, because the creatures that attacked him earlier were floating below him, brandishing a sword ...

Aaron Larner (11)
The Cotswold School, Bourton-on-the-Water

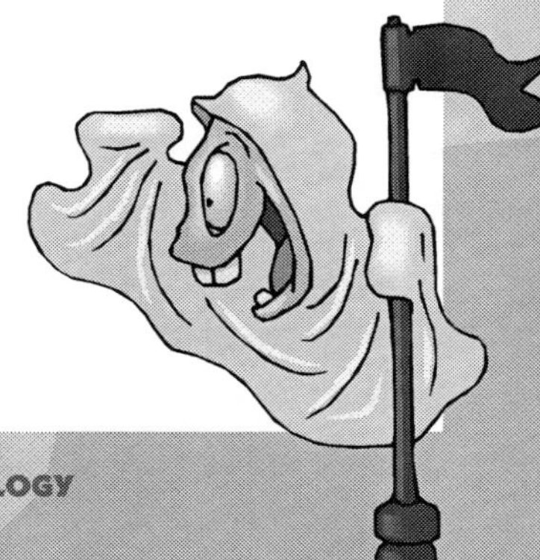

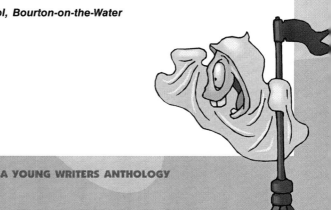

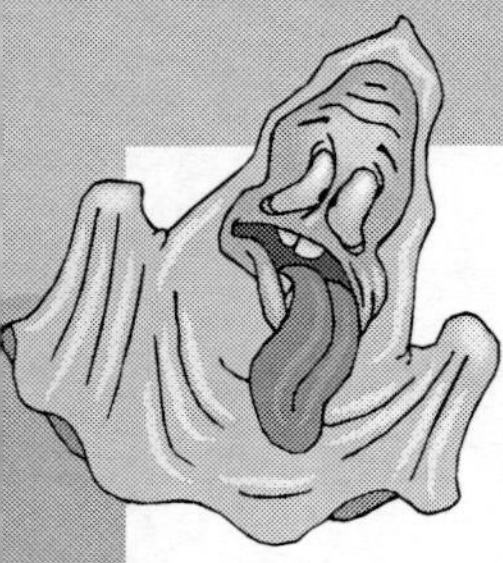

Be My Friend Forever!

'Bella stop it!' I shouted at her.

'But I *am* going to die and I want you to die with me,' Bella replied.

Suddenly the bell went, I thought, *saved by the bell.* Lately Bella's been really funny, she keeps saying that she's going to die on the 13th day of this month. Which is in one day.

Later that night Bella text me saying you know what. I didn't reply.

It's the 12th.

'Today is my last day, your last chance for us to be friends forever; oh yeah if I were you I know what I'd choose … or else,' said Bella in a heartless voice. That's all she said to me all day.

The next day. The 13th, Bella wasn't there and she's never ill. Ever.

Ela Apperley (12)
The Cotswold School, Bourton-on-the-Water

The Skeleton Cupboard

It was a Saturday evening, a thick fog was descending upon the town of Ghostville, a cold chill rang through the houses as no house in Ghostville had heating.

Andrew, a 12-year-old boy was at home helping his dad clear out the attic. He was sitting down on the sofa when his dad called him upstairs. He hurried up the squeaky staircase, and climbed up the rusty ladder to the attic.

His dad was brushing cobwebs off an old antique cupboard, 'There we are,' he said and as he opened the door to the cupboard, a skeleton arm jumped out and squeezed Andrew's dad's neck. Andrew screamed, his heart was beating faster than Concorde! His face went as white as the arm itself. Andrew looked around frantically, he picked up a large dusty broom and threw it at the skeleton's arm, it melted completely. Then, like magic, Andrew's dad's skeleton walked out of his body and crawled into the cupboard. So now a new skeleton possesses the cupboard!

Thomas Williams (11)
The Cotswold School, Bourton-on-the-Water

A Recipe for A Good Scare

Have *you* had a sleepover with no fun?

You need this guide then!

By the end of this you will have a perfect story full of scares to freak you out and scare you silly!

Ingredients

1 girl victim
1 boy victim
1 good ghost
1 haunted house (infested with ghosts)
1 creaky door
1 living door handle
2 gargoyles (that come to life at 12pm)
1 good storyline
1 spooky narrative voice
1 church bell that rings constantly after 7pm
1 hero

Instructions

Take the girl and boy victims and make them bored.

Take your haunted house and install a creaky door with a living door handle on.

Put the two gargoyles on each side of the door.

Make it 7pm and get the spooky church bell ringing.

Get the ghosts to start howling and crying.

Get your good storyline and slot these ingredients in.

Use your spooky narrative voice to tell the finished story.

Ideas for the story are …

Get the victims in the house.

Make the ghosts gang up on them.
Make it seem like there is no way out.
Get your hero in to save the day.

By the end of this recipe you will have …

1 perfect ghost story!

Imogen M Nicol (11)
The Cotswold School, Bourton-on-the-Water

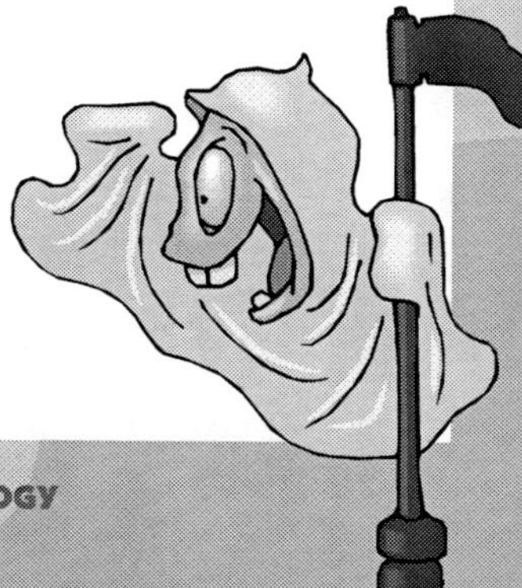

What Lurks Within?

I was walking into the abandoned shed, on the trail of my lost dog Sparkey. 'Sparkey, Sparkey!' I called. There was no reply only the darkness of the shed. The darkness clamped around me, I sat down on an ancient packing case.

After ten minutes had passed I felt something wet and greasy on my leg. It was a slug, orangey in colour. I brushed it aside then lots of slugs seemed to be crawling up my leg.

One came round my cheek and into my mouth. I bit down trying to stop it. Instead I had bitten through the slug the pus ran into my mouth. I ran for my life back the way I had come. A house stood by the entrance to the shed. On the side lay a hosepipe. I turned it on and rinsed my mouth and body, then ran to my house to have a shower.

The next day I made some lost posters for Sparkey, then made my way back to the shed. Outside was a chain. As I approached the shed, was it me or did the chain begin to move? It wrapped around me, squeezing, squeezing squee ...

Christopher Dyer (11)
The Cotswold School, Bourton-on-the-Water

Paddy Filyous

In the mist of Marie Moor surrounded by the Flich Bog and in the wreck and ruins of his ancestral home, the once-glorious and grand Filyous Mansion was where the poor Paddy Filyous lived. He survived purely on bog fish and moor bear.

One day he was warming himself by his small fire. He heard a voice, 'Paddy, Paddy, why do you live in such shambles, when you sit on such great riches? Come, come, to me.'

Paddy got up from the rock on which he always sat and looked around to see where the voice had come from.

'Push the rock,' came the voice again.

So Paddy pushed the rock. He pushed with all his might and soon he had moved the rock to reveal a small hole, just big enough for him to climb through. Down the hole there was a passageway lit by wooden torches. He followed the passage until he came to a door. Through the door was a grand room, full of the family treasure that had gone missing just before the fire that had ruined the house and for one last time he heard the voice, 'Be wise Paddy Filyous, be wise,' and for a glimpse he saw the giver of the voice.

Suddenly Paddy realised what he had to do. His thoughts were blurred. *Fire stop, thief stop, been have should it like right everything make ...*

Lachlan Mulholland (12)
The Cotswold School, Bourton-on-the-Water

I Am Her!

15th February 1999

The car screeched to a halt.

'Oh my God please don't be dead!' whispered Sarah, a tall, dark woman with dark green eyes and perfectly painted nails.

She could smell a deathly smell and taste a sickly taste. A shiver shot down her spine as she opened the door of her car and stepped out. The air was cold and there was a damp mist.

She stepped slowly towards the girl lying motionless, her heels clicking as she went. 'Please don't be dead, please don't be dead,' she muttered to herself, with her fingers digging into the sweaty palms of her hands. She knelt down beside the girl, picked up her hand and put two fingers on her wrist. Her heart seemed to skip a beat. The girl was dead. Sarah lay down on the cold tarmac and sobbed to herself.

15th March 2004

'She's so beautiful,' said Sarah staring down at her newborn child.

'What should we call her?' asked Sarah's husband Mark.

'Well we planned for her to be called Dani so that shall be her name.'

15th March 2015

'Happy birthday love,' said Dani's mum.

'It seems like only yesterday that I was going into hospital to see you when you had just been born.'

'Yeah whatever Grandad,' said Dani.

'Well someone had to say it,' said Dani's gran.

That night as Dani lay asleep a nightmare formed in her mind. She became a girl, who was walking across a field. After a while she got to a road and crossed over. She suddenly heard a car screeching towards her. She looked. It hit her and she felt no more ...

Harriet Hayward (11)
The Cotswold School, Bourton-on-the-Water

Dead Blade

My mum and I had just stepped out of the alley by our house when we heard dustbins being rattled and footsteps moving across the cold concrete floor. There was no movement just silence. The wind had dropped and my throat had gone dry.

'Er!' Mum fell on the floor with a shining, metallic, circular blade sticking out of her neck. Blood was squirting everywhere, my white shirt was now blood-red.

I turned just in time to see a short black figure scurry around the corner. I wasn't going to stick around to see what it was so I ran as fast as a cheetah until I was home.

I knew something was wrong but I didn't know what it was. I had to find out and fast, there were lives at risk. I lost my mum. I want revenge.

Christopher Lamb (12)
The Cotswold School, Bourton-on-the-Water

Sleeping With The Enemy

His hand struck my face! Every ounce of my body went numb. His evil laugh pierced through my ears. It was time for payback. Day after day, year after year, I went through the same atrocious pain! Now it was my turn to turn him into a squealing little boy!

He came in drunk, as he tried to kiss me I could smell beer and cigarettes! His hand moved up my leg. I viciously pushed him away. He tried again, this time he grabbed my neck and banged my head hard on the icy floor. I heard his laugh.

I traipsed downstairs in utter pain. This was it, the final. I took a shining sharp knife out of the drawer. Up the stairs I went. His body lying flat out on the bed.

'Bye-bye,' I whispered.

The knife raised up and quickly down it went. He screamed in pain. Blood spilled to the floor, this time his not mine. I sliced down his back, his insides poured out. This time no sound came from his dead bloody body. I'd done it. I trembled with fear but also excitement.

I picked up the knife and looked at his blood on it! I laughed. But suddenly I heard a sound ... footsteps, then the doorknob turned! What was it? Surely he was dead, or was he?

Kaeli Spires (13)
The Cotswold School, Bourton-on-the-Water

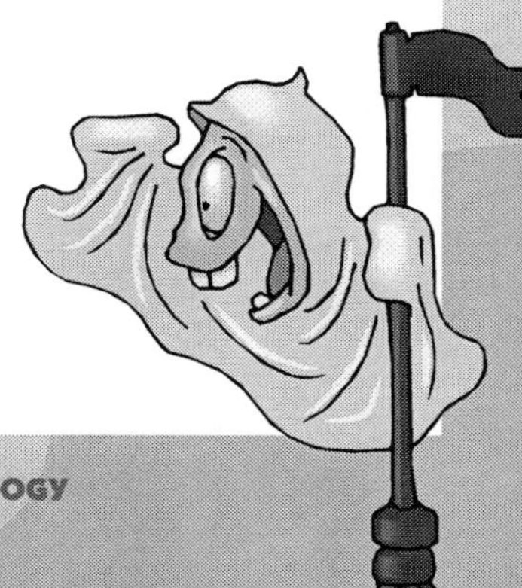

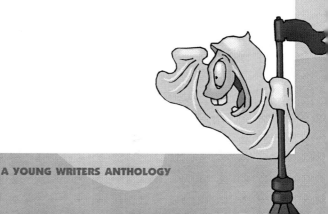

The Underground Tunnel

It was the middle of the afternoon and I was sitting under an apple tree minding my own business when the ground started to move underneath me and I could see a thin line all around me and the tree, and I was sinking down into the ground and then. Everything was still. I saw that I was in an underground tunnel. Five times the size of me.

It was dank and dark and ivy was everywhere and the walls were made of stone and crumbled a bit and the floor was covered with splodges of dark red paint.

I started to walk down the tunnel, the air was cold and musty and it was hard to breathe. Then behind me I heard a huge almighty scream and a whoosh and this huge dark red figure flew past but its legs didn't touch the ground and from that, I fainted. My mouth open, agog and my hands froze.

I woke up a few minutes later, my face white and pale and with no recollection of what happened before. But I had heard of 'The Lady in Red' and I felt a chill down my spine and the hair on my neck prickled.

But I could not see behind me where I had come so I had no choice but to carry on forwards but the ground moved again and I found myself in a dark, dense underground dungeon and on the floor I noticed that water was leaking through a hole in the wall.

An hour later ...

Zoë Willis (11)
The Cotswold School, Bourton-on-the-Water

I'm Alive

September 3rd 2000

I knew this house was haunted ever since we moved in. I keep trying to tell people, but they won't listen. It's like I'm not here sometimes.

Take today for instance, I saw somebody sitting in our old oak rocking chair, but when I tried to tell my parents, I was ignored.

September 4th 2000

Today I saw another one, walking down the stairs, towards me. I ran into the living room, shouted at Mum and Dad, but they seemed not to hear.

September 5th 2000

A moment ago I saw yet another ghost coming through the door, I shouted at it in the hope it would listen. 'Please leave this place and leave me be.' But I shouted in vain and once again I was ignored.

September 6th 2000

Now I truly believe no one cares what I have to say, it's like I'll never speak again.

September 7th 2000

It's like nobody can hear me, that I'm the only one that's left alive, that everybody is a ghost except me.

Jack Howarth (12)
The Cotswold School, Bourton-on-the-Water

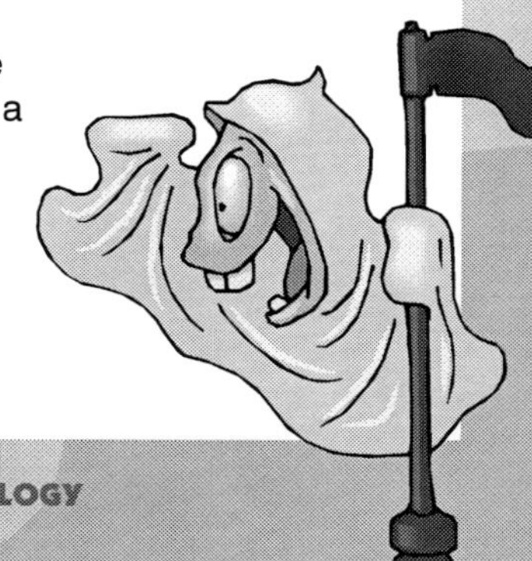

The Monster Of Fathersham Hall

It was raining heavily and was almost dark even though it was midday. Emma Kirk's carriage rolled through the gates of Fathersham Hall. She was eighteen years old and was quite pretty, with blonde hair. Suddenly she heard an enormous thump and the carriage halted. Everything was quiet. Then a ghastly face appeared at the window. It was white, with dark eye sockets that seemed to have nothing in. It reached for her neck. Emma screamed, reaching for the other door. Then it was gone. The carriage rattled along for three more minutes until it reached the impressive gothic façade of Fathersham Hall.

The next morning, after breakfast with Lady Fathersham, Emma wandered into the library. *What was that beast?* she thought thinking of the day before. Something caught her eye. She walked over to a book called 'Vampires'. Cautiously she pulled it from the shelves. Suddenly the rug on which she stood fell through a hole underneath, taking Emma with it.

She landed on the hard, stone floor of a room with arched ceiling and gothic columns. It was dark, with flickering candles lighting up the grim walls. There in front of her lay a wooden box. She knew what it was. She walked over to it and looked in. There lay the thing she had seen the previous day. She turned to run but the monster had appeared in her way. It reached for her neck. Screaming loudly, she tripped and fell. You can probably imagine what happened next …

Michael Cradock (12)
The Cotswold School, Bourton-on-the-Water

24th Street House Ghost

Rain clouds blotched the sky, making the sun look pale. Bridgestone School sat in the middle of a working Thursday. Class 6B was noisy and Dan Pike, the class bully, was yelling across the room. 'Oi, Jonny boy! There's a hedgehog on your head! Oh wait! That's just your hair!'

Jon glared at Dan and Andrea turned round and shouted, 'Dan, your hair looks like a dead hedgehog - smells like it too!'

The class burst out laughing.

'Tell you what, Andrea,' Dan said, 'I dare you and your ...' Dan looked round at Jon and Becca, Andrea's best friend, '... mates to stay at 24th Street House, tonight!'

The class gasped as Andrea nodded.

'Are you sure about this, Andrea?' Becca asked anxiously a little later standing in front of the door to the derelict house.

'Yes,' Andrea replied stubbornly.

Jon looked at the house. Windows were cracked and some were smashed.

'Let's go in,' Andrea said stiffly.

The door creaked open, the sound echoing round the large room. Footprints showed in the dusty hall.

'Somebody else has been here,' said Jon shakily, but Andrea knew perfectly well that no one had lived there for decades.

Suddenly there was a mighty bang and the door shut. Jon ran forward and tugged at it but it was shut fast.
Becca screamed.

Suddenly a door slammed and there was a rush of footsteps, then silence. Becca's shallow breathing was the only noise that could be heard.

Chloe Guy (12)
The Cotswold School, Bourton-on-the-Water

The Ghost Ship

1899

People waltzed as the music played. Suddenly the music stopped and the boat went silent. Then out of nowhere there was a sudden scream, the people ran to see what the horror was! There was another high-pitched scream as they saw the sailor lying on the floor with his eye scarily wide open.

What's happened to him?' everybody shuddered. They then saw a large footprint on the floor and white paint tipped all over the floor.

Then suddenly *crash!* everybody flew over as the boat crashed into the icebergs.

2005

'I think we have found our fortune,' shouted the captain of the salvaging team. It was a cool summer evening, the sun had just set on the shimmering sea.

They had been out at sea for nearly two weeks and at last had found what they were looking for.

They clambered onto the boat with a bang. As they were walking along the soggy wooden decks they heard a whisper, 'Come my fellow friends.' They turned round, suddenly they saw a little white ghost girl.

'I recognise that little girl,' said Hilary.

Then it clicked in her head. 'That's my daughter!' She was confused. 'But my daughter only died 4 years ago.'

Then the little girl spoke out, 'Mummy, it's me, I've come to get you now, I miss you!'

Suddenly an anchor fell on Hilary's head and the boat sank ...

Bethany Lake (12)
The Cotswold School, Bourton-on-the-Water

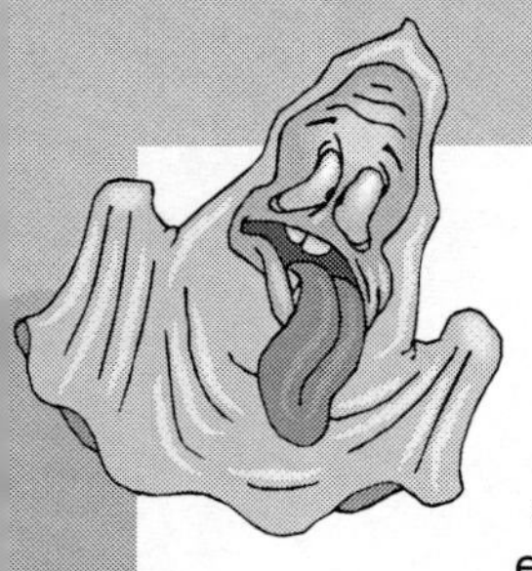

Freddie Vs Jason!

It was an eerie night, thunder and lightning gathered and savaged the night skies that swirled above the village of Green Valley. The trees cuffed each other in the violent wind, houses shook and seemed to hurl themselves at the racing shadows.

The war had started, Freddie and Jason, two bitter and angry spirits, mutilated and destroyed during childhood. Both determined to conquer the power of evil in the other.

Lethanial jerked up in bed, sleep forgotten, his heart in his mouth. Something was wrong. He had his first GCSE in the morning, and his mind was spinning, but that wasn't what he was worried about now!

Dark shapes, and sinister feelings invaded his bedroom, silent noises screamed inside his head and his body shook with dark premonition. Tonight the battle of evil was alive around him and there was no escape.

With horror, Lethanial remembered the legendary wars his grandfather told him as a child, in this very room. It was a battle as old as time, evil forces that never conquer.

He remembered stories of terrible destruction, disastrous consequences and helpless victims, whose terrified screams forever haunted those who heard. Nobody ever knew where these ferocious battles would take place, when or why because there were never any witnesses to tell.

It was then that Lethanial felt the air become heavy and too hot to breathe. He realised that his body was paralysed, just before he tried to move towards the door and a moment after he heard the terrible wail that was coming from his mouth.

Matthew Mackee (11)
The Cotswold School, Bourton-on-the-Water

Look If You Dare

Mare and her dad were treasure hunting in an old house; they had been there for a week.

Mare's dad, Bill called out, 'I've found it!'

A chain rattled, footsteps echoed. A strange howl ran through the house.

Bill looked round, he let out a piercing scream and ran through the corridor.

Mare looked at the landing, a wire noose appeared, her dad was looking behind him, he ran into the noose. It cut into his neck, it was oozing deep red.

He and the noose shot across the house, Mare ran after, she lost him.

Black muck dropped on her head, she looked up; a floating pen was gorging Bill's eyes out. His eye fell in her hand. The pen plummeted through it. Mare dropped the eye onto the now red carpet.

A stapler appeared. Staples were flying, Mare was running, ducking and diving for her life. At last she got to a phone, she picked the rusty old phone up. 'Police, my dad, he has been-been murdered.'

The phone went dead. A fiery figure appeared, Mare sprinted down a large blue corridor, into a cupboard, the figure moved through the door, it touched Mare ...

50 mins later the police came. All they found was ash ...

Melanie Norman (12)
The Cotswold School, Bourton-on-the-Water

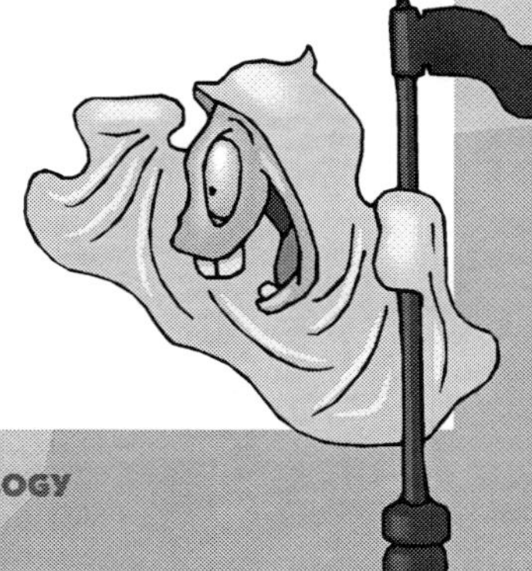

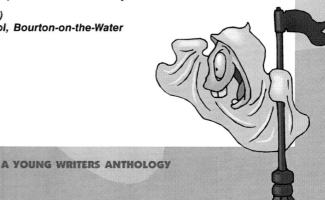

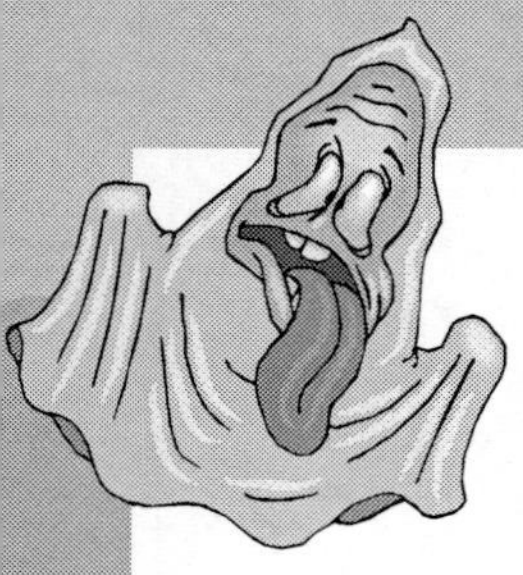

The Haunted House

I knew my little girl had gone in the haunted house. Someone had to get her out. It might as well be me.

I crept up towards the doors, silently pushing them open and I walked to the stairs. The doors squeaked as they shut. I tiptoed up the stairs and came to three doors. With my hands shaking, I reached for the first doorknob, I gripped it and pushed, nothing happened. I tried again, pushing all my weight against it. The door came off its hinges. The door fell down on the floor and there was her T-shirt, stained with blood. I stepped back, I turned to the second door. Just on the floor by it was her shoe, full of blood.

I came face to face with the last door. I didn't want to look in it, I knew it was going to be bad news, but I hoped I might be wrong. I opened the door and froze she was hanging by barbed wire with blood everywhere, a puddle of blood was underneath her. Her face had been battered. I turned around and walked to the stairs, a crash came from the second door and It opened. A little creature came out, it had yellow saliva coming out of its mouth, claws as big as pencils, teeth as sharp as needles. It ran towards me, jumped up and hit me, its claws came down and ...

Lee Rogers (12)
The Cotswold School, Bourton-on-the-Water

The Last Day Of Summer

Emily and I were in the dormitory of our boarding school in England. It was summer, the last day of school and it was almost midnight.

'I'm sleepy,' said Emily, yawning.

'Get to bed girls! It's far too late,' whispered Mrs Roberts.

'But I can't,' said Emily, 'I'm very tired, but I feel cold and frightened and I don't know why.'

Mrs Roberts put the light out and left the room.

As the clock struck midnight we heard a strange wailing noise coming from a cupboard against the far wall. My blood turned to ice and I froze. The room started spinning and I saw a white mist rising from the floor.

'Don't scream; I won't hurt you,' pleaded a distant voice. 'Please don't be scared - I need your help.'

Emily and I couldn't move.

'It was the last day of summer and I was packing my bags,' said the voice of a girl. 'I was late and running along the dormitory when I remembered that I'd left a pair of shoes in the cupboard. I went to get them, saw them right at the back and crawled inside. All of a sudden the doors closed and I heard the key turn. I think it was the cleaner, but she didn't know I was in there and left quickly. I screamed for help, but everyone had gone. I banged on the door and scratched on the wood until my hands bled, but it was too late. No one could hear me. I was cold, afraid, starving hungry and I couldn't breathe. I died!'

'That's awful! How can we help you?' I asked.

'All my family was buried in the same grave,' said the voice. 'I need to go there. Tell your teacher that a little girl is in here and needs help.'

The next morning Emily and I ran to Mrs Roberts and told her the story.

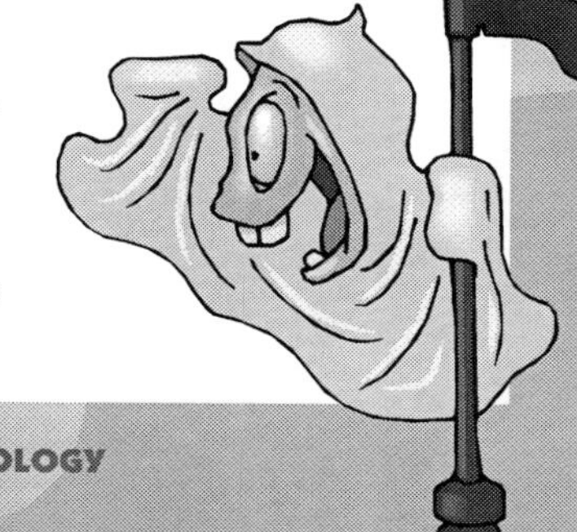

'Well girls, that's the silliest thing I have ever heard,' she said. 'Come on, get on the bus!'

'But ... but!' stuttered Emily.

No one could help that girl so, from that day forth, she still haunts the dormitory.

Rhyanna Owen (11)
The English International College, Marbella

The Haunted Mansion!

It was on the 25th February 2005. We were all starting to pack and I was helping my baby brother called Darren who is only two years old. My dad came in our house about a week ago shouting, *'We are all going on holiday!'*

That was a surprise, we never go on holiday because of my dad's work. Every time we try to go on holiday we always have to come back home early or at least he does and me, my mum and my brother go home when the date is up.

9pm we were all ready to go. Me and my baby brother Darren brought our pillows so we could have a sleep in the car. We all looked puzzled. After five hours we ended up at a very scary hotel or as I should call it House of Horror. My mum was even scared and that isn't like her.

'Come on, look properly at the map,' Jane whispered. 'This can't be where we are staying!'

'It's not that bad!'

Dad made us go in!

'Good morning children!' said the lady who owned the place.

That was the bit where we all got scared.

She had three fingers on the left hand and there weren't really any on the right hand. She had about 20 teeth missing. Her hair was the worst of anything on her body. It looked like she had been pulled through a hedge backwards. It's hard to describe the other person because he was a disgrace.

Our parents looked at us as if they wanted to desperately rush home, then the noises began ...

Rebecca Wallington (12)
Thomas Keble School, Stroud

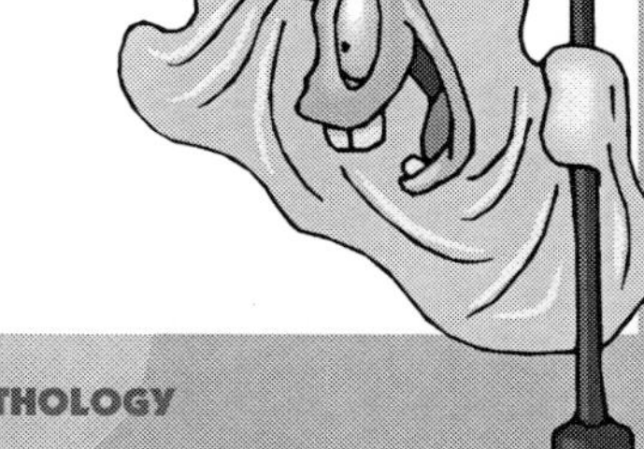

The Haunted Coach

One day, there were two girls called Shannon Poole and Georgia Wood. They were going to the Everyman Theatre. They were sitting on the coach together waiting for the coach to go.

Shannon wasn't too sure about going, she was getting travel sickness. Georgia was sitting next to the window. It was very dark outside, so dark that you couldn't see anything. Georgia was very tired and had fallen asleep on the coach. She had a dream, that she would open the ashtray and find a note saying, 'He or she who sits in these two seats shall die and suffer just like we *did!*'

Georgia then looked at the note to see who the names were on the note. It looked like this: 'L Clark and L Brown'. Then Georgia noticed that it was her two best friends, Lucy Clark and Lisa Brown.

Georgia then got really scared and woke up. Everything she did was exactly the same as what she did in the dream. Shannon, Georgia's first best friend, was wondering what was the matter with Georgia. She showed the not to Shannon and made her look at the two signatures. That's when Shannon started getting freaked out. Then all the way and back from the Everyman Theatre, they kept getting messages from Lucy and Lisa.

They just turned up outside the school. The teachers were telling everyone to get off the coach. Everyone except from Georgia and Shannon. The teachers started getting mad like angry crocodiles, but it didn't look like Georgia and Shannon were breathing, so the teachers checked Georgia's and Shannon's pulses and they were *dead!*

And this happened to everyone who sat in those two seats.

By the way, Georgia and Shannon died by being scared to *death* by Lucy and Lisa haunting both of them.

Georgia Wood (12)
Thomas Keble School, Stroud

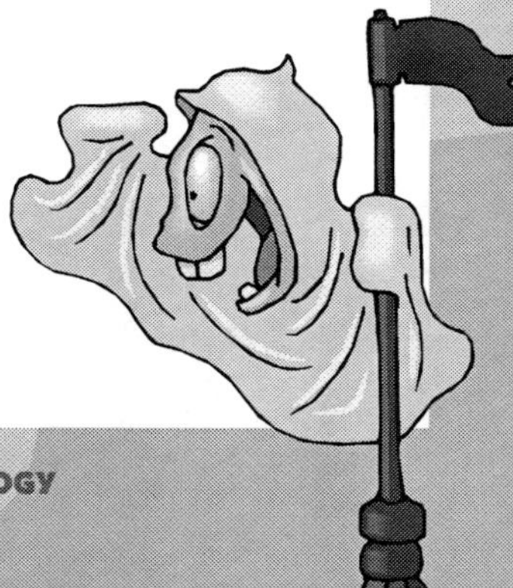

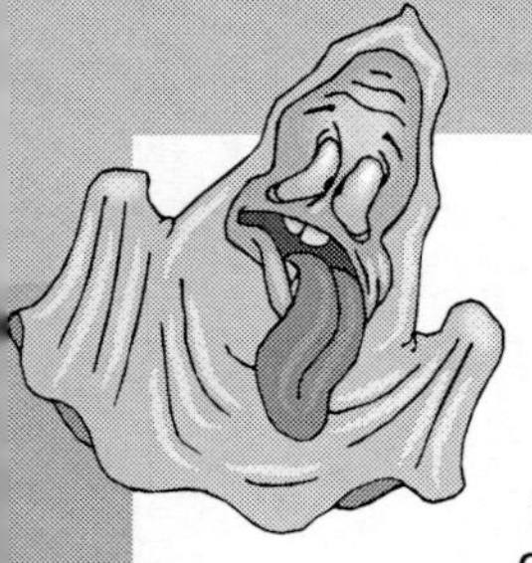

The Spooky Woods

It all happened in the woods at Marsh Hill. Nobody had been in them for 50 years. It was a terrible storm that night and a group of teenagers decided to go for a walk in the woods (the silly fools). So that night they set off at about 8.30, not knowing what would happen to them.

A boy called Steve led the way and into the spooky woods they went. They only took a torch and a drink of water.

A girl called Emily said, 'Turn the torch on Steve, we can't see anything!'

So Steve turned it on for Emily's sake, then the other four heard a howling noise coming from the other side of the woods.

The other four were scaredy-cats, so they would have heard something. Steve and Emily were fighting over who should hold the torch, but one of the scaredy-cats called Simon said, 'This is no time for fighting, us four have heard something.'

'Oh it was probably just the wind,' Steve said, feeling proud of himself because he was holding the torch.

Then they came to what looked like a creepy hut or den. Steve of course went inside because he was the leader of the group.

'Look there's nothing here,' Steve said, and then something grabbed Steve on the leg and pulled him down. 'Argh!'

'Oh no, where's Steve gone? Steve! Steve, where are you?'

'Where can he be? I didn't know there was a church around here. Come on, we have to find Steve.'

'But we can't, let's just go home. He'll make his own way back.'

'No, he's one of our friends, we can't just leave him here.'

'Oh come on Emily.'

Emily felt bad about leaving one of her best friends maybe to die.

And Steve has not been seen to this day. That taught the silly fools!

Joanna Northcott (12)
Thomas Keble School, Stroud

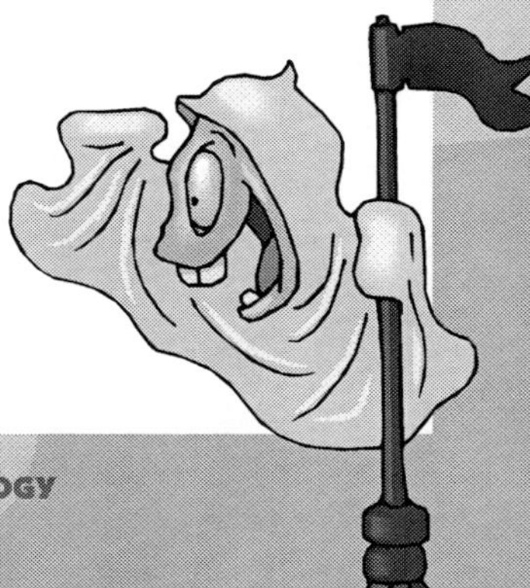

The Screamer

It all started on a stormy grey night when my friends and me, Chris, Will, Sarah, Becky and Adam, were walking down the lane. Adam said that he was bored and that we should play a fun game like dares or something, so we decided to play dares!

Will was first, he dared Becky to kiss Chris. She screamed out, 'No way!' So then Sarah dared me to go into the haunted mansion down the lane. I said that I would only do it if they came with me. They agreed. I thought that they would say 'no' because at the moment there had been a rumour that the house had been on the market for something like £112,000, but nobody would buy it because it was haunted by the ghost of Mrs Marble, the witch who had been killed there about 15 years ago by the supposed murderer Scythe Robins. We said that we would do it after school the next day.

We were walking home and nobody mentioned it until we were so bored that if nobody had spoken I would have died. We said that we would all go home and get changed, then we would meet up on 5th Street, and anybody that didn't would be cursed by the evil demon that supposedly possessed Sarah. Although none of us believed her, we all knew we just had to turn up.

When we all came to 5th street we started to slowly make our way to the house. It took us about fifteen minutes to get there, and when we got there, we tried to force the front door open, but it would not budge and that then meant we had to wade through the long grass. Chris climbed on the bin and lobbed himself through the window, the door opened shortly.

The girls quickly alarmed us when they screamed at

the top of their voices. The boys and me ran to see what the problem was. We got there and looked in horror at the pool of blood. Chris examined the blood, he then confirmed it was … red paint.

We carried on searching the house. When I saw a door, I pulled it open and found the stairs to the cellar. I started to walk down the stairs, then I saw a blurred image. Then, when it got closer, I saw that it was an old woman walking towards me. I told Chris to stop messing about, but I got more scared when I heard his voice behind me.

Then there was a horrible sickening sight. The old lady rose off the ground and floated towards me. 'Aarrgghh!'

Anton Richardson (12)
Thomas Keble School, Stroud

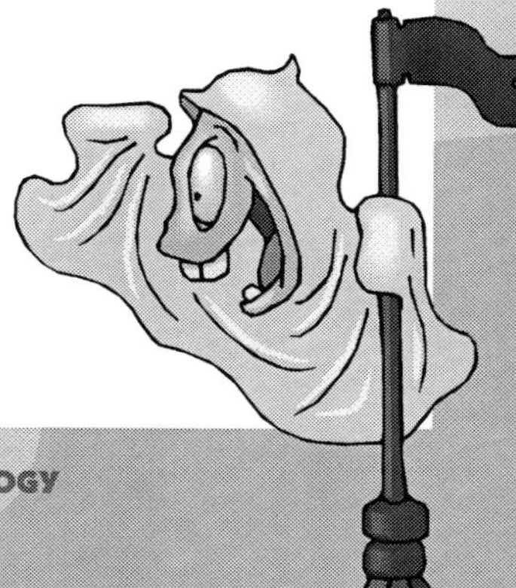

The Evil Teacher

It was a Monday and that was the day we had DT in TK school. We all hated Mr Swift, he was evil, but today was different, a lot different. In his back room there was always a creaking sound. We all walked in, then he said, 'All come in to the back room.' Then he locked us in and suddenly opened a trapdoor. Then we were all forced down.

All the girls were crying in fear. Then we saw the axe on the floor, with blood all over it.

Mr Swift said, 'Who is going to be first then?'

Then ugly little Jimmy, the dumb one, shouted, 'Me, me! Let me go first!'

(I knew he was dumb, but I didn't think he was that dumb.)

Mr Swift got the axe and chopped off his head. Blood spattered, big time. Then he prowled through the others with the axe. I ran to the door. Luckily I had spent my money on picklocks, and had taken the time to practise. I unlocked the door with ease.

I told the Head and he said, 'What a load of lies! But just in case …'

We ran back to the room. There was nothing but a load of blood and some chopped up heads. We called the police. Mr Swift went to jail but got out, but we caught him again, this time it was for life!

Now we have a new teacher, his name is Mr Smith. We have so much fun with him and got rid of the trapdoor …

Jack Youhill (12)
Thomas Keble School, Stroud

The Clearing In The Forest

'Where are we?' asked Lisa.

'In a forest, it looks like. You can come home with me, but under one circumstance, *get me out of here!'* bellowed Claire, whimpering.

'I have an idea!' Lisa yelled, and Claire jumped. 'If we split up, we have more of a chance to find the way out.'

'That's a good idea! Let's all get lost in the woods and worry ourselves to death. Oh I can't wait!' Claire exclaimed sarcastically.

'Do you have a better idea? No? So don't be sarcastic! I will go this way and you go that way.'

They split up and went into the dark, misty woods with no wind or movement.

They both headed in opposite directions. After five minutes, Claire found a clearing and started to look around. Something made her look forward, and Lisa jumped out on Claire and made her scream. They were talking, when a branch of a tree came down and they heard a laugh and a squeal. Cold air brushed past them and they thought they saw a figure in the air, when suddenly, they both turned round to find a ghost! It looked like a mother ghost. A boy and a girl played, while a baby ghost fell on them. Then the dad told everyone to be silent.

'We don't want to harm you, but this is our home.'

'That's all right, but how do we get out?' Lisa asked.

The mum replied nicely, 'You can't!'

Johanna Barton (11)
Thomas Keble School, Stroud

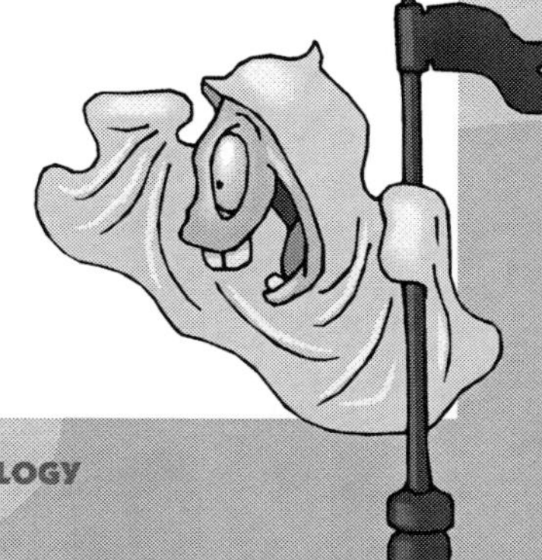

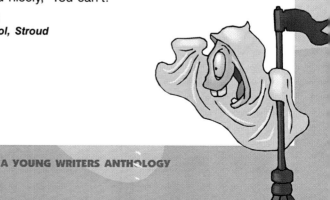

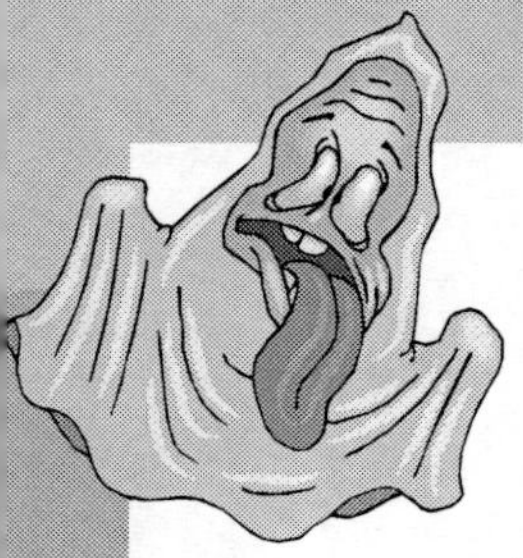

Follow Me Home ...

It was dark outside. The wind was howling around the tall walls of my school and I was alone, waiting for the return of my teacher to let me go. I wasn't looking forward to my long walk home, but there was nothing I could do ...

I felt very alone in the small room, yet I had a feeling someone was watching me, staring at me with evil eyes. The school was empty after hours and there was a sense of danger in the air. Only a few people walking around in the deserted corridors. Then I heard footsteps coming closer to the room, getting faster and louder as they approached. A click of the door handle led me to believe my teacher was there. I started putting my things away and stood up from my chair, but no one entered the room. Looking out of the small window in the door I saw nothing, just a dark emptiness.

Hearing footsteps again, I made my way to the front doors of the school. My mum was probably getting worried as she couldn't contact me - I have no signal at school. But I couldn't think about her right now, I had too much to worry about!

The path I take home was pitch-black by now, only lit up by one single street lamp right in the distance. When you're alone, you notice things you don't normally see, and hear things you don't normally hear.

My heart was thudding as I began to make my way home. It took me ages to get as far as the lamp as I was being so careful about where I was treading. Then I heard it, the noise I was dreading. Someone was behind me.

I sped up, almost to the point where I was running, but it didn't work. I couldn't lose them. Scared as ever, I made a right turn hoping I could confuse the stranger, but it was no use - the mysterious stalker wouldn't go away. The tension was almost too much to cope with. I couldn't turn around to see who it was. I couldn't run - it would make things worse, so I took a left.

To my horror it was a dead end. My heart stopped. I couldn't think. The footsteps got louder. I had to turn around as I felt a cold, stiff hand on my shoulder! There was nothing there ...

Kelsey Ross (12)
Thomas Keble School, Stroud

The Trapped Ghost

Jack and his mother walked quickly up the drive to the huge manor house. They were going to a fancy dress party and they were already late. Two massive fir trees loomed up like giants protecting the doorway. As they walked past the trees, Jack said, 'I'm bursting!'

'You can go when we get inside, OK?' replied Jack's mother.

'Why did your boss have this party here? It's spooky.'

When they entered, a frail old man gave Jack directions to the toilet. Jack went straight through the oak doors at the other end of the hall. He took a left and then he heard it. Someone was cursing him. Someone was telling him to go back.

It was a horrible voice. It was not just spoken, it seemed to appear in Jack's head. Jack turned back frantically through the door he had entered. It was locked. He started to run. What could it be? He took a right. Was it a murderer? He went through a door and, 'Argh! You gave me a fright.'

There in front of him was a boy. He was about 16, the same age as Jack, but he was dressed as a Victorian.

'You must be lost,' the boy said. 'Follow me, I know the way back.'

The boy led Jack down a few corridors and through a door. He then headed for a staircase.

'I'm going back, the hall is on this floor,' Jack said.

'No you're not!'

Jack froze, it was that voice, the voice that had appeared in his head.

'That's right.' It was the boy, 'It was me! They call me Poltergeist.'

Jack ran for a door, but it was locked.

'I want out of this cursed house,' the boy said, 'and I need a human body to do it, for I am bound to this house.'

Jack found a door that was not locked and ran through it. The boy, who seemed deeply annoyed at this, chased after him. Suddenly Jack tripped. The boy leapt down upon him and then, darkness.

Jack awoke to find that he was lying on the lawn outside the house. Flashes of what happened came back to him: he remembered smashing through a window. What had happened? Was it a dream? Would anyone believe him? Then he heard the voice in his head again.

'Thanks,' it said.

Thomas Moore (13)
Thomas Keble School, Stroud

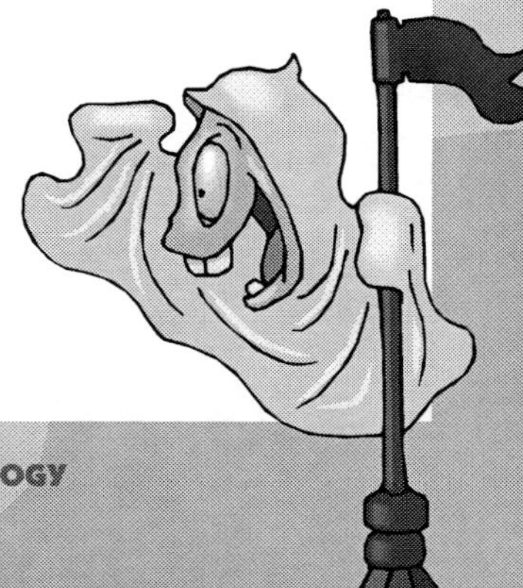

Lost?

It was a dare, just a stupid dare. I was told to go into the forest for only half an hour, but unfortunately, it turned out to be a lot longer! It wasn't scary at first, but then my torch lit the way. The forest floor crawled under the dark, damp leaves as I stepped slowly through the forest. I looked up for a second and saw that the trees seemed to go on forever. That was when I noticed it. Hiding quietly behind a tree. Frozen. I couldn't move. Then suddenly, my torch went out - leaving me in total darkness. The trees came alive, their branches reaching out, grabbing at my clothes. But all I could think about was the creature, breathing loudly, lurking close behind me.

I shut my eyes tightly for a moment, and when I opened them, I was surprised to see the moon's silver rays stretching through the treetops. I could still hear the unknown creature rustling behind a nearby tree. That was it - I couldn't bear it any longer. I ran as fast as hunted prey. I heard the creature leap out and start to chase me. Dodging trees and low branches, I stumbled desperately, looking for an escape route. Leaves brushed by me, thorns and branches tore my clothes and scratched my flesh. I heard birds fly out from trees high above me. I did not dare look behind me, for I feared the beast that was frantically grabbing at my heels. Then my worst nightmare happened.

I felt a claw grasp my ankle; I lost my balance as I gasped for breath. I lay helplessly on the forest floor, cold and struggling for breath, dreading what would happen next ...

I gathered enough courage to finally roll over and stare at the face of the snarling beast. I hoped it was all a dream and I would wake up with the sun glaring through my window. But that was all too easy.

The air felt cold as I slowly turned over. The sight was a nightmare!

The bright green eyes stared at me frightfully, surrounded by black heavy fur. The moonlight revealed pointed fangs, as sharp as needle points. I was frightened, terrified. I swallowed loudly, trying not to cry. I could smell its heavy breath brushing against my face; hot, smelly breath. I closed my eyes, waiting for something terrible to happen. But nothing happened, not even a howl.

'Scaredy-cat, scaredy-cat!'

I opened my eyes. My mates had come, the ones who had dared me into the forest. I told them the whole story while looking around for the beast that had chased me. They just laughed at me, joking and smirking. Then from behind the bushes, a gigantic howl - the beast had returned.

Katie Shaylor (13)
Thomas Keble School, Stroud

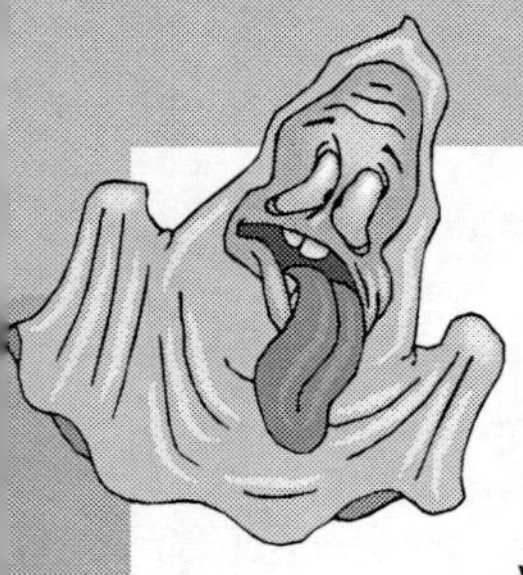

The Grace

We were walking, walking along the desolate beach at Staithes. As the roaring waves ate at the giant boulders of the breakwater, men in bright yellow coats appeared from around the corner of the jagged Yorkshire coast. They were carrying something. It was long - about the length of a fully grown man, like a stretcher, or one of those fluorescent body bags they carry dead bodies in ...

It was cold, the kind of weather you would expect in February, but this was May. I will never forget that stormy weather: wind that took your breath away, grabbing at the side of the cliff and throwing sand and soil in your face and eyes. But it was that bag, the bag that sent the shiver down my spine - not the weather.

We carried on, stumbling through the howling gale.

'I wonder what happened to him?' Anna asked.

I knew what she meant but I didn't know the answer, how did he die?

All of a sudden a man appeared. He was small with dark eyes and a crooked nose. A tattered orange jacked with 'RNLI' written on it, covered his bony shoulders. 'Couldn't help overhearing you,' he said, in a strong Yorkshire accent, 'but this is a dangerous part of the coastline. Why, back in the 20s there was a terrible shipwreck, 'The Grace' to be precise, went down just a mile out. Rough seas swallowed the lifeboat an' all, nobody survived.'

We turned to look at the ferocious ocean. By the time we looked back, the man was gone.

We decided to leave the beach then - it was starting to get even colder. There was a small junk shop two minutes away from the beach, so we went in. Shelves and shelves of books, postcards, sweets and photographs lined the walls of the old shop. A large black leather photo album lay on the counter. I opened it. Black and white photos filled the aged pages. Hundreds of men's faces stood staring back at me. They were pictures of all the lifeguards Staithes had ever had. Everyone was wearing orange jackets with 'RNLI' printed in bold letters on the back of them. A few of the photos were of certain lifeboat crews and their captains; there was one picture that had something written underneath it: *'This boat sank trying to save 'The Grace' - no one survived'.* In the centre of the picture was the lifeboat captain. He was small with dark eyes and a crooked nose. A jacket with the letters 'RNLI' covered his bony shoulders.

Jess Kirkland (13)
Thomas Keble School, Stroud

The Manor

It was raining, the wind was howling, but Grandad was ill and I wanted to be with him, so did my family, so we drove in our Ford Focus to the old manor that he had inherited from his grandad, who had inherited it from his grandad, and the same had happened for over fifty generations, me being the fiftieth.

When we got there the rusting sixty-year-old gates, slowly creaked open with an ear-piercing screech.

'Have to oil that,' Dad commented.

Lightning flashed, thunder roared but the manor on top of the hill stood still not one single shake.

As we entered the manor I felt a strange chill down my spine, then the warmth as Mum closed the door. Grandad looked worse than ever. He was as white as a sheet, as he carted towards us in his wheelchair. 'Mark, son is that you? I haven't seen you in ages; and who's this little lot then?' Grandad said quite slowly almost ghostly like. He had forgotten us.

'Grandad, it's me, John,' I said. I was worried, it looked like he was on the verge of dying.

'Oh, oh yes Johnny. You're getting the house.'

What? What did he mean? 'The house?' I enquired.

'In my will you get the house, Mark gets half my money, Claire gets the other half and this young one will get ...' he collapsed to the floor.

'Grandad!' I yelled.

Dad took his pulse and shook his head.

A note fell from his pocket. I grabbed it, and started to read: *'Beware the horrors of the manor on the 30th day after you inherit this place,*

Hell will arise. To save your life and to spare the others, you must leave'. I started to ask Dad to read the note, when it crumbled.

A month passed, and we moved into my property. We all had large rooms and we had made the rusty, horrible gates shiny and they made not a sound when you opened them. On the 30th day I was scared, but nothing happened. Then things went from amazing to hell. Everything was covered in mould and we were watching the television when there was a horrific storm. The house shook, the winds howled and everything went icy cold. Was it me? Mum was shaking, Dad was hugging her and Lauren was crying. The dog, that we had bought a few days ago, was barking violently, then crystal shapes hovered and a bolt of lightning struck a tree next to the house. Now Roxie was barking madly and the window shutters were opening and shutting faster than ever. Was it a tornado? No, this was England. The Ford Focus' alarm went off and Dad went to shut it up, but he returned without the door being opened. It looked like he was going to cry. I grabbed the keys from him and I was thrown off my feet. I hit a wall and my head was bleeding. The last thing I remember was Mum screaming and hugging me, then blankness ...

I woke and the house was rubble. The *thing* was searching through the rubble. I grabbed the nearest weapon, a rusty axe used to chop down trees and I hit it again and again but it did nothing. It ran as soon as I picked up a picture which had a message on the back, *'The manor is yours, congratulations'.* Yet the only thing I had left was this painting and my family and the car.

We drove back to the old house, but it was rubble, as was the whole street. I feared that this was the end and I warn all who wish to live nearby to beware the creature, beware its wrath and if it comes to your house or street, run, drive, just get out of there if you want to live. Who knows where it is now? It could be coming your way.

Sam Westerby (12)
Thomas Keble School, Stroud

The Carpet Fitters And The Thing

In the basement of 'Haunted House Corner' something was moving.

It was a dark and dingy day, when two carpet fitters, whose names will stay anonymous, received a phone call, telling them to measure every room in 'Haunted House Corner' for carpets. The person that rang, must not have known about the myths that have been told about that house. The fitters went. While they were driving, the wind started to howl and the rain was streaming from the sky, like an upset child.

Finally they arrived. They collected all their equipment together and crept further towards the house. They knocked on the door and it creaked open like an old man's walking stick.

The thing heard something moving. He thought long and hard about what he should do. He decided to try and talk to the people. The fitters had finished their job so they had a nose around the house. The thing was at the top of the staircase when the fitters came out of the room that they had measured.

'Argh!' screamed the thing and the fitters.

The fitters ran to the car and the thing retired back to his lonely basement.

'What was that?' enquired the first fitter.

'I don't know. Let's get out of here,' said the other.

They drove off while the thing was crying.

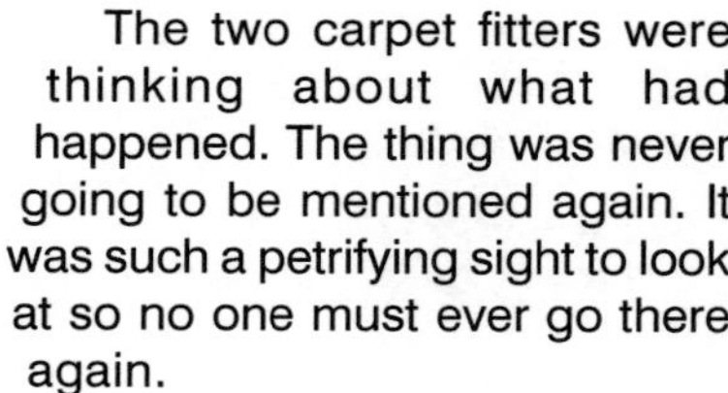

The two carpet fitters were thinking about what had happened. The thing was never going to be mentioned again. It was such a petrifying sight to look at so no one must ever go there again.

Hannah Bucknell (12)
Thomas Keble School, Stroud

The Haunted Corner

The day I knew, it wasn't all dark and windy. In fact it was a beautiful sunny day, where everybody and everyone was out playing or walking their dogs - but from then on my life would never be the same again.

You see, it was the day I was going up to Cumbria to see my dad. As I got up there it started to rain. It sounded like footsteps, but no one was there. Then all of a sudden it turned into the worst storm since last year, in this month and on this day.

As we were driving up to my auntie's farm, my dad told me a real story. He said that one hundred years ago today, on a tree just a mile up this road, a lady was hanged and ever since, on the anniversary of this day, there has been a horrifying storm.

The corner was just coming up, but I still couldn't see. Now I could see it. I could also see a lady pacing up and down under the tree. She was dressed in a wet, white nightie. I thought it might have been a confused old lady, so my dad pulled over and opened the door to ask her if she wanted a lift back home, but all of a sudden, she disappeared ...

Hannah Howson
Thomas Keble School, Stroud

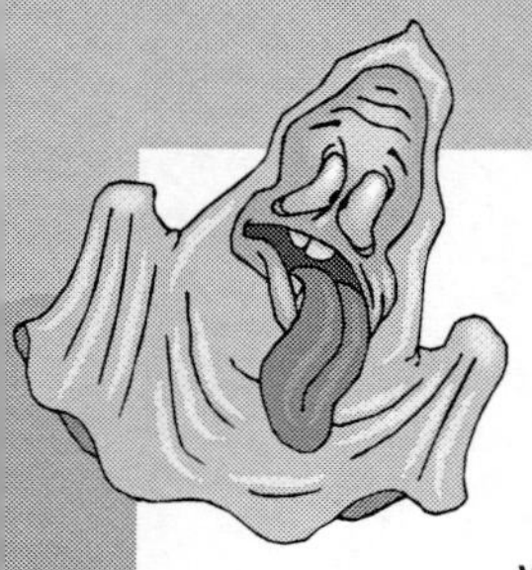

The Face At The Window

I was sitting in my room like normal. It was about 10.30 and my mum told me to switch off my light. So I reached out to switch it off and that's when it happened ...

I screamed, there was something's head! It looked as though it had been dead for about 10 years. It was saying my name. I froze, I shut my eyes praying it would go away. I dared not open them, but I had to and the head was still floating outside my window. I was petrified but curious. As I reached the window, I could hear the wind howling like a dog and the trees outside looked like they were reaching out to grab me. I edged forward to open the window. I reached out but as I was about to touch it, it disappeared. All I could feel was air. I looked down to the ground and I could see its yellow teeth smiling up at me. I thought to myself, *is this really happening?*

I looked behind me as I thought I heard my mum coming up the stairs, but it wasn't, it was the face. I tried screaming but nobody heard. It was staring straight at me and it had a look in its eye like it was going to kill me. I stepped backwards and fell onto my bed. I just curled up into a ball and fell asleep.

I woke up and thought it was a dream. But was it ... ?

Anika Ponting (12)
Thomas Keble School, Stroud

Clown Doll Of Death

Every year a travelling circus comes to town. One of these towns was called Sunnyvil. The circus is just like any other, but it has a dark secret, which only the clowns know about ...

'Mummy, Mummy, I wanna go to the circus,' whined the little boy.

'Alright, we can go to the circus,' sighed his mum

It was a normal day in Sunnyvil and a travelling circus was coming. When they got there it was just an ordinary circus, nothing amazing about it.

When it had all ended a clown came up to the little boy, his breath smelt like dead animal guts and his face was repulsive. He thrust a clown doll in front of the little boy's face and growled like a wild animal, 'Take this doll but play with it every day or else!' he then walked away.

The boy looked at the doll. His eyes were staring all around even thought they weren't moving. His hand was in the form to hold a weapon.

When the boy got home, he put the doll on the kitchen table and ran off into bed. It was midnight and the little boy was asleep. He woke up and he heard a voice which laughed evilly, 'Hee, hee, hee, time to kill.' He heard, 'One step, I'm on the stairs, two steps, I'm on the landing, three steps, I'm in your room,' then the little boy saw the clown doll . . .

Ben Free (11)
Thomas Keble School, Stroud

Dead?

'What was that?' I cried. I heard something move. Well, the house is old, nearly 200 years. I could hear it repeatedly. Suddenly I could hear someone screaming so as fast as lightning, I ran to the grand living room. I opened the door to see who was in there screaming. 'Maddy! I yelled. 'You scared me? What's wrong?'

'Nothing,' she laughed.

Little sisters, they always lie. Maybe she isn't lying this time. My parents had been away for 2 days and I was here going mad!

Later that night when I put my sister to bed, I heard someone say, 'Come here my child!' I was mortified.

Out of the blue the doorbell rang! It was an old lady asking about the job in the newspaper to look after Maddy for me. Scared out of my wits, I let the old haggard lady in. She told me how she used to own the house.

Later that night I heard something say, 'Are you alive?'

Someone was downstairs.

As soon as I could I grabbed Maddy and then ran downstairs. There were people *viewing* our house! What were they doing?

Opening the door, the old lady said, 'They have found us now.'

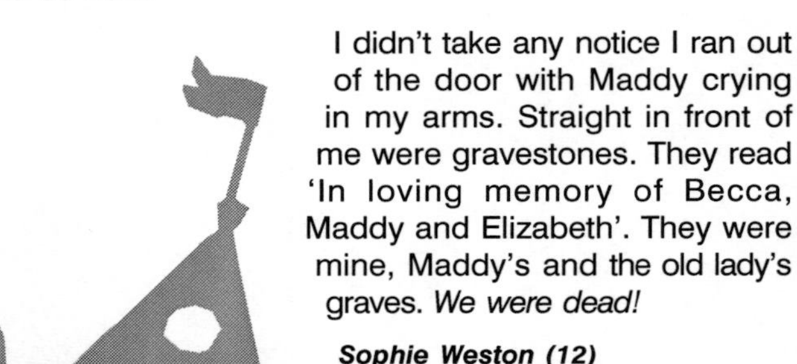

I didn't take any notice I ran out of the door with Maddy crying in my arms. Straight in front of me were gravestones. They read 'In loving memory of Becca, Maddy and Elizabeth'. They were mine, Maddy's and the old lady's graves. *We were dead!*

Sophie Weston (12)
Thomas Keble School, Stroud

The Log Cabin

It was a normal day, a day like any other. But today a scream was heard from the forest. Today someone was killed.

It was a Wednesday and Leo was going to school, but on the way to the bus, he heard a scream. Only, it wasn't any old scream, it was the most terrifying, blood-curdling scream ever imaginable. He ran, his heart beating as if a drum were inside him. The trees made grabs for him and the roots of the trees tripped him up; then he heard that absolutely terrifying scream again. He ran deeper into the forest to get the bus, but he was too late - he was stuck in the screaming forest.

He ventured around trying to pull himself together when he came to a log cabin. This log cabin was not your ordinary log cabin, this one had a strange factor about it. The door was weathered and the old metal door handle was starting to rust. Leo reached out, turned the old rusty door handle, and saw the petrifyingly pale, white-as-a-sheet victim. Dead!

Hannah Wynter (12)
Thomas Keble School, Stroud

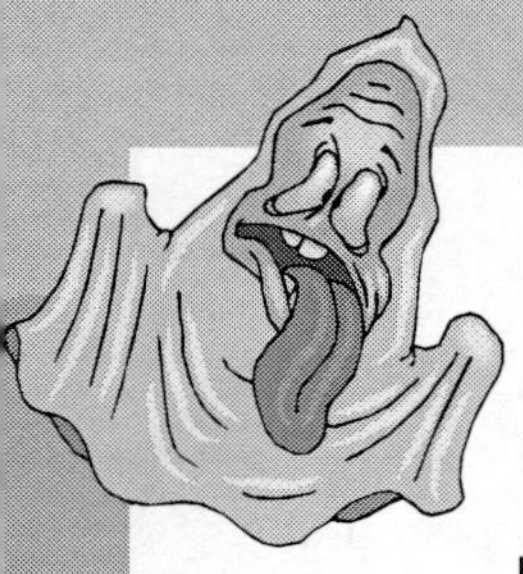

The Old Lady Next Door

It was a terrifying night in Unfortunate Lane, but every night seems terrifying when you live next door to a creepy old lady, with a graveyard in her back garden. It's usually hard to sleep when all you can hear is chuckles and chainsaws, scraping and screaming.

One even spookier night - than usually spooky nights in stories - my friend Annabel dared me to walk into her house and bring back the old lady's murderous clown doll. I took on the challenge. At first I felt terrorised, but as I started walking along the long winding pathway and smelt rotting corpses, I felt like this was my duty, like the adrenaline in my body would make me stronger. Besides, I would be a chicken if I did not do the dare. As I gripped the door handle or the rickety house, I heard raucous laughter. It was as if the old lady knew I was there.

I ran as fast as my legs would carry me and then I ran blindly into a six-foot hole. I heard footsteps and mud and soil fell down on me.

Suddenly, it hit me - I was being buried alive ...

Annie Chaplin (11)
Thomas Keble School, Stroud

The Shadowghoul

It was a cold night in the mystical land of Talwar. A chill wind gathered, carrying spirits on its wings. After all - what else could make a sound so ghostly as the wind, that it could fill peaceful Talwarian's sleep with nightmares?

Two goblin guards were on their night shifts, they were really feeling the sudden change in the weather. One had a ring through his nose and a face that was covered with scars of many a battle. His companion, however, was quite young for his profession and looked frightened. The wind whistled past their faces, chilling them to the marrow. 'Hey Bog,' said the first goblin, 'tonight, something strange is going to happen, I bet.'

'How d'you work that one out, Clad?' the young goblin asked sarcastically.

'Spirits. I can feel it,' replied Clad,

'Yeah, yeah, Wrinkly. I hardly believe in ghosts anymore.'

A sudden gust of wind nearly blew them over and something strange *did* happen. Something *evil* happened. There came the sound of blood-curdling screams, mournful moans and rattling chains, and a demonic black figure emerged from sudden ghostly mists. Bog had his back turned to it and Clad was warning him, but he thought it was just a joke. The demon spirit loomed up behind him and Clad only had a brief glimpse of his friend being torn limb from limb before he ran.

Far away, a Talwarian awoke, and all he heard was a distant scream saying, 'The Shadowghoul ... !'

Evie Skinner (11)
Thomas Keble School, Stroud

A Ghostly Story

This cruise was going great! Well . . . until I discovered something that I shouldn't. The deep, damp dusk. Under the deck and close above the sea was the cellar of the boat. The circular windows of the ship were snowing with thick layers of dust. That awful smell that made me want to be sick . . . but then I discovered what the smell came from!

The rotting, decaying bodies. Hats still resting on their heads. Was this going to happen to all of us on the boat? I quickly created a booming screech. No one, no one at all replied, not even my dad came to my rescue! I was shocked.

I hurried up the cobwebbed stairs, which whispered to me as I stomped, and took a fierce look around. Nobody was here, nobody was there and nobody was on the ship! But where? Where could they have gone? I slowly edged up to the side of the ship and looked over into the deep blue ocean. Could that have really happened? The terror of loneliness was slowly being created.

I was brave, extremely brave, in fact I was so brave I forced myself back down to the cellar! I took another look at the dead bodies. I rubbed my eyes and looked again. 'No, no!' I screamed to myself - this was like a dream.

My sister, my sister. It really was. I could not believe what I was going through, and then, and then all of a sudden . . .

Billie Wiseman (11)
Thomas Keble School, Stroud

The Thing

We were all playing rugby outside of the haunted house, when Ben, the stupid fool, kicked the ball over the wall right down the end next to the house. Of course I had to go and get my ball. As soon as I entered the garden, a heavy lightning storm started and all my friends ran home. As I got closer to the house the rain pounded against the back of my head and neck like a jackhammer. I heard something behind me and that's when I saw it ...

I stood there staring at it, it had dark brown, crusty skin and was dripping in slime and gunk. It smelt like rotten and decaying old food that had been left in someone's old gym sock behind the lockers for years. I stood there petrified, I didn't dare move. I stood there for hours when finally I had enough courage to move. I picked up my ball and walked towards the wall.

'Move once more and I'll carve you up into bits smaller than you can imagine,' the thing said.

I stopped dead. On the ground I saw something shining on the ground. It was a torch. I picked it up.

'Just take is easy, wouldn't want to hurt anyone now, would we?' snarled the beast.

I turned the torch on and shone it at him. He started to dissolve; within seconds he was just a pile of slime. I trod on him and fell to a never-ending pit ...

Freddie Hayden (12)
Thomas Keble School, Stroud

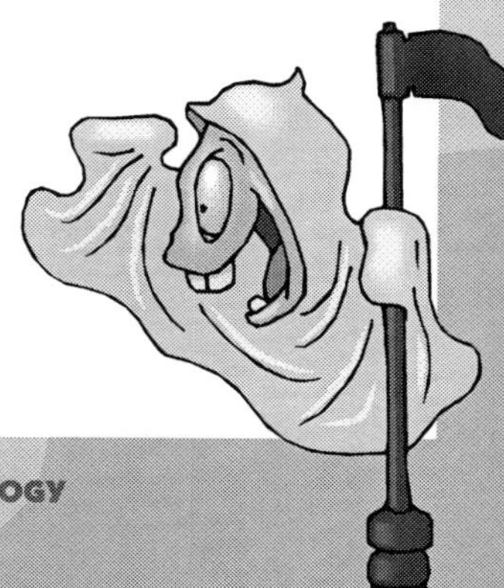

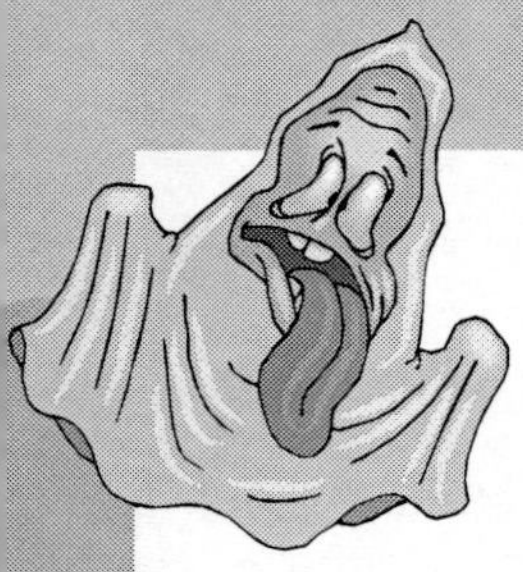

The Birthmark

Boom!

'What was that?' asked Jerry. He stopped the car to have a look. It was pitch-black outside. The darkness felt as if it was hugging him.

Five minutes had passed but Jerry still hadn't come back. 'Jerry, where are you?' shouted Tanya, his girlfriend. She was worried.

I got out of the car to see where Jerry had gone. He was nowhere to be seen. I called out his name. No reply.

'Jerry!' sobbed Tanya.

Something cracked beneath my feet. I looked down and there was a china voodoo doll, lying there on the ground like a dead animal. The doll had tyre marks on it, covered with a red quilt of blood.

The police came an hour later. I had called them as soon as we'd seen the doll. When they examined it, the only distinctive thing about it was that it had a brown mark on the left-hand side of the front. Tanya mentioned that Jerry had a birthmark but on his back on the right. Everyone was confused. The only thing the police could do was search for Jerry.

A year to that day, an old woman was walking her dog. Hanging from a tree was a mangled body. Jerry's body. He was almost a skeleton. His torso had been twisted round so his back was facing the front. In other words, his birthmark was on the left.

Miles Lewis-Iversen (12)
Thomas Keble School, Stroud

The Pacific Sailor . . .

'Goodnight Mum, Dad and Carl!' I shout.

'Goodnight,' they all reply.

Here I am with my two dogs, my brother and my mum and dad in the middle of the Pacific Ocean. It is great fun trying to travel the world.

It is 12 midnight, my family are all asleep now, the boat is bobbing up and down in the rough seas. I can hear the mast going from left to right, I can hear it creaking, and it feels like it is going to collapse on us. But it won't, I keep saying to myself, over and over again.

I've just turned my light off but I can hear a noise. It is my dogs so I race out on deck because they don't normally bark over nothing. It's all misty, I can't see anything, they're just barking at the sea but there is something there and whatever it is, I am going to find out.

I tiptoe towards my dogs, 'Hey what's wrong?' I whisper to Dave and Kali. I have just frozen with horror. I am not going to wake Mum and Dad though because they might go mad.

I'm still standing on deck when suddenly this voice is saying to me, 'Go away you horrible boy.' He is dressed in a sailor suit. It's the man who travelled the world but died here in the 1980s. I have got to find a way to get away from him. So I decide to move the boat, so I sail far away and I've never seen him again ...

Jordan Frapwell (11)
Thomas Keble School, Stroud

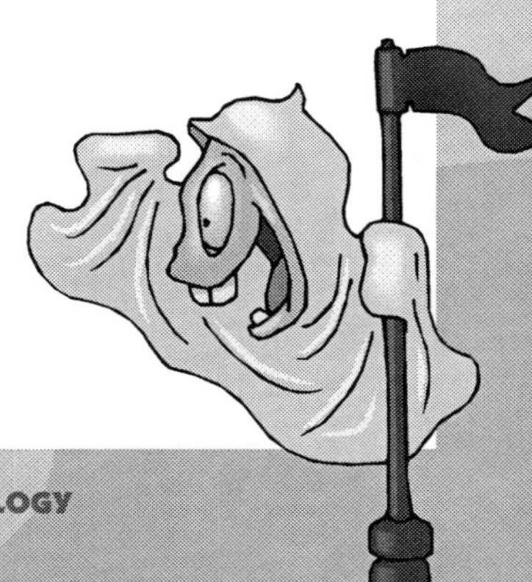

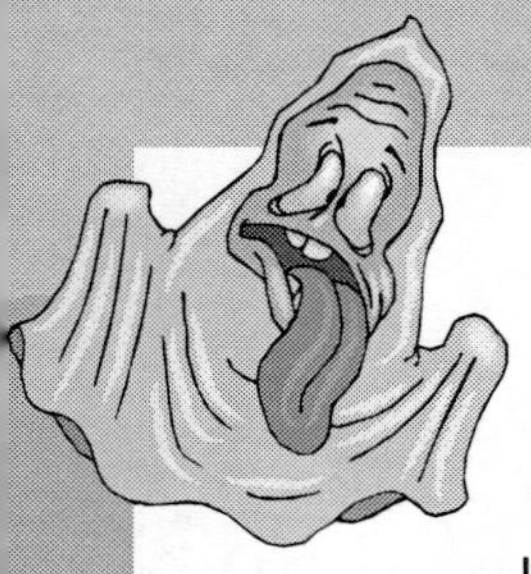

The Haunting Ghost

I knew it would happen. My mum kept saying that ghosts weren't real, but they are, they come out at night and haunt you. That's what happened last night and now my mum has disappeared, she is nowhere to be seen.

I ran downstairs as fast as my legs would carry me to tell my dad, but he had disappeared too. I was all alone in this big haunted house, I had to get out, but where to go?

I went downstairs to hide and thought to myself, *everything is going to be OK.* I kept repeating that in my head but suddenly I heard a noise coming from my bedroom upstairs. I had to go and see what was up there but I was too scared.

I forced my legs to move as I crept up the stairs. The floorboards creaked, I couldn't see where I was going because it was dark outside and the wind was howling like an angry wolf. As I got to my bedroom I slowly pushed the door open, just so I could see inside, but there in front of me was a huge white ghost with my parents beside it.

As I ran for the ghost, it disappeared, but just before it did, it said, 'You are never going to see your parents again,' and with that the ghost was gone and my parents with it. I was alone in the world, frightened and scared.

Ashton Harrison (12)
Thomas Keble School, Stroud

Blood On The Wall

'What was that?' I gasped.

'Nothing! Now go back to sleep, stupid!' said my brother, Danny.

'I am not joking. I can hear something in the garden.' I could hear something in the garden. I did try to ignore it, but I was filled with curiosity. And that's when I saw it at the window . . .

A dark shadow of a man with no face. It was caped in darkness, and I could see little red eyes giaring out from the cape.

'Danny, Danny! Look at the window,' I whispered.

'What? There's nothing there!' Danny blurted back to me.

I looked over and it had gone. The wind was still blowing outside, like a giant fan in the sky. I slept shivering till morning, tossing and turning with fear.

In the morning I went straight out into the garden to investigate. I was there in the hedgerows, when I found a trail of blood. It led to a wall. I looked at the wall, and there written in blood was, *'Beware, or you will be next'*.

I screamed, I ran, I fell. I thought that I had broken something. I lay on my back squinting at the sun. Then, something touched me on my back. I looked round, but there was nothing there. Something touched me again. I looked forward, and right there and then, I was dead.

There, my life was over. I don't really know how I died, but there we go. Just remember, watch your back ...

Kayleigh Adams (11)
Thomas Keble School, Stroud

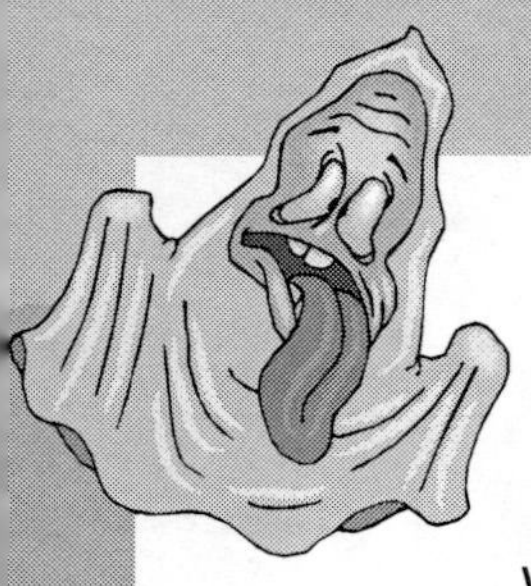

Is Anyone There?

It was Dom's big night, his friends had all arrived and everything was perfect. *This is going to be the best night ever,* he thought. Well, was Dom right? Would it be the best, or would it be filled with horror?

'What do you want to do?' Dom said excitedly.

'I don't know,' his friend Max sighed.

'I know, let's play Ghost Hunter on the computer!' Mark shouted. There was a sudden rush over to the computer. 'Can I be the shooter?' Mark yelled.

'Yer, I'll direct the gun, and you can look for ghosts,' Dom explained.

They were on the second level when all of a sudden the sound effects were getting louder, as if the ghosts were in the room. Mark spotted a ghost on the computer so he shot and as he did a bullet came smashing through the window.

'Do that again!' Max exclaimed.

So following orders, Mark pressed down on the shooting button, and sure enough, another bullet came rushing in through the window.

None of them knew what to do. There was silence. All that could be heard was the wind giggling like little children. They were all standing at the window, when something brushed past them.

'That felt weird,' Max said curiously.

They all looked behind them and to their surprise a ghost was floating around in the corner of the room.

'Argh!'

Jasmine Hicks (11)
Thomas Keble School, Stroud

The Haunted Mansion

It was a normal day, until we walked into a big, tall, gloomy, abandoned house. It wasn't normal.

Sam and me were in the mansion, you couldn't see anything. The dark surrounded us, luckily we had a torch.

When we were walking through this giant house Sam said, 'This is the ghost of Zebedia Springfield's house.'

I thought he was joking. Then we suddenly heard this groan and then something whizzed past us.

We went to check it out, the rocking chair was moving and nothing was there.

Then all of a sudden, 'Boo!'

We jumped out of our skins. I believed Sam now. Zebedia was floating there, staring at us. We started to run. We hid behind a dusty old cabinet; he had gone just like that - he vanished! We continued to wander around. We went upstairs, the floorboards were creaking like an old door. We turned round, nothing was there. We turned back round and the ghost was there. Sam picked up a sharp stick and hit the ghost. The ghost was knocked out, but it couldn't be a ghost if it was knocked out. We took the mask off the ghost and it was the school bully, so we left him there.

A month later at school, a whole load of people were claiming that they'd seen a ghost, so was it the bully or a real ghost ... ?

Callum Churchill (12)
Thomas Keble School, Stroud

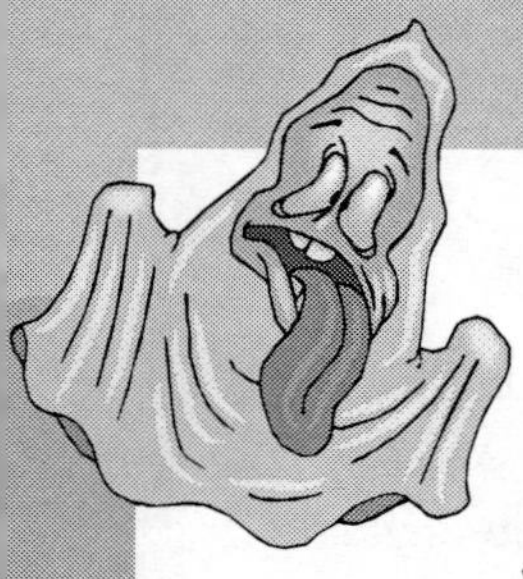

A Ghostly Story!

It was a cold and windy night in the middle of December. Two girls were walking home from school. It was a Friday, but not just any Friday, it was Friday 13th.

The two girls both arrived back home safely. Emily, one of the girls called out, 'Mum we're home,' but there was no reply. They began searching everywhere, still no luck.

Jade, the other girl, plucked up courage and started to walk towards the cellar.

Jade started to walk down the cellar stairs, which were squeaking like a mouse. She heard a drip behind her. She suddenly turned around and fell. Was it blood or just thick water? She stood up and carried on walking. She tried turning on the light, but it wouldn't work. 'I can do this,' she said.

While she was down in the dark cellar Emily was looking around upstairs.

As Jade started to walk she felt as if she was under pressure, the cold darkness began to close in on her as well as the misty cobweb clinging to her face. She felt as if she was being watched, but then she felt a cold, bony hand on her shoulder, it was pulling her back down and down.

There was a sudden piercing scream and everything went silent. Emily came running down the stairs and saw Jade lying on the cellar floor with cold, wet blood around her.

Whatever it is, it could be out to get you!

Hannah Bloomfield (12)
Thomas Keble School, Stroud

The Graveyard Ghost

'Woooooo,' came from the graveyard next to Sam's house. The graveyard was packed with tombstones covered in moss and mould and it hadn't been visited by a soul for thirty years. Sam jumped out of bed to see what the sound was. At first he could only see the swaying trees in the graveyard but as soon as his eyes adjusted to the light, he saw something so terrifying he froze.

He couldn't get back to sleep so he decided to investigate. He jumped over the crumbling wall and ventured into the weeds and dead branches, which were trying to engulf him. He scrambled out of the small ditch he had fallen into, and saw a bright yellow pulsing light, like a glow-worm trying to escape, in the clearing in front of him. Suddenly everything went dark. The pulsing light stopped and the moon went behind a cloud. He was left in darkness and he had the sensation that someone or something was behind him watching him.

Again the light started and the moon came out as if it was trying to watch everything, but this time a buzzing joined in. Soon the buzzing got so loud, Sam had to cover his ears. It began to sound like a scream. A scream from someone being dragged into a grave. Then Sam realised it was his own scream. He was the one being dragged into the grave.

Sam Mincher (11)
Thomas Keble School, Stroud

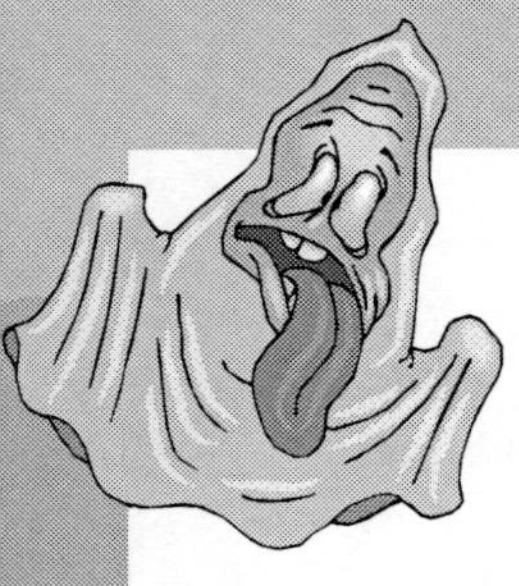

Knock, Knock

'I normally like bad weather,' said Jess to herself.

'Argh!' screamed Rebecca.

'What now?' asked Jess.

'We're out of milk,' replied Rebecca.

'Hey, where have Mum's knives gone?' asked Jess.

Then there was the sound of something falling, something metal, like a knife.

'Is your house haunted Jess?' wondered Rebecca.

'You have been watching the X-Files too much,' said Jess.

Jess went upstairs, then there was a big bang.

'What was that?' demanded Rebecca.

'Quick look at this,' shouted Jess.

There were red lights floating around one with the knife, it shot down at them. As Rebecca flew down the stairs she slipped. There was a scream. Rebecca turned to Jess. Jess was flat on her face and then she got up. She just stared at Rebecca.

'What?' asked Rebecca.

'Nothing,' said Jess.

The two went downstairs and there was a butcher's knife stuck in Jess' first teddy. Above it in blood it said 'You're next Rebecca'.

'What does that mean?' asked Rebecca. She then noticed that Jess had blood on her finger.

Knock, knock.

'Someone is at the door,' Rebecca said to Jess, but Jess was gone. 'Jess, Jess!' Rebecca screamed.

Knock, knock again at the door. Rebecca went to open the door to see to her horror a body, it was hers! 'How can I be in two places at once?'

'Because you're dead,' said Jess, 'and we're stuck here forever ...'

Kenny Walker (11)
Thomas Keble School, Stroud

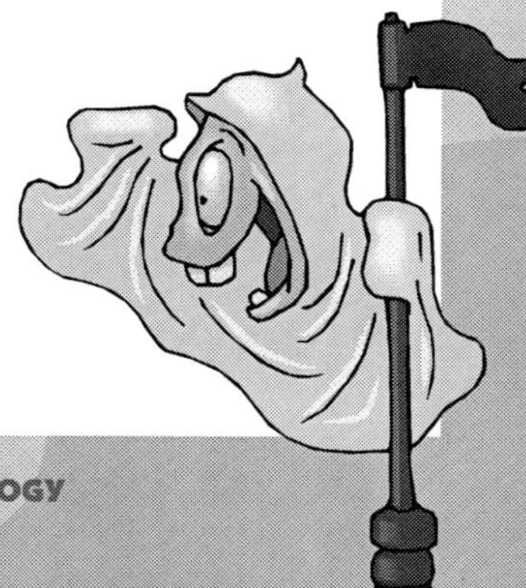

The Chain's House

'Dead! What do you mean dead? He can't be gone!' The person on the TV was screaming as I sat watching a horror film. It was a dark and dismal night up there in the Chain's house. A house where mad things happen, since being built three people had been found dead and two people had gone missing from there. 'What was that?'

There was a noise coming from the Chain's house. I heard people shouting and someone screaming. I got up from my chair and crossed the room to the window. I drew the shade back to see people making their way up to the house with a struggling girl in their arms. The girl, from what I could see, was crying.

I ran to the phone, to dial 999 as I heard another scream that came from the house. That was when I got a knock on my door. I jumped and walked to the door slowly. I opened the door. There was no one there. *It must have been the wind*, I thought.

I went back to the phone. As I did so, I pinched myself. I picked up the phone and called 999. When they got to the Chain's house it was too late, the girl was dead. The killers were gone too.

A little while later the police knocked at my door. I got up and answered the door. The police told me that the girl was dead and told me it was my sister.

Roberta Wilkes (12)
Thomas Keble School, Stroud

A Trip To France

On July 18th 2005 my mate Tom and I went on a school trip to France. We had just got off the ferry and were on our way to where we were staying in Normandy. Tom and I were gazing out of the window saying, 'Look at that, look at this!'

At about three o'clock we arrived at the place, somewhere in Normandy. So we went and dropped off our gear and down to the chill out room.

At about nine thirty we were getting tired so we went up to our room. 'Let's go to sleep so we're not tired for tomorrow,' Tom said.

'OK,' I replied.

The lights went off. After about five or ten minutes I heard some strange noises. The windows were rattling and the lights started to come on and off every second. *We were scared big time.*

The noises went.

'What was that?' I asked Tom.

Tom replied, 'I don't have a clue!'

We tried to go back to sleep, but after five minutes someone or something just touched me. 'Stop messing around Tom!'

'Messing around with what?'

'You are poking me!'

'I am not,' Tom replied. 'Do you think it was a ghost?'

'*No* and stop teasing me.'

'He is not teasing you,' said a deep voice coming from the dark corner! 'I am the ghost of this hotel, you are in the same room as I was in 299 years ago. Somebody came in and killed me with a gun, right in the head.'

Tom and I have not spoke to anyone about this ...

George Price (11)
Thomas Keble School, Stroud

Roadside

It was past midnight but still Sasha and her mum Sandra were driving along the almost empty motorway. They had not stopped driving for four hours and Sasha was getting bored and hungry.

'Mum,' Sasha pushed out the words in a whiny way, 'we haven't stopped for hours and I'm really hungry not to mention bored.'

'The services aren't for miles dear. Also we have to keep going if we want to get to the airport on time,' Sandra replied as she had done at least twenty times in the last half an hour.

Both of them sighed heavily and Sasha turned away and looked out of the window.

Suddenly a shabby road sign appeared, with the words, *Twenty-Four Hour Café* splashed onto it in red paint. Instinctively Sandra drove the way it directed and Sasha grinned, suddenly happy.

Sandra stopped the car in front of the café. She thought to herself, *this really is the pits. It looks like a tin matchbox magnified a few times and with a portaloo dumped beside it.* Although she didn't want to she grabbed Sasha's hand and stomped towards the café. Her stomach felt queasy at the sight of the cracked windows with at least an inch of grime on them. She breathed deeply, squeezed Sasha's hand and called out to her above the loud wind, 'Let's make it a quick cup of cocoa.' She then banged her knuckles against the grey shack's door. The door creaked and ground open a crack and a voice as cold as the air on top of Mount Everest whispered, 'We have been expecting you!'

They walked in, stepping carefully around the worn bits in the brown cork floor.

They sat down at a faded plastic table and a man walked towards them. He had a large cigar in one of his chalk-white hands, he was bristly and had a wild mane of greasy grey hair. His nose was bulbous and his teeth were brown as were his glowering eyes. He was the owner of the icy voice and soon after they had sat down his voice penetrated the air, 'I have made your cocoa already Sandra and Sasha.'

Sandra replied, 'How do you know our names?'

'Ha, ha, ha, ha,' he cackled and put two frothy mugs of hot chocolate down on the table. As far as they were concerned everything was okay. The place was warm and they sucked at the hot chocolate for ten minutes. Yes the place was a bit strange and the place was a bit old but it was cosy enough.

The clock struck three and suddenly the room went freezing cold.

'We had better get going,' Sandra called out to the man, but no sooner had the words escaped her mouth than the door groaned open. The look on the three pale faces that entered fixed Sandra and Sasha to their places. They decided from that moment on that they were trapped. After a while their minds blanked and they didn't hear the person on the right say, 'New meat I see Harry.' They didn't even hear Harry say, 'Yes, new meat and very tasty I'm sure for ghosts like us!'

Sasha and Sandra were transfixed, trapped and were never seen again.

Jemma Lewis (13)
Thomas Keble School, Stroud

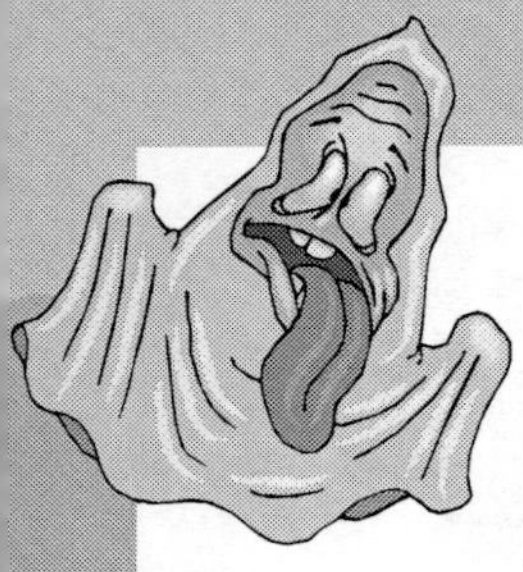

Get Them Out!

There was a cool breeze that carried a few leaves and blew through Sara's hair. She was rolling out her sleeping bag next to her twin, Seamus.

'This is great!' whispered Seamus. 'The first time out camping on our own.'

'Hopefully we won't mess up,' replied Sara.

It was getting darker and a full moon had appeared.

'Uh-oh!'

'What?' questioned Sara. 'You haven't forgotten something?'

'No. I just … need to go!' He was shuffling from side to side with his legs crossed.

Sara sighed. 'The stable's loo is closer than home,' standing up and putting her coat on. 'If we leave now there will be some light.'

The gate creaked as they tiptoed across the yard. There was a weird clicking noise but where was it coming from?

'Look! All the doors are open!' yelled Sara.

'Never mind that, I need the loo!'

As they crept the clicking didn't stop.

After, Seamus whispered, 'What is that clicking? It's really starting … what was that?'

A white figure of a boy ran across the yard, screaming, 'Get the horses out! Quick! Quick!'

'Hey!' called Sara, running over. 'Chill out. There aren't any horses!' but the boy didn't stop.

'Someone get Maze out, quick, it's spreading!' shouted the boy.

Sara and Seamus looked up and saw the stables on fire and horses panicking madly. They ran to open the doors but they were all stuck. They turned around, the boy had gone. The flames had died out and the horses had disappeared.

Emily McCollum (13)
Thomas Keble School, Stroud

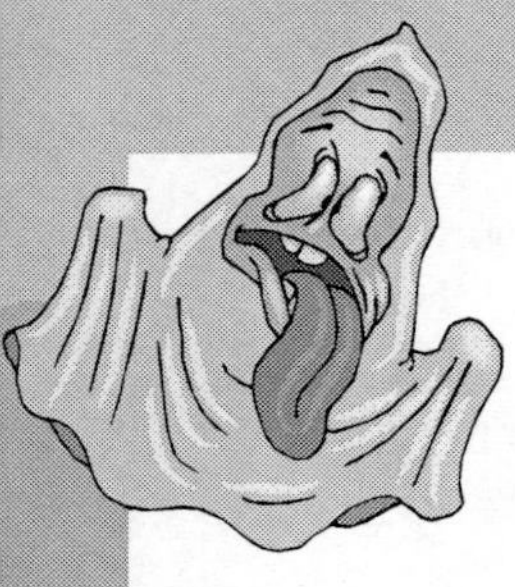

The Severed Heads

On one cold and stormy December night, Sam and his friends Jay, Archie and Tom, decided to go to the house. The haunted house.

At twelve o'clock that night they went in. They snuck around looking for interesting items, but all they saw for a moment was old dusty furniture. But then, they saw it! They saw the thing the people in the village had been talking about. It was the ghost ...

The ghost was there, he saw them, they saw him. The ghost ran off and seemed to go upstairs, they followed keeping their distance, but he was nowhere to be seen!

They searched and searched, but nothing. They looked in every nook and cranny, but still nothing. After about one and a half hours they gave up. As they were wandering down the stairs, they saw something, it was terrible. They froze on the spot. They saw the ghost holding the severed head! Ripped from a body. It was not any dead body, it was Jay's body and head, but then they saw more. There were bodies hanging from the ceiling like meat, all with their heads severed, lying on the floor next to them. The victims were all from the village. There was Mrs Smith, the post office worker, Bill Walker, the old man that Archie used to do jobs for.

They chased the ghost out of the house. They stood there and watched it enter another house.

Was that house yours?

Sam Assanakis (12)
Thomas Keble School, Stroud

Obsessions

'Master you haven't eaten in several days,' Jeeves the butler mumbled. Mr Jefferson just stared out of the old stained glass window in the old family mansion. Weeks earlier Mr Jefferson was signed up to do some bungee jumping but now he looked like an old, chair-ridden, frail man.

At first it was just a strange obsession to watch a small Victorian pale girl who sat down by the musty gates but now he lived on seeing her. The girl never stared at him though; she stared at the tree with knots that looked like faces.

In time, Mr Jefferson, to his dismay watched the old tree grow over the window blocking his view; he got really annoyed. 'Jeeves, write to the council and ask if I can cut down the tree!'

'Yes, master.'

Mr Jefferson couldn't wait for the reply so in the middle of the night he got a sudden urge. He rose from his sleep and raised a chainsaw above his head and slashed the tree to pieces!

The next morning Jeeves woke. Mr Jefferson was nowhere. After 8 months of searching, Jeeves got the family fortune. Jeeves was creeped out with the disappearance so he moved out. As he was driving away he noticed the tree had changed shape into a man with something strange in his hand ...

Megan Baker (12)
Thomas Keble School, Stroud

House Of The Unholy

'Shut up, you arrogant man,' scolded Sara.

'Get out of my house!' Sara's father exclaimed.

Sara left the small town of Dinkley. This was the worst day of Sara's life. The arrogant, snobby girl moved to a damp cottage called Delvi-on-Ilch in a small village. Staring round her leaking home, for it had been raining for weeks, she left the disturbing place to get some food. Passing puddles, striding forever forward. Suddenly an old man started to talk unannounced, 'Time for the end to pass my dear,' it was spiteful and barbaric. Sara ran without thinking; however her mind was fixed on the old tyrant.

Failing to understand what the old man had meant, she pampered herself for a date. A cupboard caught her eye, it was jewel encrusted, that wasn't there before. The door creaked open. A rank smell of flesh and sulphur coursed through the air. The only thing it could be was a rotting corpse, sickly staring at the tall, bluish girl. Edging back Sara broke into a run, the floorboards spewing up dust from long-gone years.

Screaming for her life she ran and left the house, the girl was appearing in her mind.

'Troubled are you my dear?' spat the old man.

'Help me, who are you?' she exclaimed.

'The house is my house, that girl is you!' he smirked. He dragged her off to the unholy house where countless girls had been taken. Is she alive? I don't know, do you?

Richard Amphlett (13)

Thomas Keble School, Stroud

Claws!

'Lottie, Chad, tea's ready,' said Mrs Potts.

'Coming Mum,' said Lottie.

Lottie and Chad charged downstairs for tea.

'This is lovely Mr and Mrs Potts,' said Chad.

'Why, thank you Chad,' replied Mrs Potts.

'Lottie, I need you to go to the cabbage patch and pick some cabbages for our supper,' said Mr Potts.

'OK, I'll go now,' said Lottie.

'I'll come with you,' said Chad.

Lottie and Chad went to the cabbage patch to collect the cabbages. Suddenly, Chad's mum called him from Lottie's house to tell him he had to go. Chad said goodbye and ran off. Lottie was now alone.

All of a sudden it became windy, Lottie heard a repeating beep, she thought it was a watch. She knew somebody was in her patch. The scarecrow stick wobbled. She gulped and stumbled to it. She turned and looked around at the scarecrow and ...

Argh!' she screamed and ran to the farmhouse. She ran in and locked the door and turned to see a man. He had a handmade T-shirt saying 'Claws'! He made a run for her and she ran trying to open the door, she couldn't do it. He grabbed her and took her away.

Mr Potts went to collect her and he ran crying. They phoned the police. They came around straight away, they also phoned up Chad, he was in a state.

The years passed and Lottie was still not found. Is she still alive? I wonder, where is she kept?

Jade Shelton (12)
Thomas Keble School, Stroud

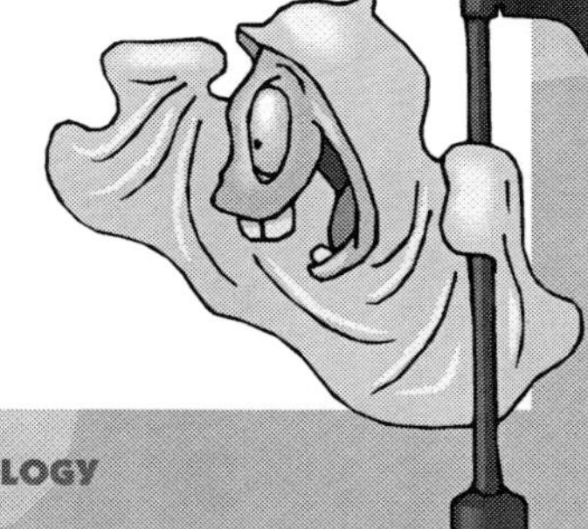

What Have We Done?

It was 8am and James arrived at the airport ready for Shilo. Finally Shilo arrived. James was holding up a sign saying *Shilo*. James shouted out, 'Shilo!' Finally Shilo arrived at the waiting area.

Shilo ran up to James and said, 'You James, yes?' in an excited voice.

James replied, 'Ummm, yes I am.'

'Great let's go,' said Shilo.

James' family drove Shilo to his house. The day passed and it was time for school. 'It's great a school.'

A huge overgrown boy ran up to Shilo and said, 'You the new kid?'

'Yes, why?'

'Just wondering.' Nathan thumped Shilo on the arm and walked off.

'Don't worry about him he's just the school bully. Just stay away from him in future,' whispered James.

'Hey, let's go to my hideout.'

'OK,' shouted Shilo. Nathan stalked them there. The place had rusty old bars and old chairs.

'Almost fit for a king.'

'Yeah,' muttered Shilo.

Nathan hid in a box, there was a creak.

'Did you hear that?'

'Hear what?'

'Shhh,' whispered James. 'Quick.'

James and Shilo grabbed rusty poles and searched the area.

Suddenly Nathan jumped out and screamed horrifically loud noises. They panicked and they both beat Nathan to death. After the beating they realised it was Nathan and they thought to themselves, *what have we done?*

After the accident they burnt down the hideout. As they burnt it down they heard a faint voice in the flames. Was it Nathan? No one knows ...

Jay Newman
Thomas Keble School, Stroud

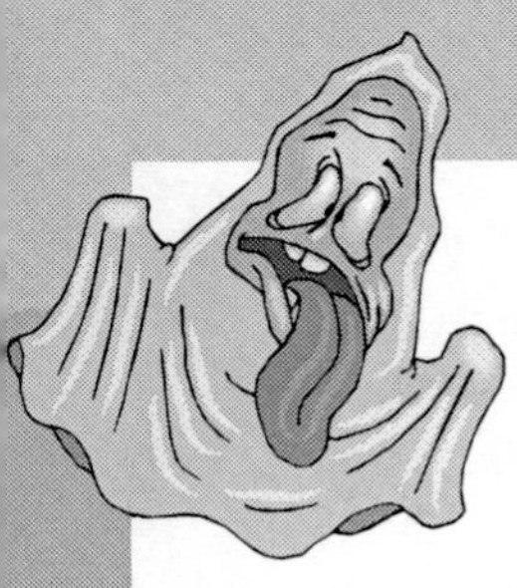

The Locker Girl

Getting ready to jump in, flapping his arms and *splash!*

'Oi you!' shouted a tubby boy called Jimmy. 'Get back here!'

'The pool is closing in 10 minutes.' Everyone rushed out to get changed, except for Jimmy and Callum.

Callum was chased into the changing rooms. The changing room doors went slam and a clicking noise was heard. Both boys rushed to the door.

'Great, I have to spend the night in a ruddy old swimming pool with you,' moaned Jimmy.

'Well, it's not my perfect idea either.'

Crash, bang, crash!

'D-d-d-did y-y-y-youu just h-hear th-that?' whispered Callum.

'Hear what?'

'The locker go bang!'

'Don't be stupid.'

'Awwwwrrr!' screamed Jimmy.

Jimmy had seen it. 'Let's get out,' panicked Jimmy, 'there must be another way out, there has to be.'

Bang, it happened again. A pale-faced girl appeared around the corner, it looked like she was wearing a Victorian swimming costume.

'What do you want?' asked Jimmy.

'And you're the school bully,' piped up Callum. 'So much for that!'

'I just want to get out of here!' the pale-faced girl exclaimed.

It was getting light outside and the two boys hadn't had a wink of sleep. They headed for the fire escape, but this meant passing the pool.

'What is your name?' Callum asked.

'Elizabeth,' she replied. Jimmy tried to open the fire door but it wouldn't budge. They suddenly saw Elizabeth on the other side of the door. The alarms sounded, they could hear sirens, but there was no escape!

Kalan-Mai Waite (13)
Thomas Keble School, Stroud

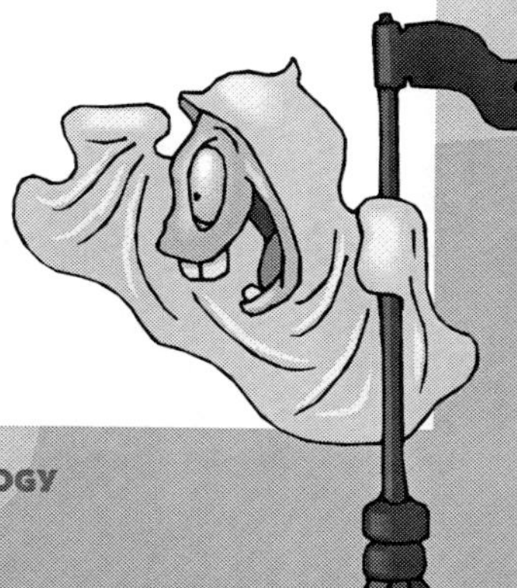

Under The Ladder

Nicole, Will and Jess were walking home from school. Nicole was waving one last time at her friends, Jess was already hunched under her bag, probably in another bad mood. The path they always took home was squishy due to building works. Will was just about to step under a ladder when Jess shrieked, 'Don't go under that, it's … !'

'Bad luck,' finished Will sarcastically stepping under it.

'You'll be cursed forever,' giggled Nicole.

Jess looked uncomfortably at Will.

A man was blocking the path in front of them. Beside him a black arrow pointed the way onto another footpath Will had never noticed before.

'Is this the way we go because of the building works, through this wood and into Crickally Village?' asked Nicole.

The man nodded coldly.

As they entered the woods Jess looked back, there had been something unsettling about the man; he was now peering at her through his hollow white eyes. He seemed faded around the edges. She ran on not wanting to lose the others and the darkness dissolved her.

'We're lost,' sighed Will.

'Let's follow the path back,' answered Nicole.

Something tapped Will on the shoulder and he spun around, tripping over a root. Gasping, as the trees seemed to bend towards him, stretching out their bony fingers to clutch at his shadowy figure. Then he was out, panting into their well-known lane.

The man had gone, but in his place, sitting stiffly in the middle of the path, was a black cat.

Kate Oboussier (13)
Thomas Keble School, Stroud

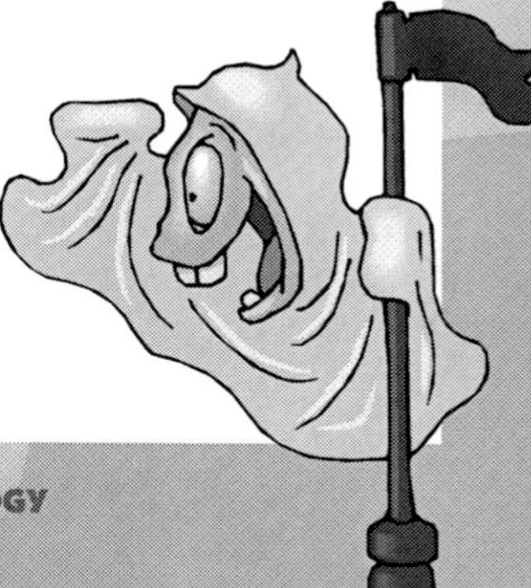

Inhabitants

Yes, I can remember that day very well; it was out of the ordinary. I ran home from school with my sister, it was 2004, I could see them, see them, the soldiers marching around the street like they owned the place, I wanted to kill them, kill them all for the hell they had brought here, but I knew I couldn't even touch them unless I was wanting to commit suicide. When I got home I gave my dad his medicine for his illness. He wouldn't tell me what it was because he didn't want to scare me.

It was midnight, all of us were hungry, but we couldn't go outside, oh no, night is always dangerous here. All I could hear were bombs and gunshots. *Would you really want to go outside right now?* I thought not, yes, those evil even sadistic creatures were still out there, waiting, waiting to strike. My father said he needed to eat or his illness would get worse. I decided to go around my neighbours; they were always willing to give us food.

I crept out the front door like a mouse scavenging for food. I crouched behind some barrels when I saw a patrol heading my way. They were talking in another language. Just as they passed me, my sister Eka stepped out of the house calling me and asked me what I was doing. I froze as they heard her as she was standing half asleep outside the front door, yes they heard her. I watched them aim their guns at her, she turned her head towards them slowly. In my eyes it was painful to watch, they killed her. I was frozen with tears running down my face, my little sister was dead.

'I must get that food, I must,' I said to myself, I told myself to focus on the task at hand and carried on. Finally, I got to my neighbour's house and I banged on the window. I saw a silhouette of a person approached the window, as the image came clearer I noticed it was one of them! I ran but he called for more men, I was surrounded, I'd failed. They said to me, *'Game over.'*

Francesca Cratchley (12)
Thomas Keble School, Stroud

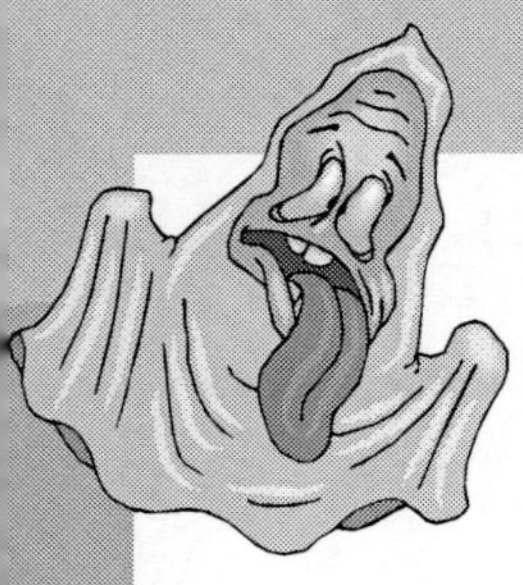

The Ghost Train

'Everybody off,' said the stationmaster.

'Tom, Jordan, let's get you a drink in the café.'

'OK Uncle Dave,' they said.

Having finished their Coke, they headed towards the door to leave. The café was empty except for Tom, his friend, Jordan, Uncle Dave and the stationmaster.

'It's locked,' said the stationmaster from the corner of the room. It's been locked from the outside, but I've called for help. We don't have another train until 7am.'

'If you don't have one, what's that I can hear coming?' said Tom.

'Let's go and have a look,' said Uncle Dave. 'Hey the train has a gun on top of the carriage.'

The men were wearing German uniforms.

'I've heard a story about a train that crashed here during the war,' said the stationmaster.

'It must be the ghost train!' said Uncle Dave.

The train rattled through the station but later came back and stopped. The soldiers walked towards them.

'What do we do?' said Tom

'There is a gun behind the counter, if we shoot at them they will go away and we'll go back down the track and we can change the points. They will go down the track that has a 134-feet drop to the bottom of the quarry,' said the stationmaster.

So they fired the gun, but the ghosts shot back, hitting Tom in the stomach, killing him.

'No!' said Jordan.

Jordan fired the gun until the bullets ran out. The ghosts returned to the train and down the track. Jordan had changed the points.

The train fell into the hole.

The next day nothing was there. What happened to the train? You decide ...

Tim Williams (11)
Thomas Keble School, Stroud

Video 101

Matt and I were walking to the video shop. We were bunking off school knowing we shouldn't, but we had done it so many times. As we got to the shop, we heard a scream but we thought it was a joke. It was sunny outside but, as we walked into the shop, it got stormy and the lights went off. When we got the video we wanted, we went over to the counter. There were splatters of blood all over the counter and the wall and Matt and I ran to the front door. It was jammed shut.

We heard the scream again, then again and it died out. We saw the glow of the evil ghosts so we ran to the fire exit but that was jammed as well. We looked around and there were bodies hung up on the wall by their feet.

We heard the ghost walking like someone pounding the floor. We saw the evil ghost, half its face was missing. It started running towards Matt so I grabbed a pole and I stabbed the ghost in the head. It fell to the floor. The ghost got back up so I stabbed him again and again. Matt and I ran to the front door and there were two people there so we were able to escape.

But where will he strike next?

Jack Gyles (12)
Thomas Keble School, Stroud

The Killing

Screech ... crash ... silence...

'Hi, my name is Doc Carden - you've just had a car crash.'

'Argh!' The people outside were having their flesh ripped off.

'What is that noise? Where am I?'

'Those were the things outside ... they are not human. It seems to be when they bite you, you turn into one yourself.' There was a short pause and then he said, 'We are in hospital and I think they may be breaking their way in. We need to find a safe place soon! What is your name?'

'My name is Sam and the safest place would probably be the shopping centre, it has reinforced windows which would make for some protection.'

The doctor then remembered to remind Sam of an important fact. 'You will want to grab something heavy and hard for protection, the only way they can be stopped is a swift blow to the head.'

Sam spotted an unused walking stick and smiled, 'This should do nicely.'

They got to the entrance of the hospital and the doctor spotted his car across the parking lot, 'OK 1 ... 2 ... 3 ... run! Run! Get in the car.'

The doors slammed. The car didn't start, he tried again, no luck. Third time lucky. *Brummmm ...*

'Get the hell out of here!' Sam screamed in a panic-stricken voice. 'You got any food?' he asked.

'Ummm ... yes, I think there is some chocolate in the glove compartment, I keep it for emergencies.'

Sam forced a smile knowing that today was going to be a bad day.

Sam Evans
Thomas Keble School, Stroud

The Storm

I'm going to tell you a story, a story that some of you won't believe and some of you will. I don't mind if you don't believe.

The storm swept over the Cornish coast like swarm of locusts. Tim and Sarah sat at the top of Michael's Hill watching the storm creep closer towards them. As they sat there a cold gush of air passed by them. Tim whispered to Sarah so as not to disturb the music of the birds. 'I'll race you to the bottom.' They both leapt to their feet and sprinted off down the hill, only leaving behind a bum print in the grass and the birds singing.

As they walked through the front door of their parents' four-bedroomed detached house, the storm had reached them. It began to rain and thunder. Tim quickly slammed the door closed, just to make sure the storm didn't open it.

The rain echoed throughout the house. The tiny sausage dog was barking continuously. Their mother shouted from the other room, 'It's going to be a bad one.' It was just reaching 9.30pm. The lights were flickering and the swing outside was swaying from side to side damaging the frame. The rain lashed against the windows like someone was hosing their house. Tim and Sarah rushed upstairs so they didn't feel the cold that loomed throughout the house, as if there were a ghost.

Both children were tucked up in their beds letting the sound of thunder and lightning lull them to sleep. The bells from the local church rang, signifying midnight. Sarah suddenly woke. The rain was still beating on the house and the thunder and lightning were still booming like a colonel shouting at his troops.

Sarah could hear the side gate bashing against the wall. She had a sudden urge to get up. It was cold - she could feel it on her face - but still she pulled off the quilt. She stepped out and onto the landing. While she stepped out she was suddenly hit by the coldness and the uncontrollable urge to go downstairs. She hastily walked down the steps, she heard the wind rushing into the kitchen. She burst through the kitchen door only to be confronted by the back door wide open and the rain and wind gushing in. She wondered to herself, *why hadn't Mum and Tim heard it?* That didn't bother her.

She went closer to the door to close it, then she noticed a little white figure staring right back at her, completely oblivious to the rain around her. It suddenly turned and ran to the end of the garden, opened the gate and ran off up the path that led to Michael's Hill. Sarah plunged out of the door and now she chased after the little white figure. She didn't know why she wanted to go after it - she just did.

As soon as she reached the foot of the hill she saw the white figure at the top wave at her and she began to laugh. As Sarah chased after her; the figure ran off.

Sarah got to the top of the hill and looked around. She didn't see anyone or anything - well that was to be expected seeing as it was one o'clock in the morning. Suddenly a white figure grabbed her hand. The hand was warm and loving, even though she did not know what or who it was. She felt safe and secure. She trusted it.

They were getting closer and closer to the edge of the cliff face that covered the north side of the hill. Sarah tried to break free but she couldn't.

Suddenly a man called from the other side of the hill. 'Stop! Stop!' he shouted. Sarah tried to turn around. The edge was only a foot away. The man was running frantically towards them, but she took that one step and fell to her death.

That man was me 20 years ago. To this day everyone blames me for her death. They believe I pushed her, but I know what I saw up there that stormy night ...

Charlie Bond (13)
Thomas Keble School, Stroud

Different Déjà Vu

There was nothing wrong about today, nothing different. It was the same but somehow I had known what I was going to do, somehow it felt familiar. I knew what I was going to feel like, or act like. It was just - different!

Walking up the hill from school with some of my mates, I heard a high-pitched scream - the type a young girl makes when she is frightened, or like a screech from a newborn baby's lungs.

At first, I thought my mates were just mucking about, but they were all in front of me, walking, as if nothing had happened, as if they had not heard it.

I then thought nothing of it until the next day when the same thing happened, *again!*

Whether it is a feeling or not, I don't know, but I felt a feeling, no, more a sense of déjà vu, though this time it was colder, there was more wind. I could feel a harsh breath going down my back; it felt more like a tornado than anything else. I could smell the sweet but saccharine smell of burning rose petals; I was nearly sick so I sat down in an alley, part way up the hill. All of a sudden the sky went pitch-black, but my friends didn't notice. I dropped my phone in the panic, my hands were fumbling around in the midnight fury.

Then I heard a youngish man's voice whisper to me threateningly, 'You didn't see that OK, got that?'

'Didn't see what?' I shouted after him, but there was no one there. How was that possible? Was it my imagination? Was I going mad, or was I just paranoid?

My friends teased me for ages after that, until about three days later when it really did happen; a man, in his mid-20s had burnt an old woman to death. When the details were released as a missing person, they said she smelt the roses and she had breathing problems so she had a heavy breathing rhythm.

After that all my mates started calling me psychic, as if I could see what was going to happen or something.

Ever since then I have never been able to walk past that same alley without turning cold.

I think I had a premonition. I should have told someone, warned them before it happened.

It all fits into place now. I could smell the old woman burning. I could feel her breathing down my back. I saw that it was going to be at night and I heard the man's voice ... *I must be psychic!*

Carly Mallinson (13)
Thomas Keble School, Stroud

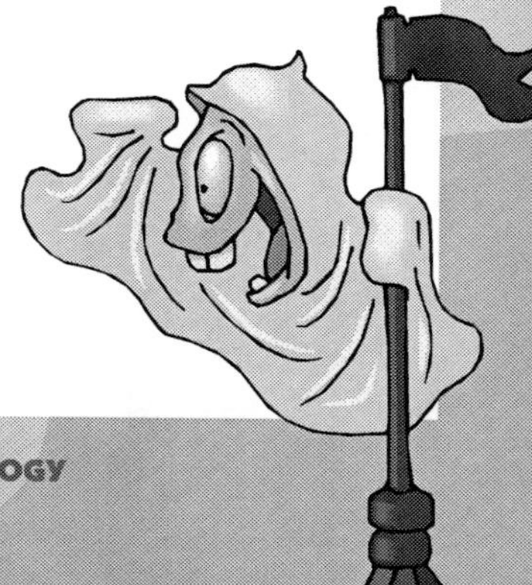

Camping In The Woods

Although everyone knows that terrifying encounters occur in the woods (even more so when it's pitch-black), Louise, Miranda, Lauren and Mel thought it would be a great laugh to go camping in the woods overnight, but they didn't have a clue about what they had let themselves in for.

They set off early that morning so they would have a full day to set up. However, soon enough it started to get dark. Lauren managed to get a small fire going and the rest of the girls collected small branches for it. Soon enough they were crouching round the fire, toasting marshmallows and swapping ghost stories.

Finally, they got to bed and as soon as their heads hit their pillows, they were out like someone switching off a light. Suddenly, a rustling sound coming from the tent woke up all four girls. They started to get scared and cuddled up to each other. After a while, the rustling came to a sudden halt and the girls realised that they had got frightened over nothing, but the worst was yet to come.

Soon after, a distant shadow appeared outside the tent. The shadow was quite large and it looked like it had been injured because what looked like arms were waving frantically about. When the girls spotted this unusual shadow, they soon started shaking and a silence descended throughout the woods. All they could hear were trees whistling. Miranda stood up proudly. She wasn't scared. She unzipped the cover and quickly yanked it across to reveal … nothing, but then, footsteps ran through the crunchy leaves scattered on the muddy ground. Where had this creature gone? It was a mystery, but the girls didn't think that much of it.

After that spooky night, Miranda, Mel, Lauren and Louise promised to start listening to scary encounters in the woods.

One day though Louise was watching the news with her family and a newsflash came on. 'There has been a murder in Frithwood, a girl was the innocent victim, only 13 years of age. The killer was an older man who was quite large and had arms that waved around.'

Louise was very shocked and her whole body froze like ice. Very, very spooky!

Amy Bloomfield (13)
Thomas Keble School, Stroud

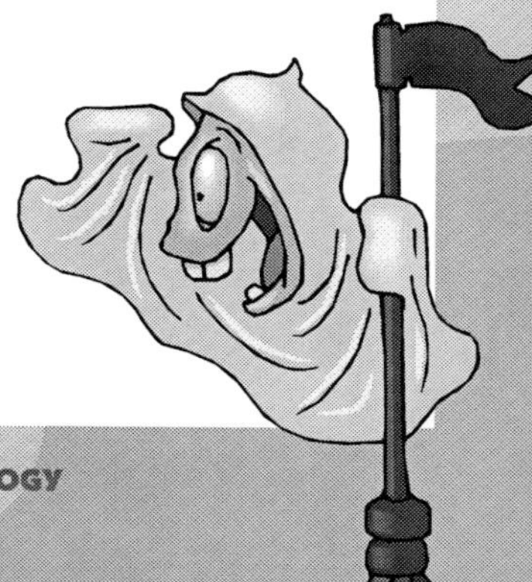

The Haunted Theme Park

One day a security guard got a new job at Camelot. On the same day at midnight the park was closed. The security guard was walking around one of the indoor rides when all of a sudden he heard strange voices so he shouted, thinking that there were intruders, 'Show yourself.' No one came, so he shouted again, 'Show yourself now!' Still no one came, so he followed the sound and suddenly he saw King Arthur's knights around the Round Table. He dropped his flashlight in shock and rubbed his eyes thinking he was seeing things.

He walked slowly towards the Round Table where the knights were sitting to see if they were real or if they were ghosts. One of the knights turned round and saw the security guard and all of a sudden the knights floated off - some went through the walls and some went through the ceilings.

The security guard shouted, 'Wait, don't go. I won't harm you.'

One of the knights turned around and said, 'Why?'

The security guard said, 'Look at me closely, what do you see?'

The knights went up to him and said, 'Arthur, is that you?'

The security guard said, 'Yes it is me, your king. I've taken human form while I keep a watchful eye on my realm.'

Roy Wise
White Ash School, Oswaldtwistle

Spooky Australia

It was a starlit pitch-black night when Paul and Brian broke down in the Australian outback with no means of contacting anybody for help. They decided to try and find their own way back.

After two days without food or water, lost and close to death, they were amazed to see a dog in the distance. As it got closer Paul was reminded of his dog who died 10 years ago. As Paul and Brian lay exhausted the dog ran up to them, barking and wagging its tail.

'It is Shep,' shouted Paul, overcome with emotion, 'I would know him anywhere but how can he still be alive and out here 200 miles from home?'

Shep set off at a trot, he kept on turning around as if he wanted them to follow him. Paul and Brian found new strength and set off after Shep.

Little more than a couple of hours later they came to a road. Shep waited until Paul and Brian hitched a lift off a pick up that came along. They got in the back and called Shep to join them but he turned and trotted off and vanished into the heat-haze like a ghost returning to its own dimension.

Brian Pearson (16)
White Ash School, Oswaldtwistle

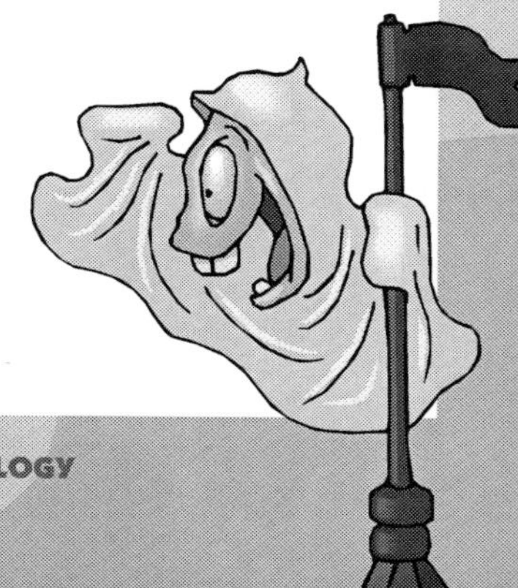

Ghost Wave

The surfers' beach was in a panic because in the last three days five surfers had gone missing, just vanished into thin air as they surfed a big wave.

First rumours were of a gigantic shark, possibly a rogue great white that could swallow a surfer and his board whole and leave no trace. The surfers' group decided to stay out of the water and keep watch for the shark.

After two days of watching there were no sightings of a shark so they thought it was safe to go back.

One surfer, braver than most, went into the sea. He paddled far out and picked up a promising looking wave which rapidly grew in height.

The surfer was up on his board now as the wave grew bigger and bigger and as it started to curl over into a huge breaker, the watchers were horrified to see gigantic teeth and a malevolent eye appear, as the wave transformed into a huge evil being with jaws that curled over and engulfed the surfer, and as the wave flattened out onto the beach ... the surfer had gone.

Efraz Hussain (9)
White Ash School, Oswaldtwistle

The Knock

One dark, dark night Sophie saw a dark, dark figure. She crept closer; it was a body on the tracks of a train station. When she got home she heard a voice.

'You should've helped me.'

Sophie thought she was hearing things. *Knock, knock,* the door began to creak. Sophie sprinted into her room and the door slammed shut.

Next day, when Sophie went to work, she saw the body had gone from the rusty tracks, but the tracks weren't closed. All day Sophie was questioning herself, 'Why weren't the tracks closed? Maybe someone had hidden her body. Don't think so.'

Before she went to bed Sophie heard, 'You should've helped me!'

Knock, knock, the door began to creak and slammed shut again.

The next day was the worst day ever. All Sophie heard was, 'You should've helped me.'

Knock, knock, the door creaked then slammed shut.

Sophie screamed, 'I can't take it anymore!'

She swung the door open. There was a tiny boy with blue eyes and brown hair. The boy gave her a piece of paper saying, 'You should've helped me'.

The next day Sophie was cleaning the attic and found a newspaper dated 7/1/1960. There was a dead boy that looked like the body that Sophie had seen on the tracks. He had been murdered. Sophie read on, he'd lived at her house and she now knew he was still there!

Rowan Pugh (10)
Winnington Park CP School, Northwich

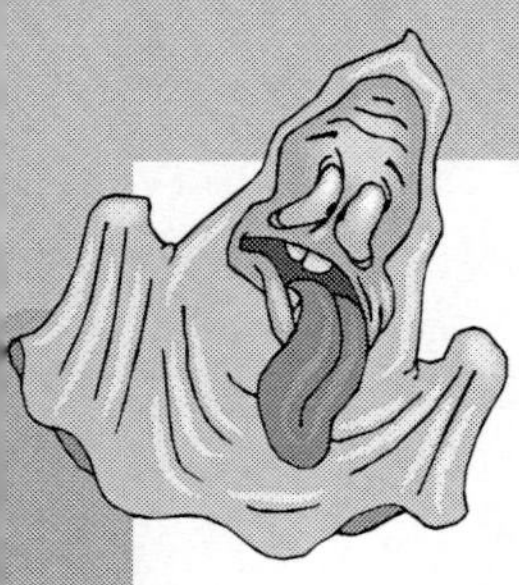

The Secret Door

One foggy morning a family moved into an old mansion. They didn't know that there was something in it that would scare the living daylights out of them.

The family had a girl called Charlotte and two brothers, Jamie and Scott. They decided to explore the mansion. Downstairs was a huge lounge with an enormous fireplace. At the far end was a grand piano and a tall grandfather clock. They played for a while until Charlotte exclaimed, 'Come on, let's find where we're sleeping tonight.'

They all ran upstairs to find their new bedrooms.

Charlotte's room was the biggest. As she jumped on the bed she noticed a little door in the corner. Excitedly she went to open it but it was locked. She ran to tell Jamie and Scott that she had found a secret door in her room.

It was night-time already. The children couldn't wait to go to bed. Mum kissed them goodnight. Charlotte couldn't get to sleep. A knock came at the door. In ran Jamie and Scott. 'Can we sleep with you? We can't get to sleep.'

Charlotte replied, 'I can't either, shall I read you a story?'

'Please!'

Suddenly they heard a door swing open. They saw two red eyes peering from the secret door. A green hideous monster staggered towards them. The children screamed. What was it? What did it want?

In a cold whisper the monster said, 'Can you read a story to me as well?'

Michelle Fryer (10)
Winnington Park CP School, Northwich

Caves Of Shadows

It was the day of the school trip to the caves. We were all excited. The coach was so noisy, as we told scary stories about caves.

When we got off the coach, the teacher shouted, 'While we are in the caves we must keep to the left. Never turn right. If you keep to the left it will fetch you back to where we started.'

We each had a torch, but I had to keep banging mine because it kept going off. I think the batteries were running out.

I crept into the cave full of spiders' webs. I looked around. There was no one else there but me and my friend, Ayesha. We must have turned right by mistake. We began to panic.

'What are we going to do now?'

'Shhh! Shhh!' whispered Ayesha. 'Can you hear something?'

I strained to hear. Then I heard it. An echoing voice. *'Now I've got you! Now I'm going to eat you!'*

As we went further into the cave, the same words got louder and louder. My torch went off again. My heart felt like it was in my mouth. We heard the words again, loud and clear. Finally I got my torch working again and there, in a corner, was a huge shadow.

'Now I've got you! Now I'm going to eat you!'

I shone my torch around the cave. There stood the teacher, picking his nose, saying, *'Now I've got you! Now I'm going to eat you!'*

Becky Healey (10)
Winnington Park CP School, Northwich

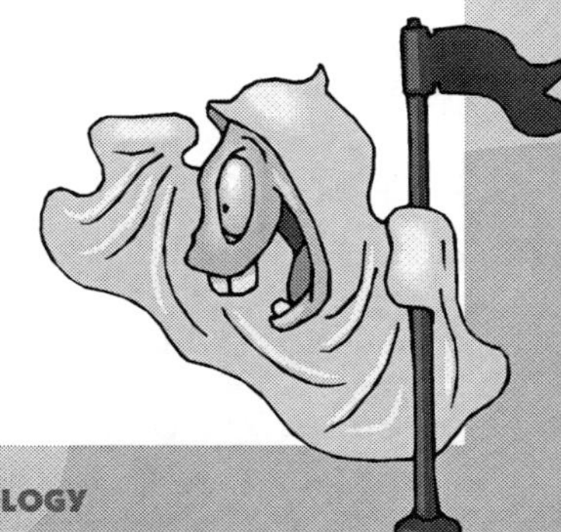

Lay One For Me

It all started one dark night when a young woman broke into an old man's house. A grave mistake - literally, as it turned out. As she crept up the stairs they creaked underfoot. The old man threw a vase at the creaking, killing the intruder stone dead. Not wanting to go to prison, he entombed the body under the stairs and bricked up the opening.

Years later a new family moved into the house. One night the daughter was laying the table. She heard an eerie voice. 'Lay one for me ... ' Again she heard it. 'Lay one for me ... '

The voice was cold, dead and it cut through her like a blade. She ignored it, but strange things began to happen around the house; the cat hissed at the wall under the stairs, the house was always cold and the family heard scraping in the night.

The girl was scared now. Her mother rang a medium to find where the voice was coming from. The medium revealed that it was coming from behind the bricked up wall, under the stairs.

The family called in builders to break down the brick wall. They found three disturbing things; a skeleton with pieces of flesh hanging off it, scratch marks on the wall, as though someone had tried to claw their way out and finally, they found a crumpled piece of paper with words scrawled on it. The girl picked it up and read the words aloud. 'Lay one for me ... '

Tom Fishwick (10)
Winnington Park CP School, Northwich

Ghost!

If you get scared easily, I wouldn't dare read this terrifying but true story.

It all started one dark, stormy night. The wind howled like a wild pack of fearsome wolves, making the old garden gate swing open, then slam shut abruptly. Sophie was sitting, alone, on the sofa watching a horror movie, unaware of the terrifying night that was ahead of her.

Suddenly she heard an ear-shattering scream. What was it? Why did it haunt her? Sophie realised it was only the girl in the movie and, relieved, carried on watching.

Just when everything seemed all right again, she heard a door creak open, then quietly close shut. This time the sound was definitely real. What could it be? Alone in the house, far away from anyone else in the village, Sophie remembered a half-forgotten rumour. It was thought that a dear old lady had been brutally murdered in this very house, stabbed to death by a mysterious figure. What was Sophie to do?

Gradually, she felt the old breath of a person, or maybe a ghost, on her stiff neck. Trembling, she turned around and saw the face of a ghost. It was pale and white, with cold, dead eyes as dark as swamp water and long black hair that swayed eerily as the phantom sat down next to her.

'W-w-w-what d-d-do you want with m-m-me?' Sophie stuttered, scared to death.

In an old, croaky voice the ghost asked, 'Do you mind if I watch telly too?'

Kathryn Hooker (9)
Winnington Park CP School, Northwich

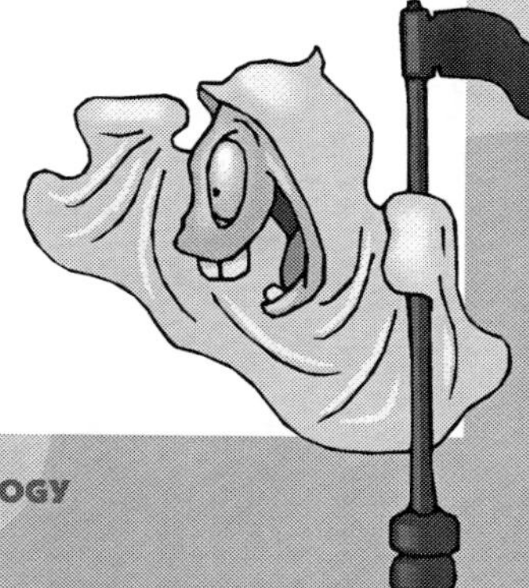

Mary, Mary!

As I sit in the dusty junk shop, I assure you the story I tell is absolutely true, so if you have young children send them to bed, now!

A girl, Mary, was walking through town when she came upon a toy shop which she had never seen before. As she peered through the window something caught her eye. It was a scruffy, old doll. Mary ran into the shop, picked it up and took it to the counter. But there was no one there. Just then she heard a girlish, yet creepy voice. 'Buy me ... '

A skinny man walked out of the shadows; the shopkeeper.

'This doll please,' the little girl asked.

'Are you sure you want this one?' enquired the shopkeeper.

'Yes please.'

The shopkeeper shook his head. 'There's a curse on it.'

Unbelieving, Mary bought it, despite the warning.

That night, Mary was tucked up in bed. She heard a mysterious voice, like a little girl, speaking. 'Mary, Mary! I'm at the bottom of the stairs.'

Mary looked, but there was no one else in the house except her and the doll.

Suddenly, there it was again, but even closer. 'Mary, Mary! I'm halfway up the stairs.' Then again. 'Mary, Mary! I'm on the landing.' Then again. 'Mary, Mary! I'm in the closet.'

Mary turned and looked at the closet door. She heard the voice one last time.

'Mary, Mary! You are *dead!*'

'Mary should have listened to the shopkeeper and not bought me.'

Daniel Payne (10)
Winnington Park CP School, Northwich

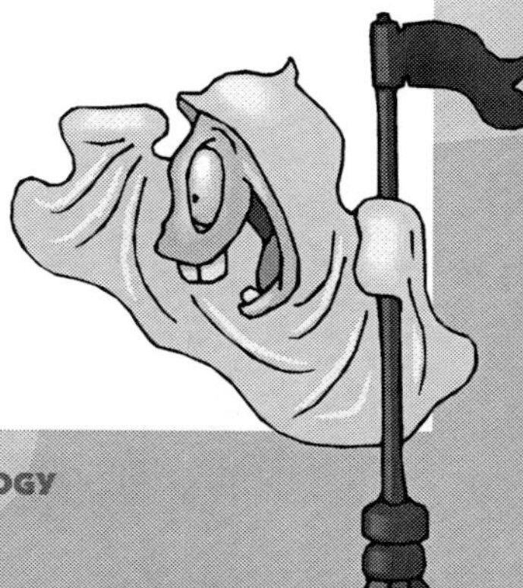

The Devil's Ditch II: The Terrible Laughter

It all started when Wendy was watching her favourite horror movie 'The Devil's Ditch'. It was about an evil killer doll. As the film finished she heard something strange from upstairs. It was laughter, eerie laughter. It couldn't be her parents - they were out. What was it?

Scared but intrigued, Wendy climbed the long, narrow staircase to see what the laughter was. It seemed to take forever. She heard it again and again until she could stand it no longer.

Eventually Wendy reached the top of the stairs. Desperately she searched, room by room, until she came across the last room, Dad's room. Finally she came to Dad's cupboard. She opened the cupboard doors and saw a shadow moving, as though it was dancing.

Suddenly a long, withered hand reached out from the shadow. It grabbed at Wendy, but she moved, just in time. Abruptly, it attacked. Wendy tried to dodge it but it got her. She screamed. What was it? She didn't know. The strange, horrible thing clawed its way up her. Wendy was sweating like a waterfall, scared stiff. She shook it, but the thing wouldn't get off her. The shadow which hid the thing fell like bed covers and she was face to face with her worst nightmare. It was a doll! The killer doll from 'The Devil's Ditch'.

The doll spoke evilly, 'Are you ready for the sequel to 'The Devil's Ditch'?'

Dean Jones (10)
Winnington Park CP School, Northwich

The Old House

One dark, cold, misty night, a mysterious figure approached a crooked, ancient, gloomy house. A man called Mr Davies had lived there for a long, long time. Beside the crooked, ancient, gloomy house was a graveyard.

Meanwhile, Mr Davies was asleep in his bed. Suddenly he was woken up by a tapping of nails on his bedside table. He was extremely terrified, as he had just been having a nail-biting nightmare, in which his long-lost friend Peter had been shot dead by Mr Davies himself in a robbery. But he knew it wasn't a dream, nor a nightmare. Long ago he *did* kill Peter, who was his only friend. But in those days money was much more important to him.

The clock struck twelve, and in the dark, dark graveyard a dark, dark figure was walking to the dark, dark house where Mr Davies lived. Peter was on his way to avenge his death. He planned to kill Mr Davies and bring him to the grave with him.

Peter was now at the crooked old door. He twisted the handle silently and walked into the house. Mr Davies heard footsteps stamping up the stairs, and then his bedroom door opened. A skeletal figure staggered into the bedroom. His eyes were as red as a blazing fire and his claws scratched on Mr Davies' bedside table.

Then Peter whispered in a cold, scratchy voice, 'I have come to take you to the grave!'

No one heard Mr Davies' final scream.

Ryan Moore (9)
Winnington Park CP School, Northwich

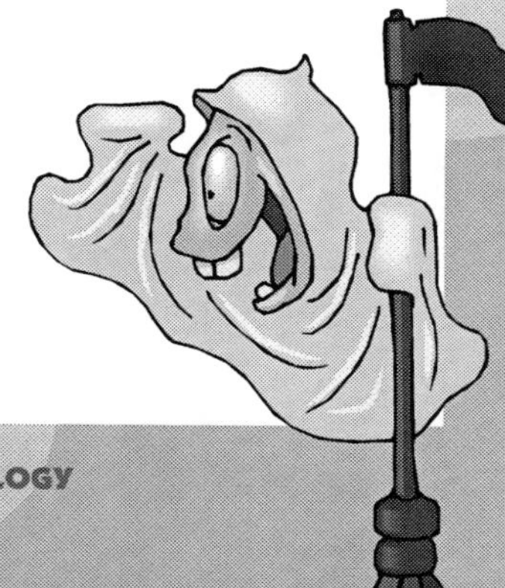

The Haunted Chest

It all began on a lovely sunny Saturday morning. Peacefully, we villagers lived, but all this was all about to change. A new family was moving in. Some way or another, they looked very strange, as though something was wrong.

The mysterious new family were unloading luggage. They were almost finished when they dragged out a gorgeous treasure chest and left it in the middle of the overgrown garden. I went up to the family and asked them, 'What is that gorgeous treasure chest doing in your garden?'

But they just ignored me and shut the door in my face.

A few days went. I was walking past the mysterious house when, lightly, I heard a ghostly voice. It was coming from the chest. I fetched my dad's hammer, which was harder than a rock. With one mighty slash, the chest began to creak open. Inside was a beautiful gold medallion. Slowly, I took the medallion out.

Another week went by and I heard the ghostly voice again. This time, it was coming from upstairs in my house. One step at a time, I walked upstairs. What could it be? What was it? Who was it? Slowly, I opened the bathroom door. It was full of mist. Then I saw a dark, dark figure in the fog. It crept up to me and bellowed, 'I have been looking for you for weeks! Now I have got you right where I want you, can I have my medallion back?'

Sam Hunt (10)
Winnington Park CP School, Northwich

The Trunk

There once lived a boy called Aiden. One spooky day, on his eleventh birthday, the greedy boy received fifty pounds. Aiden walked excitedly to the shops, when he spotted, on a window sill, a trunk, a big, old and rusty trunk. *That would be a good place to keep all my games and toys,* he thought.

His kind mum came and bought the trunk for ten pounds for him, but one thing was wrong. The lock wouldn't open. Even when they got it home they still couldn't open it. Aiden's dad tried and tried, but it was no use.

Dad said tiredly, 'I will take it to the locksmith tomorrow. Anyway, it's time for bed.'

The boy went upstairs, while his dad put the trunk beside Aiden's bed. His mum and dad gave him a kiss and then left his room.

The room was dark and spooky. Suddenly, there was a creaking noise that sounded like the trunk opening. There appeared at the edge of his bed a pale, weird-looking ghost. It looked as if it had come from out of the trunk. Aiden hid under the covers as the ghost floated scarily towards the bed.

Before Aiden had a chance to say anything, the weird ghost quietly said, 'Hello, would you like to play a game of Twister?'

Aysha Barrett (10)
Winnington Park CP School, Northwich

The Thriller

Lightning lit up all the rooms in the house. A girl called Rowan woke up in fright.

'I think I'll get a drink of water.'

Once she got to the kitchen, she turned the tap. Something was strange. Blood was pouring out of the tap, redder than you could ever imagine.

Hmm, maybe I should have some pop instead, she wondered.

Hearing a creepy noise, she turned around. A sinister figure was standing there, in the backyard. What was it? What did it want? She didn't know. The last thing she ever remembered was that the thing was standing in front of her …

A year later, on a sunny morning, I moved into the very same house.

'Wow! This is a brill house!' I said in amazement. 'I'm going to pick a room, Mum.'

'OK,' Mum replied.

So I headed upstairs. Before I knew it, I was standing outside a creepy bedroom. Suddenly I heard a voice.

'Come in,' it whispered. 'Come in!'

It became louder and louder each second. The door slammed shut!

'Wh-o a-r-e y-y-ou? Show y-y-yourself!' I stuttered bravely.

'OK,' said the voice, 'but don't scream, promise?'

'I promise,' I murmured.

'Well, here goes.'

A ghost staggered towards me. White as snow, in the shape of a creepy little girl with pigtails, it came towards me, wailing spookily.

'Right, *I'm getting out of here!'* I screamed.

Shelby Renhard (10)
Winnington Park CP School, Northwich

The Monstrous Hydra That Haunts The Lake

I am a Hydra. I have three heads and I bite. My bites are deadly. I live in an underwater lair. I am a snake-like creature, propelling myself through the water with two sets of fins. I measure three metres in length. I am extremely strong and my heads sometimes fight with each other. Every so often, if one of my heads is bitten, it will be poisoned and die. Within weeks, I will grow a new, stronger head.

I am the most vicious creature in the world. I trap my prey by lying at the bottom of my lake motionless. When humans come by, I lurch and snatch them with my jaws, before swimming back to my lair to devour them.

I love sleeping and being warm. So, on hot sunny days, I crawl out of the water and sunbathe on the rocks. It is here, on the rocks, that I shed my tough old skin. My skin is replaced by a new soft, shiny one. Until my new skin becomes tougher. I am vulnerable to attack from my only natural predator, the fire dragon. The fire dragon emits long hot flames that can burn my new soft skin. So, to avoid this happening, when I finally shed my old skin, I quickly climb back into the water and descend to the bottom. Here, I remain for two weeks, whilst allowing time for my skin to toughen up. All in all, the life of a Hydra is quite enjoyable.

Daniel Cain (11)
Winnington Park CP School, Northwich

The Crooked House

It was a cold, misty night. I was getting ready for bed. All of a sudden I saw a strange figure go past my bedroom door. As I turned again, the clock on the wall downstairs struck twelve. As I slammed the door in fright, a figure came through the closed door. All of a sudden, the figure disappeared and I heard a loud scream from the room next door. It was my friend who was staying with me.

Suddenly, I thought of the dreadful murder of my other friend, Peter, who had stayed in this house and had been shot in a robbery. That was my other friend Peter, who had an annoying habit of tapping his fingernails on his bedside table.

The house became quiet and eerie. I looked out of the window and saw a ghostly figure disappear ...

Jack Mainwaring (9)
Winnington Park CP School, Northwich

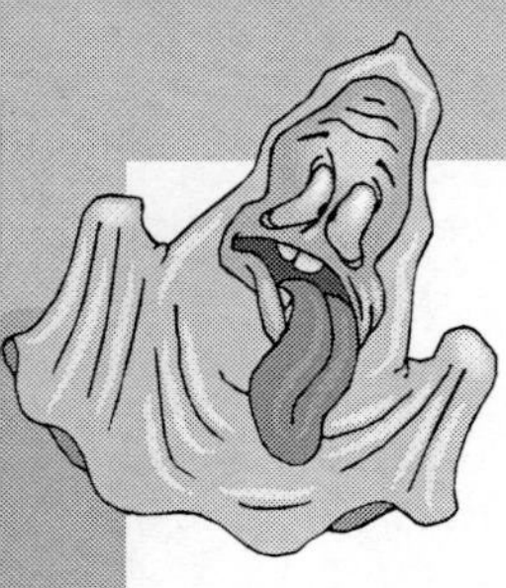

Information

We hope you have enjoyed reading this book - and that you will continue to enjoy it in the coming years.

If you like reading and writing drop us a line, or give us a call, and we'll send you a free information pack.

Write to:

Young Writers Information, Remus House, Coltsfoot Drive, Woodston, Peterborough PE2 9JX Tel: 01733 890066 or check out our website at www.youngwriters.co.uk.